THE VALENTINE GUEST LIST

A British Seaside Cozy Mystery

Copyright © 2026 Sherlyn Harlock
All rights reserved.

No part of this book may be reproduced, stored, or transmitted in any form or by any means, electronic or mechanical, including photocopying, recording, or by any information storage and retrieval system, without prior written permission from the author, except for brief quotations in reviews.

This is a work of fiction. Names, characters, places, and events are either products of the author's imagination or used fictitiously. Any resemblance to actual persons, living or dead, or actual events is purely coincidental.

First published in 2026.

TABLE OF CONTENTS

Chapter 1: Crowe Cards & Vows, morning
Chapter 2: The contract and the manager
Chapter 3: Guest list intake
Chapter 4: Suspect lineup begins
Chapter 5: Arrival day and backstage access
Chapter 6: The first switch
Chapter 7: Compatibility banquet begins
Chapter 8: Death in the corridor
Chapter 9: Storm and lockdown

Chapter 10: The list becomes evidence
Chapter 11: First interrogation wave
Chapter 12: Paper trail trap
Chapter 13: Penny's warning
Chapter 14: Second attempt, near miss
Chapter 15: The portal logs
Chapter 16: Reveal mechanics
Chapter 17: Culprit cornered
Chapter 18: Aftermath and hook
<u>AUTHOR</u>

CHAPTER 1

Crowe Cards & Vows, morning

Valentine Row looked as it always did when it wanted to be photographed. The lane was narrow enough to force strangers into accidental intimacy, as if the bricks themselves believed in romance. Salt in the air. Damp on the paving stones. A gull perched on the lamppost like an unpaid critic, watching the early tourists aim their phones at anything with bunting.

My shop sat halfway down the row, squeezed between a holiday-let key safe business that pretended it was not a key safe business, and a boutique that sold "artisan" candles in the scent of things nobody actually wanted their house to smell like. Crowe Cards & Vows had been a registrar's office on paper for years in my head, even after I stopped being one. I could not help it. Some habits lodge in the bone.

I unlocked the door at eight-thirty, because eight-thirty is a civilised hour for being in love and an uncivilised hour for being near other people's feelings. The brass key was cold, the lock was stubborn, and the wooden frame gave its usual protest, a small groan like an elderly aunt forced into a group hug.

Pip came in behind me, paused on the threshold, and sneezed once at the sea air, as if Hartcombe itself had offended him.

"Good morning to you too," I told him.

He ignored me, because he was a border terrier and therefore constitutionally incapable of acknowledging the obvious. Pip was wiry honey-brown with a darker muzzle, and he wore his confidence like a badly fitted jumper. His left ear half-flopped, with a tiny notch at the tip as if someone had tried to fold it neatly once and given up. His red collar and brass tag jingled as he made a beeline for his favourite place, the exact spot under the counter where the floor was warmest and the world was least likely to ask him to perform.

He wedged himself in, nose to paws, and gave a satisfied sigh.

There are people who say dogs can sense danger. Pip could sense drama, which in Hartcombe amounted to the same thing.

I flicked on the lights and the shop came alive in soft pools: shelves of thick card stock, ribbons in tidy spools, envelopes stacked by colour and weight. The smell of paper and ink, clean and slightly sweet, the way a new notebook promises a person they will become organised. My old registrar's instincts found order in the chaos, even when the chaos was mine.

On the counter, beneath the acrylic sign that read WEDDING STATIONERY, VOWS, CEREMONIES, and, because I could not resist, NO REFUNDS FOR COLD FEET, someone had pushed a stack of flyers through the letterbox overnight.

Bright pink. Heavy gloss. The kind of paper that thinks it is doing you a favour by being expensive.

SECOND-CHANCE ROMANCE WEEKEND, the headline announced, with a heart made of two interlocking anchors, because this was Hartcombe and the sea had to be involved even when nobody was going anywhere.

Below that was the Mariner's Crown Hotel logo, and beneath it, smaller, as if it was shy about being seen with them, VALENTINE HERITAGE TRUST.

I stared at the flyers the way you stare at a stranger who is already too familiar.

The Trust had been buying properties on Valentine Row for years. Quietly. Through shell charities and "community initiatives." People spoke about it in the same tone they used for mould, or relatives with a history of borrowing money. Officially, the Trust restored heritage and brought in visitors. Unofficially, it collected leverage the way other people collected sea glass.

I took my Pocket Log from my peacoat pocket, flipped it open, and wrote:

08:33. Flyers through letterbox. "Second-Chance Romance Weekend." Mariner's Crown. Valentine Heritage Trust named.

I wrote in ink, because pencil is for people who plan to change their minds. I had spent over two decades watching what people did when they thought no one was paying attention, then writing it down anyway. I called it prickliness. The police called it "useful." The town called it "a bit much."

The kettle clicked on behind the counter. Tea first. Always. If you cannot make tea in a crisis, you cannot be trusted with anything more complicated than a balloon arch.

I was halfway through sorting the flyers into a neat stack of no, absolutely not, thank you, when the bell above the door chimed.

Cal Reeve stepped inside with the calm of a man who had spent his life being thrown around by weather and learned not to take it personally.

He was fifty-eight, retired lifeboat coxswain, and looked like he had been carved from driftwood and stubbornness. Weathered face. Blue-grey eyes that missed nothing but did not make a fuss about it. He wore a navy jumper and a jacket that had seen better decades, and he carried a small canvas bag as if he had come to do me a favour and would deny it if asked directly.

Pip did not move. That in itself was a review.

"Morning, Hattie," Cal said, and nodded at the flyers. "Looks like love has exploded again."

"Love explodes constantly in Hartcombe," I said. "It is one of our main exports."

Cal's mouth twitched. He glanced around the shop the way he always did, as if checking the place was still standing and I was still inside it. It was not possessive. It was the habit of a man who had hauled people out of rough water. You do not stop counting heads just because you are on land.

He set the bag on the counter. "Brought you those hinges you asked about."

I had asked him about hinges last week in the way a person asks about a mild headache. I was not convinced it mattered until it started interfering with my life.

"My hero," I said dryly, which made him laugh under his breath because he knew exactly what I meant and what I did not.

He took the hinge out, turned it in his hands, and frowned at it with practical concentration. Cal did not do romance branding. He did function. The world would be a better place if more people worshipped function.

"Door sticking again?" he asked.

"Only when I'm in a hurry," I said. "So, always."

He nodded, then looked at the flyers again. "That weekend at the Mariner's Crown. High-profile lot coming in."

"High-profile," I repeated. In my experience, high-profile meant someone with a public reputation and a private habit of making it everybody else's problem.

Cal leaned an elbow on the counter, eyes narrowing slightly. "I heard it down at the harbour. Hugh Mercer's been going on about it like it's the Queen's visit."

"Hugh Mercer," I said, and my tone made it clear I had opinions.

Hugh was the general manager of the Mariner's Crown Hotel. Charcoal suits. Controlled smile. The kind of man who treated optics like oxygen and looked faintly annoyed that the rest of us breathed without a strategy.

"He's got sponsors breathing down his neck," Cal went on. "Trust lot, the council, all those folks who think Hartcombe should be a brochure and nothing else."

I poured tea into my mug and watched it cloud from amber to proper strength. "And how does that concern me?"

Cal gave me a look. "You're on Valentine Row. Everything concerns you. Even when it shouldn't."

That was annoyingly accurate.

Pip shifted under the counter, the scrape of his claws faint on the floorboards. I looked down and saw his eye watching Cal. Calm. No stare-freeze. No bark. Pip approved of Cal. It was one of his few character flaws.

"I'm not doing weddings," I said, as if the statement could ward off fate. "I did my time. Twenty years of other people crying into tissues and pretending it was joy."

"You do vows," Cal said.

"I do stationery," I corrected. "Paper behaves. People do not."

Cal reached into the bag again and pulled out a small packet. Two sausage rolls from Nisha's café, wrapped neatly.

"You've already eaten," he guessed.

I opened my mouth, then closed it again, because I was not going to lie to a man who could tell the difference between a calm sea and a dangerous one from the colour of the sky.

"I had tea," I said.

"Tea isn't breakfast," he said.

"It's a start."

He slid the sausage rolls closer. "Eat."

I narrowed my eyes at him. "You cannot order me around."

"I can," Cal said mildly, "if it's for your own good."

It would have sounded smug on anyone else. On Cal, it sounded like weather advice. Ignore it at your peril.

I took a bite of the sausage roll to prove I was making my own choices. The pastry was warm, the sausage peppery, and I felt myself re-enter my body in a way that annoyed me. Being alive was inconvenient.

Cal went back to examining the hinge. "Anyway," he said, casual, because he was never casual when it mattered. "This weekend. I'd keep your head down."

"That implies my head has been up," I said.

His eyes flicked to mine. "Hattie."

I sighed. "Fine. Why."

"Because those types love a scapegoat," Cal said. "And you've got a shop that says vows on the front window. They'll pull you in. Vendors. Paperwork. Sign a thing, agree to a thing, and suddenly you're responsible for their story."

The word story landed with weight.

In Hartcombe, story was currency. People traded it for attention, for favour, for cover. Romance branding was the most lucrative story of all. It made everything palatable, even the bits that should have tasted like rust.

"I'm not interested," I said, and I meant it. My life had only just settled into something I could tolerate. The shop did not make me wealthy, but it made me mine. I had rent to pay and pride to preserve, and those two were already a full-time job.

Cal finished turning the hinge over and gave a grunt of approval, as if the metal had passed a moral test.

"The Mariner's Crown asked Nisha first," he said.

I paused mid-bite. "For what."

He shrugged. "Catering, maybe, or a 'Hartcombe experience' package. She said no. Too much hassle. Too much control. They like telling people how to be helpful."

I made a small sound that could have been a laugh if I had been in the mood to be charitable. "So they'll come to me."

Cal looked at me as if he could see the exact moment my

stubbornness would be overridden by arithmetic.

"How's business?" he asked, carefully.

I hated that he knew. I hated more that he had asked anyway.

"January is January," I said. "Tourists vanish. Locals hide. Everyone pretends they are saving money while buying things online at midnight."

Cal nodded. "And the rent's still the rent."

"There it is," I said. "The heart of romance in Hartcombe. Rent."

He smiled then, properly. It softened him. It made him look younger and more dangerous, which was an unfair combination.

The bell chimed again, and this time it was not Cal. It was Nisha Patel, sweeping in like a woman who ran a café and therefore owned time.

Nisha was in her thirties, practical, and dressed in a way that said she did not care what strangers thought but still managed to look sharp. She carried a tray with a covered cup.

"I saw Cal's bike outside and assumed you were being bullied into eating," she said, setting the cup down. "So I brought reinforcements."

"Tea?" I asked.

"Proper tea," Nisha said. "Not the sort you make when you're spiralling."

I narrowed my eyes at her too. "I do not spiral."

Nisha lifted one eyebrow. "Hattie."

Apparently, my name was now a tone.

Pip shifted again under the counter. His collar tag jingled. He did not like applause or camera flashes, but he loved people arriving with food.

Nisha glanced at the flyers. "Oh, good. That circus is back."

"You've heard," Cal said.

"Hugh Mercer came in yesterday," Nisha said, her mouth tightening. "All charm, no warmth. He said the weekend will 'redefine Hartcombe as a destination'. Like we're a bag he's trying to rebrand."

I took a sip of the tea she had brought and felt my shoulders unclench one millimetre. "And what did you say."

"I said Harbour Kettle is not an accessory," Nisha replied. "He asked me to supply a 'curated couples' breakfast experience'. I asked if he wanted me to spoon-feed them their feelings as well."

Cal made a low appreciative sound. "Good."

Nisha's eyes moved to me. "Don't tell me you're considering it."

"I'm not," I said instantly. Too instantly, if we were being honest, which we were not.

Nisha watched me for a beat. "Hattie."

I hated that everyone knew my tells. It was what came of spending years reading other people. You learn the patterns, then forget you have them too.

"I am opening a shop," I said. "I am drinking tea. I am not attending any romantic weekends."

Nisha tilted her head. "So you won't take their stationery contract."

"I did not say that," I replied, because my mouth did not love me.

Cal's smile was a private one.

Nisha crossed her arms. "You told me you were done with drama."

"I am," I said. "I am done with emotional theatrics. I am not done with paying rent."

Nisha exhaled slowly through her nose. "If you take that job, you keep copies of everything."

"I keep copies of everything anyway," I said. "I'm not a

monster."

Cal lifted a finger. "Actually, keep originals too, if you can. And write down who asks for changes."

I looked at him. "Why do you sound like you're giving me a safety briefing."

Because he was.

Cal's voice stayed even. "Because these things attract trouble. Money, attention, egos. And the Trust. When the Trust gets involved, people stop behaving like they're in a seaside town and start behaving like they're in a boardroom."

Nisha nodded grimly. "And boardrooms have a higher body count than people admit."

That earned her a look from me, because we did not joke about bodies. Not properly. Not with Pip under the counter, warm and trusting. Not with Valentine Row outside pretending it was all hearts and bunting.

Nisha caught my expression and softened. "I didn't mean," she said. "I mean trouble. You know what I mean."

I did.

The bell chimed again. Three customers drifted in, smelling of wet wool and curiosity. An older couple in matching waterproof jackets. A teenage girl with a bright scarf and a bored face. Tourists. They hovered near the window display where I had arranged a collection of wedding invitation suites in creams and navy, with a small silver anchor charm on one. Hartcombe did not know how to stop being itself.

"Morning," I called, switching tone. Shop voice. Friendly enough to be safe, not friendly enough to invite a confession.

"Morning," the older woman said, looking at the display. "Oh, how lovely. Are you doing Valentine's Day specials."

"Not unless Valentine himself comes back from the dead and requests it," I said lightly. "But I can help with cards, certainly."

The teenage girl stared at Pip under the counter. Pip did not

13

appreciate being stared at, so he turned his head away and pretended the floorboards were fascinating.

"He's cute," the girl said.

"He's tolerant," I corrected.

The couple wandered to the card racks, fingertips brushing paper edges. The texture of thick card stock, the tiny raised ink on a letterpress heart, the whisper of envelopes sliding out and back. Paper is quiet company. It does not demand anything. It waits.

Nisha leaned in while I wrapped a card for the older man, who wanted something "romantic but not too soppy," which described most of Hartcombe's marriage proposals.

"If Hugh asks you," Nisha murmured, "say no to the portal thing."

I paused. "Portal thing."

She nodded, eyes narrowing. "He's making vendors use some shared system. Uploads, edits, approvals. It's supposed to be 'efficient'. It's also a way to control what you send and when."

My pen stilled. Fountain pen in my hand. Habit. Comfort.

"Did he mention that to you," I asked.

"He tried," Nisha said. "I told him I have an email address and a phone number and if that's not enough for him, he can go and curate his own toast."

Cal's mouth twitched again. "Good."

I wrote in my Pocket Log without looking down, because my hand knew the motion:

08:52. Nisha: Hugh Mercer pushing vendors onto shared portal. Control mechanism.

The teenage girl watched me write. "Do you always do that," she asked.

"Do what," I said, sealing the wrapped card with a neat sticker.

"Write things down," she said.

"Yes," I replied. "It stops people lying to me later."

Her eyes widened. The older couple laughed, as if I was joking. I let them think it.

By nine-thirty the shop had its usual gentle flow. A man buying apology flowers he had not brought, in the form of an apology card. A woman selecting wedding thank-you notes with the grim determination of someone choosing a coffin lining. Two holiday renters looking for "something romantic" because their cottage had a hot tub and they felt obligated to match the brochure.

Through it all, Valentine Row moved outside like a living postcard. The wind pushed salt up the lane. Bunting snapped. Somewhere, a busker played an out-of-tune love song and made it everyone's problem.

Cal replaced the hinge on my door with silent competence. He did not ask for thanks. He did not need it. He only looked at me occasionally, as if he expected the door to be the least of my sticking points.

When the last of the early customers left, Nisha drained her tea and stood. "I've got to go," she said. "Lunch prep. People can't flirt on an empty stomach."

"You'd think they could," I said. "Given how much of it is hot air."

Nisha smirked. "If Hugh comes, you send him away."

"If Hugh comes," I said, "I will be busy."

"With what," she asked.

"With breathing," I replied.

She rolled her eyes and left, bell chiming behind her. The lane swallowed her in damp light and gull noise.

Cal finished tightening the final screw and stood. "Door should behave now," he said.

"It will," I said. "Until it decides to punish me for my optimism."

He reached for his jacket. "About that contract."

I lifted my chin. "I didn't say I was taking it."

"You didn't say you weren't," Cal replied.

We stood in the quiet, the shop humming with paper and possibility. Pip shifted, then crawled out from under the counter, stretched long, and walked to me. He pressed his shoulder against my shin, steady and warm. He did it when he sensed I was making a decision I did not want to admit to myself.

I looked down at him. "Traitor," I murmured.

Pip blinked slowly. His stare was calm, almost bored. No freeze. No bark. He was not alarmed, but he was attentive. He wanted sausage rolls, yes, but he also wanted my feet on the ground.

Cal watched the exchange like he understood exactly what it meant. "I'm not saying don't take it," he said. "I'm saying take it like you're walking onto a slippery deck."

"I know how to walk on a slippery deck," I said. "I spent two decades watching people fall over their own feelings."

Cal nodded. "And you kept them standing."

"I kept paperwork standing," I corrected.

He stepped closer, lowered his voice. "Hugh's got a lot riding on this weekend. Sponsors, press, the council. If anything goes wrong, they'll want it contained. Managed. If something goes very wrong, they'll want it blamed on someone convenient."

I felt my stomach tighten, not with fear, exactly, but with recognition. I had seen the mechanics of blame. It was as procedural as anything else, if you knew what to look for.

"Convenient like the little shop on Valentine Row," I said.

Cal's eyes stayed on mine. "Convenient like the woman who keeps notes."

There was that too. People who recorded reality were unpopular in towns built on branding.

I took a breath, then opened my Pocket Log to a fresh line.

09:41. Cal warning: Mariner's Crown weekend. High-profile. Sponsors. Optics. "Contain. Manage. Blame."

I snapped the book shut.

"Fine," I said, and the word tasted like surrender even though it was only strategy. "If they ask, I'll listen. I'll set my terms. I'll keep my copies. I'll keep my originals. And if they try any portal nonsense, I'll tell them no."

Cal's mouth lifted at one corner. "Good."

"It's not good," I said. "It's rent."

Cal looked around my shop, at the card racks, the ribbon spools, the work table with its neat stack of envelopes and the wax seal kit I rarely used because I did not trust sentimentality that needed a stamp.

"It's yours," he said quietly.

That did something to my chest I did not like, so I ignored it.

The bell above the door chimed again.

Pip froze.

Not his usual lazy attention, not a casual glance. Full stillness. His head lifted. His eyes fixed on the doorway. He did not bark yet. He stared first, like he was measuring the shape of what had entered.

I felt it too, the shift in the air, the sense of a story walking in before it announced itself.

A man stepped into the shop in a charcoal suit that looked expensive enough to be an insult. Controlled smile. Eyes that skimmed the room like a checklist. Hugh Mercer, in the flesh, bringing his optics with him like cologne.

"Harriet Crowe," he said, as if he had rehearsed the name to make it sound like a favour. "How fortunate. I was hoping to catch you."

Pip held his stare.

SHERLYN HARLOCK

I adjusted my glasses on their chain, lifted my Pocket Log, and uncapped my fountain pen.

"Were you," I said. "How convenient for both of us."

CHAPTER 2

The contract and the manager

Hugh Mercer did not browse.

He assessed.

He took in my shop the way an insurer takes in a flooded kitchen, already calculating what could be blamed on poor maintenance. His suit was charcoal and too clean for Hartcombe's salt air, which meant either he had a dedicated dry cleaner or he did not spend enough time outside to understand how weather works. His hair was neatly controlled. His smile was neatly controlled. Everything about him suggested a man who believed mess was a personal failing.

Pip stayed frozen, staring, body angled forward but not moving. The single bark had not come yet. That was Pip's warning system in its first stage, the quiet one. He only barked when it became necessary to make the rest of us pay attention.

I kept my fountain pen uncapped. The nib hovered over my Pocket Log like it had its own opinions.

Cal shifted beside me, not in front of me. Cal never did that. He positioned himself the way a lifeboat positions itself in rough water, close enough to steady, not close enough to take over.

"Hugh," Cal said, his voice flat. "Didn't expect to see you down here."

Hugh's smile twitched in the direction of Cal, as if acknowledging a minor weather event. "Cal Reeve. I was unaware you'd moved into stationery."

"I've moved into retirement," Cal replied. "I do small repairs. For neighbours."

Hugh's eyes flicked to the hinge Cal had just replaced, then back to me. "Ms Crowe. I'm sorry to intrude. I'm sure you're very busy."

I looked at him for a beat. "I'm open," I said. "Busy would imply I'm enjoying myself."

A normal person would have laughed. Hugh did not. He kept the smile, adjusted it half a millimetre, and continued as if my tone was a minor typo.

"We're finalising vendors for our Second-Chance Romance Weekend," he said. "The Mariner's Crown is hosting a curated programme. Elegant. Safe. On-brand."

On-brand. There it was. The phrase that made people like Hugh feel soothed.

"It sounds exhausting," I said.

Hugh's smile tightened. "It will be highly publicised, Ms Crowe. The Trust are partners. The council are involved. We're expecting media attention. We want the guest experience to be seamless."

I wrote in my Pocket Log.

09:43. Hugh Mercer in shop. "Curated. Elegant. Safe. On-brand. Seamless."

Hugh watched me write, the way some people watch a security camera. Not fear, exactly. Irritation at being recorded without consent.

He glanced down at Pip, still staring. "And your... dog."

"Pip," I said. "He hates camera flashes and sudden applause. He's already suffered enough."

Pip's stare did not waver. Hugh did not like that. People who live on optics do not enjoy being seen clearly by something that cannot be managed.

Hugh cleared his throat. "I'd like to discuss a contract for your services. We need place cards, table plans, vendor instruction sheets, and printed materials for the weekend."

"You have printers," I said.

"We have printers," Hugh agreed, as if that were a concession. "But not your aesthetic. Not your... craft."

Craft. Another soothing word. It told him the work would look handmade, while still being controlled.

Cal's eyes moved to mine for a moment. He did not nod. He did not shake his head. He let me decide. That, I realised again, was his particular brand of steadiness. He did not push. He simply stayed.

"Fine," I said. "If you want me, you email me details and I'll send a quote."

Hugh's smile widened slightly, as if he had just won a small battle. "Excellent. We're on a tight timeline. I'd prefer you come to the hotel today for a brief meeting. My team are there. We can finalise details in one sitting."

I didn't like "finalise" any more than I liked "seamless." Both implied a person wanted to remove my ability to change my mind later.

"I'm not leaving the shop," I said.

Hugh's eyes flicked to the empty lane outside. "There are other shops on Valentine Row. Surely you can close for an hour."

"I can," I said. "I won't."

Cal's mouth twitched again, faint approval.

Hugh inhaled as if he could smell stubbornness. "Ms Crowe, this weekend brings significant revenue to Hartcombe. We're supporting local vendors. You're part of this town."

I felt my jaw tighten.

I was part of this town the way a barnacle is part of a boat. Attached, useful, and not asked permission.

"I'm part of paying my bills," I said. "If you want my work, you accommodate my hours."

Hugh held my gaze. Then he smiled again, like a man realising a different tactic was required. "Of course. I understand. Perhaps I can persuade you with efficiency."

He reached into his coat and pulled out a slim folder.

"Here," he said. "Contract. Terms. Standard."

Pip made a low sound from his throat, not a growl, not quite. A disapproving commentary.

I took the folder and did not open it. "I don't sign anything in my shop," I said. "I read it first."

Hugh's eyebrows lifted. "It is routine."

"So is paperwork," I said. "And yet people still manage to be surprised by it."

Cal shifted his weight and looked at Hugh. "You heard her."

Hugh's controlled smile faltered, just for a breath. Then it returned. "Very well. I'll have my assistant schedule the meeting. It would be best handled at the Mariner's Crown, Ms Crowe. Our staff can answer questions. We have the vendor portal set up."

There was that phrase again. Vendor portal. Nisha's warning flashed in my mind like a lighthouse signal.

"My normal email works," I said.

Hugh's eyes cooled. "For this weekend, we require all vendors to use the portal. It logs approvals. Tracks versions. Protects the brand."

Protects the brand. Like it was fragile. Like it was alive.

"I'm not a vendor," I said. "I'm a supplier."

Hugh's smile became more patient, which is another way of saying condescending. "For the purposes of this weekend, Ms

Crowe, you are a vendor."

Cal's gaze hardened. Pip's stare sharpened. I felt my fountain pen in my fingers, the familiar weight of decision.

I opened the folder, not because he had earned it, but because I needed to see how badly he planned to tie my hands.

The contract was two pages of polished language that pretended it was fair. It wasn't. It was full of clauses designed to keep me responsible for anything that made Hugh look bad.

The line that made my stomach go cold was buried halfway down page one, wrapped in the soothing cotton of "best practice" and "quality control."

All print files must be submitted through the Mariner's Crown Vendor Portal. The Hotel reserves the right to request revisions, hold publication, and approve final output to ensure brand consistency.

I did not need a registrar's training to recognise control when it was dressed up as professionalism.

I wrote in my Pocket Log without looking away from the page.

09:46. Contract: mandatory "Vendor Portal" submission. Hotel reserves approval, revisions, hold publication. "Brand consistency."

"Standard," Hugh said, watching me read. "It ensures our guests receive a unified experience."

My mouth tightened. "A unified experience," I repeated.

Hugh nodded, pleased. "Exactly."

"What it ensures," I said, "is that you can edit my work without my consent, delay my output, and then blame me if it goes wrong."

Cal let out a low breath, like he'd been expecting that.

Hugh's smile held, but his eyes sharpened. "That is not the intention."

"Intention isn't enforceable," I said. "The clause is."

Hugh's jaw tightened almost imperceptibly. "Ms Crowe, our sponsors are strict. The Trust are particularly sensitive about… presentation."

Ah. There it was. The Trust. The real client behind the curtain.

I closed the folder. "I'll meet you at the hotel," I said. "Today. One hour. I'm not signing anything until I've had time to read it properly, and I will not be uploading my files to any portal that gives you approval rights over my output."

Hugh smiled wider, as if humouring a child. "We'll discuss it."

"No," I said. "We won't. I'm telling you."

A silence settled in the shop, thickened by the salt air and Pip's unwavering stare.

Then Pip barked once. Sharp. Clean. A line drawn in sound.

Hugh flinched. He recovered quickly, but it was there.

"I see," Hugh said softly, as if Pip had spoken English. He looked back at me. "Very well. One hour. Today. I'll have my office expect you."

He stepped backward, as if leaving before he said something regrettable. "Cal," he said, the controlled smile returning. "Always a pleasure."

Cal did not return it. "Aye," he said. "Same."

Hugh left. The bell chimed. The lane swallowed him like it swallowed everything, with salt and wind and the faint pretence of romance.

Pip unfroze and shook himself, as if dislodging Hugh's presence like sand. Then he walked to my foot and sat on it.

"Fine," I told him. "I'm going."

Cal studied me. "You don't have to."

"Yes," I said. "I do. Because if I don't, he'll spin it as me being difficult, and then he'll find someone else who will let him do whatever he wants with my name attached. I'd rather see the trap while I'm still standing outside it."

Cal nodded slowly. "Smart."

"It's not smart," I said. "It's defensive."

"That's the same thing most days," Cal replied.

I capped my pen, slipped my Pocket Log into my coat pocket, and reached for my scarf. The wind outside had teeth. Hartcombe did that. It looked pretty while it bit you.

"Take Pip home," I said to Cal.

Pip lifted his head sharply. His eyes widened with offence. He hated being excluded. He also hated applause. Pip's relationship with attention was complicated.

"You can't bring him into the hotel anyway," Cal said, as if this were settled.

"I could," I said. "But Hugh would have him removed for not matching the brand."

Cal snorted. "Aye."

Pip made a small protesting noise. Then he trotted to Cal's side, because Pip liked Cal, and Pip also liked warm kitchens, and Cal's house had fewer strangers.

I locked the shop, checked the latch twice because I was that woman, and set off up Valentine Row toward the Mariner's Crown.

The lane was busier now. Tourists in bright jackets. Couples holding hands as if it proved something. A photographer with a long lens angling for content. Bunting everywhere, flapping like it was trying to escape.

Hartcombe sold romance the way seaside towns sold fish. Fresh, plentiful, and not always honest about the smell.

As I walked, the Mariner's Crown rose ahead, all polished windows and curated charm. It sat at the edge of the harbour like it owned the view. The building was old enough to look respectable and renovated enough to look expensive. People loved that combination. It let them feel they were buying heritage without inconvenience.

Inside, the lobby smelled of citrus cleaner and money. Everything gleamed. The floor was the kind of stone that punished cheap shoes. A vase of roses stood on a table as if it had been instructed to look effortless.

A receptionist in a neat black blazer looked up. Her smile was trained.

"Good morning," she said. "Welcome to the Mariner's Crown."

"I'm here to see Hugh Mercer," I replied.

The receptionist's eyes flicked over my navy peacoat, my sensible boots, my scarf that did not match the roses. She took in my glasses on their chain. She took in the lack of performance. Then she brightened slightly, as if realising I was not a guest but an obligation.

"Name," she said.

"Hattie Crowe. Crowe Cards & Vows."

Recognition hit her face. "Ah. Yes. He's expecting you. Just a moment."

She picked up the phone and spoke softly. I could hear the vague murmur of Hugh's name, the careful deference of someone who knew where their pay came from.

While she spoke, I took out my Pocket Log and wrote:

10:12. Mariner's Crown lobby. Citrus cleaner, roses. Receptionist trained smile. "Expecting you."

The receptionist ended the call and looked up. "If you'll follow me."

She led me across the lobby to a side corridor that smelled less like guests and more like work. Carpets that muted footsteps. A door marked ADMINISTRATION.

My registrar instincts flared. Back corridors were where truth lived. Front halls were for stories.

We passed a board with a printed schedule pinned to it. SECOND-CHANCE ROMANCE WEEKEND: a neat column of events with names like "Compatibility Banquet" and "Sunrise

Vows Renewal." It made my skin itch.

At the end of the corridor, the receptionist tapped on a door and stepped aside. "Mr Mercer will see you now."

I walked in.

Hugh's office was exactly what you would expect from a man who could say "brand protection" without blushing. Neutral colours. No personal photographs. A framed aerial shot of Hartcombe harbour that made the town look like a toy set. A desk immaculate enough to suggest he did not do his own paperwork.

Two people sat at a small meeting table. A woman in her late thirties, crisp blouse, tablet in hand, eyes that flicked to me and away as if scanning. An older man with a lanyard and a folder, the type who looked like he had been recruited from a corporate chain to bring "standards" to a town that did not ask for them.

"Hattie Crowe," Hugh said, standing. His smile was back in place. "Thank you for coming."

"I came because you walked into my shop," I said. "Not because I enjoy corridors."

The woman blinked. The older man's mouth tightened. Hugh's smile stayed smooth.

"This is Melissa Shaw," Hugh said, gesturing to the woman. "Events operations. And Martin Goss. Sponsor liaison."

Sponsor liaison. Translation: watchdog.

I sat without being invited, because I refused to start a meeting already at a disadvantage.

Hugh sat opposite, hands folded. Melissa's tablet was angled like a shield.

"Ms Crowe," Hugh began, "we're delighted to bring you on board. Your work is known for its quality."

"I'm not on board," I said. "I'm in a chair."

Hugh's smile did not move, but his eyes tightened again. He

was not used to people refusing the script.

"Fine," I continued. "Tell me what you need. Tell me your deadlines. Then we'll discuss your contract clause that tries to make me your employee."

Martin cleared his throat. "It's standard vendor language."

"Standard for who," I asked, and looked directly at him. "Hotels. Trusts. Councils. People who like control."

Melissa tapped her tablet, pretending not to listen while listening hard.

Hugh leaned forward, voice softening into persuasion. "The portal is not about control, Ms Crowe. It's about protection. We've had incidents in the past. Miscommunications. Errors."

"Errors like what," I asked.

Hugh hesitated half a beat, then recovered. "Last-minute changes not reflected on print materials. Incorrect dietary information. Seating confusion. It's chaos. Our guests are paying for a curated experience."

There was that word again. Curated. Like humans were a display.

My pen moved.

10:16. Hugh: portal "protection" due to past "incidents." Claims miscommunications, seating chaos, dietary errors.

I looked up. "So you're worried about paperwork."

Hugh brightened, relieved I had said something he understood. "Exactly."

"And your solution," I said, "is to centralise control in a system that can be edited by someone you're not naming."

Hugh's smile twitched. "The system logs edits. It creates accountability."

"Accountability for who," I asked.

Melissa finally spoke. "For everyone," she said, too quickly.

I turned my gaze to her. "Do you have individual logins."

Melissa blinked. "Yes."

"And does the portal use generic accounts," I asked, "like 'vendor admin'."

Melissa's eyes flicked to Hugh. She did not answer. That was an answer.

I wrote again.

10:18. Melissa avoids confirming generic admin account. Noted.

Hugh lifted a hand. "Let's not get lost in technicalities."

"Technicalities are where people hide," I said. "I am not lost. I'm looking directly at the mechanism you plan to use to hold me responsible for something I didn't do."

Martin leaned forward. "Ms Crowe, the Trust are investing heavily in Hartcombe's brand. We cannot afford anything that undermines public confidence."

There it was. The Trust speaking through a man.

"Public confidence," I repeated. "In romance."

In the silence that followed, I felt something shift. Not fear. Not certainty. Something sharper. A sense that this weekend was not just a silly hotel event. It was a pressure point.

Hugh's voice turned gentle, like he was offering me a favour. "You'll be compensated well. We're prepared to pay a premium for speed and discretion."

Discretion. Another key word. People who asked for discretion rarely wanted it for innocent reasons.

I leaned back in my chair. "You want place cards, table plans, vendor instructions, and printed materials. Fine. My terms are simple. You tell me exactly who can edit files. You do not upload my print files into a system I don't control. You send change requests by email, with a named person responsible. I print from my end. If you need emergency prints on-site, I bring sealed originals and a hard copy approval sheet that gets signed."

Melissa's eyes widened slightly, as if she had never heard anyone demand a signed approval sheet in her life.

Hugh's smile became strained. "That's… extensive."

"It's basic," I replied. "You're the one obsessed with protection."

Martin gave a tight smile. "We require uniform process."

"You require plausible deniability," I said. "There's a difference."

Hugh's eyes cooled. He sat very still. "Ms Crowe. Perhaps you're not suited to this partnership."

There it was. The threat.

I held his gaze. "Perhaps you're not suited to transparency."

Melissa made a small noise like she had swallowed a word.

Hugh's voice turned sharper. "The portal is non-negotiable."

I paused, letting the silence stretch. Then I said, "Then I'm non-negotiable too."

Hugh blinked. Not often. But he did.

I stood, slowly, and took the contract folder from my bag. "You walked into my shop, Hugh. You want my quality because your in-house printers can't match it, and because you need someone local to hold the blame if your 'curated' weekend goes sideways. You can do that without me, or you can do it with my rules. Choose."

My heartbeat was steady. That was the registrar in me. When people threatened, you did not flinch. You let them show their hand.

Hugh's jaw clenched. Martin looked irritated, but uncertain. Melissa looked like she wanted to disappear under the table.

Finally, Hugh exhaled. "Sit," he said.

I remained standing. "Answer."

Hugh's controlled smile came back, but it was thin now, the kind you wear when you realise you might lose. "We'll allow email submission," he said. "Provided you also upload final versions to the portal for archive."

"No," I said.

Hugh's eyes flashed. "Ms Crowe."

"I won't upload anything into a system that gives you the power to swap it later," I replied. "If you want an archive, I'll provide a PDF copy with a timestamp and my signature line, and I'll keep a duplicate. If your portal is about logging, you can log my email."

Melissa's fingers tightened around her tablet.

Hugh stared at me for a long moment. Then he nodded once, sharp. "Fine. Email, plus signed PDF archive. You will receive all change requests through Melissa, in writing."

Melissa looked like she had just been assigned a bomb.

I sat back down.

"Good," I said. "Now, tell me what the weekend actually is."

Hugh's smile recovered slightly. "Second-Chance Romance Weekend. Couples, singles, a featured relationship coach, press coverage, curated dinners. It's a significant event for the town."

"And who is your relationship coach," I asked, pen poised.

Hugh's smile warmed, almost genuine. "Dr Lucian Vale."

The name landed like a bad smell. It was not a name you forgot, even if you had never met the man. The sort of celebrity therapist who made a living telling strangers what they were doing wrong, with enough charm to make them pay for it.

I wrote it down anyway.

10:24. Featured coach: Dr Lucian Vale.

"Fine," I said. "Deadlines."

Melissa recovered, tapped her tablet, and began listing needs: place cards by Friday. Seating plan drafts by Thursday night. Vendor instruction templates by Wednesday. Dietary notes to be finalised by Thursday morning. The speed of it was absurd.

As she spoke, I noticed something else.

A file tray on Hugh's desk. A neat stack of papers, clipped together, with a Trust logo on the top sheet.

VALENTINE HERITAGE TRUST. GRANT CONDITIONS.

My eyes did not linger long. I didn't need to. I could feel the weight of it. Money with strings.

Hugh followed my gaze and slid the tray slightly, as if moving it could erase my noticing.

I smiled, just a little. "You're being sponsored," I said.

Hugh's expression remained neutral. "We're supported."

"By the Trust," I said.

Martin leaned forward. "The Trust's mission is to protect Hartcombe's heritage."

"By buying it," I replied.

Martin's smile tightened.

Hugh cut in smoothly. "Ms Crowe, our aim is to provide guests with an exceptional experience. Your role is crucial. We want everything polished."

Polished. That was a warning word too. Polished meant scrubbed. Polished meant nothing sharp could show through.

"And if something unpolished happens," I said quietly, "what do you do."

Hugh's eyes held mine. "We handle it internally."

There it was again. Contain. Manage. Blame.

My pen moved.

10:29. Hugh: "handle internally."

I glanced up at Melissa. "Do you have a list of who has access to your documents and files."

Melissa blinked. "Access."

"Your portal," I said. "Your printers. Your office. Your staff corridors. Who can walk into your admin area and pick up a folder."

Hugh's smile returned, brittle. "Ms Crowe, you're here to print place cards, not conduct a security audit."

"I'm here to protect my name," I replied. "And to keep you from rewriting my work and pinning it on me."

A silence.

Then Melissa spoke softly, "Only authorised staff."

"Names," I said.

Melissa's eyes flicked to Hugh again. Hugh's jaw tightened.

"I'll need them," I said. "If I'm going to meet your deadline, I need a single chain of communication. One named person to approve changes, one to sign off final files, one to collect prints and confirm receipt."

Hugh stared at me. Then, slowly, he nodded. "Melissa," he said. "You'll be Ms Crowe's contact. All changes route through you. Nothing else."

Melissa nodded like she was trying not to show fear. "Understood."

I made a note.

10:32. Hugh assigns Melissa as sole contact. "Nothing else."

"Good," I said. "Now, about your contract clause. Brand protection."

Hugh's mouth tightened.

I slid the contract across the table and tapped the clause with my pen. "You want the right to hold publication. That means you can delay my work and still demand deadlines. Remove it."

Hugh's eyes flashed. "It's standard."

"It's leverage," I said. "Remove it."

Martin opened his mouth, but Hugh raised a hand.

Hugh's voice dropped lower. "Ms Crowe. Do you want this contract or not."

I held his gaze. "Do you want my work or not."

They stared at each other across the table, two people who both believed in procedure but for different reasons. Hugh believed procedure protected him. I believed procedure protected reality.

At last, Hugh leaned back. "We can amend the clause," he said, the words tasting unpleasant in his mouth. "Limited to objective errors. Spelling. Formatting. Not content."

"And not approvals," I said.

Hugh exhaled. "And not approvals."

I wrote it down.

10:36. Clause amended: only objective errors. No hold publication. No approval rights.

Melissa looked relieved, which made me curious. People like Melissa did not get relieved about minor contract language unless they had seen it used as a weapon before.

I gathered my papers and stood. "Send me the amended version by email today. From your named account. Not a generic one. I want full metadata."

Hugh's smile did not reach his eyes. "Of course."

I turned to leave, then paused. "One more thing."

Hugh's eyebrows lifted. "Yes."

"The portal," I said. "You insisted on it as non-negotiable. Who insisted, exactly."

Hugh held my gaze. Then he said, carefully, "It's policy."

"That's not an answer," I replied.

Hugh's voice became smooth again. "It's the Trust's preference."

There it was. Clean. Finally.

I nodded. "Noted."

And it was. In ink.

10:38. Hugh admits portal preference driven by Trust.

I left the office with my stomach tight and my mind already running through mechanisms. The Mariner's Crown wanted control. The Trust wanted a paper trail they owned. Hugh wanted the weekend to look perfect no matter what happened behind the scenes.

Outside, the lobby was full of soft music and staged calm. I walked through it like a person exiting a different world. The air smelled of roses and cleaner and something else I couldn't name. Not danger. Not yet. More like pressure, building slowly.

On the way out, I spotted a small sign near reception advertising the weekend. A glossy poster with smiling couples and the words SAFE, CURATED, UNFORGETTABLE.

I wondered, briefly, what Hartcombe would do if it became unforgettable for the wrong reason.

Then I stepped back into the salt air and headed toward Valentine Row, Pocket Log heavy in my coat, and the unpleasant sense that I had just agreed to stand very close to someone else's carefully constructed story.

Behind me, the Mariner's Crown doors shut with a soft, expensive click, like a lock being turned.

CHAPTER 3

Guest list intake

By the time I got back to Valentine Row, the wind had upgraded from irritating to personal.

It funnelled down the lane with the enthusiasm of a gossip who'd been saving a story all morning. Bunting snapped. Shop signs creaked. A gull hovered above the roofline, judging my life choices with the calm certainty of an animal that never had to file a tax return.

I unlocked Crowe Cards & Vows and stepped inside, shutting the door on the salt air as if it was a rude relative. The shop settled around me at once. Paper. Ink. Quiet. The particular calm you only get from things that do not have motives.

Cal had already brought Pip home. I knew because Pip's red lead was back on its hook by the counter, and because there were faint paw marks on the mat that meant he'd done his usual turn in a circle before deciding where to lie. He left evidence everywhere and then acted offended when anyone noticed.

I hung my peacoat on the hook, unlooped my scarf, and stood for a moment without moving.

It wasn't that I felt threatened. Hugh Mercer was not a man who did threats openly. He did policies and consequences. He did meetings and "brand consistency." He did calm, curated pressure until someone signed what he needed them to sign, then he smiled as if it had been their idea.

But something about that office, about Martin Goss and his sponsor lanyard, about Melissa's quick obedience and quicker fear, had sat in my stomach like undercooked pastry.

I pulled my Pocket Log from my pocket and wrote before the day could blur into something I would regret forgetting.

11:07. Back in shop. Contract pending amendments. Portal preference confirmed: Trust. Named contact: Melissa Shaw. Sponsor liaison: Martin Goss.

I snapped the notebook shut and went behind the counter to the kettle.

Tea first. Always.

The kettle clicked on, filling the quiet with a gentle threat of boiling. I set a mug down and stared at the stack of glossy flyers on the counter again.

SECOND-CHANCE ROMANCE WEEKEND.

The Mariner's Crown logo.

The Trust name, smaller but still there.

It was remarkable how romance branding could make almost anything look harmless. A heart on a poster and everyone assumed the worst you were selling was disappointment.

The bell above the door chimed.

I didn't have to look up to know who it was. Only one person managed to enter my shop as if she was briskly delivering common sense to a world that refused to accept it.

Nisha Patel swept inside with a paper bag tucked under her arm. She smelled faintly of coffee and cinnamon, the way Harbour Kettle always did, as if even the air over there was trying to be comforting.

"I saw you coming back from the hotel," she said, voice sharp. "So I brought a sandwich in case you decided to live on tea and spite again."

"Tea and spite are a balanced diet," I replied.

Nisha put the bag on the counter and leaned in, eyes narrowed. "Tell me you didn't sign anything."

"I didn't sign anything," I said. "I did, however, spend an hour being politely bullied by a man in a suit who believes the word 'curated' is an oath."

Nisha's mouth tightened. "And the portal."

"He insisted," I said. "I refused. We negotiated. He admitted the Trust prefers it."

Nisha made a low sound of disgust. "Of course they do."

I poured the tea and let the steam hit my face. It smelled like black tea and relief. "I want everything in writing," I said. "Names, timestamps, approvals. If they try to wiggle, I want proof."

Nisha's gaze flicked to my Pocket Log on the counter. "You always want proof."

"Yes," I said. "It's one of my better qualities. It saves time."

Nisha snorted. "It also makes you unpopular."

"That's fine," I said. "I don't run a popularity contest. I run a stationery shop."

Nisha leaned closer, voice dropping. "Hattie. Be careful. That hotel runs on secrets. And the Trust doesn't like anyone keeping their own record."

"I noticed," I said, and meant it.

The kettle clicked off. I poured the tea, then unwrapped the sandwich. Ham and mustard, on decent bread, no nonsense. Nisha did not feed people because she was sentimental. She fed people because she understood that hunger makes you stupid.

"I'm going to my office," I said. "The guest list is coming today. I want to see it before anyone starts changing it."

Nisha's eyes sharpened. "You think they'll change it."

"I think they already have," I replied.

Nisha straightened. "Call me if it gets weird."

"It's Hartcombe," I said. "It's always weird. The question is what kind."

She gave me a look that said she didn't enjoy my humour when I used it to dodge fear, then she left.

The bell chimed. The door shut. Quiet returned, soft and complete.

I carried my tea and sandwich into the back office.

It wasn't glamorous. A narrow room with a desk that had been second-hand even when it was first purchased. A printer that was temperamental in cold weather. Stacks of thick cardstock, envelopes, and sample swatches. Shelves lined with labelled folders, each one the tidy remains of someone else's "special day."

A registrar's office without the public.

I sat down, woke my laptop, and waited for the day's first email to arrive like a confession.

It came two minutes later.

From: Melissa Shaw.

Subject: Vendor Onboarding, Second-Chance Romance Weekend.

I opened it.

Melissa's email was brisk and impersonal, the kind that suggested she had been trained to keep emotion out of anything that could be forwarded. It included an amended contract draft attached, plus a link to the Mariner's Crown vendor portal, with login credentials.

There it was. Even after the negotiation, the portal had made itself unavoidable. It was the hotel's spine. Everything ran through it. Hugh could call it "archive" and "logging" and "policy" all he wanted, but it was control dressed as compliance.

I took out my Pocket Log and wrote.

11:19. Email from Melissa Shaw. Contract amendment attached. Portal link provided anyway. Login issued.

Then I printed the email. Not because I needed it. Because paper does not vanish when someone decides to "update" the system.

The printer whirred, then spat out the page with a faint, familiar pattern at the edge. Not visible to most people. A tiny registration dot that my machine left on every run, a practical quirk that had saved me more than once when someone claimed I'd printed something I hadn't.

I slid the page into a new envelope and wrote on the front in black ink:

SECOND-CHANCE ROMANCE. PORTAL EMAIL. 27 JAN. 11:20.

Then I signed the flap with my initials, because I did not do half measures.

I opened the contract amendment next.

The clause about "hold publication" had been softened, as promised. It now read like a polite suggestion rather than a leash.

Still a leash, though.

I marked the changes with a pen, made a note to read it properly later, and moved on. The contract could wait. The guest list could not.

I clicked the portal link.

The site loaded with that particular bland efficiency that corporate systems loved. White background. Grey navigation bar. A heart icon in the corner as if the software itself was trying to flirt.

I logged in.

A dashboard appeared with categories: Vendor Documents. Guest Management. Seating Plans. Dietary Notes. Upload History. Edit Logs.

Edit logs. That was the one that mattered.

My cursor hovered there for a moment before I clicked. My hand felt steady, but my chest tightened anyway. Some instincts don't die. They just change costumes.

The edit logs page opened with a list of recent activity, each entry time-stamped and labelled.

A neat column of dates and times. A list of file names. A column labelled Edited By.

I scrolled slowly, letting my eyes catch what they wanted to catch.

Melissa Shaw. Hugh Mercer. Guest Team. Vendor Admin.

There it was.

Vendor Admin.

Not a person. A generic account. A mask.

I wrote in my Pocket Log before I let myself get annoyed enough to become careless.

11:27. Portal edit logs show generic account: "Vendor Admin." Not named. Concern.

Then I clicked into the Guest Management section.

A file labelled: Guest List and Dietary Notes, Version 3, was available to download.

Version 3.

I had not seen Version 1 or 2.

I downloaded the file and opened it.

The document appeared on my screen with the polished formatting of a hotel that wanted to look effortless. Table numbers. Guest names. Meal preferences. Allergy notes. A column for "relationship status" because apparently that was now a logistical requirement.

I scanned the top of the list first. The names meant nothing to me yet, but patterns always did.

And the patterns were wrong.

There were multiple guests listed with near-identical names.

Not just similar. Suspiciously similar.

Two "S. Harrington" entries. One "Sally Harrington." One "Sarah Harrington." One "Sara Harrington." No surnames to distinguish. No middle initials. No dates of birth. Nothing that would separate a person from a typing mistake.

A "James Whitcombe" and a "Jamie Whitcombe." Same surname, no relationship noted. That could be real. It could also be sloppy. Sloppy was usually a door someone walked through on purpose.

I scrolled further.

A cluster of names that looked like they had been copied from somewhere else entirely. The spacing was slightly off. The font size shifted by a fraction. The alignment of the columns didn't match the surrounding entries. It was the kind of thing you noticed if you'd spent twenty years watching people try to make paperwork lie and fail by half a millimetre.

I highlighted one block and zoomed in.

The kerning was different. Tiny, almost imperceptible. The letters sat too close together, like they'd been squeezed into a shape they didn't belong in.

I wrote it down.

11:34. Guest list contains copied blocks. Font/spacing inconsistent. Near-duplicate names.

I printed the guest list.

Not the whole thing yet. Just the first two pages, because printing twenty pages of chaos without understanding it was how people ended up drowning in paper and blame. The printer hummed. Pages slid out warm and crisp. My hands relaxed a fraction at the feel of them.

Paper was honest about what it was. Digital files were not.

I marked the pages with a small dot at the corner in my own pen, a habit from my registrar days. An invisible signature if you didn't know to look.

Then I went back to the screen and scrolled down to the dietary notes section.

The column was a minefield.

No nuts. No shellfish. Gluten-free. Dairy-free. Vegan. Low sugar. High protein. "No coriander" which I thought was less an allergy and more a personality.

Some notes were sensible. Some were performative. Some were the kind of thing people wrote when they wanted attention more than they wanted safety.

But the dates were what caught me.

Several dietary notes had been edited after midnight.

Not last week. Not earlier that day. After midnight last night.

And the editor on those changes?

Vendor Admin.

I stared at the screen for a long moment, then took a sip of tea that had gone lukewarm.

In my Pocket Log, I wrote:

11:41. Dietary notes edited after midnight. Editor: "Vendor Admin." Why.

I clicked into the version history.

Version 1 had been created three days ago. Version 2 had been created yesterday morning. Version 3 had been created at 00:17 today.

Someone had been awake, editing guest details, in the small hours of the morning.

There were plenty of innocent reasons for that. Late arrivals. Last-minute cancellations. A hotel team working late.

But there were also reasons that were not innocent.

I had spent long enough in registry work to understand the simplest truth about lists. If you controlled the list, you controlled the reality. The list decided who belonged. Who had rights. Who was invited. Who sat where. Who got served what.

People fought over lists more viciously than they fought over love. Love was messy. Lists were power.

I reopened the guest list document and started examining it properly.

I pulled my chair closer, made my office lamp brighter, and did what I always did when someone handed me a polished document and expected me to trust it.

I looked for the seams.

I clicked into one of the suspicious copied blocks.

A name near the middle: "Louise Pennington."

The name itself wasn't odd. The way it sat in the document was.

There was a faint line beneath the name, like a watermark half-hidden, misaligned. Not visible unless you zoomed in, and even then it was easy to dismiss as a printing artefact.

I zoomed in further.

The watermark wasn't a line.

It was a stamp.

Oval. Slightly skewed. The ghost of ink that had once been pressed onto paper with a heavy hand.

And I knew it.

Not because I'd seen it on a hotel document.

Because I had used it.

Hartcombe Registry Office.

Old-style. The kind we used before everything became slick and digital. Before the fire. Before the archives were "relocated" and people started using words like "revitalisation" to cover up ownership grabs.

My throat tightened.

I leaned closer, eyes narrowing at the bottom of the page.

The stamp wasn't in the visible body text. It sat in the footer area, clipped by the template edge. Someone had copied and pasted a block of names from an old document that still carried the stamp mark in the footer. It hadn't been cleaned properly. It hadn't been scrubbed.

It was a mistake.

Or it was a tell.

I stared at it long enough that my eyes started to ache. Then I sat back slowly, as if moving too quickly might make it vanish.

My fingers went to my Pocket Log. The pen felt heavier than it had five minutes ago.

11:49. Guest list footer shows old Hartcombe Registry Office stamp mark in copied name block. Should not exist.

I underlined should not exist twice.

The kettle in the front of the shop clicked faintly as it cooled. Outside, the row went on pretending it was a romantic destination. Inside my office, my past had just slid into my present through a formatting error.

I did not panic. I did not gasp. I did not do any of the things people expected from a woman discovering something "shocking."

I did what I'd done for twenty years.

I secured the evidence.

I printed the page with the stamp mark.

Then I printed it again, because printers jam and portals "update."

The two pages slid out warm. I held them to the light of the lamp. There it was. The faint oval ghost. The words barely readable but unmistakable if you knew them.

HARTCOMBE REGISTRY OFFICE.

It was like seeing an old scar. Not painful, exactly. Just proof that something had happened that people preferred to forget.

I slid the pages into a fresh envelope and labelled it carefully.

GUEST LIST V3. STAMP MARK FOOTER. 27 JAN. 11:55.

Then I wrote a short note on a separate sheet, because context mattered.

Faint registry stamp appears clipped in footer beneath "Louise Pennington" block. Indicates copied text from older template. Stamp should have been removed.

I signed and dated it, then put that sheet into the same envelope.

There were people in Hartcombe who would have told me I was being dramatic. That I was seeing ghosts. That a stamp mark was nothing.

Those people were usually the ones with something to gain.

I went back to the portal and clicked into the document properties.

Author: Vendor Admin.

Last modified: 00:17.

Source template: Valentine_GuestList_Master_2013.dotx.

My breath stopped for a fraction of a second.

2013.

That was before my shop. Before I left the registry office. Before the fire year everyone spoke about like a myth they couldn't quite agree on. Seeing a template from that era inside a modern hotel portal was like finding a coal ember in a clean fireplace.

I wrote it down.

12:02. File properties show template: "Valentine_GuestList_Master_2013.dotx." Author: Vendor Admin. Last modified 00:17.

I didn't know what it meant yet. I wasn't arrogant enough to pretend I did.

But I knew what it suggested.

Someone had access to old registry materials.

Someone had copied from them.

And someone had done it quietly, at night, inside a system designed to look official.

I closed the laptop for a moment and sat with my hands flat on the desk.

The paper stacks around me were silent. The printer sat warm and faintly smug, as if pleased to have been useful. My fountain pen lay on the desk, uncapped, waiting.

I thought about Hugh's office. The Trust grant conditions on his desk. Martin's line about "public confidence." Melissa's fear. The insistence on the portal. The phrase "handle internally."

Then I thought about the stamp.

I had not seen that stamp in years. It was supposed to have been destroyed, or at least secured, after the registry office moved operations. That was the story. The official version. The version everyone nodded along to because it was easier than admitting they didn't know what had happened.

But stamps do not walk away on their own.

Templates do not resurrect themselves.

Someone had held onto them.

And now they were inside a hotel's romance weekend paperwork.

A list.

Always a list.

I opened the laptop again and went deeper.

I compared Version 2 to Version 3.

The portal allowed a side-by-side view, as if it was doing me a favour.

Names added. Names removed. Dietary notes changed. Seating placeholders adjusted.

And then, near the top, a guest block that had been inserted wholesale.

A chunk of names appeared that weren't alphabetised. They

were grouped as if they'd come from a different list entirely.

There was a "Penny Harrow" in there.

The name snapped my attention like a string pulled tight.

Harrow was a local name. Not rare, but not common either. I'd heard it on Valentine Row. I'd seen it on old property forms. I'd filed it, years ago, when I still sat behind a registry desk and watched people become legal in front of me.

I didn't know Penny Harrow. Not yet. But if she was on this guest list, she was not here for the romance.

Hartcombe locals did not pay for curated weekends at the Mariner's Crown unless they were trying to be seen, or trying to see something.

I circled her name on the printed page and wrote beside it: LOCAL.

Then I wrote another note.

12:15. Penny Harrow appears in inserted block of names. Local. Why in romance weekend list.

A sound came from the front of the shop. The bell chimed.

Then, from behind the door, Pip barked once.

Sharp. Clean.

Cal's voice followed, calm as ever. "Hattie."

I stood, went to the shop front, and opened the office door.

Cal stood near the counter with Pip at his side. Pip's wiry coat looked slightly damp, and his darker muzzle was dusted with sand. He'd been down near the harbour, then. Cal's cheeks were pink from the wind.

"You're back," I said.

Cal nodded. "Thought you might forget to eat again."

"I ate," I said, gesturing vaguely. "Nisha fed me."

Cal's mouth twitched. "Good."

Pip walked straight to my foot and sat on it. Anchor behaviour. He looked up at me, then glanced toward the back office door as if asking why I was making that particular face.

Cal noticed too. "What is it."

"Guest list," I said.

Cal leaned an elbow on the counter. "Just names."

"No," I replied. "It's never just names."

I went behind the counter, poured fresh tea, and handed Cal a mug without asking if he wanted one. He did. Everyone did. He took it with a quiet nod.

I didn't invite him into the back office. Not yet. Those pages needed to stay as contained as possible. Cal was steady, but the fewer people who touched evidence, the better. I didn't have to be in an investigation to know that.

I pulled my Pocket Log out and flipped to the relevant page. "The portal edit logs show a generic account," I said. "Vendor Admin. It made edits after midnight. And the guest list file has a copied block from an old template."

Cal's eyes sharpened. "Old how."

I kept my voice even. "Old enough to have a registry office stamp mark in the footer."

Cal stared at me. The humour left his face entirely.

"That stamp shouldn't exist," he said.

"No," I agreed. "It shouldn't."

Pip made a small huff and leaned harder against my boot, as if he approved of the seriousness.

Cal lowered his mug slowly. "Did you print it."

"Twice," I said.

Cal nodded, like a man hearing a safety check report. "Good."

I took a breath. "I don't know what it means yet," I added, because I refused to inflate a clue into a story before I had facts.

Cal held my gaze. "But it means something."

"Yes," I said. "It does."

Outside, someone laughed in the lane. A bright, carefree

tourist sound. Inside my shop, the air felt tighter, as if the paper itself was listening.

Cal spoke carefully. "You're working that weekend."

"I'm printing for it," I replied. "That's what I agreed."

"And you're using their portal," he said.

"I'm using it to download what they send," I corrected. "I am not letting them upload my files into it without my own archive."

Cal nodded again. "Keep doing that."

"I intend to."

Pip shifted, then froze suddenly, staring toward the shop window.

A camera flash popped outside.

Pip barked once, furious and betrayed.

I glanced through the glass and saw a tourist couple taking photos of the bunting, the shopfronts, the "romantic" lane. They didn't mean anything by it. They were collecting moments like souvenirs.

But Pip's reaction hit a nerve in me anyway.

This town had learnt to live under observation. Under branding. Under stories sold to strangers. It made people behave differently, even when they insisted it didn't.

Pip hated the flash because it forced attention. Because it startled. Because it demanded performance.

That, I realised, was why I hated the portal too.

It demanded performance from paper.

It made a list into a stage.

Cal followed my gaze and watched the tourists. "You all right," he asked.

I took my glasses off, wiped them with the corner of my scarf, then put them back on the chain. A small ritual. A way to buy myself a second.

"No," I said. "But I'm functional."

Cal's mouth twitched, faint humour returning. "That's about as good as it gets."

I nodded, then picked up my Pocket Log again. "I'm going back to the list," I said. "I want to map every change. I want to know who is being added and who is being removed. If someone is controlling this weekend through paperwork, I want to see their fingerprints."

Cal lifted his mug. "Call me if it gets worse."

"It's paperwork," I said. "It's always worse."

He didn't argue.

Pip stayed on my foot until Cal drained his tea. Then Cal whistled softly and Pip trotted to him, not happily, but willingly. Cal clipped on the red lead.

At the door, Cal paused. "Hattie."

"Yes."

His voice was low. "This is the sort of thing that starts small. A list. A stamp. A late-night edit. Then it turns into a mess you can't scrub out."

I held his gaze. "I know."

Cal nodded once, then left.

Pip gave me one last look over his shoulder, as if warning me not to do anything stupid in his absence, then he was gone too.

The shop fell quiet again.

I went back into the office and laid out the printed pages on the desk.

Guest list pages. Dietary notes. The stamp-mark page in its envelope. My notes, signed and dated.

I created a new folder on my computer too, because I wasn't sentimental about paper at the expense of practicality. I saved the downloaded file with my own naming system, not theirs.

GUESTLIST_V3_DOWNLOAD_27JAN_1119.

Then I downloaded Version 2 as well, so I could keep my own record, regardless of what the portal claimed later.

As the files saved, I caught myself thinking, briefly, about the women I used to deal with at the registry. The ones who came in smiling, clutching bouquets, pretending marriage was a simple matter of signatures and love. The ones who arrived later, alone, asking quietly how to retrieve records, how to prove things, how to fix what a story had broken.

Paper always mattered more after the romance ended.

Hartcombe, it seemed, just liked to speed up the lesson.

I clicked into the portal again and pulled the edit log for the guest list file.

00:17. Vendor Admin. Insert block. Template 2013.

00:22. Vendor Admin. Modify dietary notes.

00:31. Vendor Admin. Adjust seating placeholders.

00:40. Hugh Mercer. Approve Version 3.

Hugh had approved it. That meant he either knew what it contained, or he trusted the system enough not to check. Neither option made me feel better.

I wrote the approval time down.

12:44. Hugh approved Guest List V3 at 00:40 after Vendor Admin edits.

Then I leaned back in my chair and stared at the ceiling for a moment.

This was how it started. Not with a scream. Not with a body. With a list. With a stamp mark. With a late-night edit account that didn't have a name.

In Hartcombe, romance was the cover story.

Paper was the real plot.

I picked up my fountain pen again, turned to a fresh page in my Pocket Log, and began doing what I did best.

I started reconstructing the truth, one timestamp at a time.

And somewhere in the neat, polished rows of names on the Mariner's Crown guest list, a faint oval stamp sat like a bruise, refusing to be scrubbed out.

CHAPTER 4

Suspect lineup begins

The calendar reminder on my laptop chimed at ten to two, as if it was doing me a kindness.

SECOND-CHANCE ROMANCE WEEKEND, it said, in that cheerful font that always looked smug to me. PRE-WEEKEND PLANNING CALL.

I stared at it for a moment and considered the many ways a person could ruin a day without leaving their chair.

Then I took a slow sip of tea and adjusted my reading glasses on their chain, because I did not believe in facing nonsense without proper vision.

Pip lay under the desk with his chin on his paws, red collar visible, brass tag catching the light when he breathed. He was not asleep. Pip did not do asleep when he sensed activity. He did alert, which for him meant stillness and a sort of offended watchfulness. His left ear half-flopped, notch at the tip making him look permanently unimpressed.

"Don't start," I told him.

He blinked once, as if he would never dream of it.

My office smelled of paper and printer toner, with a faint note of mustard from the sandwich Nisha had forced on me earlier. Outside, Valentine Row was busy in that mild winter way, tourists in bright coats pretending the wind was romantic. Inside, my shop felt like a different country. A quieter one. One where words stayed where you put them.

I opened my Pocket Log to a clean line and wrote the time.

13:50. Planning call start in 10 mins. Tea. Pip present.

I did not write "nerves" because I wasn't nervous. I was alert, which was more useful and less dramatic.

The email from Melissa Shaw sat in my inbox with a link to the call and, naturally, a reminder to "ensure your camera is on to foster connection."

Foster connection. I had spent twenty years watching people foster connection in registry offices, and half of them still ended up hating each other over a dispute about who kept the good towels.

I clicked the link anyway.

The screen loaded into a familiar grid of faces, some with cameras on, some with their names floating over black squares like anonymous threats.

Melissa Shaw's face appeared in the top left. Crisp blouse. Hair pulled back. Events operations energy, which meant she looked permanently as if she was running late even when she wasn't. Her smile was polite and faintly strained.

"Harriet Crowe," she said, brightening when she saw me. "Hi, Hattie. Thank you for joining. Can you hear us all right?"

"I can hear you," I said. "Whether I enjoy it remains to be seen."

Melissa's smile flickered, then recovered. "Right. Well. Good. We're just waiting for a few more to join."

A man with a neat beard and a headset hovered in another window, expression fixed in that neutral influencer look that suggested he had trained his face not to show surprise. Beside him was a woman with glossy hair and a white jumper, lips slightly parted like she was mid selfie even when she wasn't.

Their name labels read: Miles & Saffy Hartwell.

Influencer couple, then. Names that sounded curated to match.

Saffy glanced sideways at Miles, then back at the camera. Miles adjusted something off-screen and did not look up. The tension between them was the quiet sort. Not a fight. A performance rehearsal.

A black square labelled PENNY HARROW sat below them. No camera yet.

Another black square labelled IMOGEN BAIRD, VHT.

VHT. Valentine Heritage Trust.

And then there was a man who had his camera on, sitting in what looked like a hotel suite with a headboard visible behind him, hair perfectly styled, teeth bright enough to power the Mariner's Crown lobby lights.

Label: Dr Lucian Vale.

He smiled at the camera like he thought it owed him money.

"Hello, hello," he said, voice smooth in that practiced way, as if he was greeting an audience rather than a planning call. "Are we all here to make love happen?"

Pip shifted under the desk. Not a freeze. Not yet. But his eyes opened wider.

I felt my mouth tighten. Love happen. Like it was a firework display.

Melissa's smile turned brighter, a woman grateful someone else had taken over the oxygen. "Dr Vale, lovely to have you. We're just waiting for Penny Harrow and Imogen Baird to join."

"I'm here," the black square labelled IMOGEN BAIRD said, voice sharp and clipped. Camera still off. "I'm listening."

Melissa's shoulders straightened, as if she'd been yanked upright by a string. "Wonderful, Imogen."

Of course.

Trust rep, then. Quiet hostility, the kind that didn't need a raised voice to make the room colder.

A chime sounded. PENNY HARROW joined, camera on for a second, then off, then on again, as if she was fumbling with settings. Finally her face appeared.

Penny Harrow looked like someone who knew how to be noticed and was trying not to be. Early thirties, maybe. Dark blonde hair pulled into a loose knot. No obvious makeup. A soft scarf around her neck. Journalist, then, but not the flashy kind. She sat in a small room with a plain wall behind her and a mug in her hand.

"Sorry," she said quickly. "Signal's odd."

"Not a problem," Melissa said, voice bright. "Welcome, Penny."

Penny's eyes flicked across the grid, taking in faces and names fast. She paused when she saw mine.

"Hattie Crowe," she said. "Crowe Cards & Vows."

"That's me," I replied. "You're Penny Harrow."

Penny nodded once, sharp. "Yes."

Dr Vale leaned forward slightly, eyes narrowing as if he'd found something amusing. "How wonderful," he said. "The local paper people. We love local texture."

I wrote in my Pocket Log.

13:59. Dr Vale: "We love local texture."

Pip made a small huff, offended on behalf of the entire town.

Melissa clapped her hands once, brisk. "All right. Thank you, everyone. This is our final pre-weekend alignment call. We'll cover the run-of-show, guest experience, media guidelines, dietary needs, seating, and any last-minute changes. The goal is to ensure everything runs seamlessly."

Seamlessly. Another soothing word.

I took a sip of tea, because my patience had limits.

Melissa continued, "Dr Vale will be leading the Compatibility Banquet segment and the morning session. Penny will be joining as press, and Miles and Saffy will be our official social partners."

Saffy smiled brightly, teeth perfect. Miles nodded once, as if acknowledging his own existence.

"And Imogen," Melissa added, voice careful, "is here representing the Valentine Heritage Trust."

Imogen's black square remained black. Her voice was calm and cold. "We are funding this weekend. Yes."

There was a silence that landed like a paperweight.

Dr Vale chuckled softly. "Fabulous. Sponsors are love, aren't they."

Imogen did not respond.

I wrote:

14:01. VHT rep: "We are funding this weekend."

Melissa cleared her throat. "Right. So, first item, guest list."

My fingers tightened slightly around my mug. Guest list. The list that had been edited at midnight by a generic account. The list with an old registry stamp mark hiding in the footer like a confession.

Melissa shared her screen. A spreadsheet appeared, names and notes neatly arranged.

"This is the final guest list as of this morning," she said. "Any changes must come through me in writing."

Good. At least that part had stuck.

I leaned forward. "I've downloaded Version 3 from the portal," I said. "There were edits after midnight. Who made them."

Melissa's eyes flicked away from the camera for a fraction of a second. "The guest team."

"The guest team is not a person," I replied. "Names."

Miles shifted, looking bored. Saffy glanced at him with the faint irritation of a woman who had to carry the charisma for two.

Dr Vale smiled wider. "Hattie, darling," he said, as if we were friends. "It's a romance weekend. Lists change. Love doesn't respect office hours."

I did not look at him. I looked at Melissa. "Who made the edits."

Melissa's smile tightened. "It was… an admin account."

My tea went slightly more bitter.

"Vendor Admin," I said.

Melissa hesitated, then nodded once.

Imogen's voice cut in, sharp. "The portal exists to ensure compliance. It logs everything. That is the point."

I wrote:

14:04. Melissa confirms edits via admin account. Imogen: portal for compliance.

Penny's camera was on now. She watched without speaking, eyes moving between faces, absorbing. Journalist behaviour. I respected it. Silence first. Notes second. Questions later.

Miles finally spoke, voice smooth and practised. "Can we keep this upbeat," he said. "Our audience responds to positivity."

Saffy nodded vigorously. "Yes. We're here for romance and transformation."

I stared at my screen. "You're here for content," I said. "Romance is the set dressing."

Saffy's smile faltered. Miles' eyebrows lifted as if he was unused to being spoken to like an adult.

Melissa rushed in. "Right, yes, thank you. We'll stay focused on logistics."

I took a breath. "I'm focused on logistics," I said. "And the logistics are that a generic admin account can change the guest list, dietary notes, and seating placeholders after hours. That's a liability. If something goes wrong, it will be blamed on whoever printed the wrong version. Which is me."

A pause.

Imogen's voice was cool. "If you are concerned, Ms Crowe, you should use the portal to ensure you have the most current version."

"That assumes the portal is trustworthy," I replied. "And that the edits are accountable."

Dr Vale laughed softly, like I'd made a charming joke. "Oh, Hattie. You're adorable. You're living in a little paper world, aren't you."

The words landed with the neat cruelty of a man who believed he was being kind.

My face stayed still. My stomach did not.

I picked up my pen and wrote in my Pocket Log, exact, because that was how you kept truth from being rewritten.

14:06. Dr Vale: "You're adorable. You're living in a little paper world, aren't you."

Then I looked up at the camera. "Yes," I said. "I am. It's called reality. Paper is what keeps people honest when their stories don't."

Dr Vale's smile stayed on his face, but his eyes cooled slightly. He wasn't used to being pushed back on. He was used to being adored. Adoration makes men lazy.

Melissa cleared her throat, voice strained. "Okay. So, dietary notes. We have several gluten-free requests, nut allergies, and one severe shellfish allergy. The kitchen has been briefed."

"I've seen dietary notes edited after midnight," I said.

Melissa's cheeks went faintly pink. "Yes, one guest updated their requirements last night."

"Which guest," I asked.

Imogen cut in, voice sharp. "That is private."

Penny's eyes narrowed slightly. She didn't speak, but she noted it.

I kept my tone even. "I don't need to know the medical detail,"

I said. "I need to know that the edits are legitimate and that there is a named person responsible. If you want privacy, fine. But then you provide a signed approval sheet that confirms the version number and the time it was finalised. Otherwise you're setting up a situation where you can say the printer made a mistake."

Miles sighed audibly. "This is so intense."

I looked at his camera. "People with allergies don't find it intense. They find it necessary."

Saffy's smile returned, but it was brittle. "We absolutely care about safety," she said. "We're going to highlight how thoughtful the hotel is."

Thoughtful. Another soothing word.

Imogen's voice came in again, calmer now, which was somehow worse. "Hattie Crowe," she said, using my full name like she was reading it from a form, "your role is print production. The Trust expect professionalism."

I smiled slightly. "So do I."

A beat.

Melissa moved the call forward. "Right. Seating plan. The Compatibility Banquet involves a table rotation segment led by Dr Vale. Guests will have assigned seats for each course."

My jaw tightened.

Assigned seats. Seat swaps. Dessert targets. I didn't know the murder yet. I didn't know the method. But my instincts were already watching the mechanics. People got hurt in the gaps between assigned and actual.

Melissa continued, "Hattie will produce place cards and table plans. We will distribute them through the ballroom team."

I interjected, "I will hand off sealed packets, and I want a named person to sign receipt."

Melissa nodded quickly. "Yes. Of course."

Imogen did not speak, but I could feel her displeasure through the silence.

Dr Vale leaned closer to his camera, voice turning warm as if he was soothing a nervous bride. "Everyone, let's remember why we're here," he said. "These guests are brave. They're opening their hearts again. We need to create a safe container."

Pip's head lifted under the desk. He hated applause. He also hated fake sentiment. He didn't bark, but his stare fixed on the screen with the same stillness he'd shown when Hugh walked into my shop.

Dr Vale continued, "We're going to do a moment at the start of the banquet where we invite everyone to applaud themselves for showing up."

Saffy squealed softly. "Oh my gosh, yes."

Miles nodded like he'd just been handed a brand deal.

Penny's face remained neutral.

I did not speak, but my pen moved.

14:12. Dr Vale plans applause moment at banquet.

Pip made a low warning sound.

"Dr Vale," Melissa said, "we'll coordinate with audio and lighting for that."

"And the press," Dr Vale added, smiling at Penny's square. "Penny, darling, you'll capture the magic, yes."

Penny's smile was polite and cold. "I'm here to observe," she said. "Not to sell."

Dr Vale laughed as if she'd made a clever joke. "Observation is selling, sweetheart. You just pretend it isn't."

I wrote:

14:13. Dr Vale to Penny: "Observation is selling, sweetheart. You just pretend it isn't."

Penny's eyes flicked to mine for a fraction of a second. Not agreement. Recognition. She understood what he was.

Imogen's voice cut through. "Dr Vale, please refrain from

antagonising press. The Trust are sensitive to negative coverage."

Dr Vale's smile didn't waver. "Imogen, my love, I don't antagonise. I provoke transformation."

Saffy laughed too brightly. Miles smiled.

I stared at the screen, because there are few things more dangerous than a man convinced he's doing people a favour.

Melissa moved on quickly, as if trying to keep the call from turning into theatre. "Media guidelines. Miles, Saffy, you'll have designated filming zones. No filming in staff corridors. No filming private guest rooms. No filming kitchen areas."

Miles raised a hand. "We need behind-the-scenes."

Melissa smiled tightly. "We can arrange staged behind-the-scenes content."

Saffy nodded. "Yes, like, a cute moment with the chef plating."

Melissa's eyes flicked to Imogen's black square, then back. "Yes. We can do that."

I wrote:

14:16. Influencers want behind-the-scenes. Hotel offers staged version.

Pip shifted. He did not like staged anything. He liked sausage rolls and honest smells.

Penny spoke for the first time in a way that wasn't purely defensive. "Will there be access to the vendor portal logs for press," she asked, tone neutral.

Melissa blinked. "Portal logs."

Penny's smile was polite. "You said transparency. I'm curious how it works."

Imogen answered instantly. "No."

Penny's face stayed calm. "Noted."

I liked her.

Dr Vale leaned in, eyes bright. "Penny, darling, if you want transparency, you should ask the guests. They'll tell you everything when they're emotional."

Penny's smile became thinner. "I don't exploit people's emotions," she said.

Dr Vale's voice turned patronising again, honey-coated. "Oh, everyone does. Some of us just admit it."

My pen hovered. I didn't write that one. Not because it wasn't useful. Because my page was already full of him. I didn't want him to take up more space than necessary.

Melissa cleared her throat again. "All right. Any other concerns."

I raised my hand slightly. "Yes. The guest list document contains a copied block from an old template. It shows a registry stamp mark in the footer."

The call went quiet.

Even Miles and Saffy stopped smiling, though they looked confused rather than worried.

Melissa's face went blank. "A stamp mark."

Imogen's voice was sharp. "That is not relevant."

"It's relevant to me," I replied. "Because it suggests the list has been cobbled together from older documents, and if it's older documents, it raises questions about where those documents came from."

Imogen's tone turned colder. "You are overreaching."

Penny's eyes sharpened. She didn't speak, but she leaned closer to her camera.

Dr Vale chuckled. "Oh, Hattie. Darling. This is exactly what I mean. You can't bring the bureaucracy into the bedroom."

I looked directly into my camera for the first time in the call. "And you can't bring the bedroom into public policy," I said. "Yet here we all are."

Miles frowned. Saffy looked lost.

THE VALENTINE GUEST LIST

Melissa's voice was strained. "Hattie, can you send me a screenshot of what you're seeing."

"Yes," I said. "I've printed it too."

Imogen's voice snapped, "Do not distribute Trust materials outside the portal."

I smiled slightly. "You might want to update your contract. It does not say I can't print what I'm required to print."

Silence.

Then Melissa spoke, carefully, "Imogen, we'll handle this internally."

The phrase landed again, like a door closing.

Penny's lips pressed together. She wrote something down, I could tell. Journalists had their own version of Pocket Logs, even when they called them something else.

Dr Vale leaned back, bored now that the conversation had turned to paper rather than feelings. "Can we return to the guest experience," he said. "We're building hope here."

Imogen answered immediately. "Yes."

Melissa took control again. "Right. So, Dr Vale's sessions. The Compatibility Banquet will begin at seven. Guests will be seated at seven-thirty. Dessert service at nine. Rotation segment at eight-fifteen. Hattie, your place cards must be final by Friday noon."

"Final," I said. "Meaning no edits after Friday noon."

Melissa hesitated. "Ideally."

"No," I said. "Meaning no edits after Friday noon. If you want edits, you pay for a rush and you sign the approval sheet. Otherwise you accept the risk."

Imogen's voice came in soft, controlled. "We do not accept risk, Ms Crowe. We manage it."

"Then manage it with a deadline," I replied.

Melissa nodded quickly. "Yes. Friday noon. We'll lock the list."

I wrote:

14:24. Melissa agrees: lock guest list Friday noon. Approval sheet required for changes.

Penny spoke again, quiet. "Who has access to the admin account," she asked.

Melissa blinked. "Penny, that's internal."

Penny's smile didn't change. "So is the weekend. Yet here I am."

Dr Vale laughed. "Oh, I like her. She's spicy."

Penny didn't smile back.

Imogen's voice was sharp. "This is not an interrogation."

Penny's tone stayed even. "It's journalism."

Imogen's black square remained black. "The Trust do not appreciate hostile framing."

Penny's eyes narrowed. "Then don't give it."

I felt a small, reluctant spark of admiration. Penny Harrow had more backbone than most people Hartcombe produced. Or maybe she'd developed it in self-defence. Either way, it was useful.

Melissa hurried the call toward closure. "All right. Thank you, everyone. We'll send out a follow-up email with action points. Hattie, I'll email you directly for the print specs and final guest list sign-off. Dr Vale, we'll coordinate the run-of-show. Miles and Saffy, we'll provide filming guidelines. Penny, your press pass will be ready at check-in. Imogen, we'll keep you copied."

Imogen's voice was flat. "Ensure compliance."

Dr Vale smiled. "Ensure love."

Miles and Saffy smiled too, as if they'd been told to.

Penny didn't.

"Before we end," Dr Vale said, eyes on me again, "Hattie, darling, you should loosen up. If you keep gripping that pen, you'll give yourself wrinkles."

I held his gaze, calm. "Wrinkles are proof I've survived," I said.

"I'd worry more about what your teeth are trying to hide."

For the first time, Dr Vale's smile faltered.

Pip barked once, sharp, as if punctuating my point.

Melissa's laugh came out too loud. "Right. Thank you, everyone. We'll see you this weekend."

The call ended.

My office went quiet so fast it felt like someone had shut a lid.

Pip crawled out from under the desk and stood with his body stiff, staring at the laptop screen, even though the faces were gone. He froze, then gave one single bark at nothing.

"All right," I told him, voice low. "I heard you the first time."

He looked up at me, dark eyes intent, then pressed his shoulder against my shin.

Anchor.

I reached down and scratched behind his half-flopped ear. "You don't like him," I murmured.

Pip sneezed once, which was his version of an opinion.

I picked up my Pocket Log again and read over what I'd written, because that was how you turned a call into evidence instead of letting it dissolve into feelings.

Dr Vale: patronising. Treats people like props. Likes to provoke. Likes applause.

Penny Harrow: controlled. Observant. Not easily managed. Asked about admin access.

Influencer couple: hungry for behind-the-scenes, will push boundaries, will frame anything for content.

Imogen Baird: Trust rep. Hostile to questions. Insists on compliance. Hates mention of stamp mark.

Melissa: anxious, trying to keep everyone happy, likely trapped between Hugh and Trust.

I didn't write "suspects" because it was early. No one was dead. No crime had been committed that I could prove. But the mechanics were already there. Pressure. Control. Lists. The urge to manage perception.

That was how it began.

Not with blood. With brand.

I opened my email and started drafting a message to Melissa.

Subject: Guest List Lock and Approval Process.

Short. Clear. No room for interpretation.

I wrote that the guest list would be locked Friday at noon. Any changes after would require a written change request from Melissa, a signed approval sheet acknowledging version number and time, and an additional rush fee. I wrote that I would print only from the final version provided by email, and I would maintain my own archive of that file and all correspondence.

Then I attached a photo of the printed page showing the faint stamp mark clipped in the footer.

I hesitated for one second before hitting send.

Not because I was afraid.

Because I knew what would happen next.

When you show people a flaw in their perfect story, they either fix it or they punish you for noticing.

I sent it anyway.

Pip sat at my foot, steady.

Outside, Valentine Row kept selling romance to strangers.

Inside, my Pocket Log sat open on the desk, ink drying on the line where Dr Lucian Vale had dismissed my work as a "little paper world."

If he thought paper was small, he was about to learn what paper could do when it stopped playing along.

CHAPTER 5

Arrival day and backstage access

Friday arrived with the particular confidence of a day that believed it owned me.

Valentine Row was already awake when I opened the shop, not because anyone in Hartcombe enjoyed mornings, but because tourists treated cold air as a novelty and romance as an activity. The bunting was back. It always came back. You could take down a heart, but someone would replace it with two, as if doubling down could make sentiment less embarrassing.

I unlocked the door, flicked on the lights, and listened to the shop settle around me. Paper has a sound when it warms, a faint soft shift that is probably imaginary and yet I could swear I heard it. Ink and card stock and ribbons were my normal weather, reliable, honest. The Mariner's Crown was not.

Pip wasn't under the counter. The gap felt wrong, like discovering you'd put your keys somewhere sensible and now couldn't remember where. Cal had him at home for the day. That was the plan. Pip hated camera flashes and sudden applause, and the weekend promised both in industrial quantities. Keeping him away from the hotel was not just kindness. It was basic safety.

Still, the empty space under the counter tugged at me.

"You're fine," I told the silence, which was a habit I had never admitted to until I caught myself doing it.

I made tea, because tea is how you prove you still control something, and laid out my final printed materials on the worktable.

Place cards, thick and clean, names in a classic typeface that didn't flirt with anyone. Table plans, folded and labelled. Vendor instruction sheets with my signature line at the bottom and a tiny dot pattern near the corner from my printer, consistent across my run. If anyone tried to substitute my work later, I wanted proof.

I checked each pack twice, not because I was anxious, but because I had spent too many years watching people pretend they were organised when they were actually improvising.

My Pocket Log sat open beside the stacks. I wrote as I went.

08:12. Arrival day. Final place cards, table plans, vendor instructions packed. Dot pattern consistent. Sealed packets prepared. Pip with Cal.

I used brown paper envelopes for the key items and sealed them with plain tape, then signed across the tape with my initials. It wasn't dramatic. It was practical. It turned "I don't know" into "Here's exactly what happened."

I slipped the sealed packets into a canvas tote and added a staff-only folder, sturdy and unromantic, with a bright tab that read STAFF USE ONLY in block capitals. I wanted no confusion about what belonged where.

A message popped up on my phone from Nisha.

You eating today or doing your usual martyr act?

I stared at it, then typed back.

Eating. Calm down.

Her reply came fast.

Good. Also, do not let them shove you into any photos. You'll hate it.

I almost smiled.

I did hate it. Photos turned everything into a performance. They flattened truth into angles. Pip knew it too. That was why he reacted the way he did, freezing and staring, then that single bark when he'd had enough.

I zipped the tote, locked the shop, and stepped back into the wind.

Hartcombe's harbour air was sharp, salty, and loud with gulls that behaved like they were on a commission. I walked up the lane with my tote banging lightly against my leg, each step making me more aware of the weight I was carrying.

It wasn't heavy in the physical sense.

It was heavy in the way responsibility is heavy when people are already arranging how to blame you.

The Mariner's Crown sat at the edge of the harbour like it had been built to impress strangers and intimidate locals. Its windows shone. Its front doors were polished enough to reflect your faults. The lobby inside smelled of citrus cleaner and roses, exactly as it had earlier in the week, as if they refreshed the scent every hour to keep reality from creeping in.

A sign at reception announced:

WELCOME TO SECOND-CHANCE ROMANCE WEEKEND
SAFE. CURATED. UNFORGETTABLE.

I didn't trust any event that promised "safe" before it promised "honest."

Melissa Shaw met me near the side corridor, not in the lobby. That told me two things. First, she didn't want me seen carrying my practical, unglamorous tote through the front like a tradesperson. Second, she didn't want me overheard.

Melissa's smile looked stretched thin today. Her eyes had the faint shine of someone who had already had three conversations that morning and lost all of them.

"Hattie," she said, stepping forward briskly. "Thank you for coming early. We're turning the ballroom over in two hours."

"I came early so I could leave early," I replied.

Melissa did a small laugh that sounded like pain. "Right. This way."

She led me through a staff door and into the service corridor.

The difference was immediate. The front of the hotel was perfume and soft music. The back was bleach, carpet glue, and the faint metallic smell of stacked chairs. The lights were harsher. The walls were scuffed. It felt like the building's true face.

I preferred it.

We passed a linen trolley. A chef in a white jacket carrying a crate of bottled water. A young staff member taping directional signs to a wall, her fingers moving fast. Everyone looked busy, but only some of them looked competent.

Melissa glanced back at my tote. "You brought everything."

"Not my patience," I said. "But yes."

She gave me a look, then opened a door marked BALLROOM SERVICE.

Inside, the ballroom was half finished and already loud.

Tables were set in neat rows, white cloths pulled tight. Centrepieces were being placed, pale roses and greenery arranged to look effortless, which is always how effort presents itself when it's expensive. A small stage stood at one end with a microphone being tested. Speakers hummed. A lighting rig glowed faintly overhead.

Someone was running through a playlist of romantic songs, because obviously they were. A slow piano intro drifted across the room like a threat.

Melissa raised her voice to be heard. "We'll set the place cards on tables once the chairs are finalised. The table plan will go on the easel near the entrance."

I nodded, scanning the room the way I always did. Not for

beauty. For flow. For access points. For where people would hover.

The staff corridor door was propped open. A second door at the far side led toward the kitchen. Another led to what looked like a small office.

Backstage access.

I wrote in my Pocket Log while walking, because I could.

09:03. Ballroom set up in progress. Multiple access doors. Staff corridor door propped open.

Melissa saw me writing and didn't comment. She'd learnt at least that part.

We reached a long table at the side of the room where staff were stacking programmes and name badges. A clipboard sat there. A young woman with a tight bun and nervous hands looked up.

"This is Chloe," Melissa said. "Ballroom supervisor."

Chloe's smile was polite and brittle. "Hello."

I pulled out my sealed packets and placed them on the table. "I need a signature for receipt," I said.

Chloe blinked. "Receipt."

Melissa jumped in quickly. "Yes, Chloe. Hattie requires a sign-off. Version number and time."

Chloe looked confused, then flicked her eyes toward Melissa as if asking if this was really necessary.

Melissa's smile didn't budge. "Please."

Chloe reached for the clipboard. I handed her my approval sheet, already prepared, with the version number, date, and time, plus a line for her name and signature. It was not complicated. It was just inconvenient for people who preferred things vague.

Chloe signed.

I took the sheet back, checked the signature, then wrote my

own initials beside it. Chain-of-handling. Simple.

"Thank you," I said.

Chloe looked relieved, as if she'd completed a task without being yelled at.

I set my STAFF USE ONLY folder down beside the packets. "These instructions are for staff," I said. "Not guests. They include the final table plan and handling notes. If you need changes, you come through Melissa in writing."

Chloe nodded quickly. "Understood."

Melissa's shoulders loosened a fraction. She looked like someone who had been holding her breath for days.

We moved deeper into the ballroom to set the table plan on the easel.

As we walked, I noticed the usual early arrivals.

The influencer couple, Miles and Saffy Hartwell, were near the stage filming something with a phone held at a perfect angle. Saffy's smile was on, bright and fixed. Miles stood slightly behind her like a backup dancer.

A hotel staff member hovered nearby, looking unsure whether to stop them or encourage them.

No behind-the-scenes, Melissa had said. No staff corridors. No kitchen. Yet here they were, already blurring boundaries, because content always wanted more.

Saffy spotted Melissa and waved with manic cheer. "Hi, babes. We're just getting a quick teaser."

Melissa's smile turned even tighter. "Please stay within the designated filming area."

Miles nodded like he was agreeing, while still filming.

I didn't look at them for long. Influencers were not my main problem. They were a nuisance, a noise layer, a way the hotel could claim everything was "documented" while still controlling the narrative.

My main problem was the list.

I placed the table plan on the easel, checked it was stable, and stepped back to view it.

The table numbers were clear. The names were legible. The layout flowed.

Perfect, if you believed perfect existed.

Melissa leaned in and lowered her voice. "Hugh wants you in his office briefly."

My stomach tightened.

"Why," I asked.

Melissa's eyes flicked toward the office door at the far side. "He wants to confirm you're aligned."

Aligned. Another word people used when they meant obedient.

"I'm aligned with being paid," I said.

Melissa's mouth twitched, but she didn't laugh. "Just five minutes."

Five minutes in Hugh Mercer's world meant a conversation where you walked out owing him something.

Still, refusing would give him an excuse to paint me as difficult. I had no interest in giving him material.

"All right," I said. "Five minutes."

Melissa led me through another staff corridor and into Hugh's office.

The space was immaculate, as always. Desk clean. A framed photograph of the harbour. A scent like expensive aftershave, faint and persistent.

Hugh stood when we entered, smile ready. He looked the same as he always did, which meant he had the luxury of still being himself.

"Hattie Crowe," he said. "Thank you for your efficiency."

"Thank you for your signature," I replied, and held up the receipt sheet.

His smile faltered slightly, then recovered. "Naturally."

Melissa hovered near the door like she wanted to vanish into the wall.

Hugh gestured for me to sit. I didn't.

He began in the smooth voice he used when he believed he was offering calm. "This weekend is an opportunity for Hartcombe. The Trust are watching. The council are watching. Press will be present. We need everything consistent."

"I've delivered consistent," I said. "If you want anything else, you request it in writing."

Hugh's eyes tightened. "About the stamp mark you mentioned."

Ah. There it was.

"The guest list footer," Hugh continued. "It's been handled."

"Handled," I repeated.

"Yes," Hugh said, smile controlled. "The guest team used an older template by mistake. It has been corrected."

"And who is Vendor Admin," I asked.

Hugh's smile didn't move. "It's an internal account."

"Names," I said.

Hugh's gaze hardened. "Hattie."

I held his stare. "You're asking me to take risk for your brand. I'm asking you to take accountability for your system."

Melissa shifted, eyes fixed on the floor.

Hugh's voice remained calm, but something sharper edged it. "The Trust require compliance with the portal process."

"Then the Trust can put their name on their edits," I replied.

Hugh exhaled slowly, like a man deciding how far to push. "I'm not going to debate internal permissions with a vendor."

"I'm not going to be blamed for your internal permissions," I said.

A beat of silence.

Hugh's smile returned, slightly warmer, because he was switching tactics. "I appreciate your professionalism," he said. "I do. It's refreshing. But this weekend is not the time for conflict."

"Conflict is a choice," I replied. "I'm choosing clarity."

Melissa looked up quickly, then back down.

Hugh's eyes flicked to her, then to me. "Melissa will remain your single contact," he said. "You'll be copied on any changes. That should satisfy you."

"It doesn't," I said. "But it's what I can get today."

Hugh's jaw tightened. "Good. Then we're done here."

I nodded once. "Yes. We are."

As I turned to leave, Hugh spoke again, voice soft as if offering an extra kindness. "Try to remember, Hattie, that this is a romance weekend. Guests are vulnerable. We can't have them unsettled by administrative tension."

I paused at the door and glanced back. "If your guests are unsettled," I said, "it won't be because I asked who edited their dietary notes. It'll be because someone in your building thinks control is more important than safety."

Hugh didn't respond. His smile stayed fixed. His eyes didn't.

I left.

The staff corridor swallowed me again with its bleach smell and its scuffed walls, a relief after Hugh's polished air.

Melissa followed, voice low. "Thank you for not making it worse."

"I didn't," I said. "He did."

Melissa swallowed. "I know."

That single sentence told me more than she intended.

Back in the ballroom, the set-up had shifted closer to ready. Chairs were aligned. Table numbers placed. The stage microphone was now live, producing a faint feedback squeal that made staff wince and then pretend not to.

I helped Chloe set the place cards, not because it was my job, but because it protected the chain. I didn't want someone else placing them and later claiming I'd done it wrong.

We moved table by table, the rhythm of it calming. Names placed carefully. Cards aligned. Fingers smoothed the edge of paper against cloth. The little tactile details that grounded me.

Every so often I thought of Pip, safe at Cal's house. Probably asleep now, or pretending to sleep while listening for danger. I missed the weight of him under my counter. I missed the steady presence that didn't require words.

I wrote a quick note in my Pocket Log in between tables.

10:11. Placing cards myself to protect chain. Pip absent, missed.

Dry humour didn't stop you missing a dog. It just made you less likely to admit it out loud.

Chloe watched me with a mix of respect and confusion. "You're very thorough," she said.

"I'm very untrusting," I replied. "It looks similar if you squint."

Chloe gave a nervous laugh.

As we worked, I noticed Penny Harrow in the doorway.

She wasn't in the ballroom itself yet. She stood at the threshold, half in the corridor, half in the room, as if deciding how visible she wanted to be. She wore a plain coat and held a notebook, not a phone. Her eyes moved in the same pattern mine did, scanning flow, watching people, marking who hovered near staff doors.

Her gaze met mine.

She nodded slightly, a simple acknowledgement, and then she moved away, slipping back into the corridor.

Journalists, I thought, were like cats. They appeared when they wanted, left when they wanted, and pretended you didn't matter right up until they needed you.

No, I reminded myself. My series didn't have cats. My life did not need cats.

I kept placing cards.

When we finished the last table, Chloe exhaled like she'd been holding her breath all morning. "Thank you," she said.

"Don't thank me yet," I replied. "Wait until the guests start moving."

Chloe's eyes widened. "They'll move."

"They always do," I said. "Assigned seats are a suggestion. Human beings treat suggestions as personal insults."

Melissa approached, looking harried. "Dr Vale is here," she said. "He wants to see the ballroom."

"Of course he does," I said.

She gave me a brief look that was almost apology. "Just stay out of his way."

That was not a request I could promise to honour. I didn't chase conflict, but I didn't retreat from it either.

Dr Lucian Vale entered the ballroom like he was walking onto a stage.

He wore a dark coat that looked tailored, hair perfect, smile ready. He moved with the confidence of a man who had never had to wonder whether a room would accept him. People stepped aside automatically, staff and guests alike.

He clapped his hands once.

Chloe flinched. Melissa flinched. A server carrying glasses flinched and nearly dropped them.

I thought of Pip, and felt briefly grateful he was not here.

"Hello, beauties," Dr Vale announced. "This is where the magic happens."

He caught sight of Melissa. "Darling. Have we got the applause moment set?"

Melissa's smile turned bright and brittle. "Yes, Dr Vale. We're coordinating it."

"And the press," he continued, eyes scanning the room, seeking a camera. "We'll need them to capture the atmosphere."

Penny Harrow was not in sight, which I suspected was deliberate.

Dr Vale's gaze landed on me. "Ah," he said, smile widening. "Hattie. Our little paper world warrior."

I didn't move. "Dr Vale."

He stepped closer, lowering his voice as if offering intimacy. "I was thinking. We should do something special with the place cards. Something that encourages vulnerability. Perhaps a question printed under each name. A prompt. 'What do you want to risk?' Something like that."

My mouth tightened. "No."

His eyebrows lifted, amused. "No?"

"No," I repeated. "The place cards are already printed. And I don't put therapy prompts on paper that will be photographed and posted online. That's not vulnerability. That's content."

His smile stayed in place, but his eyes cooled. "You're very cynical."

"I'm very experienced," I replied.

He chuckled softly. "Experience is just fear with better vocabulary."

I stared at him. "And charisma is often just cruelty with better lighting."

His smile faltered for a fraction of a second again.

Melissa stepped in quickly. "Dr Vale, Hugh would like to see you in the lounge. We're preparing for the welcome mixer."

Dr Vale's eyes lingered on me, then he smiled again, bright as a blade. "Hattie, darling," he said. "Try not to choke on your own seriousness this weekend."

"I won't," I replied. "I'm saving my choking for the hotel's portal."

He laughed as if I'd made a joke, then swept away with Melissa in tow.

Chloe exhaled. "Is he always like that," she asked quietly.

"I've met seagulls with more self-awareness," I replied.

Chloe's laugh was real this time. It steadied her.

I checked my Pocket Log.

10:47. Dr Vale proposes adding prompts to place cards. Refused. Notes: he seeks cameras, uses applause, patronising.

Then I moved out into the service corridor to drop my staff-only folder into the staff staging area, exactly where it belonged.

A wall board there held the staff notices. Seating plan printed large and pinned up, with table numbers and a clear map of the ballroom. Next to it were staff schedules and a list of "VIP sensitivities," which made me itch.

The seating plan was the heart of the weekend. Who sat where. Who rotated when. Who received which dessert. Who was in line of sight. Who could reach the staff doors without being noticed.

It was also the easiest thing to tamper with, because people assumed maps were neutral.

I pinned my own smaller table plan beside it, my version number at the bottom, my tiny dot pattern near the corner, and a note in marker.

FINAL VERSION. DO NOT SUBSTITUTE. ALL CHANGES THROUGH MELISSA SHAW IN WRITING.

A server walked past and glanced at it, then nodded at me as if grateful someone had said out loud what everyone was thinking.

I turned to leave.

That's when I saw him.

A man stood a few metres down the corridor, close enough to the board to be clearly reading the seating plan, far enough away to pretend he wasn't hovering. He wore a black lanyard, the kind staff had, but his clothes were too neat for service work. Not a suit like Hugh. More like "smart casual," a uniform for people who wanted to look like they belonged everywhere.

He held a phone in his hand.

He wasn't typing.

He was angling it.

He lifted it slightly, the movement quick, smooth, practised, and took a photo of the seating plan on the wall.

No flash, thank God. Pip would have lost his mind.

But the action itself hit me like cold water.

He took a photo, lowered the phone, and then looked up, eyes meeting mine briefly, as if to gauge whether I'd noticed.

Then he smiled, a small bland smile, and walked away down the corridor like he belonged there.

No hurry. No awkwardness. No guilt.

Just a person who expected access.

My body stayed still, because surprise is useless if you let it show. My fingers went to my Pocket Log automatically.

10:59. Male, smart casual, staff lanyard. Photographed seating plan on staff wall. No flash. Walked away like staff. Unknown.

I underlined Unknown.

I glanced at the board again, as if checking it hadn't shifted while I watched him.

It hadn't.

Yet.

I walked down the corridor after him, not rushing, not making it obvious, just moving as if I had a reason to be there. The corridor split near the kitchen door. He turned left, toward a staff-only staircase, and disappeared.

I stopped at the junction and listened.

Footsteps faded. A door clicked. Then nothing.

I didn't chase further. Chasing makes you look panicked. Panicked people are dismissed. I wasn't going to hand anyone an excuse to tell me I was "overreacting."

Instead I went back to the staff board and took my own photo of the seating plan, my version number visible. Proof of what was posted at 10:59. Proof of what could be compared later if it changed.

Then I went straight to Melissa.

She was in the corridor outside the ballroom, headset on, talking to someone about welcome mixer timing. When she saw my face, she paused mid-sentence.

"Melissa," I said quietly. "Someone just photographed the seating plan on the staff wall."

Melissa blinked. "What."

"Just now," I said. "Male. Staff lanyard. Not Chloe, not ballroom team. Walked away like he belonged."

Melissa's mouth opened, then closed. Her eyes flicked toward the corridor as if she could see the man still there.

"Who," she whispered.

"I don't know," I replied. "That's the point. Who has access to staff areas. Who has a lanyard. Who thinks photographing the seating plan is normal."

Melissa's face went pale. "It could be someone from AV," she said quickly, too quickly. "Or security."

"Then he can introduce himself," I said. "Because that seating plan decides everything."

Melissa swallowed. Her headset crackled with someone calling her name. She ignored it.

"I'll check," she said, voice tight. "I'll speak to Hugh."

"Yes," I said. "And you'll document it."

Melissa's eyes met mine. There was fear there, real and sharp.

"I will," she said.

I watched her for a beat, then nodded once and stepped away.

Back in the service corridor, the staff board sat there like a quiet target, everyone pretending it was harmless.

I looked at the seating plan again, names and tables in neat rows, paper pretending it could hold back chaos.

Somewhere in the building, a man I didn't know had a photo of that plan on his phone.

And he'd walked away like he belonged.

CHAPTER 6

The first switch

The Mariner's Crown looked prettier at dusk, which was the sort of thing that made me suspicious.

Lights warmed the windows. The harbour beyond was a smear of steel and black, boats bobbing like they were trying not to be noticed. Tourists drifted in scarves and optimism, clutching overnight bags as if romance could be packed neatly between pyjamas and a curling iron.

I stood outside for a moment with my hands in my peacoat pockets, letting the wind do what it always did, scrub the day's chatter out of my head. My tote was lighter now. The place cards and table plans were already in the ballroom, signed for, sealed, and supposedly safe.

Supposedly was doing a lot of work.

I could still see that man in my mind, the neat lanyard, the phone angled at the staff board, the bland smile that said he'd never once been challenged on access. I'd told Melissa. She'd promised to check. Promises were lovely. Paper was better.

Pip would have hated the hotel tonight. Camera flashes, sudden applause, strangers cooing at him like he was an accessory. Cal had him at home, which was the sensible decision. I'd still put a sausage roll on the kitchen counter at my shop earlier, wrapped in paper, labelled for Pip in my own handwriting, like a small bribe to the universe.

I'd also written a line in my Pocket Log before I left.

17:22. Welcome mixer tonight. Pip with Cal. Reminder: stay calm. Stay precise.

I went in.

The lobby smelled of citrus cleaner and something floral that tried too hard. A stand of roses sat on a table near reception, arranged to look casual, which is how expensive things try to pretend they are not expensive.

A banner stretched across the far wall.

WELCOME, SECOND-CHANCE ROMANCE GUESTS.

Under it, Hugh Mercer stood like a man who'd been manufactured for this sort of nonsense. Charcoal suit. Controlled smile. Hands loose at his sides, ready to shake hands, ready to soothe, ready to contain.

He spotted me and gave the sort of nod you gave a vendor when you wanted them to remember their place.

I nodded back, because I could be civil without being obedient.

Melissa Shaw hovered near the drinks table, headset on, a clipboard in her hand. She looked like she'd already answered the same question fourteen times and had started hearing it in her sleep.

Dr Lucian Vale was on the other side of the room, laughing too loudly at something no one else had said. He was surrounded by a cluster of guests, his smile bright, his posture open, his eyes scanning for cameras.

Miles and Saffy Hartwell were near the corner, phone up, already filming. Saffy's grin was on full power. Miles stood slightly behind her as if he was there to confirm she existed.

I kept moving, keeping my shoulders loose, my face neutral. A welcome mixer was not my natural habitat. My natural habitat was behind a counter with paper, ink, and a door I could lock.

Someone called my name.

"Hattie."

I turned and saw Penny Harrow.

She was dressed more warmly tonight, coat open to reveal a simple dark jumper, scarf looped once. She had her notebook in hand, not a phone. Her eyes flicked over my face, then to the lobby, taking in the scene the way a person takes in a room when they've learnt the hard way that rooms can turn.

"You came," she said.

"I'm paid to be here," I replied.

Penny's mouth twitched. "And because you like watching people."

"I like watching lists," I said. "People just happen to be attached to them."

Penny's gaze went past me to Dr Vale. "He's worse in person."

"I'd guessed," I said.

She lowered her voice. "I asked Melissa about the admin account. She shut me down."

"She shut me down too," I said. "It's almost like they don't want anyone knowing who edits things."

Penny's eyes sharpened. "I saw your email about the stamp mark."

"You did," I said, careful.

Penny nodded once. "That wasn't a mistake. Not at this scale."

I studied her face. She wasn't fishing. She wasn't flirting. She wasn't trying to make me say something dramatic for a quote. She looked like a woman who had found a loose thread and was trying not to pull it in public.

"What are you here for, Penny," I asked.

Her eyes held mine. "Work," she said. "The romantic kind, apparently."

"Lovely," I said, because it was the safest thing to say.

Penny's gaze dipped to my Pocket Log, tucked into my peacoat pocket. "Still keeping your own record."

"Always," I replied.

A sharp voice cut through the noise.

"Hattie Crowe."

Melissa was striding toward me, eyes wide, expression strained.

Before she could speak, a young staff member appeared at her shoulder, breathless, cheeks flushed, hair escaping its bun. She had a name badge that read ALICIA. Her hands were empty, which was never a good sign. Empty hands meant she wanted to borrow something, or blame something, or both.

"Sorry," Alicia said, not sounding sorry. "We need you to reprint three place cards."

I didn't move. "No."

Alicia blinked, as if she'd never heard that word before. "It's for VIP preferences."

"No," I repeated, because the first time had not been unclear.

Melissa's face tightened. "Hattie. It's just three. There's been a request."

"A request from who," I asked.

Alicia cut in, voice sharper now. "From the VIPs."

"Names," I said.

Alicia's mouth opened, then shut.

Penny watched us with quiet interest, pen poised over paper.

"I don't change place cards on verbal requests," I said, keeping my tone flat. "You want reprints, you send written approval through Melissa, with the specific names, table numbers, and seat numbers. Then you sign for them. That is the process."

Alicia's eyes flashed. "It's a welcome mixer. People are already here."

"And I am still not changing a seating plan because someone

smiled at you and called themselves important," I replied.

Melissa stepped closer, voice low. "Hattie. Please."

I looked at her. "Melissa. The list was edited after midnight. Someone photographed the seating plan today. I am not handing anyone a chance to manipulate this and pin it on me. Written approval."

Alicia huffed. "It's not manipulation. It's just, you know, preferences."

I smiled slightly. "Preferences are how manipulation introduces itself at parties."

Alicia glared.

Melissa closed her eyes briefly, then opened them again. "Fine. I'll send you an email."

"Not from the portal," I said.

Melissa's expression tightened. "Hattie."

"Email," I repeated. "From your named address. With a timestamp. With the exact change request."

Alicia looked like she wanted to throw a flute of prosecco at my head, but she didn't have one.

Melissa turned to her. "Alicia, can you tell me the names and table numbers."

Alicia's voice went stiff. "It's for Miles and Saffy. They want to sit closer to the stage. And also Dr Vale wants one person moved, because he thinks it will help their 'journey'."

Penny's pen moved fast.

I wrote too.

18:11. Alicia requests reprint 3 place cards. Reason: "VIP preferences." Names given verbally: Miles Hartwell, Saffy Hartwell. Dr Vale wants one person moved for "journey." Refused. Written approval required.

I looked up. "Which person."

Alicia hesitated. "I don't know. Melissa has it."

"Then we wait," I said.

Alicia's jaw clenched. "This is ridiculous."

"It's procedure," I replied. "It keeps you from being blamed later."

Alicia rolled her eyes. "No one blames staff."

I stared at her. "Do you work here."

Melissa made a small sound, somewhere between a cough and a laugh, and turned away to pull out her phone.

Penny leaned closer to me, voice low. "They're moving influencers closer to the stage."

"Of course they are," I said. "Cameras like good angles."

"And Dr Vale wants a seat moved," Penny added. "That matters."

"It does," I agreed.

Alicia stood there, arms crossed, the shape of irritation. Her eyes kept darting to the lobby where Miles and Saffy were still filming.

"They're making a fuss," she said, loud enough for me to hear.

"Of course they are," I replied. "Drama keeps people watching."

Alicia's cheeks flushed. "They said someone is trying to sabotage them."

Penny's eyebrows lifted slightly.

I kept my face still. "Sabotage."

Alicia nodded quickly, eager now. "Yes. Their followers are obsessed with them. People get jealous. They said someone must have moved their place cards to make them look bad."

There it was.

A red herring delivered on a silver tray. Jealousy. Petty sabotage. Influencer nonsense. A neat little story that let everyone ignore the real mechanics of control.

I didn't correct her. Not yet. I just wrote it down.

18:14. Alicia claims influencers allege "sabotage" due to jealousy. Red herring risk.

Melissa's phone chimed. She glanced down, then looked up at me. "I've sent the email," she said, voice tight. "Three place cards. One for Miles, one for Saffy, and one for Penny Harrow."

Penny's head snapped up. "Me."

Melissa swallowed. "Dr Vale requested it. He wants you at Table Four, closer to him."

Penny's face went flat. "No."

Alicia looked pleased, as if she'd found her entertainment.

I held up a hand. "Stop," I said. "Melissa, does this request include table number, seat number, and the reason. In writing."

Melissa nodded quickly. "Yes. It's in the email."

I pulled my phone out and opened it, because I was not trusting anyone's summary.

The message was there. Time-stamped. From Melissa's address. It listed the three reprints with table and seat numbers. It included the phrase: Requested due to VIP preference and programme flow.

Programme flow.

A phrase that meant nothing and everything.

I looked up at Penny. "Do you want to move."

Penny's eyes were hard. "No."

"Then you don't move," I said.

Melissa looked panicked. "Hattie, please. Dr Vale is insisting."

"I don't care," I replied. "Penny is press, not a chess piece. You don't move her without her agreement."

Alicia scoffed. "It's just a chair."

"It's never just a chair," I said.

Penny's mouth twitched slightly, almost a smile.

Melissa looked like she might cry, which meant Hugh would be furious later.

"Then what do we do," Melissa whispered.

"We reprint the Hartwell cards only," I said. "If they want a better filming angle, that's their business. Penny stays where she is. If Dr Vale wants to rearrange the room like a living magazine spread, he can do it in his own house."

Alicia's eyes widened. "You're refusing Dr Vale."

"Yes," I replied. "Try it. It's liberating."

Melissa's shoulders sagged. "He's going to be angry."

"He'll survive," I said. "He has teeth. He can chew through it."

Penny's smile flashed then disappeared.

"All right," Melissa said, voice resigned. "Just the Hartwells."

I nodded. "Good. Where is the nearest printer that is not controlled by the portal."

Melissa blinked. "The hotel office printer."

"No," I said. "That one is controlled by everyone. I want a staff printer with limited access. Chloe's station."

Alicia huffed again. "That's in the ballroom corridor."

"Then we walk," I said.

Melissa led us through the lobby and into the service corridor, Alicia trailing like an annoyed shadow.

As we walked, I caught a glimpse of Hugh across the room, smile fixed, shaking hands with a couple who looked delighted to be "curated." His gaze slid to me for a fraction of a second. He didn't move. He didn't call out. But I felt the pressure of it, like a finger pressed gently into my spine.

Keep it tidy, his look said. Keep it quiet. Keep it inside.

I kept walking.

The service corridor was louder now, staff moving faster, trays clinking, radios crackling. The air smelled of hot food and bleach. A welcome mixer in the lobby meant a sprint behind the scenes.

Chloe was at her station near the ballroom door, clipboard in hand. She looked up when we approached, expression wary.

"Hattie," she said. "Problem."

"Small problem," I replied. "We need two reprints. Miles and Saffy Hartwell."

Chloe glanced at Melissa. "Are we changing the seating plan."

"We are changing two cards," I corrected. "With written approval."

Melissa held up her phone like it was a badge. "I emailed it."

Chloe exhaled. "Okay."

I opened my tote and pulled out the spare cardstock I always carried for emergencies. Thick, same stock, same cut. I set it on the table like I was laying down evidence.

Chloe gestured to the staff printer. "You can use this one."

I looked at the printer. It was not mine. That mattered. A different printer meant no dot pattern. No signature quirk. That was a problem.

I turned to Melissa. "I'm printing these from your printer. That means the dot pattern proof will not match. So I need you to sign a note stating these two cards were reprinted on hotel equipment at 18:26 due to VIP request, and the original cards remain in my possession."

Melissa blinked. "Hattie."

"Sign it," I said.

Alicia made a sharp laugh. "You're unbelievable."

"Yes," I replied, not looking at her.

Chloe's eyes flicked between us. She looked nervous, but she didn't disagree. People who had worked long enough in hotels knew exactly how blame travelled. It always travelled downhill.

Melissa grabbed Chloe's pen and signed my note with hands

that shook slightly. I signed too, then slid the note into a labelled envelope.

WELCOME MIXER. REPRINT NOTE. HARTWELLS.

I handed Chloe the original Hartwell cards from my tote, still clean, still showing my dot pattern. "These are the originals," I said. "Keep them. Do not destroy them. If anyone asks, you show them to DI Linley when she arrives."

Chloe stared at me. "DI Linley."

I nodded. "Storm season. High-profile weekend. It's sensible."

Chloe swallowed and nodded back, like she understood more than she wanted to.

I printed the two new cards carefully, matching font and layout. The hotel printer was sharper than mine, which annoyed me. It made my work look slightly softer by comparison, which was exactly the sort of detail guests would never notice and I would never forget.

I picked up the fresh cards. They felt warmer, thinner somehow, even though the stock was identical. My hands know paper. They know when something is not mine.

I wrote the time in my Pocket Log.

18:27. Reprinted Hartwell place cards on hotel printer. Written approval from Melissa. Note signed, originals retained.

Melissa reached for the cards. I held them back.

"Sign for them," I said.

Melissa closed her eyes. "Hattie."

"Sign," I repeated.

She signed the receipt sheet, time and date, and I handed her the cards.

Alicia rolled her eyes, then darted forward, snatched them from Melissa, and hurried away.

"Do not let Alicia handle anything without supervision," I said quietly to Melissa.

Melissa looked stunned. "She's staff."

"She's impatient," I replied. "That's worse."

Melissa's gaze followed Alicia down the corridor. "She's just stressed."

"So am I," I said. "Yet I'm still not stealing paperwork."

Melissa's mouth tightened. "I'll speak to her."

"Do," I said.

I tucked my Pocket Log back into my pocket and turned to leave.

That's when I saw the seating chart.

It was pinned on the staff board again, larger than my own, with the neat typed layout and the table map. Under the typed names, near Table Four, two sets of handwritten initials had been added.

Not printed. Not typed. Handwritten.

They were small, almost casual, as if someone had made a quick note for themselves. But they were visible. They were there for anyone to see. And I knew the hotel's usual pen.

Chloe always used a thick black marker for staff boards. Hugh's office pens were thin, expensive, and dark blue. Melissa's were cheap ballpoints.

These initials were written in a different ink entirely. A slightly green-black tone, fine tip. The sort of pen you used when you wanted to add something without making it look like you'd added something.

I stepped closer.

Two initials: L.V. and P.H.

Lucian Vale.

Penny Harrow.

My stomach tightened.

Penny was not in this corridor, but her name had been dragged into it anyway, reduced to two letters like a secret.

I looked at Chloe. "Did you write those."

Chloe shook her head quickly. "No."

"Did Melissa," I asked.

Melissa's eyes widened. "No."

Alicia's footsteps echoed as she returned, cheeks flushed, cards in hand.

"They're thrilled," she said. "See. Easy."

My gaze stayed on the seating chart. "Alicia," I said, voice low. "Who added initials to the chart."

Alicia blinked. "What."

I pointed. "Those."

Alicia glanced, then shrugged. "Oh. That must be Dr Vale. He's been talking about his 'pairings.' He likes to mark things."

Melissa's face tightened. "He was not authorised to write on staff documentation."

Alicia scoffed. "He's the star."

"He's a guest," I corrected.

Alicia's eyes flashed. "He's the reason people paid."

"He's the reason people will complain," I replied.

Alicia snorted. "You're so dramatic."

I turned to Melissa. "This is the first switch," I said quietly.

Melissa stared at me. "What."

"The first small change that looks harmless," I said. "Two initials, a note in the wrong pen, a shift in where someone sits. Then later, when something goes wrong, everyone will say it was just chaos. Just preferences. Just drama."

Melissa swallowed. Her eyes flicked to the initials again.

Penny Harrow's initials were there. Written by someone who wanted her moved, tracked, handled.

I pulled out my phone and took a photo of the chart, close

enough to capture the ink tone and the initials.

Then I pulled up the photo I'd taken earlier, the one from the morning, with my version number visible.

No initials then.

Initials now.

Proof.

I wrote in my Pocket Log.

18:32. Seating chart on staff board now has handwritten initials "L.V." and "P.H." added in fine green-black ink. Not hotel's usual marker. Chloe and Melissa deny writing. Alicia claims Dr Vale "marks pairings."

Alicia crossed her arms. "What does it matter."

"It matters because someone is tracking seats," I replied. "And because it's not being done through the approved process."

Melissa looked close to panic again. "I'll remove them."

"No," I said.

Melissa blinked. "No."

"No," I repeated. "Don't touch it. Don't smear it. Don't tidy it. Leave it exactly as it is. We document first."

Chloe nodded quickly, grateful someone was giving clear instructions.

Alicia rolled her eyes and made a dramatic sigh. "Fine. Whatever. I have work to do."

She stalked off again.

Penny appeared at the corridor entrance as if summoned by her own instincts. She stepped in, eyes narrowing as she took in the cluster of us and the tension.

"What's happened," she asked.

Melissa forced a smile. "Nothing. Just a small adjustment."

Penny's gaze slid to the seating chart. Then to the initials. Then back to us.

Her face hardened. "They're marking me."

I didn't sugarcoat it. "Yes," I said. "They are."

Penny stepped closer, eyes on the ink. "That's not Chloe's pen."

Chloe shook her head quickly. "No."

Penny looked at Melissa. "Did Hugh authorise this."

Melissa's voice was small. "It's Dr Vale. He's…"

"A liability," I supplied.

Penny's jaw clenched. "I'm not moving."

"You're not," I said.

Penny looked at the initials again, then at me. "You photographed it."

"Yes," I replied.

Her eyes softened slightly, a brief flicker of gratitude. "Good."

Melissa looked overwhelmed. "We're trying to keep the vibe positive," she said, as if repeating it might make it true.

Penny stared at her. "Your vibe is going to get someone hurt."

Melissa flinched.

Chloe stepped back as if the words might splash.

I kept my voice steady. "Penny, stay where you are tonight," I said. "If anyone asks you to move, ask for written approval. If they try to pressure you, call it what it is. Optics management."

Penny nodded once. "I can do that."

Then her gaze flicked down the corridor, toward the lobby. "Miles and Saffy are already telling guests someone tried to sabotage them," she said.

I felt my mouth tighten. "Jealousy story."

Penny nodded. "They're saying someone moved their cards because they're famous. People are eating it up."

"That's deliberate," I said.

Melissa's eyes widened. "Deliberate."

"Yes," I replied. "It reframes any tampering as petty drama. It makes real changes look like nonsense."

Penny's expression went grim. "And it keeps eyes off the list and the portal."

"Exactly," I said.

Chloe swallowed. "Should we tell Hugh."

Melissa's face tightened. "He'll tell us to handle it internally."

The phrase again. Always the phrase.

Penny's eyes narrowed. "Internal means buried."

"It often does," I agreed.

Melissa looked at me, then at Penny, then back at the seating chart, and I could see her fighting the urge to fix it, erase it, make it look normal again.

"Don't," I said softly. "Not yet."

Melissa nodded, small and shaky. "Okay."

I took another photo of the initials, then a wider shot showing where they sat on the chart relative to the table map. Context mattered.

Penny pulled out her notebook and wrote something down. Her pen scratched fast, the sound sharp in the corridor's hum.

Chloe looked like she wanted to disappear.

Melissa whispered, "I'll speak to Dr Vale."

Penny's laugh was humourless. "He'll call you darling and ignore you."

Melissa flinched again.

"I'll speak to Hugh too," Melissa added, voice trying to regain strength.

I nodded. "Do. And get everything in writing."

Melissa gave me a look that was half gratitude, half exhaustion. Then she hurried away.

Penny stayed, eyes still on the initials.

"I didn't come here to be managed," she said quietly.

"No one comes to Hartcombe to be managed," I replied. "Yet

somehow the town keeps finding ways."

Penny looked at me. "You know about the Trust."

"I know they prefer portals and generic admin accounts," I said. "And they don't like questions."

Penny's gaze flicked to the lobby again. "They don't like records."

I thought of the faint stamp mark in the guest list footer. The 2013 template. The fire year people spoke about like it was weather.

"I like records," I said.

Penny's mouth twitched. "I can see that."

We stood for a moment, the corridor noise around us, the chart pinned up like it was harmless.

Then the lobby sound swelled. Laughter. Clinking glasses. Someone's voice rising in an excited cheer.

Applause, starting.

Pip would have barked.

Penny grimaced. "Here we go."

I pocketed my phone and my Log. "Welcome mixer," I said. "Where they pretend everyone is safe while someone sharpens a knife behind the scenes."

Penny's eyes flicked to mine. "You think this ends badly."

"I think the first switch always matters," I replied. "And someone has already started switching."

Penny nodded once. "Then we watch."

We walked back toward the lobby together, not as friends, not as allies yet, but as two people who recognised the same smell.

Not roses.

Control.

In the lobby, Dr Vale stood near the banner, hands raised, smile wide, inviting applause like a man collecting rent.

Miles and Saffy filmed it from the side, faces bright, captions probably already forming.

Hugh Mercer stood a little apart, smile fixed, eyes scanning. He looked pleased, which in his case was never a comfort.

I found a spot near the wall where I could see the doors, the staff corridor entrance, and the drinks table all at once. Penny lingered nearby, notebook ready.

I held my tea, because I'd grabbed a cup on the way through and because having something warm in my hands stopped me from doing something reckless.

Dr Vale's voice boomed. "Give yourselves a round of applause for being brave enough to love again."

The guests clapped. Some laughed. Some looked genuinely hopeful. That part made me feel almost guilty for being cynical.

Almost.

Then a woman near the centre glanced down at her place card and frowned, turning it over as if expecting a secret message.

A man beside her leaned in to look.

A little ripple of confusion spread.

Small.

But visible.

I watched it, alert, as Dr Vale basked in his own performance.

Because confusion is how chaos enters a room.

And someone in this building had already shown me they knew exactly where to plant it.

CHAPTER 7

Compatibility banquet begins

Ballrooms are like arguments. They look polite until you notice how carefully the furniture has been arranged.

The Mariner's Crown's ballroom had been scrubbed into a kind of eager perfection. White tablecloths pulled tight enough to bounce a coin. Glassware aligned like soldiers. Candles already lit, because nothing says "second chance" like open flame near free-flowing prosecco. A subtle scent of roses fought with the more honest smells drifting in from the kitchen corridor: butter, roasted garlic, and the faint tang of industrial detergent.

The sea pressed against the windows in the distance, a dark presence beyond the warm light, reminding the whole room that Hartcombe did not exist purely for romance branding. Outside, the wind had teeth tonight. Inside, everyone pretended it was a gentle breeze made for hand-holding.

I stood near the side wall, close enough to see the entrance, the easel with the table plan, and the staff corridor door that Chloe had promised would remain closed. Close enough to hear the scrape of chair legs when people shifted. Close enough to catch the little things that mattered.

Far enough away that no one could claim I was "in the way."

A cup of tea steamed in my hands, paper-sided and faintly bitter, because hotel tea always tasted like it had been introduced to boiling water and immediately regretted it. I'd brought my own from the staff station, not because I wanted it, but because holding something warm kept my hands from doing something dramatic like grabbing the table plan and hiding it in my coat.

My Pocket Log sat open against my palm. Pen ready. Glasses on their chain. Navy peacoat still on, because I was not taking it off in a room full of strangers who thought romance was a spectator sport.

Pip would have hated this place tonight.

He'd have frozen at the first camera flash, stared like he was weighing his options, then delivered his single bark with the precision of a judge's gavel. He was at Cal's, safe, probably lodged against Cal's boot like an anchor. That thought steadied me in a way I resented, because relying on a dog for emotional regulation was not what I'd had in mind when I left the registry office and opened a stationery shop.

Still.

A vibration in my coat pocket. A text.

Cal: Pip's sulking because I wouldn't share my sausage roll. He'll live. You all right?

I read it twice, because it was rare for Cal Reeve to ask a question in writing when he could get away with a grunt.

I typed back.

Hattie: Fine. Ballroom's full of teeth. Keep him away from applause.

Then I slid the phone away and wrote in my Pocket Log.

18:58. Banquet start. Tea. Pocket Log open. Pip with Cal. Wind rising outside.

A hostess rang a small bell near the entrance. Guests began filtering in from the lobby, glossy and hopeful, as if they'd been promised not just a weekend but a new personality. Couples, singles, the slightly bewildered, the slightly determined. A few looked like they'd been dragged here by friends who believed in "fresh starts" with the zeal of a religion.

Miles and Saffy Hartwell arrived early, naturally.

Saffy wore a pale dress and a smile that didn't fit the season. Miles wore a dark blazer and the look of a man who had made peace with being filmed for a living. They drifted toward their table with their phone already up, capturing everything as if the room might disappear if they didn't document it.

They had their new place cards, printed on hotel equipment, not mine, and they held them up to the camera anyway like trophies.

"VIP preferences," Saffy said loudly, laughing as if it was cute. "We're closer to the stage now."

Miles nodded, eyes flicking over the table plan on the easel. He checked it the way a person checks an itinerary they don't quite trust.

Saffy leaned toward him, smile still on. "Everyone's being so weird about seats," she said. "It's like, babes, it's a romantic dinner, not Parliament."

I watched them sit.

Table Two, near the stage. Good view. Good filming angle. A perfect red herring.

Hugh Mercer entered after them, gliding through the room like a man who believed he was the reason the candles burned. He shook hands. Smiled. Tilted his head at the right moments. His smile tonight was too hard, too fixed. Not hospitality. Performance.

He spotted Miles and Saffy, and his smile softened just enough to look authentic. Then he spotted me and it tightened again.

Optics-first, I thought.

Hugh drifted to the easel and placed a hand lightly on the

table plan as if blessing it. Then he looked around the room, scanning. Measuring.

His gaze stopped briefly on the staff corridor door. I watched him notice it.

He gave Chloe a small nod, the sort of nod that could be interpreted as gratitude or warning depending on how well you knew him.

Chloe hovered near the door with a clipboard, shoulders stiff. She had the expression of someone trying to keep a dam from cracking with a teaspoon. Alicia moved behind her in quick darts, carrying napkins, adjusting chairs, whispering into a headset as if whispering could make the work smaller.

The event coordinator, Lorna Beckett, appeared next.

She wasn't wearing a suit like Hugh. She wore a soft blouse, dark trousers, and a lanyard with a badge that swung as she walked, which made her look both official and approachable. A dangerous combination.

Her hair was pinned back. Her smile was polite. Her eyes were not.

Lorna moved through the ballroom checking place settings, murmuring to staff, pausing at the table plan to trace a finger down the list.

Then she looked up and saw me watching her.

For a fraction of a second, her smile faltered.

Then it returned, brighter. "Hattie," she said, as if we were friends.

"Lorna," I replied, and kept my face neutral.

She stepped closer, voice low. "Everything in place?"

"Everything I printed is," I said.

Her smile tightened. "Wonderful. We just need everything to feel effortless tonight."

"Effortless usually means someone is sweating in a corridor," I replied.

Lorna gave a soft laugh that didn't reach her eyes. "That's hospitality."

"That's theatre," I corrected.

Her gaze flicked to my Pocket Log. "Still keeping notes."

"I've never met a crisis that improved by being forgotten," I said.

Lorna held my gaze, then nodded once. "Enjoy the show."

Then she turned and moved toward the stage area, where Dr Lucian Vale was about to make his entrance.

He did not walk into the ballroom like a guest. He walked in like a headline.

Dr Vale wore a dark suit that looked tailored, shirt collar open enough to suggest casual charm, smile bright enough to reflect candlelight. He paused at the entrance, letting the room register him, then spread his arms wide.

"Welcome," he called, voice carrying. "Welcome, my brave beauties."

A ripple of laughter from the guests. A few claps. Saffy lifted her phone higher.

Pip would have barked.

I tightened my grip on my tea and wrote in my Pocket Log.

19:05. Dr Vale enters. Calls guests "brave beauties." Applause beginning. Cameras up.

Dr Vale moved toward the stage, stopping at tables, touching shoulders, making eye contact like it was currency. He leaned close to a woman in a red dress, murmured something that made her laugh too loudly. He clasped a man's hand a second too long. He had the practised intimacy of someone who'd made a career out of telling strangers they were special.

He reached the stage and tapped the microphone.

The sound system gave a small squeal, then settled.

Hugh stood at the edge of the room, smile fixed, hands

clasped. Imogen Baird, the Valentine Heritage Trust rep, stood near him, camera still off in every sense. She wore black. No jewellery that caught light. Her posture was straight, as if she refused to soften herself for anyone.

She watched Dr Vale the way a person watches a dog they don't entirely trust.

Penny Harrow arrived last.

She slipped into the room quietly, coat still on, notebook in hand, scanning. She didn't look at the stage first. She looked at the doors. The staff corridor. The table plan. The bar.

Then her eyes found me.

She nodded once, a tiny acknowledgement, and moved toward her table.

I watched her name on the plan.

Table Fourteen.

Good. Far from Dr Vale.

I saw her check her place card, then sit. She kept her back straight, chin level, eyes alert. Not a guest. Not entirely press either. A person who knew the weekend had edges.

Dr Vale raised his hands again. "Look at you," he said, voice warm. "Showing up. Taking the risk. Choosing hope."

A few guests clapped. More laughter. Some genuine. Some performative.

Miles murmured something to Saffy. She giggled and panned her camera across the room.

Dr Vale continued, "Tonight is not just dinner. It's a compatibility banquet. A chance to learn what you want and what you deserve."

I kept my face still. I'd heard enough wedding speeches in my life to know when someone was selling people their own emotions.

"Our first exercise," Dr Vale announced, "is simple. I want each table to choose one person to tell us, loudly, what they're looking for. Not what you think you should say. What you actually want."

A murmur of discomfort. A ripple of nervous laughter.

Dr Vale smiled, delighted. "Yes. Discomfort means truth."

Lorna Beckett hovered near the stage, nodding like she approved.

Hugh's smile stayed too hard.

Imogen's posture did not shift.

Penny's shoulders tightened slightly at her table. She did not raise her hand.

Dr Vale pointed at a table near the front. "You," he said, cheerful. "Yes, you. Tell us."

A woman stood, flushed, and said something about kindness and laughter. People clapped. Dr Vale praised her. Moved on.

The room relaxed into the rhythm of being coached.

I did not relax. Coaching was just another form of control.

I kept watching the small movements.

Who stood. Who sat. Who leaned into the staff corridor. Who walked to the easel and checked the table plan as if they needed reassurance.

A man in a smart jumper, lanyard hanging, walked up to the plan and stared at it for a long moment.

My stomach tightened.

It was the same man from earlier, the one who'd photographed the staff board.

He held his phone loosely at his side now, not raised, but his eyes tracked the list with the same calm confidence.

Then he turned and walked away again, heading toward the kitchen corridor, not the guest toilets.

Like he belonged.

I wrote quickly.

19:12. Unknown male with staff lanyard (same as earlier

photo incident) checks table plan on easel. Walks toward kitchen corridor.

I watched him disappear through a side door.

Chloe noticed my focus and glanced toward the door too. Her face went pale for a second, then she looked away and resumed her work like she was trying not to die of stress in public.

Dinner service began with a soft swell of movement.

Starters appeared, plates carried by staff in clean lines. The smell of roasted beetroot and goat's cheese cut through the roses. Glasses clinked. Chairs scraped. Conversations rose and fell.

Dr Vale stepped down from the stage and began making rounds, drifting between tables like a friendly shark.

At Table Two, Miles and Saffy were already filming their starter plates.

"This looks divine," Saffy said, voice pitched for the camera. "Hartcombe is so romantic."

Miles murmured, "Tell them about the sabotage."

Saffy laughed brightly. "Oh my gosh, yes. Someone literally tried to move our place cards earlier. Can you believe. Jealousy is real."

A woman at a nearby table leaned over. "Jealousy?"

Saffy nodded, eyes wide, delighted. "Totally. People get weird when you're visible. It's fine though. We're staying positive."

The woman laughed awkwardly, then repeated it to her table, because people love passing along drama that costs them nothing.

Red herring, I thought.

A neat little story that made "seat changes" sound like petty nonsense instead of a mechanism.

I wrote another line.

19:18. Saffy loudly repeats "sabotage" story about moved place cards. Guests reacting. Red herring spreading.

Hugh drifted through the room, pausing at tables to offer his polished smile and controlled warmth. He checked in with Dr Vale, gave Lorna a nod, then leaned toward a server carrying a tray and murmured something.

The server nodded quickly, adjusted their route, and disappeared toward the kitchen.

Hugh watched the server go, then turned and smiled at a couple as if he'd done nothing at all.

Optics are oxygen, I reminded myself. He was breathing it.

Penny remained seated at Table Fourteen, eating slowly, watching. She didn't engage with the exercises. She didn't laugh too loudly. She didn't look like she was here for transformation. She looked like she was here for information.

A man beside her leaned toward her, speaking in a low tone. Penny's face stayed calm, but her eyes sharpened.

Not flirting. Not banter.

Something else.

I shifted slightly, using the movement of staff as cover, and angled myself to see more clearly without making it obvious.

The man was older, late fifties perhaps, hair greying at the temples, jacket too expensive for a casual weekend. He spoke with a smile that didn't fit his eyes. He gestured lightly with his fork, as if the conversation was harmless.

Penny responded with a smile of her own, polite, cold. She didn't lean in. She didn't move closer.

A whisper-free argument, I realised, as it began to take shape. Two people speaking softly enough not to draw attention, but not leaning in, not trying to hide it in body language. Tension carried on their faces, in the stiffness of shoulders, in the tightness around mouths.

The man's smile sharpened. Penny's eyes narrowed.

Then Penny pushed her chair back slightly and stood.

She didn't make a fuss. She didn't speak loudly. She simply stood, picked up her place card, and turned toward the woman seated opposite her, a brunette in a pale blue dress who looked like she'd been trying to enjoy her starter and had just realised she was sitting near something unpleasant.

Penny spoke to her briefly. The brunette's eyes widened. She shook her head once, then nodded. Penny nodded back.

Then, with the speed of someone who didn't want anyone watching to have time to interpret it, Penny and the brunette swapped seats.

Not a dramatic chair scrape. Not a drawn-out shuffle. A clean exchange.

Penny slid into the brunette's chair. The brunette slid into Penny's.

Place cards moved. Napkins shifted. Glasses barely trembled.

The man with the expensive jacket blinked, surprised, then smiled again as if nothing had happened.

Penny sat. Picked up her fork. Resumed eating.

And now she was in a different seat number.

A small change.

A huge one.

I felt my pulse quicken, not with fear, but with the sharp instinct that said, Pay attention. This matters.

I wrote quickly in my Pocket Log, hand steady.

19:26. Penny Harrow stands and swaps seats with brunette guest at Table 14 after tense low argument with older male guest. Swap fast, discreet. Place cards moved.

I added a note under it.

Seat mapping altered. Noted.

Dinner continued as if nothing had happened.

That was the nature of these things. The mechanism clicked into place silently, and the room kept laughing.

Dr Vale returned to the stage for the next segment, calling for more "bravery," praising more "honesty," soaking up applause like it fed him.

At Table Two, Saffy's sabotage story had grown. Now a man at another table was joking about "seat thieves." Someone laughed. Someone else said, "People will do anything for attention."

I stared at my tea and felt a cold line of irritation.

Attention was not the danger. Control was.

Lorna Beckett moved through the room again, pausing at the easel, checking the plan, making a small note on her clipboard. She spoke to Chloe briefly. Chloe nodded. Lorna's smile stayed polite.

I watched her hands.

No pen on the table plan. No obvious edits. But she knew where everything was. She knew how to move pieces without being seen.

Hugh stood near the bar, still smiling, still monitoring. Imogen remained near him, expression flat, eyes sharp. She looked toward Penny's table for a moment, then away.

The wind outside rose again, rattling the window frame faintly. The candles trembled, then steadied.

The room didn't notice.

I noticed everything.

Staff began clearing starter plates and setting down the main course. Roast chicken, small portions designed for elegance rather than hunger. A sauce that smelled of lemon and thyme. Potatoes arranged like they were auditioning for a magazine.

The kitchen supervisor, a stocky man with a tight expression, appeared briefly at the kitchen door, scanning the room like he was counting heads. His gaze landed on Dr Vale, then slid away. I saw a flicker of something in his face.

Not admiration.

A grudge, perhaps, or at least resentment.

I made a note, because my brain didn't let things go once it had seen them.

19:34. Kitchen supervisor (male, stocky) scans room from kitchen door. Looks at Dr Vale with visible dislike.

Alicia darted past again, whispering into her headset, adjusting a chair, smoothing a tablecloth that didn't need smoothing. She was busy in the way people are busy when they want to look useful.

She paused near the staff corridor door, glanced into it, then stepped away again as if she'd heard something.

I watched her go and wondered, not for the first time, who had taught her to treat access like a toy.

Penny sat in her new seat, face calm, eyes alert. The brunette sat in Penny's former seat now, looking slightly unsettled. The older man leaned toward her instead, smile still too sharp.

Penny looked across the table, not engaging, not giving him the satisfaction of reaction.

I admired her restraint even as I feared what it meant. People who swapped seats quickly were either very brave or very frightened.

Or both.

Dr Vale's voice swelled again from the stage. "Now," he said, "we do the rotation."

Lorna tensed slightly, ready to manage. Chloe stiffened. Staff moved into position.

Rotation meant movement. Movement meant chaos. Chaos meant opportunity.

I took a slow breath and held my tea tighter.

Rotation also meant that a seat number might soon belong to a different person again, and I'd just watched Penny alter the mapping quietly without anyone announcing it.

If the hotel was tracking seats for service, desserts, anything, it mattered.

If someone was targeting a seat, it mattered more.

I looked again at the table plan on the easel.

It still showed Penny in her original position.

Paper had not caught up with reality.

That was always where trouble began.

I wrote one more line in my Pocket Log, the ink dark and decisive.

19:39. Table plan still shows Penny in original seat. Reality now different. Rotation about to begin.

Somewhere in the room, Miles and Saffy laughed loudly for their camera, turning the whole evening into a story about jealousy and VIP drama.

Hugh smiled too hard.

Dr Vale performed.

And Penny Harrow sat in the wrong chair, by choice, with the calm face of a woman who knew exactly what she'd just done.

I watched the staff corridor door, the kitchen door, the table plan, and the guests who moved like they had permission.

The first switch had already happened.

Now the room was full of people about to switch again.

CHAPTER 8

Death in the corridor

Rotation did what it always did. It made grown adults behave like they were in Year Nine, except with better shoes and worse judgement.

Dr Lucian Vale stood centre-stage, mic in hand, smiling as if he'd personally invented second chances. Around him, the ballroom glowed with candlelight and curated optimism. Somewhere near the bar, someone laughed too loudly at a joke that hadn't been funny. At Table Two, Saffy Hartwell's phone remained held up like a holy relic, panning across faces that hadn't consented to be part of her storyline.

I watched the doors.

That was my job now. Not officially, of course. Officially I was a vendor who printed paper and kept my mouth shut. Unofficially I was a woman who understood that chaos did not arrive on its own. Someone always opened the door for it.

The staff corridor door was shut tonight, thank God, but people kept hovering near it as if they could sense there was a world behind it where things were still real. Chloe stood a few feet away, clipboard held close, her shoulders rigid. Alicia darted in and out of view like a sparrow in a shopping centre. Hugh Mercer lingered at the edge of the room, smile fixed, eyes scanning, breathing optics like air.

My tea had gone lukewarm. I took a sip anyway because it gave my hands something to do.

Dr Vale's voice sailed out over the room. "Right, my brave beauties. Table rotations. Three minutes each. Ask questions you'd never ask on a dating app."

A ripple of laughter. A few groans. Chairs scraped. Glasses trembled.

Guests stood, milled, shuffled. Some moved with excitement, some with dread, some with the blank determination of people who'd been promised transformation and intended to get their money's worth. Staff began circling the edges of the room, watching for spilled drinks, steadying chairs, anticipating the sort of accidents that always happened when people moved and tried to look charming at the same time.

I opened my Pocket Log, pen poised.

19:42. Rotation begins. Guests up. Staff circling. Staff corridor door shut. Hugh scanning.

Dr Vale stepped off the stage, moving between tables like a shepherd with an expensive coat. He guided people with a light touch and a heavy voice, placing hands on shoulders, leaning close, smiling as if he was giving them permission to be interesting.

He approached Penny's table.

I felt it before I saw it, the shift in the room's energy, the way a person's presence can pull focus without asking. Penny sat in her swapped seat, posture straight, face calm. The older man with the expensive jacket sat opposite her now, watching with an expression that suggested he liked being near unease.

Dr Vale stopped beside Penny, smile bright. "Penny Harrow," he said warmly, as if they were old friends. "Our local voice."

Penny didn't stand. She didn't smile. She looked up at him with that journalist's calm that said, I won't perform for you.

"Dr Vale," she replied.

He placed a hand lightly on the back of the chair that Penny had originally occupied, the seat she'd vacated. The brunette guest now sat there, shoulders tense, eyes darting between Penny and Vale like she was watching a tennis match she hadn't asked to attend.

Dr Vale's gaze flicked to the empty space beside the brunette, then to the chair itself. He moved as if it was the most natural thing in the world.

"I'm joining you," he announced.

No one invited him. No one needed to. That was part of his trick.

He pulled out the chair that had been Penny's original seat and sat down.

Not beside Penny. Not facing Penny.

In Penny's old seat position.

A small detail, and yet my skin tightened as if the room had dropped a degree.

I wrote quickly.

19:44. Dr Vale sits at Table 14 in Penny's original seat position (now occupied by brunette guest). Penny remains in swapped seat. Seat mapping altered further.

Penny's gaze met mine across the room for a fraction of a second. No panic. No drama. Just a look that said, Did you see.

I nodded once, tiny, and kept watching.

Dr Vale leaned forward, voice soft enough to feel intimate, loud enough to carry. "You're here for the records, aren't you."

Penny's expression didn't change. "I'm here for dinner."

He laughed lightly. "You can be honest with me. Honesty is my trade."

Penny's eyes narrowed slightly. "That and applause."

Dr Vale's smile held, but his eyes cooled. "Now, now."

The older man opposite them shifted, amused. The brunette

guest looked trapped.

I watched the table plan on the easel by the entrance. It still showed Penny in her original seat position. Paper had not caught up with reality. Again.

Staff moved around the room, keeping pace with the rotation. I spotted the man with the lanyard again, the one who had photographed the seating plan earlier. He appeared near the kitchen-side door, half in shadow, eyes on the room. Then he turned and disappeared through the side corridor as if he had a key to everything.

I made another note.

19:46. Unknown lanyard male seen near kitchen-side door during rotation. Observing. Exits through side corridor.

Alicia darted past the easel and checked the table plan, finger tracing down names. She paused at Table Fourteen, then moved on. Her lips moved as if she was counting.

Hugh's gaze tracked her. He watched the easel too, not in a way that said he cared about seating, but in a way that said he cared about control.

Dr Vale clapped his hands once. The sound cracked through the room.

Pip would have barked himself hoarse.

"All right," Dr Vale called. "Back to your seats. Dessert is coming. And dessert, my loves, is a truth serum."

People laughed, shuffled back, scraping chairs and stepping around handbags like a dance no one had rehearsed.

I didn't move. I kept my eyes on Table Fourteen.

Dr Vale remained seated. He didn't rotate. He didn't let the room tell him what to do. Guests around him returned to their own chairs, murmuring apologies and jokes, but he stayed in that seat position, the one Penny had occupied earlier.

The brunette guest, the one who had swapped seats with Penny, hovered uncertainly, holding her place card like she didn't know where she belonged anymore. Penny spoke to her briefly, a calm sentence, and the brunette sat in Penny's former seat across the table, shoulders tight.

So now the table held an extra complication.

Penny sat in the brunette's seat position. The brunette sat in Penny's original. Dr Vale sat at the seat position he'd claimed, which was still Penny's original seat position physically, but no longer her name card.

If you were serving by name, you'd be lost.

If you were serving by seat position, you'd be fine.

And that thought sat heavy in my chest like a stone.

Dessert service began with a subtle change in the air. The scent shifted from savoury to sugar, warm chocolate and citrus and something boozy that tried to smell romantic and mostly succeeded.

Staff moved out of the kitchen corridor carrying trays. Plates were small, glossy, arranged like jewellery. Most guests leaned forward, delighted, because nothing brings people together like a shared expectation of sweetness.

I watched the servers' hands.

One server, young, pale, looked slightly panicked. She held a tray with three identical desserts and a small printed sheet in her other hand. She glanced down at it, then up, then down again, like she was reading a map in a town she didn't trust.

Alicia stepped in beside her, leaned close, and pointed to the sheet.

The server nodded quickly.

Alicia pointed again, sharper, then waved her toward Table Fourteen.

The server moved.

I tightened my grip on my tea.

The server arrived at Table Fourteen and paused, eyes flicking between place cards and the physical seat positions. Her sheet fluttered slightly in her hand. She didn't look at names. She looked at the table edge.

Then she set one dessert down in front of Dr Vale.

Dr Vale smiled broadly. "Ah. Fate."

He picked up his fork as if dessert had been delivered by the universe and not by a stressed nineteen-year-old with a printout.

The server set the second dessert down in front of the older man with the expensive jacket. The third went to the brunette guest.

Penny's hands remained empty.

She looked at her plate space, then at the server, then at Dr Vale, expression controlled.

The server glanced down at her sheet again, frowned, then said quietly, "One moment," and hurried back toward the kitchen corridor.

Penny's gaze flicked toward me again, quick, sharp.

I wrote fast.

19:53. Dessert server uses printed sheet, not names. Alicia directs. Dessert delivered at Table 14 to Dr Vale, older male, brunette. Penny not served. Server returns to kitchen.

The server returned within seconds, carrying a fourth dessert.

She walked straight back to Table Fourteen and placed it in front of Penny with a small apologetic smile.

"Sorry," she murmured. "Seat mix-up."

Seat mix-up.

Not name mix-up.

My stomach tightened hard enough to make me swallow. I'd spent twenty years in rooms where one small procedural error could turn into a disaster. This was the same shape. It was just wearing a nicer dress.

Penny smiled politely at the server, then looked down at the dessert without touching it.

Dr Vale, meanwhile, had already taken his first bite.

He closed his eyes theatrically. "Mm. Chocolate. That's the language of forgiveness."

The guests laughed. Hugh's smile glinted from across the room. Saffy lifted her phone to capture Dr Vale's "charming reaction."

Penny's fork stayed still.

I stood there with lukewarm tea and the sudden certainty that the room had shifted into a different category of danger.

Alicia hustled back past the easel, headset crackling. She didn't look at me. She didn't look at Penny. She looked relieved, as if a small crisis had been patched quickly.

Patched, not solved.

Dr Vale ate.

He spoke while chewing, which was unforgivable in any room, romantic or not. He said something to Penny that made her jaw tighten. The older man laughed softly, pleased by whatever unpleasantness was occurring at that table.

Then, about a minute later, Dr Vale's expression changed.

Not dramatically. Not enough that anyone filming would catch it unless they were looking for it.

His smile faltered. His eyes flicked down, then up. He swallowed once, hard.

He pressed a hand briefly against his sternum as if adjusting his tie, though he wasn't wearing one.

Penny watched him closely, her face still, her eyes sharp.

Dr Vale stood.

He smiled again, as if he could will charm into reality. "Excuse me," he said lightly, voice pitched for the table. "Too much truth serum at once."

He stepped away from the table and moved toward the staff

corridor door.

Not the guest toilets. Not the lobby.

The staff corridor.

Chloe saw him coming and stiffened. She moved to intercept, but Dr Vale waved a hand. "I just need a moment," he said, voice airy. "You'll survive without me for thirty seconds."

Chloe hesitated, then stepped aside.

That was the problem with people like Dr Vale. They made staff forget they were allowed to say no.

He pushed through the staff corridor door.

I moved.

Not running. Not dramatic. Just moving with purpose, the way I used to move when a bride fainted or a groom's mother started hyperventilating. I followed the line of staff and dodged a server carrying a tray of coffee cups. I kept my tea in hand because it gave me cover. A woman with tea looked like she belonged in any corridor.

The staff corridor beyond the door was harshly lit, a long strip of fluorescent glare and scuffed walls. The air smelled of bleach and sugar and the damp wool of coats hung on hooks.

Dr Vale had taken about six steps before his knees buckled.

He didn't collapse like a film star. He folded, awkwardly, hand reaching for the wall. His shoulder hit it, then he slid down and landed on his side with a dull thud that sounded far too final for a romance weekend.

For a split second, the corridor was silent.

Then Chloe's voice rose, sharp with fear. "Doctor!"

Alicia shouted, "Someone call for help!"

The young dessert server froze, tray in hand, eyes wide. Her lips moved silently like she was counting steps backwards.

My own stomach turned hard, a hot flip that tried to push my tea back up. I swallowed it down and stepped forward.

Registrar instincts, I thought. This was where they lived. In the part of me that could go cold and precise when everyone else went loud.

"Call 999," I said, voice firm, not shouted. "Now. Say adult male collapsed, not breathing normally, request ambulance."

Alicia blinked at me, then fumbled for her phone.

"Chloe," I said, "get the first aid kit and tell me if you have a defib on-site."

Chloe nodded, already moving.

I crouched beside Dr Vale.

His face had gone a strange grey, sweat beading at his hairline. His eyes were half open but unfocused. His breathing was shallow, uneven, a soft wet pull that made my stomach clench again. No obvious injury. No blood. No drama. Just a body failing quietly, which was far worse.

I didn't touch him yet. I looked first, the way I always had to look before acting. Who had touched him already. Who had moved him. What was around him.

Alicia hovered, phone at her ear, voice high. "Yes, yes, he just collapsed, in the corridor outside the ballroom, yes, Mariner's Crown, yes, yes."

The dessert server stood frozen a few steps away, tray trembling slightly. The printed sheet she'd used earlier was crumpled in her hand.

I kept my eyes on it even as I watched Dr Vale's chest rise and fall.

That paper mattered.

Someone else entered the corridor, footsteps quick.

Hugh Mercer.

He arrived like a man who had been notified instantly, which, given the hotel's appetite for control, was probably true. His smile was gone. His face looked tight, pale. He took one look at Dr Vale on the floor and then looked at the staff as if deciding who to blame.

"What's happening," he demanded.

"He collapsed," Alicia said, voice trembling. "We're calling an ambulance."

Hugh's eyes snapped to me. "Hattie, you need to leave. This is staff only."

"This is a medical emergency," I replied, still crouched. "Staff only stops being relevant when someone's life is on the floor."

Hugh's jaw tightened. "We need privacy."

"We need oxygen and an ambulance," I said. "Privacy comes later."

Hugh's eyes narrowed like he wasn't used to being contradicted in his own corridor.

"Close the ballroom doors," he snapped at someone behind him. "Keep guests inside. No filming. No phones out. Tell Dr Vale's team we're handling it."

Handling it.

That phrase again, wrapped around a man collapsing like it could prevent consequences.

I looked up at Hugh. "Do not move him," I said. "Not until trained first aid arrive unless he stops breathing."

Hugh stared at me, then at Dr Vale, then back at me. "We can't have him here," he said tightly. "Guests will see."

"They will see anyway," I replied. "And if you drag him somewhere and worsen it, you'll have more than optics to manage."

Hugh's nostrils flared.

Chloe returned, breathless, first aid kit in her hands. "Defib is in the lobby," she said.

"Go," I told her. "Bring it. And tell someone competent to come with it."

Chloe sprinted away again.

Hugh watched her go, expression pinched. "This cannot become a scene," he said.

"It already is," I replied.

From the ballroom side, muffled laughter continued, then shifted into a confused murmur as someone noticed the staff door activity. A few chairs scraped. Someone's voice rose, curious.

Hugh snapped again, louder. "Doors closed. Now."

Alicia's phone call ended. She looked at me, eyes wide. "Ambulance is coming," she said. "They said storm traffic might delay."

Storm traffic.

Outside, the wind rattled the corridor's small high window. The sound made my skin prickle. Hartcombe's weather never missed a chance to remind you it was in charge.

I leaned closer to Dr Vale, watching his breathing. His lips had a faint bluish tinge, slight, but enough. His hand twitched once, fingers curling and uncurling.

"Dr Vale," I said, not because I thought he could hear, but because you speak to people in crisis. It's what you do when you want to keep them attached to the world. "Can you hear me."

His eyelids fluttered. His gaze didn't focus.

My stomach turned again, harder, and I forced it down with sheer stubbornness.

Penny appeared at the corridor door.

Hugh moved instantly to block her, arm out like a barrier.

Penny's eyes flashed. "What happened," she demanded.

"Medical incident," Hugh said quickly. "Please return to the ballroom. We're managing."

Penny's gaze went past him to Dr Vale on the floor. Her face hardened. "That's not managing. That's hiding."

"Penny," Hugh said, voice tight, "this is not the time."

"It's always the time when someone collapses in a staff corridor," Penny snapped.

Hugh's posture stiffened. "You are a guest."

Penny's mouth twisted. "I'm a journalist."

Hugh's eyes narrowed. "Not on my property."

I spoke then, calm and flat. "Penny, stay there. Don't come closer. We need space and we need to know who has been in this corridor. Don't contaminate it."

Penny's eyes flicked to me. She nodded once, controlled, then stayed at the threshold, not stepping in.

Hugh glared at me as if I'd just given Penny permission to exist. "Stop talking," he hissed.

"Stop trying to control the wrong thing," I replied.

Chloe returned again, this time with a defib and a middle-aged bartender who looked more competent than any of the event team. The bartender knelt beside me, already opening the device with practised hands.

"Is he breathing," he asked.

"Shallow," I said.

The bartender checked Dr Vale quickly, placed fingers at his neck, then looked up. "We may need to start compressions," he said.

Hugh flinched visibly. "Not here," he said, voice sharp. "Take him to the office."

The bartender ignored him, which was the first sane thing I'd seen all night.

"He needs the floor," the bartender said. "And space. Call it whatever you want, but we're doing this here."

Hugh's face tightened as if he was swallowing rage.

Penny watched from the doorway, notebook already in hand. She wasn't writing yet. She was watching, and her stillness made me think she already understood this wasn't going to end neatly.

The bartender placed the defib pads with efficiency. The device beeped. Instructions spoke in a calm recorded voice that made the whole scene feel surreal, like the corridor had become a training video.

The bartender began compressions.

I kept my eyes on Dr Vale's face, on the staff around us, on the corridor itself.

Alicia hovered, hands to her mouth.

The dessert server stood a few steps back, tears in her eyes, still holding the crumpled sheet.

Hugh stood rigid, fists clenched at his sides, watching the corridor as if the corridor was the problem.

I made myself stand, because crouching beside the body was no longer helpful. Watching was.

Registrar instincts again. When something went wrong at a wedding, people ran around doing nothing useful. My job had been to become the spine. Calm, procedural, unromantic.

"Who touched him first," I asked, voice steady.

Alicia blinked. "What."

"Who," I repeated. "Touched him, moved him, gave him anything."

Alicia's eyes darted. "No one. He just fell."

"Chloe," I asked.

Chloe shook her head. "I didn't touch him. I was going to, but Hattie said not to."

Good.

I looked at the bartender. "Have you touched anything besides him and the defib," I asked.

He glanced up. "No."

"Good," I said.

Hugh scoffed. "This is not an investigation," he snapped.

"It will be if he dies," I replied.

Hugh's face went pale.

I watched him register it, the way people do when the stakes move from PR to reality.

Penny's voice cut in from the doorway. "Why was he in the staff corridor."

Hugh turned to her sharply. "Because he needed privacy."

Penny's eyes narrowed. "Or because someone guided him here."

Hugh's jaw clenched. "Enough."

I looked at the dessert server. "What's your name," I asked.

She blinked through tears. "Ellie," she whispered.

I didn't like the softness of her voice in that corridor, so young against that harsh light.

"Ellie," I said, calm, "what's in your hand."

She looked down as if she'd forgotten it existed. "The sheet," she said. "The dessert list."

"Do not throw it away," I said. "Do not give it to anyone who asks nicely. Put it in the first aid kit box or hand it to me."

Hugh snapped, "That's hotel property."

I ignored him.

Ellie hesitated, then stepped forward and placed the crumpled sheet carefully into my open hand like she was handing me a live wire.

The paper felt cheap. Not the hotel's usual thick stock. The print looked close to official but not quite, the font slightly wrong, the spacing a touch off.

My stomach sank further.

I folded it carefully and slid it into one of my labelled envelopes from my tote. I hadn't even realised I still had them with me, but of course I did. I never travelled without paper. It was my armour.

I wrote across the envelope quickly.

DESSERT SERVICE SHEET. RECEIVED FROM ELLIE. 20:03. STAFF CORRIDOR.

Hugh's eyes burned into me. "Give me that," he said.

"No," I replied.

His voice sharpened. "Hattie."

I held his gaze. "If you want it, you request it from the police when they arrive."

"The police are not needed," Hugh snapped.

Penny laughed, short and cold. "That's adorable."

The defib beeped again. The bartender paused, listened, then continued compressions, jaw clenched.

The corridor's small window rattled. Somewhere in the building, a door banged. The wind was rising.

Minutes stretched into the kind of time that doesn't feel real. The ballroom behind the closed doors would be buzzing now, guests confused, staff making excuses, Hugh's team probably spinning a narrative about "a sudden illness" and "everything under control."

I watched Dr Vale's face.

I watched the bartender's hands.

I watched Hugh's posture, stiff as a rod.

I watched Penny, poised like a blade at the doorway.

Then I heard footsteps again, fast, heavy.

Paramedics.

Two of them, wet-haired, breathless, carrying gear, faces serious. They took over quickly, voices clipped, efficient. The bartender stepped back, sweat on his forehead, breathing hard.

One paramedic checked Dr Vale, then looked at the other. A small shake of the head.

They worked anyway. They always worked. That's the cruelty

of hope. You do the job even when you suspect it won't end the way people want.

Hugh hovered, trying to speak. "We need discretion," he started.

A paramedic cut him off without looking up. "We need space."

Hugh shut his mouth.

Penny's notebook moved now. Quick lines. Controlled.

I wrote too.

20:10. Paramedics arrive. Take over. Hugh attempts "discretion," shut down. Dessert sheet secured.

The paramedics continued for several more minutes. The defib beeped. Voices rose and fell. Someone asked for time. Someone responded.

Then one paramedic stood back slightly and looked at the other, and I knew before anyone spoke.

The recorded calm of the defib stopped. The corridor went still in the way rooms do when the outcome lands.

The paramedic turned to Hugh, face professional, voice quiet. "I'm sorry. We did what we could."

Hugh's face went blank.

Alicia made a small sound like a sob and pressed her hands to her mouth.

Ellie's tears fell silently.

Penny's eyes sharpened, jaw clenched.

My stomach turned one final time, a deep sick roll, and I breathed through it because there was no room for me to fall apart in a corridor full of people who would use it as proof I was dramatic.

Registrar instincts again. Calm. Procedure. Paper.

The paramedics began their next steps, covering Dr Vale, checking details, asking questions.

Hugh found his voice again. "We need to keep this quiet," he said, too fast. "The guests, the weekend, the Trust, we cannot have panic."

Penny snapped, "A man just died."

Hugh's eyes flashed. "Not in the ballroom," he said, as if the location changed the fact.

I stared at him. "Where do you think death belongs," I asked. "Somewhere less inconvenient."

Hugh's face tightened. "This will destroy the weekend."

"This will destroy Dr Vale's pulse," I replied. "Try to keep perspective."

Hugh's gaze went sharp, hateful, then smooth again. He turned to the paramedics. "Can you confirm this was a natural event," he asked, already grasping for a label.

The paramedic's expression didn't change. "Cause of death is for the coroner," he said. "Police will need to be notified."

Hugh flinched. "Police."

"Yes," the paramedic replied. "Now."

Hugh's jaw worked as if he was chewing glass.

Penny stepped forward slightly. "Tell them about the dessert," she said, eyes on me.

Hugh spun toward her. "There was no dessert issue."

Penny's gaze went past him to the ballroom doors. "There was a seating issue. There was a service sheet. There was a corridor. There was a death. Stop lying."

Hugh's face went pale with rage. "You will not publish anything."

Penny's laugh was thin. "Watch me."

I held up a hand, because shouting helps nothing. "We do this cleanly," I said. "We note times. We note who was where. We preserve the paper."

Hugh glared. "This is not your role."

"It became my role when you started trying to tidy facts," I replied.

The paramedic asked, "Who found him."

Chloe answered, voice shaking. "He came through the door and collapsed. Hattie told us what to do."

The paramedic looked at me. "You're staff."

"No," I said. "Vendor. Former registrar. I do paperwork and panic control."

The paramedic gave a small nod like he understood exactly what that meant. "All right. Police will want statements. Don't leave."

Hugh opened his mouth to object.

The paramedic looked at him. "Don't move anything in the ballroom either," he said. "Dessert plates, table plan, anything connected to his last movements. Leave it."

Hugh's eyes widened. "We need to clear the room."

"You need to leave it," the paramedic repeated, voice harder. "If you clear it, you contaminate it. You want that on your conscience."

Hugh shut his mouth again.

The ballroom doors remained closed, but I could hear the muffled roar of confusion behind them now, voices rising, chairs scraping, the energy of a crowd that sensed something and didn't yet know what.

Hugh turned to Alicia. "Go tell them it's a medical situation being handled privately," he said quickly. "No one leaves. No phones."

Alicia nodded and rushed off.

Penny muttered, "He's more worried about Instagram than a dead man."

I didn't correct her because she wasn't wrong, but I was watching the corridor.

The unknown lanyard man appeared briefly at the far end,

near the kitchen-side door. He stood there for a second, just long enough for me to see the silhouette, the calm posture, the slight tilt of his head like he was observing a scene he'd expected.

Then he turned and disappeared again.

My skin went cold.

I wrote it down anyway.

20:14. Unknown lanyard male briefly visible at far corridor end during paramedic declaration. Observes. Leaves.

Hugh began talking again, voice low, urgent, directed at Chloe and the bartender. "We need to move him to a private room. Guests must not see."

The paramedic cut him off. "We're not moving him until police arrive and we record the scene."

Hugh's eyes flashed. "This is my hotel."

The paramedic's expression was flat. "This is a death."

Silence fell in a sharp line.

I looked down at my Pocket Log, at the ink marks, at the times.

Then I looked at my envelope with the dessert service sheet inside it.

Paper in my hand. A corridor full of people trying to control the story. A ballroom full of guests being told everything was fine.

And a man who'd been alive ten minutes ago now lying under a sheet because someone in this building had been serving dessert by seat position.

My stomach turned again, smaller this time, but it didn't go away.

Hugh stepped closer to me, voice low and dangerous. "Hand over whatever you took."

I met his eyes. "No."

His smile tried to return and failed. "Hattie, don't be difficult."

"I'm not being difficult," I said. "I'm being exact. You should try it."

He leaned in slightly, voice hissing. "You'll regret this."

I didn't raise my voice. I didn't flinch. "I've regretted agreeing to this contract since Tuesday," I said. "You're not special."

Hugh's eyes burned.

From the ballroom, applause erupted suddenly, loud and wrong, as if someone had instructed the crowd to clap to drown out confusion.

Pip would have barked until he choked.

The sound made my skin crawl.

Hugh's gaze flicked toward the ballroom doors, then back to me. "Go back inside," he said. "You're upsetting staff."

"Staff are upset because a man died," I replied. "Not because I'm holding paper."

The paramedic said, "Everyone stays put," and Hugh finally had no choice but to stand there and wait.

I waited too.

I watched the corridor.

I listened to the ballroom noise spike and dip behind closed doors.

I felt the weight of my fountain pen in my hand and the familiar comfort of ink.

And I understood, with a clarity that made my throat tighten, that the first switch had not been a harmless scribble of initials or an influencer's jealousy story.

The first switch had been practice.

This was the outcome.

And someone was already trying to tidy it.

CHAPTER 9

Storm and lockdown

The Mariner's Crown lobby had been dressed for romance and ended up looking like a waiting room. Not the soothing kind, with magazines and soft music. The other kind, the one where people sit too straight and pretend they are not listening to the word "urgent" being said behind a door.

Staff had moved a pair of velvet ropes across the main entrance to the ballroom corridor, as if velvet could hold back reality. The banner still hung on the wall. WELCOME, SECOND-CHANCE ROMANCE GUESTS. The letters were cheerful in a way that now felt personal, like the hotel was mocking us.

Hugh Mercer stood in the centre of it all, shoulders squared, suit immaculate, face controlled. He looked like he wanted to iron the whole evening flat.

Guests clustered in loose groups, murmuring, clutching glasses they had forgotten to drink from. Some stared at the staff corridor door as if it might confess. Others stared at their phones, thumbs twitching, desperate to turn the moment into content before anyone could stop them.

Saffy Hartwell was already filming. Not openly, because Hugh had ordered "no phones," but she held her device at waist level with that familiar influencer posture, chin tipped down, eyes bright, pretending she was checking messages while recording every flinch and whisper and scandal-shaped shadow.

I stood near the reception desk with my tea gone cold again, Pocket Log open, and my tote hugged close like it contained something explosive, which it did.

The dessert service sheet sat inside a labelled envelope. I'd folded the paper with care, even though it had been crumpled in Ellie's shaking hand. The ink on the envelope was my own, sharp and clear.

DESSERT SERVICE SHEET. RECEIVED FROM ELLIE. 20:03. STAFF CORRIDOR.

My fountain pen felt heavier than usual. The sort of weight you notice when you realise you might need to defend what you've written.

Chloe drifted past, face pale, eyes glassy. She looked like she'd aged five years in ten minutes. Alicia hovered near Hugh, hands twisting, posture frantic. Ellie, the dessert server, sat on a chair near the staff door with her head bowed, trembling as if she was trying not to be sick on the carpet.

I watched Saffy, then looked away before my irritation turned into something unhelpful.

Penny Harrow stood near a pillar, coat still on, notebook in hand, expression tight and unreadable. She looked less like a guest now and more like someone who had wandered into the middle of a story and decided she would not be written out of it.

Someone near the bar said loudly, "It was probably an allergy."

Someone else replied, "He was under so much stress."

Someone else, sharper, said, "Or someone wanted him quiet."

Hugh's head snapped toward them. His smile flickered on like a light. "Ladies and gentlemen," he said, voice smooth. "Please. This is a medical situation. We ask for privacy and patience."

Privacy and patience. Two words that always sounded reasonable when you were using them to stop people asking questions.

Penny's mouth twisted. She didn't speak, but I saw the tension in her jaw.

I wrote in my Pocket Log anyway, because I wrote when my stomach wanted to fold in on itself.

20:22. Lobby. Guests gathered. Hugh framing "medical situation." Phones in hands despite request. Rumours starting.

Hugh moved toward the Hartwells, smile on, voice low. "Saffy, Miles, please put your phones away."

Saffy widened her eyes innocently. "Oh, I was just texting my mum."

Hugh's smile stayed fixed. "Now."

Miles slipped his phone into his pocket quickly. Saffy hesitated just long enough to make it a performance, then did the same.

Hugh nodded, pleased with himself, then turned away. The second his back was turned, Saffy's hand slid to her pocket again.

I made a mental note. People who filmed everything did not stop filming because they were asked nicely.

From outside, the wind hammered the lobby doors. Rain streaked the glass in slanted lines. The sound made the building feel smaller, like the storm was pressing the hotel into a tighter box.

A receptionist leaned toward Hugh and murmured something. Hugh's expression tightened.

He raised his voice again. "Everyone, please stay in the lobby area. Due to the weather, there are road closures. We are waiting for police to arrive and we will update you shortly."

A low murmur rose, annoyed, frightened, curious.

Road closures meant what it always meant in a small coastal town in a bad storm. Fallen trees. Flooded lanes. A slip on the cliff road. The kind of damage that turned a hotel into a sealed room with too many stories inside it.

I felt the familiar cold settle in my spine.

Closed circle.

Not as a cosy trope. As a logistical fact.

A guest near the fireplace said, "We can just leave, can't we."

Hugh's smile sharpened. "At present, it would be unsafe. And we need to take statements."

Statements, I thought. That was new. That was not "medical situation." That was death.

Penny's eyes flicked up. She caught the word too.

Hugh caught himself, smoothed his face. "We are cooperating fully," he added quickly, as if cooperation were a gift.

Someone at the edge of the lobby began to cry softly. Another person put an arm around them, then looked over their shoulder to see who was watching.

I stood very still, because I could feel panic trying to rise in the room like heat.

I also knew what would happen next.

If police were delayed, Hugh would step into the vacuum. He would control who talked to whom. He would control what papers were moved. He would control what was cleaned. He would control the narrative the way he controlled linen.

And if he could, he would control me.

My phone vibrated in my pocket again. I checked it.

Cal: Storm's nasty. Coast road's blocked by fallen tree. Police being diverted. You still at the hotel?

I stared at the message for a second, then typed.

Hattie: Still here. Death in staff corridor. Hugh trying to mop up with words. Keep Pip inside.

I didn't send more because I didn't have the patience to explain the shape of the danger in a text.

I slipped my phone away and looked up.

Hugh was walking toward me.

Of course he was.

He stopped a little too close, smile on, voice low. "Hattie. You need to go back to your room."

"I don't have a room," I said. "I live in the real world. It's unpleasant, but I manage."

Hugh's smile tightened. "Then go home."

"You just told everyone the roads are closed," I replied.

His eyes flicked. "This isn't the time."

"It never is, when someone has something to hide," I said.

Hugh's jaw clenched. "I'm trying to protect my guests."

"You're trying to protect your brand," I corrected. "Your guests are just the props."

His smile faltered for a fraction of a second, then returned. "I'll say this once. Hand over whatever paperwork you took from staff."

I looked at him. "No."

His eyes cooled. "Hattie, don't make this difficult."

"Stop saying that," I replied. "You sound like a man who's never been told no by anyone who wasn't being paid."

Hugh's nostrils flared. "You are a vendor. You are not law enforcement."

"I'm also not stupid," I said.

His smile vanished completely. "If you interfere, you will never work with this hotel again."

I held his gaze. "I didn't want to work with this hotel the first time."

Hugh stared at me like he couldn't decide whether to threaten or charm.

Penny drifted closer, notebook still in hand, eyes sharp. She didn't speak, but her presence was a reminder that Hugh could not bully quietly if someone was watching.

Hugh noticed Penny, smile flicked back on. "Penny. I'm asking everyone to remain calm and respect privacy."

Penny's voice was flat. "Privacy is for bathrooms. This is a death."

Hugh's smile tightened. "We don't know that it's suspicious."

Penny's eyes narrowed. "You don't know it isn't."

Hugh turned away from her and back to me, voice low again. "You're going to cause panic."

"No," I replied. "You're going to cause a cover-up. I'm going to cause a paper trail."

He stared at me, then leaned closer, voice edged. "Where is it."

"In a labelled envelope," I said. "Like a sane person."

Hugh's eyes flashed. "Give it to me."

"No," I repeated.

Hugh's jaw worked. Then he forced his smile back on as if it was armour. "Fine. Then you can hand it to the police when they arrive."

"That was always the plan," I said.

Hugh turned away sharply, moving back into the lobby like he was returning to his stage.

I watched him go and felt my stomach tighten again, not with fear, but with the clear understanding that he would try another route. He would find another way to get that paper out of my hands.

The receptionist spoke again to Hugh, urgent.

Hugh's shoulders tensed. He turned and raised his voice.

"Everyone," he said, "I need you to listen. The storm has caused significant damage on the coastal road and the lane toward the village. Police are delayed. For your safety, we are locking down the premises. Please remain in the lobby until further notice."

Locking down. Another phrase that sounded like care and meant control.

The murmurs grew louder. Someone swore quietly. Someone laughed in disbelief. Someone said, "Are we prisoners now."

Hugh smiled too hard. "No one is a prisoner. We simply need order."

Order, I thought. Like candles and place cards. Like a table plan that matched reality.

A crash sounded from somewhere outside, a bin perhaps, thrown by the wind. Guests flinched.

That was when the front doors opened.

A gust of rain and salt air tore into the lobby, sharp and cold. For a second, everyone turned as one body.

A woman stepped in, coat dark with rain, hair pulled into a tight bun that stayed neat despite the weather. Her face was pale with cold, eyes sharp, expression tired in the way that suggested she had already seen too much of the world's nonsense today.

DI Sera Linley.

She shook rain from her sleeves with a brisk motion, took in the lobby with one glance, and walked straight toward Hugh Mercer as if he were an obstacle in her path rather than the manager of the building.

The room changed immediately. It always did when someone with actual authority entered.

Hugh's smile snapped into place. "Detective Inspector Linley," he said, voice warm, as if he were greeting a friend. "Thank God. We've had a medical incident."

Sera didn't smile. "I've had three 'medical incidents' this week that turned into crimes," she said, voice dry. "Show me where he is."

Hugh blinked. "He's in the staff corridor. We've kept things discreet."

Sera's eyes flicked over Hugh's face. "Discreet," she repeated, and somehow the word sounded like an accusation.

She turned slightly, scanning the lobby. Her gaze landed on Saffy's pocket, where the outline of a phone was visible. Her gaze landed on Penny's notebook. Then, finally, her gaze landed on me.

Not because I was important, but because I looked like someone who had been taking notes instead of flapping.

Sera's eyes narrowed slightly. "You," she said. "Harriet Crowe."

I didn't pretend surprise. "Detective Inspector."

"You're the printer," she said.

"I prefer stationer," I replied. "Printer makes me sound like machinery."

Sera's mouth twitched. Not quite a smile. "Are you involved."

"I was in the corridor when he collapsed," I said. "I told staff to call 999. I kept track of who touched what."

Sera's gaze sharpened. "Good. Where is your note-taking."

I held up my Pocket Log slightly, not waving it, just showing. "Here."

Sera nodded once, then looked back at Hugh. "Take me to the scene."

Hugh gestured quickly, stepping into motion. "Of course. This way."

Sera held up a hand. Hugh stopped like a dog who'd been trained by someone he respected.

"Before we go anywhere," Sera said, voice clear, carrying just enough to cut through the lobby murmur, "no one leaves. No one goes into the ballroom. No one cleans anything. If I catch anyone wiping a surface or moving a plate, I'll treat it like you've tried to interfere with evidence. Clear."

The room went quieter.

Hugh's smile tightened. "We've maintained control," he said

quickly.

Sera looked at him. "You've maintained something," she replied. "We'll discuss what, exactly, later."

Penny's eyes flashed with satisfaction.

Sera turned to the reception desk. "Who's on CCTV tonight."

The receptionist blinked. "Er, security monitors it."

"Get him," Sera said. "Now. And tell him not to touch anything. I want the footage preserved."

Hugh opened his mouth to speak, then closed it again. Sera had taken the space.

Sera turned to me. "Harriet. Come with me."

Hugh's head snapped up. "Hattie is not staff."

Sera didn't look at him. "I didn't ask."

Hugh's face went pale with irritation. "This is highly sensitive."

Sera finally looked at him. Her eyes were sharp enough to cut glass. "Death is always sensitive. That doesn't mean it's yours to control."

Hugh swallowed.

Sera headed toward the staff corridor door without waiting. I followed, Pocket Log in my hand, tote close to my side.

Penny moved too, stepping as if she intended to come along. Sera's gaze flicked back.

"Penny Harrow," Sera said, naming her without question.

Penny stopped. "Detective Inspector."

"You can wait here," Sera said. "You can also decide whether you want to be helpful or you want to be a nuisance. I'm not your editor. I'm not your audience."

Penny's mouth tightened. "I want the truth."

Sera nodded once, curt. "Then stop turning everything into a performance. You'll get your statement when I'm ready."

Penny's eyes held Sera's for a long moment, then she nodded.

"Fine."

Sera continued into the corridor.

The staff corridor looked worse under Sera's gaze, as if the fluorescent light had sharpened. Dr Vale lay further down, covered. Paramedics were gone. The bartender stood nearby, face drawn. Chloe hovered close to the wall, hands clasped, looking as if she wanted to disappear into plaster.

Sera moved like a person used to stepping into rooms where the air had changed.

She crouched, glanced at the covered body, then looked up at the bartender.

"Who are you," she asked.

He told her. She listened, asked brief questions, then looked at Chloe.

"Who found him," Sera asked.

Chloe's eyes flicked to me. "He came through the door and collapsed. Hattie gave instructions."

Sera looked at me again. "Time."

I opened my Pocket Log. "He collapsed at 19:58. Paramedics arrived at 20:10. They declared at 20:13."

Sera's gaze sharpened. "You're sure."

"I write exact times," I replied. "It's what I do."

Sera nodded once. "Good."

She turned to Hugh, who had followed us in, face tight. "I want the ballroom locked down. I want the dessert plates left exactly where they are. No clearing. No stacking. No 'tidying'."

Hugh's mouth opened. "Guests are upset."

Sera's eyes were flat. "Guests can be upset in the lobby. Evidence stays where it is."

Hugh swallowed hard. "We need to feed them."

Sera's voice stayed calm, which somehow made it more threatening. "You can feed them later. Right now, you can stop creating new problems."

Hugh's jaw clenched.

Sera turned back to me. "What do you have."

I hesitated for a fraction of a second, not because I didn't want to give it to her, but because I wanted to make sure it was done properly.

I pulled the envelope from my tote and held it out.

"Dessert service sheet," I said. "Handed to me by the dessert server, Ellie, in this corridor. I labelled the envelope with time. I did not show it around. I did not give it to Hugh."

Hugh's eyes flashed. "That was hotel property."

Sera didn't look at him. She took the envelope carefully, as if it mattered, because it did.

Sera checked the label, then looked back at me. "Good work," she said, plain.

It wasn't praise. It was acknowledgement, the kind that meant, You did the sensible thing.

I felt my shoulders loosen slightly. Not relief. Just a fraction less tension.

Sera slid the envelope into her own evidence pouch. "You'll write a statement about how you obtained it and who handled it," she said.

"I already have notes," I replied.

"Good," she said. "Now tell me, from the beginning. Not your feelings. Not your theories. Facts."

I took a slow breath and gave her the facts the way I'd given them at hundreds of weddings when someone decided to sabotage a seating plan and the bride wanted to cry.

"Dr Vale performed in the ballroom," I began. "Rotation began at 19:42. Dessert service followed. At Table Fourteen, there was seat swapping earlier. Penny Harrow swapped seats with another guest after a tense quiet argument with an older male guest."

Sera's eyes sharpened. "Quiet argument."

"No leaning in," I clarified. "Low voices. Tense faces. Then seat swap. Fast. Discreet."

Sera nodded. "Continue."

"Dessert was delivered using a printed service sheet. I saw Alicia direct the dessert server toward Table Fourteen. The server set dessert down by seat position rather than by name. Penny was not initially served, then was served after the server returned. Dr Vale ate. He left the table and went through the staff corridor door. He collapsed about six steps in."

Sera's gaze flicked to the corridor door. "Why did he come into staff areas."

"He said he needed a moment," I replied. "Chloe hesitated to stop him."

Hugh shifted. "He was a guest. A VIP."

Sera looked at him. "He was a person," she said. "VIP means nothing to me."

Hugh went still.

Sera turned back to me. "Who else was in the corridor when he collapsed."

I checked my notes. "Chloe. Alicia. Ellie. The bartender. Hugh arrived quickly after."

Sera's eyes narrowed. "Quickly how."

"Within a minute," I said. "Maybe less."

Hugh's face tightened. "I was informed."

"By whom," Sera asked, looking at Hugh now.

Hugh's smile tried to return and failed. "Staff," he said vaguely.

Sera didn't accept vague. "Name."

Hugh swallowed. "Alicia."

Alicia, I thought. Of course.

Sera looked down the corridor. "Where is Ellie."

"Lobby," Hugh said quickly.

Sera turned to Chloe. "Where is Alicia."

Chloe hesitated. "She's in the lobby too."

Sera nodded. "Good. No one leaves."

She stood, straightened her coat, and looked at Hugh. "Now we go to the lobby. I want staff lined up. I want the dessert server and anyone who handled the dessert sheet. I want the kitchen supervisor. And I want your security monitor."

Hugh nodded stiffly. "Of course."

Sera paused. "Also, I want the original guest list file."

Hugh blinked. "We have printed copies."

Sera's gaze went sharp again. "I didn't ask for printed copies. I asked for the original file. The one that shows who uploaded it and when. The one that shows edits."

Hugh's face tightened. "We manage that through our vendor portal."

Sera's eyes narrowed. "Portal."

Hugh nodded, forced. "It centralises documents."

"Centralises control," Sera corrected. "I want the file and the portal access logs. Now."

Hugh's smile returned as a grimace. "That may take time. The system is proprietary."

Sera held his gaze. "You will give me access, or I will obtain it through a warrant, and you can explain to your board why you obstructed a death investigation."

Hugh swallowed hard. "We will cooperate."

Sera's eyes flicked to me. "Harriet. That guest list file went through this portal."

"Yes," I said. "Hugh insisted."

Sera nodded. "Did you receive the original file."

"I received a version," I replied. "It had unusual formatting. And an old stamp mark in the footer that shouldn't exist."

Sera's gaze sharpened. "What stamp mark."

"An old style Registry Office stamp mark," I said. "In the footer of one guest name block. Not a real stamp, a mark like a template remnant. It stood out."

Sera's eyes didn't change, but I could see her interest sharpen like a blade. "You told someone."

"I told Melissa Shaw," I said. "And I noted it."

Sera looked at Hugh again. "Melissa," she said. "She's on your event team."

"Yes," Hugh replied quickly. "She's managing the weekend."

"Then she's now managing a crime scene," Sera said, and the way she said it suggested Melissa would not enjoy the promotion.

We returned to the lobby.

The murmur rose as soon as Sera appeared. People leaned forward. Phones twitched. The urge for information pressed against the air like steam.

Sera raised her voice, clear, calm. "I'm Detective Inspector Linley. There has been a death on these premises. Due to the storm, roads are compromised and additional officers will be delayed. That does not mean this will be treated casually. It means you will cooperate, you will stay where you are, and you will stop filming."

Saffy's eyes widened innocently.

Sera looked straight at her. "Put the phone away. If I see it again, I will take it."

Saffy's mouth opened, ready to protest.

Sera's tone stayed flat. "Test me."

Saffy closed her mouth and shoved the phone deep into her bag like it was suddenly toxic.

Miles shifted uncomfortably. He looked like he'd just remembered he was not in control of this story.

Hugh stepped forward, attempting to reclaim the room. "Everyone, we're handling this with the utmost discretion."

Sera turned to him. "Stop saying discretion," she said. "It sounds like you want to hide something."

Hugh's face went tight. "I'm trying to protect the guests."

"You can protect them by not lying," Sera said. "Now, I want staff. Chloe. Alicia. Ellie. Melissa Shaw. Kitchen supervisor. Security monitor. Bring them to reception. Now."

Staff moved quickly, heads down.

Sera turned to me again. "Harriet. You stay near me."

Hugh's head snapped. "She has no reason to be involved."

Sera's gaze didn't flicker. "She has notes. You have opinions."

Hugh fell silent.

Chloe appeared first, still pale. Ellie came next, eyes red. Alicia arrived with her face arranged into something that tried to look professional and failed. Melissa Shaw followed, hair slightly loosened, eyes wide, cheeks flushed, looking like a person who'd been trying to keep the weekend alive and had just realised it was dead.

The kitchen supervisor arrived, jaw tight, arms folded, expression defensive.

Finally, a security monitor, older, with a damp jumper and a harried look, appeared from a side door.

Sera looked them over like a person reading a list.

"Right," Sera said. "Phones off. No one talks to anyone else. Hugh, you will provide a room for interviews."

Hugh nodded stiffly. "Conference room."

"Good," Sera said. She turned to the security monitor. "You. Show me CCTV coverage of the staff corridor door, the ballroom entrance, the easel with the table plan, and the kitchen corridor. Preserve footage from 18:30 until now. Do not scrub. Do not 'compress.' Do not 'lose' it."

The man nodded quickly. "Yes, DI."

Sera turned to Melissa. "You manage the vendor portal."

Melissa swallowed. "I manage the events. The portal is… shared."

"Shared by whom," Sera asked.

Melissa glanced at Hugh. Hugh's smile returned, too smooth. "It's an admin account. Standard practice."

Sera's eyes hardened. "Standard practice is how fraud hides in plain sight."

Hugh's jaw clenched.

Sera looked at Melissa. "I want the original guest list file," she said. "Not your printed copy. The digital file as uploaded. I also want the portal's edit log. Who edited it, when, and what was changed."

Melissa's hands trembled slightly. "It logs edits," she said. "But sometimes it only shows the admin account."

Sera's eyes narrowed. "Admin account."

Melissa nodded, voice small. "Generic vendor admin. It's used for multiple things."

"Convenient," Sera said.

Hugh stepped in quickly. "It's for efficiency."

Sera looked at him. "It's for deniability," she replied. "You're going to give me access."

Hugh's smile held. "We will comply."

Sera turned to me. "Harriet. Your copy of the guest list, was it also through the portal."

"Yes," I said. "Hugh insisted I submit and receive through it."

Sera nodded. "Then you will forward me every email and every file you received, including attachments and timestamps. You will not delete anything."

"I don't delete anything," I said. "I keep it all in labelled folders like a person with trust issues."

Sera's mouth twitched again. "Good. Keep those trust issues."

The lobby buzzed with restrained panic behind us. Guests murmured. Someone tried to edge toward the door and was quietly stopped by a staff member.

The wind battered the glass again, hard. A branch struck the window with a crack that made several people jump.

A man near the fireplace said, "We're trapped."

Sera didn't turn. "You're safe," she said loudly, voice carrying. "You're also not leaving. Both things can be true."

Hugh flinched at the bluntness.

I admired it.

Sera moved toward the conference room, staff lined up behind her like reluctant schoolchildren. She glanced back at the guests once, eyes sharp.

"If anyone has information," she said, "you will speak to staff and they will bring you to me. If anyone tries to create drama for the internet, you will learn what police patience looks like."

Saffy stared down at her bag as if it might bite her.

Penny watched Sera with something like respect, tempered by frustration. Penny hated being told to wait. Penny also understood when the person telling her to wait had earned the right.

Sera led us into the conference room, a bland space with beige walls and a table too long for its own good. Hugh's staff had placed a tray of tea and biscuits on the sideboard, as if sugar could smooth this out.

Sera looked at the tray. "Tea," she said.

"British crisis response," I replied.

Sera's mouth twitched. "It helps. Don't quote me."

She turned to the staff and began, efficient, clipped.

"Ellie, you start. Tell me exactly what you did with dessert. Who gave you the sheet. Who told you where to go."

Ellie's voice shook, but she answered. She mentioned Alicia. She mentioned a printed sheet. She mentioned being told to serve by seat position because "it's quicker."

Sera's eyes sharpened. "Serve by seat position," she repeated, and the way she said it made the phrase sound like a loaded gun.

Alicia tried to interrupt. "It's normal. It's just how we do it when we have rotations and changes."

Sera held up a hand. Alicia stopped.

Sera turned to Alicia. "You spoke to Ellie."

Alicia swallowed. "Yes, I directed her."

"Why," Sera asked.

Alicia's eyes flicked to Hugh. "Because there were changes. VIP preferences."

Sera's gaze hardened. "VIP preferences again."

Alicia's cheeks flushed. "It was chaos."

"Chaos is a gift to anyone who wants to hide," Sera said. Then she looked at me. "Harriet. You heard this. You noted it."

"Yes," I said. "I noted Alicia directed Ellie and that Ellie used a sheet, not names."

Sera nodded.

She turned to the kitchen supervisor next. "Who prepared the desserts."

He bristled. "Kitchen did."

"Name," Sera said.

He gave it. Sera wrote it down. Then she asked who plated, who carried trays out, who had access to the staff printer that produced the sheet.

The man started sweating. Not from guilt, necessarily. From the fact that Sera was treating "service" like a system, not a vibe.

Hugh tried to steer. "DI, we should focus on reassuring guests."

Sera looked at him. "Reassure them with truth," she said. "Not slogans."

Hugh's jaw clenched again.

Sera turned to Melissa. "Portal," she said. "Open it."

Melissa hesitated. "The login is in Hugh's office."

Sera's eyes narrowed. "Then we go to Hugh's office."

Hugh said, too quickly, "Of course."

We moved, Sera leading, Hugh stiff beside her, me following with my Pocket Log, tea left untouched in the conference room because I didn't trust it not to be used as a prop later.

Hugh's office was immaculate. Too immaculate. Not a paper out of place. A framed photo of the hotel in sunlight. A framed certificate about hospitality excellence. A small bowl of mints that looked untouched.

Sera looked around once, then went straight to the computer.

"Login," she said.

Hugh gestured to Melissa. Melissa sat, hands trembling slightly, and logged in.

The vendor portal opened with a bright interface that tried to look friendly and modern. My irritation rose. Friendly interfaces were always hiding sharp edges.

Sera leaned in. "Find the guest list," she said.

Melissa clicked. A folder labelled Second-Chance Romance Weekend opened.

Inside, a file named GuestList_Final_FINAL_v3.

Sera's mouth tightened. "Final final," she said. "Wonderful."

Melissa clicked again. The file displayed. Names. Dietary notes. The same mess I'd seen in my office.

Sera pointed. "Edit history."

Melissa clicked a tab.

A log appeared.

Timestamps. Actions. User.

My stomach tightened as I read.

Several edits. After Hattie approval. User: VendorAdmin.

Not a person. A mask.

Sera's eyes went cold. "VendorAdmin," she said.

Hugh's voice came in smoothly. "As I explained, it's a shared admin account."

"Shared accounts exist so no one is responsible," Sera replied. "Who has the password."

Hugh's smile held. "Multiple members of staff."

Sera turned her gaze to him fully. "Name them."

Hugh hesitated. "I'd have to check."

Sera's voice stayed calm. "You have thirty seconds."

Hugh swallowed. He listed names. Melissa. Lorna. Someone in IT. Possibly even the Trust rep, though he didn't say that, and his eyes flicked away when the thought crossed his face.

Sera watched him like she was reading a confession in his posture.

She pointed again at the log. "These edits happened after the event vendor approval," she said. "Meaning someone changed information after Harriet Crowe signed off."

Hugh's smile tightened. "It could be minor corrections."

Sera's gaze didn't move. "Minor corrections don't hide behind generic accounts."

I leaned closer, eyes scanning the log. One timestamp caught my eye. 00:47. A bulk edit. Multiple entries altered at once.

My throat tightened.

Sera noticed my focus. "You see something," she said.

I nodded slightly. "That timestamp," I said. "After midnight. That's when the list changed. That's when I said it changed."

Sera nodded once. "Good."

She turned to Melissa. "Download the original as uploaded. Then export the edit log. Now."

Melissa obeyed, fingers quick.

Sera looked at Hugh. "And you will not touch this system again until my team arrives," she said. "If I find logs wiped or files altered, I will treat you as a suspect in obstruction."

Hugh's face went pale. "DI, that's outrageous."

Sera's tone stayed flat. "So is a man dying at your branded romance weekend."

Hugh stared at her, stunned into silence.

Sera looked at the screen again, then at me. "Harriet. That stamp mark you saw in the footer. Was it in the current file."

Melissa clicked, scrolled. The footer showed up, faintly.

There it was.

The old style Registry Office mark. Not a stamp, not real, but present, like a ghost of a template that should have been dead.

Sera's eyes narrowed. "That's not normal," she said.

"No," I replied. "It shouldn't exist."

Sera leaned back slightly, eyes sharp, tired. "And yet it does."

Hugh tried to speak again, still clinging to his version of reality. "It's probably a formatting glitch."

Sera turned her head slowly toward him. "A formatting glitch doesn't explain why a guest list is being edited under a generic admin account after midnight," she said. "And it doesn't explain why you insisted all files be handled through this portal."

Hugh's smile wavered. "It's policy."

"Policy is made by people," Sera said. "People can be questioned."

Hugh's eyes flashed. "This hotel has standards."

Sera nodded. "Then show me."

She moved away from the desk, already deciding her next

steps. "Right," she said. "We lock down the ballroom and preserve every plate and printed sheet. We pull CCTV. We take statements. We identify who had access to the portal, who had access to staff printers, and who had access to the table plan."

She looked at me. "Harriet. Stay available. You're my clearest witness right now."

I didn't feel proud. I felt tired.

Sera's gaze softened by a fraction, just enough to read as human. "And drink some tea," she added. "You look like you're running on spite."

"I usually am," I replied.

Sera's mouth twitched. "Spite is useful. Just don't let it make you sloppy."

"I'm not sloppy," I said.

"I can see that," she replied.

Outside, the wind struck the building again, hard enough to make the windowpane tremble. The hotel lights flickered once, then steadied.

The storm had locked us in.

The portal had logged edits under a name that belonged to no one.

And Hugh Mercer, standing in his immaculate office with his immaculate smile, looked like a man who was realising that this time, paper was not going to let him tidy his way out.

CHAPTER 10

The list becomes evidence

My room at the Mariner's Crown was not mine. It was a temporary holding pen for a woman who asked inconvenient questions and wrote everything down. Hugh Mercer had given it to me with the expression of a man paying a fee he didn't believe he owed. It was on the second floor, facing the sea, which meant the view was dramatic and the window rattled like a warning. The corridor outside smelled of wet wool, carpet cleaner, and the faint metallic tang that always followed a storm into a building, even when the building pretended it was impervious.

Sera Linley had been the one to make the decision, not Hugh. She said, in her dry voice, that she wanted me contained, comfortable enough to function, and close enough to fetch when she needed answers. She didn't say she was protecting me from Hugh, but she didn't need to. I could read a room. I'd made a living doing it.

The key card worked on the first try, which surprised me. The hotel's competence was selective.

Inside, the room was beige and well behaved. A double bed with pillows stacked like small, smug clouds. A desk with a lamp and a kettle, because we are a nation that has faced war and famine and still decided the essential item was boiling water on demand. A small tray held two biscuits in plastic wrap, as if the hotel believed sugar could undo death.

I shut the door behind me and turned the bolt. Then, because I was not stupid, I hooked the little security chain too. It wasn't a fortress, but it was a clear statement.

I stood for a moment with my tote still on my shoulder, listening.

The storm filled the space beyond the glass. Wind in hard pulses. Rain like thrown handfuls of gravel. Somewhere lower down, a door banged. The hotel was an old building wearing a modern suit, and storms always found the seams.

My stomach rolled again, softer than earlier, but persistent. The corridor. Dr Vale's body under a sheet. Hugh's voice saying discretion like it was a prayer. Ellie's trembling hands handing me the dessert sheet. Sera's sharp eyes pinning the portal to the wall like a specimen.

I set my tote on the desk and took out my Pocket Log first. That came out before anything else, always. People thought the important thing about record-keeping was writing. It wasn't. It was ordering your world when someone else wanted to scramble it.

I wrote.

22:07. Room 214, Mariner's Crown. Given key by Hugh under DI instruction. Door bolted and chained. Storm ongoing. Evidence: my Pocket Log, personal print drafts and files only. Dessert service sheet handed to DI Linley.

I hesitated, then added another line beneath.

Hugh attempted to obtain paper. Noted.

Then I took off my peacoat, folded it, and placed it over the back of the chair. I did it carefully, because care was a habit and also because if I didn't keep my hands busy, they would start shaking.

The kettle sat there, silent and slightly smug. I filled it, flicked the switch, and listened to it begin its familiar growl. It was absurd, making tea in a room while a dead man lay downstairs, but absurdity was Hartcombe's normal state. We did the polite thing even when it made no sense.

While the kettle heated, I opened my laptop on the desk. The screen glowed in the dim light, a rectangle of control. My files were my territory. Hugh could not smile them away.

I plugged in my phone and checked for messages.

One from Nisha Patel at Harbour Kettle, time-stamped earlier.

Nisha: Heard something awful at the hotel. Are you there. Please say you're safe.

Practical ally, always. I typed back.

Hattie: I'm here. Storm has us locked in. Police on site. Don't come near the hotel. Keep your doors shut.

Then I stared at the message thread a moment longer than necessary. Nisha was a steady point on Valentine Row, the kind of person who fed you without asking you to earn it. If this weekend turned into a wider mess, she would be caught in it too. Everyone on the Row always was, eventually.

Another message came through from Cal Reeve.

Cal: Coast road's still blocked. Pip's asleep on my foot. You eat anything. You want me to ring someone.

I read it twice. It was his version of panic.

Hattie: Not hungry. Keep Pip away from the window. DI Linley's here. Hugh is being Hugh.

Cal replied almost immediately.

Cal: That's a shame. I liked him better when he was only irritating.

I snorted once, quiet, then wrote in my Pocket Log.

22:11. Text from Cal. Roads blocked. Pip safe. He offers support. I decline.

The kettle clicked off. I poured hot water into a mug, dropped in a teabag from the hotel tray, and watched the colour seep into the water like a slow bruise. I added milk, because I was not a martyr, and carried the mug back to the desk.

Then I began.

Sera had asked me for facts, not feelings. She'd also asked, with that bluntness that was either refreshing or lethal depending on the day, for my reconstruction. I could hear her voice in my head.

Tell me what happened. Cleanly.

What had happened was that paper had lied, and someone had used the gap between paper and reality to place a dessert in front of a man who died minutes later.

If I wanted to be useful, I had to show it, not merely say it.

I opened my work folder. The Mariner's Crown weekend lived there now, a neat digital line of files that had begun as a job and ended as evidence.

GuestList_Final_FINAL_v3, the portal's little joke. My own saved copies. My table plan drafts. My place card template. My print notes. My email confirmations with Melissa Shaw. My screenshots, because I didn't trust portals, and tonight I trusted them less.

I pulled up my place card template first.

It was a simple design, tasteful. Black ink. A small flourish at the bottom, the sort of detail that made people think you cared, which I did, even when I resented them. I used the same printer at the shop for all professional jobs. It was reliable, slightly noisy, and it left a tiny registration dot near the corner of the card, a micro artefact of how the printer fed and aligned the stock.

It was not visible unless you knew to look for it.

I knew. Because I'd spent years in rooms where someone tried to replace one piece of paper and expected no one to notice.

I opened a photo on my phone, taken at my shop earlier in

the week, a quick reference shot of a sample place card under bright light. I zoomed in. There it was, near the lower right corner, almost like a speck of dust that refused to move. A dot, faint but consistent.

My dot.

I wrote in the Pocket Log.

22:18. Place card print run marker: tiny registration dot near lower right corner (consistent on shop printer). Reference photo confirms.

Then I opened the print history from my laptop. File names, dates, timestamps. I didn't just create paper. I created a timeline.

Wednesday: initial draft. Thursday: updated guest list version, corrected dietary notes. Friday morning: final run printed in one batch. No late-night additions. No hotel printer. No portal edits. My job had been locked.

Or it had been until someone else decided to unlock it without permission.

I pulled up my email thread with Melissa.

Melissa had been polite, harried, and keen to keep Hugh happy. She'd sent me the guest list through the portal link, not as an attachment. I'd downloaded it, saved my own version, and worked from that. The portal wanted to be the source of truth. My hard drive had decided to be a better one.

I opened my saved copy of the guest list and scrolled. Similar names. Copy and paste artefacts. Strange template remnants. The old Registry Office stamp mark in the footer of one name block, faint and wrong. Like someone had used an old form as a base and forgotten to strip the ghost out of it.

I stared at it, the tiny mark that shouldn't exist, and felt my skin tighten. It was a clue and it was also a warning. Someone was playing with records. Not just seating charts. Not just desserts.

Records.

Valentine Row lived and died on records.

I sipped tea, now hot enough to sting my tongue, and welcomed the sting. It was proof I was still in my body.

I opened my table plan drafts next.

The ballroom tables had been numbered, of course, because hotels loved numbers. Numbers turned people into manageable units. Table Two, Table Fourteen, Table Seven, each with a neat list of names and dietary flags. The plan had been printed on thick paper and pinned to an easel like a declaration of order.

Except order had been pretend.

I clicked through my drafts, comparing them to the last version I had approved and saved.

The approved plan showed Penny Harrow in Seat 14C, if you wanted to be exact. Her chair at the table, her position relative to the stage and the service route.

My notes, my Pocket Log, showed reality.

Penny swapped seats with the brunette guest at 19:26. Dr Vale sat in Penny's original seat position at 19:44. Dessert service used a printed sheet and delivered by seat position at 19:53. Dr Vale ate and collapsed at 19:58.

Seat mapping altered. That line from my Pocket Log might as well have been a drumbeat.

I wrote again.

22:27. Table 14 mapping changed twice: Penny swap (19:26), Vale sits in Penny's original seat position (19:44). Dessert delivered by seat position (19:53). Collapse (19:58).

The storm hit the window hard, a sudden hammering that made the glass buzz. I paused, listened to the hotel creak, and imagined Pip's reaction. Freeze. Stare. One bark. Cal would have rubbed his ears and muttered about dramatic weather.

I didn't have Pip tonight. I had paper.

I took out my labelled envelopes from my tote and laid them on the desk. They made a small, neat row, each one a promise of containment.

PLACE CARD SAMPLES. TABLE PLAN DRAFTS. POCKET LOG PHOTOS. PORTAL SCREENSHOTS.

I opened the PLACE CARD SAMPLES envelope and pulled out three spare cards I'd printed at the shop. Blank, but same stock, same ink, same printer dot. I held one under the desk lamp and angled it.

There it was again, faint, stubborn.

I didn't know yet if Sera would need me to testify about dot patterns. I did know that if someone had swapped a card, this was how I would prove it.

A knock came at the door.

Not gentle. Not a tap. A firm, controlled knock, the kind of knock that said, I am allowed to be here.

I froze, pen in hand. My eyes went to the chain, then the bolt. Both still set.

I didn't open it. I didn't speak. Silence was also a tool.

The knock came again, the same rhythm. Then a voice.

"Harriet. DI Linley."

I exhaled once, slow. Only then did I move.

I opened the door as far as the chain allowed and peered through.

Sera stood in the corridor, coat still damp, bun still tight, expression tired and sharp. A uniformed constable stood behind her, slightly younger, looking as if he'd been thrown into the deep end of a very British nightmare.

Sera's gaze flicked past me, taking in the desk, the laptop, the envelopes. She approved without saying it.

"You look like you're building a case," she said.

"I'm building a timeline," I replied. "Cases are your job."

Sera's mouth twitched. "Cases are everyone's job when people start lying."

She held up a clear evidence bag. Inside was a place card.

My stomach tightened.

"I need your eyes," she said. "Not your theories."

"You'll get both if you stand here long enough," I replied, then unhooked the chain and opened the door fully.

Sera stepped in, the constable remaining in the corridor like a guard dog with manners.

Sera placed the evidence bag on the desk. "This was on the table," she said. "Table Fourteen. Near where Vale was seated."

I leaned in.

The place card read DR LUCIAN VALE in neat black type. At first glance, it was fine. At first glance, everything that killed people always looked fine.

I picked up one of my spare sample cards and held it beside the bagged one, careful not to touch the evidence bag more than necessary. I angled both under the lamp.

Then I saw it.

My sample card had the tiny registration dot near the lower right corner.

The bagged card did not.

I leaned closer, narrowed my eyes, checked the other corner in case it had shifted. No dot. No faint stubborn speck.

My throat went dry.

"That's not mine," I said.

Sera's gaze sharpened. "Explain."

"My print run leaves a tiny registration dot," I said. "Near the lower right corner. Consistent. It's a micro artefact of my shop printer. It's on every card from my run. This one doesn't have it."

Sera stared at the card through the plastic for a long moment, then looked at my sample card, then back at the evidence bag.

"What about paper stock," she asked.

I held my sample closer. "Mine are a warm white, slightly textured. This looks cooler, smoother. But that's harder to prove without side-by-side under consistent light."

Sera nodded. "Dot is better. Dot is repeatable."

I sipped my tea, realised it had gone lukewarm, and didn't care. "Someone printed a replacement," I said. "Or several."

Sera's eyes stayed flat. "Meaning someone had access to a printer."

"Hotel printer," I replied. "Or a portable one. Or a staff office machine. But not mine."

Sera took the evidence bag back and tucked it under her arm. "Good," she said. "Write it down. Describe the dot. Describe your printer. Describe how you know it's consistent."

"I already started," I said, tapping my Pocket Log.

Sera looked at the envelopes again. "You're also going to reconstruct the seating plan," she said. "Not the version on paper. The version that happened."

"I'm doing it," I replied.

Sera's gaze flicked to my laptop screen. "And you're going to tell me why Vale ended up in that seat."

"I can tell you how," I said. "Why is the part you'll need to extract from people who lie."

Sera's mouth twitched again. "Good answer."

She paused, then added, "Hugh's furious."

"I noticed," I replied. "He wears it like cologne."

Sera's expression didn't soften. "He's trying to frame this as an unavoidable tragedy. He's also trying to keep the Trust rep calm."

"Imogen Baird," I said.

Sera's eyes narrowed. "You know her name."

"I read contracts," I replied. "It's my hobby and my curse."

Sera nodded once. "Keep your door locked. Don't let staff in. If anyone asks for your notes, you refuse. You hand them to me only."

"I don't hand my notes to people who treat truth like a branding problem," I said.

Sera's gaze held mine. "That's why I'm using you."

That was not comforting. It was honest.

Sera moved toward the door, then stopped. "One more thing," she said. "The storm's getting worse. More trees down. Backup units are delayed. We're holding everyone overnight."

"I assumed," I said.

"Good," she replied. "Then don't let fatigue make you careless."

She left without waiting for acknowledgement, because Sera didn't do sentimental exits. The constable followed, closing the corridor back into silence.

I re-bolted the door and hooked the chain again.

Then I sat down at the desk and stared at my place card sample, my tiny dot glaring up at me like a stubborn truth.

A replacement place card. Not mine.

Which meant someone had planned to alter the mapping on paper, not just in bodies.

People could move on impulse. Paper moved because someone made it.

I wrote in the Pocket Log.

22:36. DI Linley brought place card (Dr Lucian Vale) from Table 14. Card lacks my printer's tiny registration dot near lower right corner. Paper stock appears smoother/cooler. Conclusion: replacement card printed outside my controlled run.

I underlined the last line, then regretted it slightly. Underlining looked emotional. I preferred crisp sentences. Still, the moment deserved emphasis.

I opened my table plan draft again and began reconstructing the reality version, line by line.

Table Fourteen: names as listed, seat positions as planned. Then changes.

Penny swapped with brunette guest at 19:26. I didn't yet know brunette guest's full name, not for certain. The list showed a few similar names, the copy-paste problem. But I had seen her face. I could narrow it later with Sera. For now, I used what I knew.

19:44. Dr Vale sat in Penny's original seat position. Which meant, if dessert service was running by seat position, Vale received the dessert intended for Penny's seat.

But Penny received dessert too, after a brief gap, which suggested the staff were trying to reconcile service with confusion. That mattered because it implied the system was not purely by name.

I typed a timeline in a document, because digital text could be copied, sent to Sera, and preserved. My Pocket Log stayed the original. The document was a working copy.

19:42 rotation begins. 19:44 Vale seated at Table 14, Penny's original position. 19:53 dessert delivery directed by service sheet, delivered by seat position. 19:58 Vale collapses in staff corridor.

As I typed, I thought about Ellie's sheet.

A printed dessert service sheet that told staff where to deliver plates.

Who printed it. Who wrote it. Who instructed it.

If the sheet was forged, like the vendor instruction sheet later in the outline, it could direct a specific dessert to a specific seat. Not a person. A seat.

Seat-targeted.

My skin tightened again.

A knock came at the door again. This time softer, cautious.

I didn't move.

"Hattie," a voice called quietly. "It's Chloe."

I paused. Chloe wasn't a threat in the same way Hugh was. Chloe was just frightened, and frightened people could be used.

"Go away," I called, voice flat.

A pause. "I just… I wanted to check you're all right."

I stared at the door. The chain held. The bolt held. Still, the safest kindness was distance.

"I'm fine," I lied. "Go back to the lobby. Don't talk to anyone."

Chloe's voice wavered. "Mr Mercer said we should… we should collect any paperwork and keep it safe."

There it was.

Hugh's second route. If he couldn't take it from my hands, he'd send someone kinder.

I felt a cold anger settle, the clean kind.

"Chloe," I said, calm. "Do not touch any paper. Do not carry anything for Hugh. DI Linley has evidence control. If Hugh asks again, you tell him to speak to her."

Silence.

Then Chloe whispered, "He'll be angry."

"I know," I replied. "Anger is his hobby."

Another pause. Then, softly, "All right."

Her footsteps moved away down the corridor, light and quick.

I wrote in the Pocket Log.

22:48. Chloe knocked. Said Hugh instructed staff to "collect paperwork and keep it safe." I refused. Told Chloe evidence control is DI Linley. Possible attempt to retrieve notes indirectly.

That was the truth of it. Hugh was not merely controlling, he was opportunistic.

I returned to my reconstruction with more urgency.

If I could show Sera that a replacement place card existed and that it was not from my run, it supported a deliberate manipulation. It also supported the idea that the hotel's internal systems, printer access, portal access, and service sheets were part of the mechanism.

I opened my file of place card dot pattern notes, a small internal record I kept after a previous job where someone had tried to replace a single card and claim it was mine.

Yes, it had happened before. Humans were predictable. They lied in the same ways. They assumed no one would notice a speck.

I added detail to my statement draft: the model of my shop printer, the card stock brand, the dot's position relative to the corner and text baseline, the consistency across my run.

Then I paused and thought about the ballroom itself.

Sera had locked it down. Plates and cups untouched. Table plan still on the easel, likely. Place cards still on tables.

Which meant the ballroom was a time capsule.

It also meant Hugh would be desperate to get in there and "reset" it before morning.

The storm prevented escape. It also prevented outside oversight arriving quickly. The hotel, the Trust, and anyone with keys would have more time than they should.

That was the ugly gift of weather.

I stood, crossed to the window, and looked out.

The sea was barely visible, a dark mass beyond rain. Lights along the promenade flickered and softened. Somewhere below, the lobby's glass doors shuddered under wind pressure.

My reflection stared back in the window, pale and stern, hair bobbed blunt, white streak like a stripe of warning. My glasses hung on their chain, catching a small glint of lamp light. I looked like I did when I used to tell grooms that no, they could not change the seating plan fifteen minutes before the ceremony because their mother had "a feeling."

I looked like a woman who was tired of people pretending procedures were optional.

I returned to the desk and drank my tea, now cold. It tasted like resignation.

Then I kept working.

The guest list was messy. Similar names, copy and paste artefacts. That wasn't just inconvenient, it was exploitable. If two people shared a surname and a first initial, you could swap them in a list and later claim it was an innocent error. If you had an admin account and edit logs that pointed to no one, you could alter entries without personal consequence.

That was a system designed for plausible deniability.

It was also a system built to hide mistakes and hide crimes.

I opened the portal screenshots I had taken earlier, the ones that showed the edit log tab. VendorAdmin. Multiple edits after midnight. A bulk edit at 00:47.

I zoomed in, reading the timestamps again. The edits were not random. They clustered around certain tables. Certain dietary notes. Certain guests.

If I wanted to be useful, I had to identify what changed. Not in abstract. In specifics.

I compared my saved guest list version to the portal's current version as best I could, using the downloaded file metadata. I didn't have direct portal access now, Sera had locked it, but I had my own copies.

Differences emerged.

A dietary note shifted from "no nuts" to "no dairy." A guest's surname corrected in one version, then "corrected" back in another. A seat assignment changed for one couple, subtle, just one seat to the left.

Small changes.

Small enough to be explained. Large enough to redirect a plate to a different person if the system used seat numbers.

I wrote these differences into my working document carefully, not as accusations, but as observations.

If Sera wanted to pursue it, she would. If she didn't, the notes would still exist.

I kept thinking of Penny. Penny had swapped seats to avoid something, I suspected, or to send a message. Penny also looked like a woman who knew exactly what she was doing and did it anyway.

And then Dr Vale sat in Penny's old seat position like fate had pulled him there.

But fate didn't print replacement place cards.

People did.

I heard movement in the corridor outside again. A door opening. A low voice. Hugh's voice, faint, clipped. Someone replied, quieter. A key card beeped somewhere. The hotel was full of access sounds now. The sort of sounds you notice when you're waiting for someone to try your door.

I didn't like it.

I pulled my tote closer to my chair and slid my envelopes inside, leaving only what I needed on the desk. If someone forced their way in, which they could, this was still a hotel, I wanted my evidence portable.

Pocket Log. Laptop. Phone. Tote. Go.

I hated thinking like that. It made my skin tight. It made the room feel smaller. But I'd worked with enough wedding parties to know that people could become vicious when their reputations were threatened.

And Hugh's reputation was not merely personal. It was institutional.

The Trust would not tolerate mess. Councillors and donors never did.

Another knock, sharp.

I didn't move. I waited for the voice.

"Hattie," Hugh said through the door, smooth as varnish. "May we speak."

May we speak, as if he had ever asked anyone's permission for anything.

"No," I called back.

A pause. Then, "DI Linley would prefer we keep communication open."

I laughed once, without humour. "Then she can come herself."

"Hattie," Hugh said, voice tightening, "this situation is delicate."

"Death isn't delicate," I replied. "It's final."

Another pause. Hugh changed tack, the way men like him always did.

"I'm concerned you're tired," he said. "You've had a shock. I don't want you misunderstanding details and creating confusion."

There it was. Undermining as care.

"I'm not confused," I replied. "I'm exact."

"Hattie," he said again, slightly sharper. "You are a vendor."

"And you're a man who thinks saying a thing makes it true," I said. "Go away."

Silence.

Then, softer, "We need the weekend to continue."

My hand tightened around my pen. "A man died," I said. "If you keep talking about the weekend like it's a soufflé that might fall, I'm going to assume you're guilty of something even if you aren't."

That landed. I could hear it in the pause.

"Hattie," he said, voice careful now. "I'm trying to protect the guests."

"You're trying to protect the Trust," I corrected.

Silence again.

Then footsteps retreating, quick, controlled. Hugh did not like losing. He also did not like being heard losing.

I wrote in the Pocket Log.

23:19. Hugh knocked. Requested to speak. Attempted to frame my fatigue as unreliability. Mentioned "weekend continuing." I refused. He left.

Then I returned to my work with a colder clarity.

I pulled up the seating plan and began mapping the dessert service routes. Not a full diagram, because I wasn't drawing a bloody battlefield, but enough to understand how staff would move.

Servers started near the kitchen door, moved clockwise. Table Two near stage. Table Fourteen mid-room. Staff corridor door near side.

If someone wanted a particular dessert to reach a particular seat without fuss, they could exploit the staff's habit of moving by seat order and service sheets rather than reading names.

Names were messy. Seats were stable, until someone swapped them.

Unless you printed a replacement place card to make the swap look legitimate.

I stared at the thought.

A replacement Dr Vale card on Table Fourteen suggested someone expected a seat change, or wanted to formalise one.

Why would Vale need a replacement card. He was the celebrity. His name would have been printed correctly from the start.

Unless the replacement wasn't to fix his name.

Unless the replacement was to place his name where it shouldn't be.

To justify him sitting in a particular seat.

To make it look intentional.

My skin went cold.

I wrote in my working document: Replacement card may have been used to legitimise seat position shift. Investigate who placed it, when, and why.

I sat back, exhausted for the first time since the corridor. The adrenaline was fading. The tea did nothing now. The room was quiet except for storm and distant lobby murmurs that rose and fell like the sea.

I thought of Pip again. His warmth, his stubborn little weight on my foot, his simple honesty. Freeze, stare, bark. No branding. No manipulation. Just a dog telling you the world had changed.

I looked at my Pocket Log, at the pages filling with times and facts.

If Pip was my anchor, paper was my weapon.

There was another tap on the door. Not Hugh this time. A shorter rhythm. Professional.

"Harriet," Sera's voice called. "Open up."

I unhooked the chain and opened the door.

Sera stood there, expression unchanged, rain finally drying on her coat. Her eyes flicked past me into the room, noted the organised desk, the closed laptop angle, the tote within reach.

"You found something," she said.

"Yes," I replied. "The place card you brought me lacks my printer dot pattern. It's a replacement. Not mine."

Sera nodded. "I want your written statement now."

"It's in progress," I said. "Come in."

She stepped inside, shut the door behind her, and leaned against the desk in a way that suggested she was too tired to sit and too stubborn to admit it.

"Talk," she said.

I handed her my spare sample card first, so she could see the dot without me lecturing. Then I described it, position, consistency, printer. I told her about Hugh's attempts to retrieve paper. I told her about Chloe being tasked to "collect paperwork."

Sera's eyes sharpened at that. "He's interfering."

"He's trying," I said.

Sera's voice stayed calm. "If he tries again, you ring me."

"I will," I replied.

Sera looked at my laptop screen. "What else."

I pointed to the file comparison notes. "Guest list changes," I said. "Small ones. Dietary notes, surnames, seat assignments. Enough to redirect service if the system used seats."

Sera's gaze went still. "Good. That's what I need."

I hesitated, then said it. "The replacement Dr Vale card suggests someone wanted his name in a specific seat position. Not to fix spelling. To legitimise placement."

Sera's eyes held mine. "That's a theory," she said.

"It's an inference," I replied. "Based on paper behaviour."

Sera's mouth twitched. "All right. Keep it in that lane. Facts first. Inferences second. No speculation."

"I don't do speculation," I said.

Sera glanced at my cold tea. "You do stubborn, though."

"It's what kept me employed for twenty years," I replied.

Sera straightened. "Get me your written statement," she said. "Then try to sleep. We're doing interviews at first light. And Harriet."

"Yes," I said.

Her tone sharpened. "Do not open the door to anyone but me or my officers. Not Chloe, not Melissa, not your retired lifeboat friend, not a sob story."

"I won't," I replied.

Sera nodded once, then paused as if she wanted to say something more human and decided against it.

She settled for, "Good work."

Then she left, quiet as a closing file.

I bolted the door again, sat at the desk, and finished my statement.

I wrote it the way I wrote everything. Time. Action. Evidence. Chain.

I described the dot pattern. I described my printer. I described my controlled print run. I described the place card lacking the dot. I described how Sera brought it to me in an evidence bag. I described my conclusion: replacement produced outside my run.

Then I saved the document in two places, emailed it to Sera's address she'd dictated earlier, and printed a copy using the hotel printer.

I stopped myself with a sharp laugh.

No, I did not trust the hotel printer.

I saved it only. Digital and duplicated. No hotel machine was touching my words.

Finally, I shut my laptop and stared at the ceiling.

The storm was still raging. Roads were still blocked. The guests downstairs were still trapped with their phones and their need to narrate.

Hugh Mercer was still thinking about branding.

And somewhere in the building, someone had printed a place card that wasn't mine and placed it on a table like a quiet lie.

I lay down fully dressed on the bed, shoes off but socks still on because I was not relaxing. The sheets were too crisp and smelled like detergent and other people's lives. I stared at the dark.

My Pocket Log sat on the bedside table. My tote was within reach.

I didn't sleep quickly. People who said they could sleep after a death had either never seen one up close or had built a wall so thick it was practically a prison.

I listened to the wind, to the building creak, to the distant lobby murmur, and to my own mind slotting paper into patterns.

Seat mapping altered.

Replacement card.

VendorAdmin edits.

Old Registry Office mark.

Romance branding as control.

In the dark, the clues didn't feel like a puzzle yet. They felt like a hand closing slowly around the town.

And I had the unpleasant certainty that this death was only the part of the weekend the hotel couldn't polish away.

CHAPTER 11

First interrogation wave

The conference room had the sort of carpet designed to forgive sins.

Beige. Patterned just enough to hide spills. The kind of room that hosted quarterly meetings and polite complaints, not deaths. Someone had switched on the strip lights, which made everyone look slightly unwell. It suited the moment.

I sat at the far end of the table with my Pocket Log open, my reading glasses hooked on their chain, and a mug of tea that tasted like it had been brewed out of obligation rather than care. The hotel had produced it anyway, because a British crisis without tea would feel dangerously foreign.

Outside, the storm worked the building like a persistent creditor. The wind hit in pulses. The windowpanes trembled. Somewhere in the corridor, a door banged hard enough to make the water in my mug quiver.

DI Sera Linley stood at the head of the table, coat off now, shirt sleeves rolled, bun still tight. She looked tired in the way that suggested she had been tired for years and simply refused to acknowledge it. Two uniformed constables hovered near the door, not sitting, not relaxing, ready to move if the hotel tried to wriggle.

Hugh Mercer hovered too, briefly, until Sera turned her head and pinned him with a look that could have stripped paint.

"No," she said.

Hugh blinked. "Detective Inspector, I'm only here to assist."

"You can assist by leaving," Sera replied. "This is an investigation, not a management exercise."

Hugh's controlled smile tightened, then he managed a nod that looked like compliance and felt like resentment. He stepped out, shutting the door as if closing it gently would prove he was a good man.

The moment he left, the air changed. Less polished. More real.

Sera glanced at me. "Harriet. You're here as a witness. You don't answer for anyone. You don't argue with anyone. You write."

"I was going to do that regardless," I said.

Her mouth twitched. "Good. If I want your voice, I'll ask for it."

I dipped my pen and wrote.

23:57. Conference room. First interviews. DI Linley. Two PCs. Hugh removed.

Sera looked at the clock on the wall, then at the file folder in her hand. The folder was plain, which meant it belonged to the police. Hugh's folders tended to be embossed, as if raised lettering could raise truth.

"All right," Sera said. "We begin with the people who had access, motive, and opportunity. We are not doing feelings. We are not doing reputation management. We are doing facts."

The door opened and the first suspect walked in.

Lorna Beckett looked like a woman who had been trained to smile through chaos and had finally reached the limit of her training. Late thirties, neat hair pulled back, makeup still intact despite the storm and the lobby and the death, a lanyard around her neck as if the badge still mattered.

She sat too quickly, hands clasped hard, eyes darting once to me, then to Sera, then to the door, as if calculating who might walk in next.

Sera didn't sit. She stayed standing, which was a quiet power move. People always felt smaller when the police stayed on their feet.

"State your name and role," Sera said.

"Lorna Beckett," Lorna replied. "Event coordinator. Contracted through Beckett Events."

Sera nodded. "You're in charge of planning and execution."

"Yes."

"You had access to the vendor portal," Sera said.

Lorna's eyes flicked. "We all did. It's the hotel's system."

Sera's gaze stayed steady. "You had access."

"Yes."

"Password."

Lorna blinked. "It's… shared."

Sera's voice stayed calm. "Who shared it with you."

"Hugh, mostly," Lorna said, too quickly. "He insists. The portal is policy. It's streamlined for vendors."

I wrote the word she used, because people revealed themselves with their preferred vocabulary.

00:02. Lorna says portal "streamlined." Claims Hugh policy.

Sera's eyes narrowed slightly. "We're not here to discuss efficiency. We're here to discuss edits made after approval."

Lorna's posture stiffened. "Edits?"

Sera opened the folder, slid a printed screenshot across the table. It was the portal log, the one I'd seen in Hugh's office. VendorAdmin. Multiple edits. Midnight. Bulk edit.

Lorna stared at it, colour rising in her cheeks. "That could be anyone."

"That's the problem," Sera said. "Generic accounts are useful for people who don't like responsibility."

Lorna swallowed. "It's not my choice."

Sera's tone sharpened. "Your choice is whether you used it."

Lorna's hands tightened. "I didn't edit anything after final approval."

Sera held her gaze. "What is final approval."

"The vendor sign-off," Lorna said. "Hattie's sign-off."

She glanced at me again, a quick look that tried to turn me into a shield.

I did not shield people who used me as a prop.

Sera turned slightly toward me. "Harriet, did you approve the guest list and seating plan."

"Yes," I said. "And I saved my copies."

Sera nodded and returned to Lorna. "After Harriet approved, edits were made. You're telling me you did not make them."

"Yes."

Sera's voice stayed even. "Then who did."

Lorna shook her head quickly. "I don't know. It could be hotel admin. It could be IT. It could be the Trust. It could be anyone."

The Trust. Interesting that she said it unprompted.

I wrote.

00:05. Lorna mentions "the Trust" without prompt.

Sera noticed too. Her eyes sharpened. "Why would the Trust edit a guest list."

Lorna's mouth tightened. "Because they're paying."

Sera waited.

Lorna shifted in her seat. "They... they care about branding. They want the guest experience perfect. They fuss over names. They fuss over dietary notes. They fuss over who sits next to whom."

Sera's gaze didn't soften. "Who from the Trust."

Lorna hesitated, then said, "Imogen Baird."

The name landed like a nail.

Sera nodded once, as if she already knew it. "Imogen will be in next," she said. "We'll return to that."

Lorna's shoulders sagged with relief, then tightened again as she realised relief was premature.

Sera leaned forward slightly. "Now tell me about tonight. Dessert service. Who gave instructions. Who printed the service sheet."

Lorna blinked. "That's kitchen and operations."

"Answer," Sera said.

"I didn't print anything," Lorna said quickly. "I didn't touch dessert."

"Did you request reprints of place cards," Sera asked.

Lorna frowned. "No."

Sera's gaze flicked briefly to me. She didn't need to ask. I'd already told her about the request at the mixer, and the replacement card without my dot.

Sera returned to Lorna. "Were you aware of seat changes during the banquet."

Lorna's eyes widened. "People move around all the time. They mingle. They swap. It's a romantic weekend."

"Were you aware," Sera repeated, still calm.

Lorna's mouth tightened. "I saw some movement, yes. Guests do that."

Sera nodded. "Did you intervene."

"No. Why would I."

Sera slid another sheet across the table. This one was my handwriting, photocopied from my statement draft that I had emailed. It felt strange seeing my words printed in a police folder already. It made the whole thing more real and more invasive at once.

"Harriet observed a seat swap involving Penny Harrow," Sera

said. "And she observed Vale seated in Penny Harrow's original seat position shortly before dessert."

Lorna stared. "That doesn't mean anything."

"Not alone," Sera replied. "It means something when dessert was delivered by seat position."

Lorna's face went pale. "You can't be saying…"

"I'm not saying anything yet," Sera said. "I'm asking questions."

Lorna swallowed hard. "Vale had enemies," she said, too fast, as if she'd been waiting for that line. "Everyone knows that. He humiliated people for money. That was his whole thing."

There it was, the red herring in full colour. It was plausible. It was loud. It was also convenient, because it invited everyone to focus on Vale's personal nastiness rather than the system that put the wrong plate in the wrong place.

I wrote anyway.

00:11. Lorna: "Vale had enemies. Humiliated people for money."

Sera didn't bite. "Who did he humiliate."

Lorna shrugged quickly. "Guests. Clients. People on his programmes. He made a living out of tearing people down and calling it healing. There were complaints. There were social posts. There were threats. I heard staff talking about it."

Sera's eyes narrowed. "Which staff."

Lorna blinked. "I don't know. People."

Sera's voice stayed flat. "Name someone or stop throwing fog around."

Lorna flushed. "The kitchen supervisor doesn't like him," she snapped. "He said Vale was a bully."

Sera noted it, then asked, "Did you see anyone photographing the seating plan."

Lorna hesitated. "People take pictures. They're influencers."

"Not guests," Sera said. "Backstage. Staff corridors. The wall plan."

Lorna's eyes flicked away. "I didn't see."

Sera held her gaze until Lorna's discomfort became visible in her throat, a swallow that barely worked.

Then Sera said, "All right."

Lorna exhaled, hopeful.

Sera continued, "You will remain available. You will not speak to anyone about what we discussed. If you do, I will know, because I will be watching the lobby and the portal. You understand."

Lorna nodded quickly.

Sera opened the door and a constable stepped forward. "Take Ms Beckett to the side room," Sera said. "Water. No phone. No contact."

Lorna stood, looking at me again. Her eyes held a plea. Not for help, exactly. For me to become the sort of woman who said, She seemed nice.

I wasn't.

She left.

Sera turned to me. "Note her phrasing. Note where she jumped."

"She volunteered the Trust," I said.

Sera nodded once. "Exactly."

I wrote.

00:18. Lorna deflects via Vale enemies angle. Volunteers Trust influence. Points to kitchen supervisor grudge.

The door opened again.

Imogen Baird walked in like a person stepping onto a stage, not into a police interview.

She was mid-thirties, sleek coat, tidy hair, a face that had been trained into pleasant neutrality. She carried a folder, naturally.

THE VALENTINE GUEST LIST

Trust people loved folders. They hid behind paper like it was a curtain.

She sat without being asked, legs crossed neatly, hands folded atop her folder as if she'd rehearsed this.

"Detective Inspector Linley," she said, voice warm. "How dreadful. We're all quite shaken."

Sera stayed standing. "State your name and role."

Imogen blinked once, smile barely shifting. "Imogen Baird. Sponsorship liaison for the Valentine Heritage Trust."

Sera nodded. "You're here because you influence this weekend."

Imogen's smile brightened slightly. "We support local businesses and community events."

Sera's expression didn't change. "Do you have access to the vendor portal."

Imogen's posture tightened, just a fraction. "No. That's the hotel's internal system."

Sera reached into the folder and slid the portal log screenshot across.

Imogen glanced at it, then back up. "I'm not sure what you're showing me."

"I'm showing you an edit log under a generic admin account," Sera said. "Edits were made after vendor sign-off. The Trust's liaison has been named as someone who cares deeply about guest lists and arrangements."

Imogen's smile remained. "Guest experience matters. That's why we sponsor. But we don't edit hotel systems."

Sera tilted her head slightly. "Do you have the password."

Imogen's eyes widened in controlled surprise. "Of course not."

Sera watched her. "Has anyone from the Trust ever had it."

Imogen's smile tightened. "No."

Sera's voice stayed calm. "Imogen, you will answer my

questions directly. If you don't, I will assume you're hiding something."

Imogen's smile softened into something vaguely hurt. "Detective Inspector, the Trust is trying to help Hartcombe. Tonight's tragedy is awful, but it's a medical situation. We should be careful about turning it into something it isn't."

Sera's gaze went cold. "I decide what it is. Not you."

Imogen's expression froze for half a second, then returned to warm neutral. "Of course."

I wrote.

00:23. Imogen frames death as "tragedy" and "medical situation." Attempts to steer.

Sera asked, "Where were you tonight."

Imogen answered smoothly. "In the ballroom, at my table. Then in the lobby after the incident. I spoke with Hugh to coordinate guest welfare."

Sera's eyes narrowed. "Coordinate."

Imogen nodded. "People were frightened. We wanted calm."

Sera's voice stayed flat. "Calm helps liars."

Imogen blinked. "That's unkind."

"It's accurate," Sera said. "Who did you speak to in the last hour before dessert."

Imogen's fingers tightened slightly on her folder. "Hugh. Melissa Shaw. A few guests. The influencer couple wanted reassurance. The journalist, Penny Harrow, asked questions."

Sera's gaze sharpened. "What questions."

Imogen's smile became cautious. "She asked about the Trust's role. About property ownership. She seemed to be... fishing."

I felt my spine tighten. Penny's line again. Fire year records. Registry seals. Trust. Property.

Sera didn't react outwardly. "Did you answer her."

"I told her the Trust operates transparently," Imogen said, too smoothly.

Sera held her gaze. "Do you."

Imogen's smile didn't falter. "Yes."

Sera leaned forward slightly. "Then you won't mind me seeing your sponsorship agreements, your communications with the hotel, and your internal notes."

Imogen's smile tightened. "Those are confidential."

Sera's eyes hardened. "Confidentiality doesn't outrank a death."

Imogen's tone stayed pleasant. "We will cooperate fully within appropriate boundaries."

There it was. The phrase you used when you intended to cooperate with nothing.

I wrote.

00:27. Imogen: "cooperate fully within appropriate boundaries."

Sera asked, "Did you request changes to the guest list."

Imogen's eyes widened slightly. "No. We don't handle operational details."

Sera's voice stayed calm. "Did you request changes to the seating plan."

Imogen hesitated, then smiled. "We make suggestions. For sponsor visibility. For VIP comfort."

Sera's gaze narrowed. "Suggestions or instructions."

Imogen held her smile. "Suggestions."

Sera asked, "Were any of those suggestions delivered through the vendor portal."

Imogen's fingers tightened on the folder again. "I wouldn't know."

Sera moved to a different angle. "Do you know what a vendor admin account is."

Imogen blinked. "I assume it's a hotel system role."

Sera nodded. "Correct. It allows edits without a name attached. Convenient for anyone who wants changes but doesn't want accountability. Now, let me ask you this: has the Trust ever pressured the hotel to 'handle things internally.'"

Imogen's smile flickered. "We prefer issues resolved discreetly, yes. For guest comfort."

Sera's gaze sharpened. "Discreetly. Another favourite word. Like privacy."

Imogen's smile returned. "We're a charity. Our purpose is town revitalisation."

Sera's voice stayed flat. "Charities can commit crimes too."

Imogen's eyes cooled for the first time. "Detective Inspector, with respect, this line of questioning is inappropriate."

Sera's tone didn't change. "With respect, you don't decide that."

Imogen took a breath, then said, "Vale was controversial. If you're looking for motive, you'll find it in his own behaviour. He made enemies everywhere."

She was doing Lorna's red herring again, dressed up in sponsor language. Vale as the problem. Vale as the lightning rod. Vale as an easy narrative.

Sera watched her. "Did he make an enemy of you."

Imogen's smile sharpened. "I barely knew him."

Sera asked, "Did you speak to him tonight."

Imogen's eyes widened. "No."

Sera's gaze held. "Are you sure."

Imogen's smile held too. "Yes."

Sera waited. Silence did the work.

Imogen finally added, "He was busy performing. He was surrounded by guests."

Sera nodded once. "Interesting. You just gave me a detail I didn't ask for."

Imogen's cheeks flushed slightly. "I was simply clarifying."

Sera said, "You can clarify less. It makes you safer."

I almost smiled, and stopped myself. This was not the time to enjoy Sera's sharpness. It was the time to watch for cracks.

Sera asked, "What is in your folder."

Imogen's smile returned. "Notes. Sponsorship deliverables. Guest feedback sheets."

Sera held out her hand. "Give it to me."

Imogen's posture stiffened. "That's Trust property."

Sera's gaze went icy. "So is the building you're buying, I suspect. Give me the folder."

Imogen blinked, then slowly handed it over, smile stretched thin.

Sera opened it and flicked through. Pages. Printed sheets. A logo watermark. Guest feedback forms with hearts. An agenda. A seating chart version.

Sera paused on that last page.

I leaned slightly, curiosity sharp.

It was a seating plan, but not the one I had printed. Different layout. Different font. It had little heart icons beside certain names.

Sponsor seating, I thought. Sponsor visibility.

Sera looked up. "You said you don't handle operational details."

Imogen's smile returned, shaky now. "That's just for sponsor notes. It's not the official plan."

Sera tapped the page. "Where did it come from."

Imogen swallowed. "Hugh provided it."

Sera's eyes narrowed. "When."

Imogen hesitated. "Earlier today."

Sera asked, "Through the portal."

Imogen blinked quickly. "I don't know. Possibly."

Sera held her gaze. "You don't know how the document arrived in your folder."

Imogen's smile tightened. "It was emailed."

Sera's eyes sharpened. "From whom."

Imogen hesitated again. "Melissa."

Sera nodded once, as if noting a small circle tightening. "We'll confirm."

Imogen tried again. "Detective Inspector, the Trust is not your enemy."

Sera's voice stayed flat. "Then stop acting like you're negotiating."

Imogen's smile wavered. She glanced at me, not pleading like Lorna, but measuring, as if deciding whether I could be intimidated.

I met her gaze and made my expression bland.

I'd spent years in offices with people like Imogen. Polished, strategic, careful. They always believed blunt women were a problem to be managed. It never occurred to them that blunt women were often the only ones in the room telling the truth.

Sera closed the folder and slid it into her own file stack. "You will remain available," she said. "You will not make calls. You will not send messages. You will not speak to Hugh about this interview. If you do, I will assume you're coordinating."

Imogen's smile cracked, finally. "This is outrageous."

Sera nodded once. "Good. You're awake now."

Imogen left with a stiff spine and a face full of controlled fury.

Sera turned to me. "She lied about access," Sera said quietly.

"She lied about influence," I replied.

Sera's eyes held mine. "Same thing."

I wrote.

00:41. Imogen possesses alternate seating chart with sponsor markings. Claims not operational. Claims emailed. Defensive on portal, confidentiality, "boundaries."

Sera rubbed her forehead briefly, just one quick gesture that proved she was human. Then she straightened again, as if she'd never done it.

"Next," she said.

The door opened and the kitchen supervisor walked in.

He was broad-shouldered, late forties maybe, hair thinning, face ruddy with anger and exhaustion. His chef whites were covered by a dark jumper now, but the smell of kitchen clung to him, hot oil and detergent and something sweet that made my stomach tighten.

He sat heavily, arms folded, eyes already hostile.

"Name and role," Sera said.

"Dean Lomas," he replied. "Kitchen supervisor."

Sera nodded. "You're responsible for kitchen operations."

"Yes."

Sera asked, "Did you like Dr Vale."

Dean's eyes flashed. "No."

Straight. Refreshing, if dangerous.

Sera held his gaze. "Why."

Dean leaned forward slightly, voice hard. "Because he was a bully. He came in earlier, made comments about the food, about staff. He treated my kitchen like a set."

Sera asked, "Did you argue with him."

Dean snorted. "He tried. I didn't give him the satisfaction."

Sera's eyes narrowed. "Did you have a grudge."

Dean's jaw clenched. "I'm allowed to dislike a man without killing him."

Sera didn't argue. She simply asked, "Who handled dessert tonight."

Dean listed names, clipped. Ellie as server. The pastry station. A commis chef. A runner.

Sera asked, "Who printed the dessert service sheet."

Dean frowned. "We don't print service sheets. Front of house does that."

Sera's gaze sharpened. "Where is the staff printer."

Dean jerked his chin. "Hotel office. Or reception. Not kitchen."

Sera asked, "Do you have access."

Dean's eyes narrowed. "I can walk into an office, sure. It's a hotel. But do I use their printers. No."

Sera asked, "Do you have access to the vendor portal."

Dean blinked. "No."

Sera slid the portal log screenshot across the table anyway, because it was her favourite kind of pressure. Evidence that existed without a face.

Dean stared at it and shrugged. "Looks like hotel admin nonsense."

Sera's eyes narrowed. "Do you know who has the VendorAdmin password."

Dean snorted. "Anyone Hugh trusts. Which is no one, really."

I wrote that down because it was too honest not to preserve.

00:49. Dean: "Anyone Hugh trusts, which is no one."

Sera asked, "Did you see Vale tonight before dessert."

Dean's jaw tightened. "He came into the kitchen earlier. Not during service. Before guests arrived. He wanted a tour."

Sera's gaze sharpened. "A tour."

Dean nodded, anger rising. "He wanted content. He wanted to film. Hugh told us to humour him. Vale pointed at my pastry chef and said, loud as anything, 'If this goes wrong, it's on your hands, love.' Like she was a fool. Like he was a king."

Sera asked, "Did your pastry chef react."

Dean hesitated. "She was upset."

Sera nodded. "Name."

Dean gave it.

Sera asked, "Did Vale eat anything in the kitchen."

Dean frowned. "No. Not that I saw."

Sera asked, "Did you see anyone tamper with desserts."

Dean's eyes widened. "No."

Sera's gaze stayed steady. "Do you know how desserts were assigned."

Dean shook his head. "Not my side. We plate. We send out. Front of house runs the room."

Sera asked, "Do you know what a seat-targeted service is."

Dean blinked. "A what."

Sera explained briefly, cleanly, without drama: dessert delivered by seat position, not by name. Seat swap changes recipient.

Dean's face tightened as he followed. "So you're saying someone could have put a plate meant for one guest in front of another because they moved."

Sera nodded. "Yes."

Dean stared at her. "That's stupid."

Sera's gaze didn't shift. "It's also effective."

Dean rubbed his jaw. "So Vale might not have been the target."

Sera watched him. "Who would have been."

Dean snorted. "Half the guests. He was the celebrity. People would love to ruin him."

Sera's voice stayed calm. "Or someone wanted to ruin someone else and he stepped in the way."

Dean shrugged. "Maybe."

Sera asked, "Do you know Penny Harrow."

Dean's eyes narrowed. "The journalist."

Sera asked, "Does the kitchen know her."

Dean hesitated. "She's around town. She's done pieces. She's asked questions. About the hotel, about the Trust, about who owns what."

There it was again. The property thread sliding into every conversation like damp.

Sera asked, "Has Penny been a problem."

Dean's mouth tightened. "Not for me. For Hugh, maybe. People who ask questions are a problem for men like him."

Sera watched him carefully. "Did Vale have any connection to Penny."

Dean shrugged. "I don't know. But Vale was the sort of man who collected people. Not friends. People."

That line was sharp enough to cut. Also probably true.

I wrote.

00:58. Dean: Vale "collected people." Notes Penny as question-asker.

Sera leaned forward slightly. "Dean. I'm going to ask you directly. Did you do anything to harm Vale."

Dean's face flushed with anger. "No."

Sera didn't look away. "Did you instruct anyone to do anything."

"No."

Sera asked, "Do you have any reason to lie."

Dean snorted. "If I wanted him dead, I'd have told him to go stand in the storm. I wouldn't risk my kitchen."

Sera's mouth twitched. "Noted."

She moved to the next angle. "Who in the kitchen has access to medication, cleaning chemicals, allergens."

Dean's eyes narrowed. "We're a hotel. We have all sorts."

Sera asked, "Who has keys."

Dean blinked. "Keys to what."

Sera's gaze sharpened. "To storage. To staff corridors. To office printers."

Dean shook his head. "That's not kitchen. That's hotel operations. Ask Hugh."

Sera nodded once, as if the answer confirmed what she already knew. The hotel was a web of access. The kitchen was part of it, but not the controlling knot.

Dean shifted in his seat, then said, "Look. Vale had enemies. Real ones. People he humiliated. People he ripped off. You're going to find threats if you look."

There it was again. Vale enemies. The red herring was gaining strength. It was tempting because it was plausible. It was also lazy.

Sera's eyes stayed flat. "We will look," she said. "We will also look at systems. Not just grudges."

Dean shrugged. "Fine."

Sera stood, ending the interview without ceremony. "You will remain available," she said. "You will not discuss this with staff. If anyone approaches you to 'align stories,' you tell me."

Dean's eyes flicked. "Align stories."

Sera held his gaze. "You heard me."

Dean nodded once, stiff. He left.

The door closed.

For a moment, the room was silent except for the storm and the faint hum of the strip lights.

Sera finally sat down, just for a second, and leaned her elbows on the table. The posture looked like relief and like a trap at once.

She glanced at me. "What did you notice," she asked.

I flipped back through my Pocket Log, then looked up. "Lorna volunteered the Trust without being pushed," I said. "Imogen came in with an alternate seating chart. Sponsor markings. She pretended she wasn't operational. She is."

Sera nodded. "And Dean."

"He hates Vale," I said. "But his hatred is clean. No polish. If he's lying, he's a better actor than half the hotel."

Sera's mouth twitched. "He's a chef. They perform all day. But yes."

I hesitated. "He mentioned Vale touring the kitchen earlier. That gives you a timeline and a cast list of who was exposed to him."

Sera nodded. "Good."

I tapped my pen once against the notebook. "Also, everyone keeps pushing the same story. Vale had enemies. Vale humiliated people. Vale brought it on himself."

Sera's gaze sharpened. "Yes."

"That story is useful," I said. "It turns this into a morality tale instead of a mechanism."

Sera leaned back slightly. "Exactly."

She stood again, back in her role. "We're not done," she said. "But this is enough for the first wave."

I looked at the clock. After midnight now, properly. The storm still had us locked in. The lobby downstairs would be full of tired people who wanted to gossip and film and turn this into content. Hugh would be in his office, calculating damage. Imogen would be planning how to protect her Trust. Lorna would be trying to decide which story kept her job. Dean would be telling his staff not to talk and then talking anyway.

Sera gathered her papers. "Harriet," she said. "Your dot pattern proof matters. It gives us something outside testimony. Keep that clean."

"I will," I replied.

Sera paused at the door. "Also," she added, "the VendorAdmin account access list Hugh gave me is longer than it should be."

I felt my spine tighten. "How long."

Sera's eyes narrowed. "Long enough that it includes someone who does not work for the hotel."

My pen stopped mid-hover above my Pocket Log.

I looked up. "The Trust."

Sera didn't answer directly. She didn't have to. Her silence was a confirmation.

She opened the door. "Try to sleep," she said. "Morning will be worse."

"Morning usually is," I replied.

Sera left, shutting the door behind her.

I sat alone for a moment, listening to the storm and the building creak, and the unpleasant new thought settling in.

If someone outside the hotel had access to the shared admin account, then the portal wasn't just a hotel convenience. It was a back door.

And back doors were never built by accident.

I wrote one last line in my Pocket Log before I went back to my room.

00:17. DI Linley indicates VendorAdmin access list includes non-hotel person. Possible Trust access. Portal is not neutral.

Then I closed the notebook, held it against my palm, and stood.

My feet felt heavy, like the hotel carpet was trying to keep me in place.

I didn't let it.

CHAPTER 12

Paper trail trap

Sleep came in thin strips, like cheap ribbon. It looked festive until you tried to use it for anything practical.

I woke to my phone vibrating against the bedside table at 05:42, the screen lighting my face an unflattering shade of hospital corridor. Outside the window the storm had not run out of spite. The sea was still a dark smear beyond sheets of rain. The hotel held its breath between gusts, then exhaled in creaks and rattles.

A message from Cal Reeve sat at the top of my notifications.

Cal: Pip's decided my foot is a permanent address. Roads still shut. You alive.

I read it twice, then typed back.

Hattie: Alive. Not delighted. Keep him away from cameras. This place will try to turn everything into a story.

Cal: Too late. He's already judging me.

That made me snort once, which felt indecently close to laughter. I didn't indulge it for long. Death had a way of draining the amusement out of you, even when you were stubborn enough to try to keep it.

Another vibration. A new message, this one from Sera.

DI Linley: Dress. Meet me outside Room 214 in ten. Bring your log and phone.

No please. No comfort. Just a directive, as if we were both cogs and she'd decided the machine needed turning.

I sat up, rubbed my eyes, and listened for the corridor.

Quiet. That brittle pre-dawn quiet hotels get when guests are asleep or pretending to be. The building smelled of damp carpet and stale perfume. Somewhere far below, a machine whirred, maybe laundry, maybe a desperate attempt at normality.

I dressed quickly, pulling on my navy peacoat and scarf out of habit more than warmth. I clipped my reading glasses on their chain. I pocketed my fountain pen, my Pocket Log, and the small stack of labelled envelopes I'd brought up last night because I didn't trust anyone downstairs. Then I checked my tote. Phone charger. A small plastic sleeve for photos if needed. A spare blank place card from my run. A strip of my own card stock trimmed down, because you never knew when you'd need a comparison.

It was ridiculous, carrying paper like a talisman.

It was also how you survived Hartcombe.

I opened my door and stepped into the corridor. The carpet swallowed sound. The strip lights buzzed softly. Two doors down, one of the hotel's fire doors was taped open with a wedge, as if someone had decided safety regulations were optional in a storm. It made my skin tighten.

Sera waited outside my room with a constable. She looked as though she'd slept even less than I had, which I found both impressive and unpleasant. Her hair was still in that tight bun. Her shirt sleeves were rolled again. Her face was set into the same expression she'd worn all night, sharp and tired and angry at the universe but too disciplined to blame it.

"You're up," she said.

"Sadly," I replied.

Her eyes flicked to my tote. "Good. We're going to the printers."

"Lovely," I said. "A romantic outing."

Sera ignored that, which was her way. "We have a window. Hugh will try to 'reset' everything the moment he thinks he can. I want the office area documented before anyone plays tidy."

"I assumed," I said.

Sera nodded. "Then move."

We walked down the corridor, the constable behind us, the three of us a small procession of purpose. As we passed the stairwell, I smelled something faintly sharp and chemical, like toner and cleaning spray. It was a smell that lived in offices, not ballrooms.

I wrote as we walked.

05:55. DI Linley escort. Destination: staff office printers. Objective: identify source of last-minute instruction prints and replacement items.

The lift brought us down to a service level that guests never saw. The hotel's public areas were all polished wood and soft lighting and smiles. The back areas were scuffed skirting boards, harsh fluorescents, and posters about handwashing.

The corridor outside the staff office held the stale warmth of machinery and too many bodies moving through it. A wall-mounted noticeboard carried laminated sheets in cheerful fonts, the kind that said TEAMWORK MAKES THE DREAM WORK, which always felt like a threat.

The door to the office had a keypad. A small red light blinked, expectant.

Sera turned to the constable. "Key."

The constable, a young woman with a patient face and a clipped ponytail, produced a master fob and keyed in a code. The door beeped and opened.

I expected Hugh to be waiting inside like a spider. He wasn't.

For the moment, the storm and sleep and Sera's explicit removal had kept him away.

The office smelled of paper, hot plastic, and coffee that had been brewed at some point and then abandoned. Two printers sat against the wall, one large and serious, one smaller and irritated-looking. There were also two desktop computers, a stack of reams, a cupboard with a keyhole, and a desk with a tray of laminated "vendor instructions" that looked like they were meant to soothe rather than inform.

Sera didn't waste time. "Find me what's been printed," she said. "And tell me how."

I approached the printer area the way I approached a wedding reception table after someone had sworn they hadn't moved place cards. Slowly, with my eyes open.

The big printer's screen glowed faintly. A multifunction machine, the kind hotels loved because it could do everything and therefore could be blamed for everything. Its paper trays were labelled with little stickers. TRAY 1: LETTERHEAD. TRAY 2: PLAIN A4. TRAY 3: CARD STOCK.

Card stock. Interesting.

I leaned closer and inspected the trays. Tray 1 held cream letterhead with the Mariner's Crown logo in the corner. Tray 2 held bright white A4 paper, too bright for my taste, the kind that made printed black look slightly cheap. Tray 3 held heavier stock, plain, no logo.

"Who loads these," I asked.

Sera turned her head. "Hotel operations. Reception. Whoever has keys."

"Which is everyone," I said.

Sera's eyes sharpened. "Not everyone. Someone's controlling access, even if Hugh pretends otherwise."

I nodded, then turned back to the printer.

I tapped the screen. A menu popped up with options. Copy.

Scan. Print Jobs. Settings.

Print Jobs was what I wanted. Print queues were the paper trail people forgot existed, because they lived in the machine, not in a folder they could shred.

I pressed it.

A list appeared. Recent jobs. Some were labelled with names. Some were not.

ROOMING LIST 05:12.
BREAKFAST ALLERGENS 04:58.
VENDOR_INSTR_00:47.
PLACE CARD REPRINT 00:52.

My stomach went tight.

I didn't touch anything else. I didn't want to alter the queue. I lifted my phone, turned off flash, and took a photo of the screen with the time visible.

Then I took another, closer, to capture the job names.

I wrote in my Pocket Log.

06:03. Printer queue shows jobs: "VENDOR_INSTR_00:47" and "PLACE CARD REPRINT 00:52." Photographed screen.

Sera leaned in beside me, gaze hard. "That's useful," she said.

"It's also damning," I replied.

Sera glanced at the constable. "Photograph the screen as well," she said. "Then we bag anything printed under those jobs."

The constable did as told, efficient and calm.

I turned to the laminated vendor instructions on the desk. There were several versions, some with coffee stains, some pristine. The top sheet was titled VENDOR INSTRUCTIONS: SECOND-CHANCE ROMANCE WEEKEND in a font that looked like my design work had been copied by someone with a nervous hand.

The layout was familiar, but wrong.

I picked it up carefully, like it might bite.

The paper wasn't laminated, despite the label tray suggesting it was. This was just plain A4, folded once as if someone had carried it in a pocket. The hotel's usual instruction sheets were either laminated or printed on branded letterhead. This was on bright white stock, smooth and slightly stiff, the kind that came from a discount ream.

The text was in black. The headings were bolded. The spacing looked right at first glance. It was meant to pass.

I turned it slightly under the fluorescent light.

The ink sat too sharply on the surface, as if the toner had fused differently. Not inkjet, then. Laser.

I looked closer at the font.

It was near my style. Near enough to flatter, which was always suspicious. The letters had the same general silhouette as the serif font I used in my templates. But the kerning was off.

Kerning was the space between letters, the subtle adjustment that kept text looking balanced rather than like it had been typed by a machine with no aesthetic sense. Most people didn't notice it consciously. They just felt when something looked slightly cheap.

I noticed it the way I noticed forged signatures.

On this sheet, the spacing between certain pairs was wrong. The capital V sat too far from the following a in Vale. The "To" in "To be delivered" had an awkward gap, as if the T was too proud to stand close to the o. The word "Table" looked slightly stretched, not in size, but in rhythm.

It wasn't my file.

It was someone's imitation.

I set it on the desk, took out my spare place card sample, and laid it beside the instruction sheet. Different stock entirely, but I wasn't comparing stock. I was comparing typography.

My place card font was a specific version with kerning tables enabled. The spacing was clean and deliberate. This instruction sheet looked like someone had used a similar font but either didn't have kerning enabled or used a default substitute.

I lifted my phone again and took a photo of the instruction sheet with the time visible on the screen of my lock screen. Then I took a close-up photo of the word VALE and the word TABLE, zoomed in to show the spacing.

Then I took another photo of my place card text for comparison, so I could show Sera the difference without sounding like a woman trying to explain art to a man who'd already decided it was nonsense.

Sera watched, arms folded, as if holding herself back from touching everything.

"You're sure," she said.

"Yes," I replied. "This is a near-match. Not my exact kerning. It looks right from a distance. Up close, it's wrong."

Sera's eyes flicked to the sheet. "What about content."

I scanned it. My stomach tightened again.

It wasn't just a generic vendor instruction sheet. It contained a line that made my skin go cold with familiarity.

DESSERT SERVICE: Apology desserts to be delivered by SEAT POSITION as per table plan. Do not delay. Discretion requested.

Seat position. Not name. Not person. Seat.

Discretion requested.

It was a mechanism written in polite language.

I felt that strange, unpleasant sensation of a puzzle piece clicking into place while you were still wishing the picture was different.

I looked up at Sera. "This isn't just forged," I said. "It's targeted."

Sera's gaze sharpened. "Explain."

"It tells staff to deliver by seat position," I said. "That turns seat swaps into a weapon."

Sera's face stayed blank, but her eyes went harder. "Photograph that line," she said.

"I already did," I replied.

Sera nodded once. "Bag it."

The constable pulled an evidence bag from her pocket and held it open. Sera didn't touch the sheet. She let me slide it into the bag by the edges, careful, as if we were both aware that paper carried more than ink.

The bag sealed with a soft crackle. The constable labelled it with date and time, neat handwriting.

Sera looked at the desk tray again. "Are there more."

I thumbed through the stack. Most were standard hotel instructions about set-up times and vendor check-in. Then I found another page half-hidden under a clipboard. This one was titled STAFF NOTE: LAST-MINUTE AMENDMENTS.

My eyes narrowed.

It was printed on a different paper stock than the forged vendor sheet. This one was on the hotel's cream letterhead. It looked official. It was also clearly printed at a different time, because the toner sat differently. The cream paper had a slight texture. This sheet looked like it had been printed too fast, the black a shade heavier.

The content was brief.

REPRINTED PLACE CARDS ISSUED FOR VIP COMFORT. USE REPLACEMENTS ONLY. DESTROY ERRORS.

I felt heat rise in my chest, the kind that arrived when someone tried to order you to destroy evidence and called it comfort.

I held the sheet up for Sera.

Sera's jaw tightened. "Bag it," she said.

The constable did.

Sera turned to the printer again. "Place card reprint job at 00:52," she said. "We need the output."

I looked at the output tray. There were a few pages sitting there, curled slightly. Mostly lists. Rooming. Breakfast allergens. A stack of place cards printed on thick stock, still warm at the edges.

I didn't pick them up. I didn't want to smear or bend anything.

Sera nodded at the constable, who donned gloves and lifted the stack carefully, sliding it into another evidence bag.

"Count them," Sera said.

The constable did, quietly. "Six," she said. "Six place cards."

Sera's eyes flicked to me. "How many were requested from you at the mixer."

"Three," I said.

"Six printed," Sera said, voice flat.

I didn't like the way my stomach dropped. "So someone doubled the 'VIP comfort' story," I said.

Sera nodded once. "Or printed extras to allow movement without questions."

I stared at the place cards through the plastic.

Names in neat black type. A few of them I recognised from the guest list. One I didn't expect to see.

PENNY HARROW.

My throat went dry.

Sera saw my reaction. "You know that's significant," she said.

"I know it's deliberate," I replied. "Penny's card shouldn't need reprinting."

Sera's eyes narrowed. "Why."

"Because her name wasn't misspelt," I said. "Because she's not a VIP to the hotel. She's a problem."

Sera's gaze stayed steady. "And if you reprint her card, you can put her name wherever you want."

"Yes," I said. "You can justify her sitting in a different seat. You can justify moving her. Or moving someone into her place."

Sera's eyes hardened. "Exactly."

The office door opened and I felt my shoulders tense before I even turned.

Hugh Mercer stood in the doorway, looking freshly dressed and freshly furious, as if he'd decided sleep was optional because control mattered more.

His charcoal suit was immaculate. His hair was neat. His smile was gone.

"Detective Inspector," he said, voice low. "What are you doing in my operations office."

Sera didn't turn fully toward him. She kept her stance angled toward the printer, as if refusing to give him the dignity of being the centre.

"We're investigating," she said. "You're interfering."

Hugh's gaze flicked to the evidence bags. His eyes sharpened when he saw the sealed plastic. "Those are internal documents."

"They're evidence," Sera replied.

Hugh's jaw tightened. "I understand your role, but there are procedures. The hotel has a duty of care to guests. If you remove operational materials, you create risk."

Sera finally turned and looked at him full on. "A man died in your corridor," she said. "Your duty of care is already a question."

Hugh's gaze flicked to me, then back to Sera. "Harriet is a vendor," he said. "She shouldn't be in here at all."

I didn't speak. I just lifted my Pocket Log slightly, as if reminding him I was recording.

Sera's voice stayed calm. "Harriet is here because she can identify forged documents. Because you, Hugh, have made a system where no one is accountable for edits."

Hugh's face tightened. "The portal is standard. It protects vendors and clients."

"It protects liars," Sera said.

Hugh's eyes cooled. "Detective Inspector, the Trust will be extremely concerned about the way you're handling this."

Sera's gaze stayed flat. "Then the Trust can speak to me. Through a solicitor. Not through you."

Hugh took a breath, then tried a different tactic. "Harriet," he said, tone softening into something patronising. "You're tired. You've had a shock. I don't want you confusing the police with design details that don't matter."

That landed like a slap, not because it hurt, but because it revealed exactly what he thought of me.

I met his gaze. "My 'design details' are the only reason you can't pretend this was a simple tragedy," I said.

Hugh's smile twitched, brief and ugly. "This is not about you."

"It's about paper," I replied. "And you keep trying to move it around."

Sera lifted a hand slightly, a quiet command for Hugh to stop talking.

Hugh ignored it. "Harriet, your contract is with this hotel. I can terminate it."

"You can try," I said. "But you'll do it in writing, and you'll do it while a police officer watches."

Sera's eyes flicked to him. "Leave," she said.

Hugh's jaw worked. "You can't order me out of my own office."

Sera's voice stayed even. "I can. Under the circumstances. You can stand in the corridor and wait if you want to watch. If you step closer to any evidence, I will have you removed."

Hugh held her gaze, the two of them in a silent contest of will. Then he stepped back into the corridor, stiff and furious, as if retreating was an indignity he would charge interest on later.

The door swung partly shut behind him, leaving it ajar, as if he couldn't bear to be fully excluded.

Sera looked at me. "Keep going," she said.

I exhaled slowly and returned my attention to the printer.

"Print jobs show place card reprints," I said. "And a vendor instruction job at 00:47. The forged sheet was here on the desk."

Sera nodded. "How do we tie it to the machine."

"Paper stock," I said, and opened Tray 2 carefully to look at the ream. The label on the wrapper read a brand I recognised as cheap, bright white, high brightness rating.

"This matches," I said. "The forged vendor sheet is on this bright stock. The hotel's branded sheets are cream. This is a separate supply."

Sera's eyes narrowed. "Meaning someone chose it."

"Yes," I said. "They wanted it to look like a quick internal print. Not like a polished hotel document. Less official. More plausible."

Sera nodded once. "Any watermarks."

I held a blank sheet up to the light. No watermark. Smooth. Clean cut edges. Cheap paper was often clean in an unsettling way. It had no character. It was designed to be invisible.

I looked at Tray 1's cream letterhead. That had the faint tooth of better stock and the slight shadow of the logo.

"This sheet about destroying errors," I said, "was printed on letterhead. That one looks like someone wanted it to look official."

Sera's eyes tightened. "Like a directive."

"Yes," I said.

I turned back to the printer screen. "We need user info," I said. "Some printers store the username that sent the job."

Sera nodded. "Can you access it without altering evidence."

"Maybe," I said.

I pressed Details on the print job list, carefully, noting each movement. The screen offered more info.

VENDOR_INSTR_00:47.
USER: VENDORADMIN.
SOURCE: FRONT DESK PC.

PLACE CARD REPRINT 00:52.
USER: VENDORADMIN.
SOURCE: FRONT DESK PC.

My throat went tight.

Front desk PC. VendorAdmin. Midnight printing. It was practically waving its arms.

I took photos again, crisp and clear. Time stamps visible. I also wrote.

06:14. Printer job details show user "VENDORADMIN" and source "FRONT DESK PC" for 00:47 vendor instructions and 00:52 place card reprint. Photographed.

Sera leaned in, eyes hard. "Good," she said. "That's what I needed."

"And it gets worse," I said quietly, because I couldn't help it.

Sera's gaze flicked to me. "How."

I pointed at the forged vendor instruction line again in my mind. Seat position. Discretion. Apology desserts. It wasn't just that someone printed a forged sheet. It was that they printed one that directed a specific behaviour at a specific time.

A trap written as a polite instruction.

Sera said, "What are you thinking."

I chose my words carefully. "Someone wrote a mechanism into the workflow," I said. "If staff follow it, they can kill someone by accident and call it procedure."

Sera's face stayed blank. "Yes," she said. "And if we prove it, the whole 'medical incident' narrative collapses."

"Which is why Hugh keeps trying to control paper," I said.

Sera nodded once, sharp. "Exactly."

The constable, still calm, said, "There's a bin."

Sera turned. "Where."

The constable pointed to a shredder bin under the desk, the kind with a lockable lid. The lid wasn't locked. The bin was half-full.

Sera's eyes narrowed. "Open it."

The constable donned gloves and lifted the lid. Inside were strips of paper, unevenly shredded, as if someone had fed sheets quickly and then stopped.

Sera's voice stayed calm. "Pull the top layer only. Don't dig. We document before we disturb."

The constable did as told, lifting just the topmost strips and laying them on the desk in a loose fan. The fragments showed bits of text. A few partial words.

SEAT.

TABLE 14.

DESTROY.

I felt my skin tighten.

Sera saw it too. "Photograph," she ordered.

I took photos from above, time visible, then close-ups of the fragments. The fragments were not enough to reconstruct fully, but they were enough to show intent.

Someone had attempted to shred evidence in the staff office.

I wrote.

06:21. Shredder bin contains partial strips referencing "SEAT" and "TABLE 14" and "DESTROY." Photographed. Possible attempted disposal of instruction sheet variants.

Sera glanced toward the half-open door. Hugh still stood in the corridor, pretending to check his phone while listening to every word. His posture was too still. His attention too sharp.

Sera stepped to the door and closed it fully.

The click of the latch was small but satisfying.

Then she turned back. "Harriet," she said. "I need you to do a comparison."

"I'm already doing one," I said.

"I need it formal," she replied. "Show me the kerning difference."

I sighed, because she was right. In court, "It looks wrong" was not enough. You needed to articulate wrong in a way that made sense to people who didn't spend their lives staring at letters.

I pulled out my spare place card and laid it beside a clean sheet from Tray 2. On the blank sheet, I wrote VALE in my own hand, then shook my head.

"That's not helpful," I muttered.

Sera watched. "What do you need."

"My template," I said. "If the front desk PC has a file, we need to see it. If it's a copied template, I can show you the exact spacing differences between my original and their imitation."

Sera nodded. "Then we go to the front desk PC."

My stomach tightened again. "Hugh will fight that."

Sera's eyes narrowed. "Let him."

We left the office with the evidence bags sealed, the printer screen photographed, the shredder bin documented. Sera had the constable guard the door as we moved down the service corridor toward reception, because Sera did not trust the hotel's idea of boundaries.

The front desk area at dawn was a strange hybrid of calm and tension. The lobby lights were dimmed. A few guests slept on sofas like shipwreck survivors. Someone had draped a blanket over an influencer's ring light as if that counted as restraint. A couple argued in a whisper near the fireplace, their faces lit by their phones, not the flames.

A receptionist sat behind the desk, eyes bloodshot, hands moving mechanically through tasks that no longer mattered.

She looked up when Sera approached and went pale.

"Morning," Sera said, which sounded like a threat in her voice.

The receptionist swallowed. "Detective Inspector."

"I need access to the front desk PC," Sera said. "Now. You do not touch it. You do not log in. You do not warn anyone."

The receptionist's eyes flicked, instinctive. Toward Hugh's office.

Sera's gaze followed. Hugh's office door was closed. The glass panel had blinds pulled halfway. It was the sort of door that said, I am hiding and also I expect you to respect it.

Sera leaned closer to the receptionist. "If you alert him," she said, low, "you will make yourself part of this. Don't."

The receptionist nodded quickly, fear making her obedient in the way hotels preferred.

She stepped aside.

Sera gestured me closer. "Look," she said.

The front desk PC sat behind the counter. A standard desktop setup, keyboard slightly sticky, mouse pad branded with the hotel logo. The screen was locked. A login prompt. No one was supposed to touch it without authorisation.

Sera nodded to the constable. "Photograph current state," she said.

The constable did.

Then Sera turned to the receptionist. "Who has login credentials for this machine."

The receptionist's mouth opened, then closed. "All reception staff," she said. "And management."

"Management," Sera repeated.

The receptionist swallowed. "Hugh."

Sera nodded once. "And the VendorAdmin portal credentials. Who has those."

The receptionist blinked, then said too quickly, "Only

authorised staff."

Sera's eyes narrowed. "Name them."

The receptionist's face flushed. "I don't know. It's... it's just a shared admin."

I felt a cold anger settle. Shared admin. Shared responsibility. Shared blame. No one held. Everyone slippery.

Sera's voice stayed calm. "Try again."

The receptionist's eyes flicked toward Hugh's office again. "Hugh. Melissa. Lorna sometimes. Imogen asked about it."

There it was.

Sera's gaze sharpened. "Imogen asked about it."

The receptionist nodded, miserable. "She said she needed to check the guest list. She said donors were sensitive about spelling."

Sera's jaw tightened. "When."

"Yesterday afternoon," the receptionist said.

Sera nodded once, then turned to the constable. "I want IT logs if they exist," she said. "And I want to image this machine if possible."

The constable nodded.

Sera looked at me. "We might not get full imaging right now," she said quietly. "Storm. Limited resources. But we can capture what matters."

"What matters is the file," I said. "The template."

Sera nodded. "Right."

She turned back to the receptionist. "Unlock the machine."

The receptionist hesitated.

Sera's gaze cut. "Now."

The receptionist typed with shaking hands. The desktop loaded.

A few folders sat on the screen. Staff schedules. Guest feedback. Vendor portal shortcuts. A folder called WEEKEND DOCS.

Sera pointed. "Open."

The receptionist clicked.

Inside were files. Seating plans. Guest list versions. A Word document titled Vendor Instructions Updated. Another titled Vendor Instructions Final.

Sera's eyes flicked to me. "That."

I leaned in and looked at the file names. My skin went tight again. Someone had been working at the front desk like it was a print shop.

Sera said, "Open the updated instructions."

The receptionist hovered her hand, then clicked. Word opened. The document loaded.

On screen, the vendor instruction sheet appeared. It looked like the one I'd bagged. Same headings. Same phrasing. Same line about seat position. Same request for discretion.

I leaned closer to the text.

Then I did what I always did when I suspected a forgery. I stopped reading content and started reading spacing.

The font was a common serif, one that mimicked my style without being my exact type. Worse, the document's kerning settings were off. Kerning option disabled. The letters sat slightly apart in certain pairs, the way they did on the printed forged sheet.

I pointed at the word VALE in the document, then at my own spare place card in my hand. "See this," I said to Sera, keeping my voice low. "On my template, the V and the a sit closer. The spacing is balanced. Here, it's default spacing. Kerning off."

Sera's eyes narrowed. "Can you demonstrate."

"Yes," I said.

I asked the receptionist, "Do you have the font menu."

She nodded quickly.

I clicked into Word's font settings and opened the advanced

typography panel. Kerning was unchecked.

I didn't change it. I didn't touch it beyond viewing. I didn't want to alter anything.

I lifted my phone and took photos of the screen showing the unchecked kerning option, and the font name.

Then I took a photo of my place card. Then I took a macro shot of the printed forged sheet in the evidence bag, showing the spacing issues. Then another of the Word screen showing the same spacing.

A set of comparison images. Time stamped. Clean. Repeatable.

I wrote quickly in my Pocket Log, balancing it against the counter.

06:33. Front desk PC contains Word file "Vendor Instructions Updated." Kerning option unchecked in advanced font settings. Font is near-match serif, not my template font. Photos taken of font name and kerning settings. Matches forged printed sheet spacing.

Sera watched my writing. "And paper stock," she said.

I nodded. "Printed from Tray 2 bright stock," I said. "Not hotel cream. Not my stock. The machine queue confirms job source as front desk PC."

Sera's gaze sharpened at the receptionist. "Who created this file."

The receptionist's eyes widened. "I didn't."

Sera's voice stayed calm. "Who did."

The receptionist's gaze flicked toward Hugh's office again. "I don't know," she whispered. "It was just there."

Sera's eyes narrowed. "When did you first see it."

The receptionist swallowed. "After midnight."

Sera's jaw tightened. "And who was on shift."

The receptionist hesitated.

Sera leaned in. "Name."

THE VALENTINE GUEST LIST

The receptionist whispered, "Chloe was helping. And Melissa came down. And Hugh was in his office. He kept asking for updates."

My chest went tight at Chloe's name, because I could see her anxious face in the corridor outside my room, repeating Hugh's instruction about collecting paperwork.

Sera nodded once, then turned to the computer again. "Print history," she said.

The receptionist clicked into Word's file properties. It showed last modified time.

00:44.

Last modified by.

VendorAdmin.

My stomach dropped in a clean, cold way.

Sera saw it. Her eyes hardened. "Photograph," she said.

I did.

Then Sera said, quietly, "That account isn't just portal access. Someone uses it as an identity."

"And that's intentional," I said.

Sera nodded once. "Yes."

She turned to the receptionist. "You are not to touch this machine again," she said. "You step away. You don't log out. You don't close files. You don't warn Hugh."

The receptionist nodded quickly and stepped back.

Sera looked at me. "Now we need the physical sheet," she said, "and we already have it. We have the queue. We have the file metadata. We have the paper stock source."

"And we have the line about seat position," I said.

Sera's gaze held mine. "Yes. That line is the spine of this."

I felt a small, bitter satisfaction. Not joy. Not relief. Just the grim satisfaction of a mechanism becoming visible.

Then a voice cut in from the side.

"Hattie."

It was Chloe.

She stood near the lobby entrance to the reception area, hair pulled back, eyes wide, clutching a clipboard like it could protect her. She looked exhausted and frightened and very young, even if she wasn't. She looked like someone who'd been told all night that if she did the wrong thing the hotel would collapse.

She looked at Sera, then back at me.

"I didn't do it," she blurted, before anyone had asked her anything.

Sera's gaze moved to her, sharp. "Chloe," she said, tone calm. "Sit. Breathe."

Chloe didn't sit. She clutched the clipboard harder. "Mr Mercer said I should help. He said… he said it was about guest calm. He said we needed new sheets."

Sera's eyes narrowed. "New sheets."

Chloe nodded, tears gathering, humiliating her. "I printed what he told me to print. I didn't know it was wrong. I swear I didn't."

My stomach tightened. Chloe wasn't clever enough to design this. Chloe was exactly the kind of person people like Hugh used. She would follow instructions because her job trained her to follow instructions.

Sera's voice stayed even. "Did Hugh tell you to print vendor instructions."

Chloe's face went pale. "Yes."

Sera asked, "Did he give you the file."

Chloe nodded quickly. "It was on the computer. He said just print it. He said it was updated because of the incident. He said it would help staff."

Sera's eyes narrowed. "Did he tell you to shred anything."

Chloe flinched. "No."

Sera asked, "Did anyone else touch the machine."

Chloe's eyes flicked. "Melissa. She said the Trust wanted the list correct."

Sera's gaze sharpened. "Melissa said that."

Chloe nodded, miserable. "Yes."

I felt my jaw tighten. Melissa Shaw, the event operations woman, harried and polite, the one who'd served Hugh's needs with a smile because that was her job.

Sera nodded once. "All right," she said. "Chloe, you will sit with a constable. You will not speak to anyone. Not Hugh. Not Melissa. Not guests. Understood."

Chloe nodded, face crumpling, and finally sat when the constable guided her to a chair.

Sera turned to me. "That's your answer," she said quietly.

"My answer is Hugh," I replied.

Sera's gaze stayed hard. "Hugh is a gate. Not necessarily the hand."

I hated that she was right. Hugh could be a mechanism too. A man who enforced secrecy. A man who took orders from above. A man who believed he was protecting the hotel when he was really protecting something else.

"The Trust," I said.

Sera nodded. "Possibly."

My mind flicked to Imogen's folder. To the alternate seating chart with sponsor markings. To the receptionist admitting Imogen asked about portal access. To VendorAdmin being a name people used like a mask.

I looked at the front desk PC again, the Word document still open, the polite instructions sitting there on screen like a smile that hid a knife.

Seat position. Discretion requested. Destroy errors.

It wasn't just forgery. It was instruction to erase.

"Take one more photo," Sera said.

I blinked. "Of what."

"Of the file list," Sera said. "The folder. Names. Times."

I did as told, photographing WEEKEND DOCS and its contents. Several versions of the guest list. Several versions of seating plans. That many versions existed because the system encouraged endless edits.

Or because someone wanted the ability to say, Oh, that was an older version, not the final one.

Plausible deniability written in file format.

I wrote.

06:44. WEEKEND DOCS folder contains multiple guest list/seating plan versions. Suggests repeated edits and confusion risk. Photos taken.

Sera stepped back, scanning the lobby.

Guests were waking now. They were checking phones. They were whispering. They were looking at the police and deciding whether fear or excitement would get them more attention.

Hugh's office door was still closed. The blinds still half-drawn. He was listening. He was calculating.

Sera leaned closer to me. "You need to be ready," she said quietly. "This will turn. They will try to make you the problem."

"They already have," I replied. "I'm a vendor who won't behave."

Sera's mouth twitched once. "Good. Keep being that."

She straightened and turned to the constable. "Guard this machine," she said. "No one touches it. If anyone tries, they get removed."

The constable nodded.

Then Sera looked at me again. "Come with me," she said. "We're going to bag any remaining printed copies from the office, and then we're going to speak to Melissa."

My stomach tightened at Melissa's name. "She'll cry," I said.

Sera's gaze stayed flat. "Let her. Tears don't wipe metadata."

We moved back through the service corridor toward the staff office. The fluorescent lights made everything look harsher. The smell of toner clung to my scarf now, faint but persistent.

When we reached the office, the constable guarding the door stepped aside. Hugh was not there. Either he'd decided to regroup, or someone had told him that hovering near police looked bad even for him.

Inside, the printer still hummed faintly, like a machine refusing to admit it was part of a crime.

Sera went straight to the desk and opened a drawer. Inside were more instruction sheets, unlaminated, stacked in a hurry. She didn't touch them. She nodded to the constable, who gloved up and bagged the whole stack.

Sera said, "If we can match these to the same stock, same file, same queue, we have a pattern."

"And if there are variations," I said, "we have intent."

Sera's eyes flicked to me. "Exactly."

I looked at the stack being bagged and felt that familiar tightening in my throat. Not fear, exactly. Anger. A clean anger at people who hid behind procedure and then used it to hurt.

I thought of Pip again. The honesty of a dog's single bark. The way he froze and stared, as if his body knew before his brain did.

If Pip had been here, he'd have barked at this office. He hated sudden applause and camera flashes, but I suspected he also hated lying. Dogs often did.

As if summoned by my thoughts, my phone vibrated again.

A message from Nisha.

Nisha: Harbour Kettle's open but empty. People are scared.

Anything you need, I can drop at the hotel entrance if police allow.

I stared at it, warmth and sadness mixing. Nisha always offered food like it could fix the world. Sometimes it almost did.

Hattie: Thank you. Don't come. Stay safe. I'll come to you when roads open.

Then I added, because I couldn't help myself.

Hattie: Keep the kettle hot.

Nisha replied with a simple heart emoji, which made my mouth tighten in that almost-smile way.

Sera watched me tuck my phone away. "Friend," she said.

"Ally," I corrected.

Sera nodded once. "Good. Keep her out of this."

"I will," I said.

The constable finished bagging the instruction stack. Sera gestured to the printer again. "Any other evidence you can see."

I scanned the area one more time, not letting my eyes slide over anything.

Then I saw it.

A pack of paper on the lower shelf, half hidden behind a box of pens. It wasn't the bright white stock in Tray 2. It was a different brand, slightly off-white, thicker.

I crouched and held it up to the light. It had a faint watermark pattern, subtle.

That was unusual for cheap office paper. It was the kind of paper you used when you wanted a document to feel official without putting letterhead on it.

I looked at Sera. "This," I said.

Sera's eyes narrowed. "Bag it."

The constable did.

I wrote.

06:58. Additional paper stock found in office shelf: thicker, faint watermark pattern. Bagged as potential source for forged documents.

Sera's gaze stayed hard. "Now," she said, "Melissa."

We found Melissa Shaw in a side corridor near the ballroom storage. She looked like she'd been awake for a week. Her hair was scraped into a bun that didn't hold. Her blazer was creased. Her face carried the kind of exhausted panic you saw in people who had built their life on making things go smoothly and suddenly realised smooth was over.

She tried to smile when she saw Sera. It failed.

"Detective Inspector," she said. "I'm so sorry. This is awful."

Sera's voice stayed calm. "Melissa. Where were you at midnight."

Melissa blinked. "Midnight."

"Answer," Sera said.

Melissa swallowed. "At the front desk. Hugh wanted updates. The storm was getting worse. Guests were asking questions."

Sera's gaze narrowed. "Did you print anything."

Melissa's eyes widened. "Print."

Sera didn't move. "Did you print vendor instructions."

Melissa's face went pale. "I… I printed what Hugh asked."

Sera's eyes sharpened. "What did he ask."

Melissa's voice wavered. "He said we needed updated instructions because staff were confused. He said it would protect guests."

Sera's tone stayed flat. "Did you create the file."

Melissa shook her head. "No. It was already there."

Sera asked, "Did you modify the file."

Melissa hesitated. Just a fraction too long.

My stomach tightened.

Sera noticed. "Melissa."

Melissa's eyes filled. "Imogen," she whispered.

Sera's gaze went still. "Imogen modified it."

Melissa nodded quickly, ashamed. "She said the Trust needed the guest list correct. She said donors would be furious if names were wrong. She said… she said it wasn't the time for sloppiness."

I felt my jaw tighten. Sloppiness. That was what they called the truth when it didn't fit their plan.

Sera's voice stayed calm. "Did she have the VendorAdmin password."

Melissa swallowed. "Yes."

Sera's eyes hardened. "Who gave it to her."

Melissa's gaze flicked, instinctive. Toward Hugh.

Sera waited.

Melissa whispered, "Hugh."

There it was. Gate and hand. Both.

Sera nodded once, as if confirming something she'd already suspected. "Thank you," she said.

Melissa blinked, startled. "Am I… am I in trouble."

Sera's gaze stayed flat. "You might be. Depending on what else you did."

Melissa flinched.

Sera continued, "But you just did the smartest thing you've done all weekend. You told me the truth."

Melissa's shoulders sagged, tears finally spilling. She wiped them quickly, humiliated.

I watched her and felt no satisfaction. Only a dull ache. Melissa was not the mastermind. Melissa was the kind of person who got used by masterminds and then blamed when things went wrong.

Sera turned slightly to me. "You got what you needed," she

said.

"Yes," I replied. "The forgery isn't just a feeling. It's settings, stock, queue, and access."

Sera nodded once. "Exactly."

Then her phone buzzed. She looked at the screen, jaw tightening.

"What," I asked, because I could hear the change in her breathing.

Sera's eyes met mine. "Penny Harrow wants to speak to you," she said.

My stomach tightened again, but this time with something else underneath. A prickling sense of consequence.

"Why me," I asked.

Sera's gaze stayed sharp. "Because she trusts paper people more than police," she said. "And because she's scared."

I swallowed. "Where is she."

Sera glanced toward the stairwell. "She's asked for the back stairwell. She says it's about the fire year."

The words landed in my chest with a cold weight.

Fire year. Registry seals. Trust property. The old stamp mark I'd seen in the guest list footer, faint and wrong.

The paper trail wasn't just about a dessert. It was about ownership. Control. Who got to rewrite the town's history and who got buried under it.

Sera's voice stayed calm. "Harriet. Take your log. Take your phone. I'll be close. You don't go anywhere alone."

"I won't," I said, though my skin prickled with the urge to run straight to answers.

Sera nodded once. "Good. And Harriet."

"Yes," I said.

Her gaze held mine. "Whatever she tells you, you write it down exactly. Word for word. Times. Names. No interpretation."

I lifted my Pocket Log slightly. "That's my only religion," I said.

Sera's mouth twitched once, then she turned toward the stairwell.

I followed, pen already uncapped, feeling the storm still battering the building, feeling the hotel's polished public story cracking at the edges.

Behind us, printers sat quietly, still warm from their midnight work.

Paper looked harmless until it wasn't.

CHAPTER 13

Penny's warning

The back stairwell smelt like wet concrete, disinfectant, and the kind of panic people tried to hide behind polite signage.

I followed Sera through a service corridor that narrowed as if the building itself was trying to squeeze us back into the bright lobby where everything was meant to look calm. The door to the stairwell had a green EXIT sign above it and a steel push bar that resisted my hand, just enough to feel like a warning.

Sera stopped with her palm on the bar.

"You asked for her to meet you," she said.

"No," I replied. "She asked for me."

Sera's mouth tightened. "Same result."

I held my Pocket Log in my left hand, fountain pen uncapped in my right, because if my hands were busy my mind stayed steady. That was the trick. Give the fear somewhere to go that wasn't my voice.

Sera looked at me, not soft, but deliberate. "You do not follow her anywhere," she said. "You do not let her steer you. You do not let anyone pull you out of sight."

"I run a stationery shop," I said. "No one's going to drag me anywhere. They'd trip over a box of envelopes."

That earned me a brief flicker of amusement in her eyes, which vanished as quickly as it arrived.

"I'll be on the landing," she said. "Close enough to hear your tone change. Not close enough to ruin your conversation."

"You're very considerate," I said.

"I'm very practical," she corrected.

She pushed the door open, then stepped aside so I could enter first. It was a small thing, but I noticed it anyway. She didn't want anyone to say the police cornered Penny. She wanted the record clean.

The stairwell was narrow, painted an institutional cream that had seen too many scuffed shoulders. A metal handrail ran along the wall, cold and slightly sticky. Emergency lights glowed faintly, washing everything in a washed-out hue. Somewhere above, a door rattled in the wind, and the sound travelled down the shaft like a message you didn't want.

I took two steps in and stopped.

Penny Harrow stood on the next landing up, angled as if she'd just happened to be there. She held a paper coffee cup in one hand and her phone in the other, her posture trying hard to say, I'm just checking signal. Nothing suspicious.

Her eyes gave her away.

They were too alert, too fast, like a rabbit pretending it was merely enjoying the view.

"Harriet," she said, using my full name as if we were in a council meeting and not a back stairwell with a dead man upstairs.

"Penny," I replied, stopping one step below her so we weren't shoulder to shoulder. I liked space. It gave you options.

She smiled quickly. It didn't reach her eyes. "Sorry to drag you out," she said. "I know you've had quite the night."

"I'd rather not repeat it," I said.

Her mouth twitched, almost a laugh, then she swallowed it

down. "Yes," she said. "Same."

She glanced past me, down toward the door we'd come through. Sera was visible through the narrow gap, on the landing below, leaning against the wall with her arms folded. She didn't look at us directly. She looked like she was waiting for a bus she fully intended to miss.

Penny's shoulders eased by a millimetre at the sight of her. That told me two things at once. Penny didn't trust the hotel. Penny did, at least a little, trust Sera.

And Penny was frightened enough to need that comfort.

Penny lifted her coffee cup as if it were an excuse. "Do you mind if we talk here," she said. "I thought… fewer ears."

"Fewer ears," I repeated. "In a hotel."

She gave a dry little nod. "I'm aware. But it's less theatrical than the lobby."

"Everything is theatrical in the lobby," I said. "Even grief."

Her eyes flickered. "That," she said quietly, "is one of the reasons I asked for you."

I raised my pen. "Say what you need to say," I told her. "And say it cleanly. I'll write it down."

Penny's gaze dropped to my notebook. The pen. The chain of my glasses. The labelled envelopes bulging slightly in my tote. Her expression shifted, just for a second, into something like relief.

"Of course you brought it," she said. "You're like a portable records office."

"Don't insult me," I said. "The records office misfiles things."

That did pull a small, genuine sound from her, halfway between a laugh and a breath.

Then her face tightened again.

"Right," she said. "Okay. I'll be quick."

I wrote the time without looking at the page, muscle memory.

06:07. Hotel stairwell. Penny Harrow. DI Linley on lower landing.

Penny took a breath. "You saw the instructions," she said.

"Yes," I replied. "And Sera has them. In bags."

Penny's jaw worked. "Good."

I kept my voice steady. "What do you mean, good."

Penny's eyes darted to the stairwell door above, then back to me. "Because they're trying to turn paper into permission," she said.

That line hit in my chest with the unpleasant clarity of truth.

"Say it again," I said, and lifted my pen.

Penny hesitated, then repeated, slower. "They're trying to turn paper into permission."

I wrote it word for word.

06:08. Penny: "They're trying to turn paper into permission."

She swallowed. "And they'll say it came from you."

"They can say whatever they like," I replied. "Ink doesn't agree with them."

Penny's gaze fixed on mine. "They're not just trying to blame you for a printing error," she said. "They're trying to scare me off a story."

My skin tightened.

"You came for the weekend," I said, "as a guest."

Penny's mouth twitched, a grim attempt at charm. "Officially."

"That word always worries me," I said.

"It should," she replied, and her voice dropped a fraction. Not a whisper. She didn't do that. She spoke like a journalist, even in fear. Low, controlled. "I came for the fire year records."

The phrase landed like a stone.

"The fire year," I repeated, because repetition forced people to be precise.

Penny nodded. "The Registry Office fire. The one everyone treats like an unfortunate accident that happened to tidy up old paperwork."

I felt my stomach tighten, because I'd grown up in a town that loved a tidy story.

"Fire year records," I said. "What records."

Penny's eyes flicked toward my Pocket Log again, as if needing to see the words become real. "Property ownership," she said. "Transfers. Old registrations. Who owned what before everything 'revitalised.'"

I wrote.

06:10. Penny: "I came for the fire year records." Tied to property ownership and transfers.

Penny's fingers tightened around her coffee cup. The cardboard creaked. "Valentine Row isn't just a lane of shops," she said. "It's an asset. It's always been an asset. The romance branding is cover. It makes tourists spend and locals shut up."

I didn't disagree. I'd watched people smile politely while being priced out of their own street.

Penny continued, "The Valentine Heritage Trust," she said, and her mouth flattened, "is not what it pretends to be."

"You don't say," I replied.

Her eyes sharpened at my tone, then softened slightly. "You know," she said.

"I know enough to be suspicious," I said. "Sera suspects too."

Penny's gaze flicked down the stairwell again. "She suspects," Penny said. "But you understand paperwork. You understand how little marks matter."

My pen paused. "Tell me about the mark," I said.

Penny's throat bobbed as she swallowed. "The seal," she said.

My spine went cold, because I'd been thinking of it since the guest list file.

"What seal," I asked, though I already knew.

Penny's eyes held mine. "An old Registry Office seal," she said. "The one they used before the fire. It should have been destroyed after. That's the procedure."

Procedure. The word tasted familiar in my mouth. Procedure could save you. Procedure could also kill you, if someone wrote it wrong.

Penny's voice tightened. "But it wasn't destroyed," she said. "Someone kept it. And if you have the seal, you can make anything look official. You can stamp a letter, a notice, a transfer, and half the town will treat it like gospel because it's got the right mark."

I wrote, careful.

06:12. Penny: "Old Registry Office seal… should have been destroyed after the fire… wasn't."

Penny leaned slightly forward. "I've been chasing it," she said. "Quietly. For months. Every time I ask at the council offices, they smile and give me nothing. Every time I request files, they tell me they're archived. Every time I push, someone tells me I'm 'creating drama'."

I felt a familiar rage flicker, the kind you swallowed down because rage wasn't evidence.

"I saw the stamp mark," I said.

Penny's eyes widened. "Where."

"In the guest list file footer," I said. "A faint stamp mark that shouldn't exist."

Penny's breath caught. "Yes," she said. "That's it."

I lifted my pen. "Say it cleanly," I told her. "For my notes."

Penny swallowed and spoke with careful precision. "The stamp mark in the guest list footer is the old Registry Office seal style. It should not appear on modern documents."

I wrote it.

06:14. Penny confirms stamp mark matches old Registry Office seal style. "Should not appear on modern documents."

Penny's gaze dropped to my page, then lifted again. "If they're using it in the footer," she said, "they're showing off. Or they're sloppy. Either way, it means the seal exists in someone's hands."

I thought of the Trust rep, Imogen Baird, her smooth smile and her folder. I thought of Hugh Mercer, his obsession with "brand protection." I thought of the solicitor name that hovered over this entire weekend like a shadow you couldn't quite pin down.

"Celia Pryce," I said.

Penny's mouth tightened. "Of course you know her name," she said, and there was a kind of bitter admiration in it. "Yes. Her. She's the town's solicitor, but she's tied to the Trust. She signs things. She stands behind people and tells them they're doing it for the good of Hartcombe."

My pen moved.

06:16. Penny flags Celia Pryce tied to Trust. "Signs things."

Penny's fingers moved on her phone screen as if she was resisting the urge to show me something. Then she stopped herself, eyes flicking to the stairwell door above again.

"You're afraid someone's listening," I said.

Penny's smile was small and unpleasant. "I'm afraid someone's always listening," she replied.

That was honest. It wasn't dramatic. It was simply a journalist's lived reality in a town that didn't like questions.

I kept my voice light on purpose. "Luckily, I'm boring," I said. "People rarely listen to boring women."

Penny's eyes flickered. "You're not boring," she said. "You're inconvenient."

"That's more accurate," I replied.

Penny took a breath that shook slightly. "The instructions," she said, steering back. "That line about seat position. That wasn't an accident."

"No," I agreed. "It was a mechanism."

Penny nodded quickly. "Yes. If you make staff believe they're serving by seat number, not person, you can target anyone who sits in that seat. And you can tell yourself you didn't do it to them. You did it to the seat."

My pen paused. My skin prickled.

"Is that what you think happened," I asked.

Penny's eyes slid away, then back. "I think," she said carefully, "Vale wasn't meant to be the one who took it."

I kept my face neutral, but my stomach tightened hard.

"Why," I asked.

Penny's lips pressed together. "Because I was meant to be in that seat," she said.

I wrote it down. Then I looked up.

"You swapped," I said.

Penny's eyes widened a fraction. "You saw."

"I saw," I confirmed. "Why did you swap."

Penny's throat bobbed. "Because someone pulled me aside," she said. "Right before dessert. A hotel staff member. Said there was a 'VIP discomfort' issue. Said I needed to move for the sponsor photos. It sounded ridiculous, but it was delivered with that smile that makes you feel like the difficult one if you refuse."

I felt anger rise again, clean and sharp. The smile as a weapon. The polite instruction as a shove.

"Who," I asked.

Penny swallowed. "Melissa," she said.

My pen moved.

06:22. Penny: Melissa asked her to move pre-dessert, framed as "VIP discomfort" and sponsor photos.

Penny flinched as she said the name, as if naming it made it more dangerous. "I didn't want to cause a scene," she added quickly, and her eyes hardened. "And I didn't want them clocking that I was watching them."

"So you moved," I said.

Penny nodded. "And Vale slid into the seat because Penny Harrow's chair was suddenly free and there's always someone willing to take a better view."

The phrasing was dry, but her hand trembled slightly as she lifted her coffee cup. She tried to hide it by drinking. The cup shook against her lip.

"You think they were aiming for you," I said.

Penny's eyes held mine. "I think they wanted a warning," she said. "A health incident. Something that would make me look reckless, unreliable. Something that would let them say, She came here to chase a story and look what happened."

"And you believe the story is the Trust and property," I said.

Penny nodded. "Yes."

I wrote.

06:25. Penny believes target was her, intended "warning" health incident narrative to discredit her and stop fire year records story.

Penny's gaze flicked down the stairwell again. Sera still stood below, posture unchanged. The presence steadied me. It seemed to steady Penny too, even as she pretended she wasn't looking.

Penny said, "They don't just buy properties," and her voice sharpened, "they buy silence. People take grants. People take sponsorship. People take free refurbishments. Then they smile and stop asking why the paperwork doesn't add up."

"I've met that type," I said. "They always use the word 'community' like it's holy."

Penny's mouth twisted. "And 'revitalisation.'"

That one made my jaw tighten. Councillor Max Hardwick's

favourite. Every time he said it, it sounded like a hymn. Every time he said it, a family shop closed.

"Max Hardwick," I said.

Penny nodded. "He's the face," she replied. "He's not the hands. He smiles for the cameras. The hands are quieter."

Celia Pryce again. Imogen again. Hugh again. A ring of people who hid behind each other, each one plausible, each one just doing their job.

"Why tell me," I asked Penny, "and not Sera."

Penny's eyes sharpened. "Because I'm scared," she said, which was an answer and not an excuse. "And because police hear 'seal' and they think wax and history. They don't hear how a mark can move money."

I nodded. "Sera hears it," I said. "She's not stupid."

Penny's gaze flickered. "No," she conceded. "She's not. But she's alone. And she's blocked by roads and storms and politics. You're in their ecosystem. You see what they try to hide."

That landed unpleasantly close to truth. My entire work depended on being invited into people's plans. Weddings. Events. Guest lists. Seating arrangements. All of it was power dressed up as romance. I'd left the registrar job because I'd tired of being used as the pen that made people's lies official.

Now I was back in it, just with prettier paper.

Penny leaned closer. "If you see that stamp mark again," she said, "keep it. Screenshot it. Print it. Whatever you need. Because if I'm right, that seal is the key to everything."

I wrote.

06:31. Penny: "If you see that stamp mark again, keep it… the seal is the key."

A sound above us made my muscles lock.

Footsteps. Slow, careful, coming down from the upper floor. Not the sloppy stomp of a guest. Not the clatter of staff in a hurry. Measured.

Penny froze. Not theatrically. Instinctively. The way Pip froze before he barked.

She pressed her back against the wall, coffee cup held close, eyes wide.

I didn't move, but I shifted my weight slightly so I could pivot if I needed to. My pen stayed in my hand. Ridiculous weapon, but it was what I had.

Sera's head turned below. She'd heard it too. Her posture changed, almost imperceptible. Ready.

The footsteps came closer. A silhouette appeared on the landing above. A man, older, wearing a hotel robe like armour, hair sticking up, looking annoyed rather than frightened.

He blinked down at us. "Can't sleep," he muttered, voice thick. "Storm's got the whole place rattling."

Penny's shoulders sagged a fraction in relief that looked like shame. She lifted her coffee cup in a bland gesture.

"Sorry," she said, tone too bright. "We'll be out of your way."

The man grunted and continued down the stairs, passing us without really seeing. He smelled of aftershave and stale wine. He didn't look at my notebook. He didn't look at Penny's face. He barely looked at Sera.

He went through the door at the bottom, and the stairwell fell back into tense quiet.

Penny exhaled shakily.

"You're jumpy," I said, not unkind.

Penny's mouth twisted. "I'm alive," she replied. "That comes with side effects."

I wrote that too, because it was the kind of line people remembered.

06:34. Penny: "I'm alive. That comes with side effects."

Penny looked at my page, then at my face. "You're going to tell her," she said, nodding toward Sera.

"I'm going to tell her what you told me," I replied. "Yes."

Penny's eyes tightened. "Tell her the seal part," she said. "Not just the target part. The seal is bigger."

"I understand," I said.

Penny's jaw worked. "And Harriet," she added, voice tightening, "be careful at breakfast."

I felt my stomach drop again, because the outline in my head knew where this was going.

"What do you know about breakfast," I asked.

Penny's eyes flicked away, then back. "They like to fix narratives with food," she said. "An apology. A special treat. A small gesture to show the hotel cares. It looks lovely. It photographs well."

"And it can be used," I said.

Penny nodded. "If someone offers me an apology dessert," she said, and her voice went thin with fear she tried to flatten, "don't let me take it."

The words hit like a bell.

I wrote them down exactly.

06:37. Penny: "If someone offers me an apology dessert, don't let me take it."

Penny swallowed hard, then tried to smooth it over with forced lightness. "Which makes me sound mad," she added. "I know. I can hear myself."

"It makes you sound observant," I said. "That's different."

Her eyes flickered with gratitude that she didn't allow to settle.

"I should go," she said, shifting her coffee cup as if it suddenly weighed too much. "If I stay here too long, someone will notice. And then I'm not just scared. I'm suspicious."

"Women always are," I said.

Penny's mouth twitched, humour and bitterness tangled together. "Exactly," she said.

She took one step down, then stopped and looked at me again.

"One more thing," she said.

"Yes," I replied, pen ready.

Penny's voice dropped, controlled. "They'll try to paint you as a meddler," she said. "They'll say you're enjoying this. They'll say your little shop is getting attention."

I felt my jaw tighten. "My shop isn't a stage," I said.

"They don't care," Penny replied. "They care about the story that protects them. If you threaten it, they'll make you the villain."

I wrote.

06:40. Penny warns: they'll scapegoat Hattie as "meddler" and attention-seeker to protect their story.

Penny nodded once, as if that was all she could afford to give. Then she moved down the steps, smoothing her expression into something passably casual as she passed Sera. She didn't stop. She didn't speak. She simply walked out through the lower door and into the corridor beyond, disappearing into the hotel's belly.

I stood still for a moment, listening to the wind battering the building, feeling the cold creep from the stairwell walls into my gloves.

Sera climbed two steps up toward me.

"What," she said, not as a question, but as a demand for data.

I looked down at my Pocket Log. "She came for fire year records," I said. "Property ownership. She says the old Registry Office seal should have been destroyed after the fire, but it wasn't. She believes it's being used to mark documents, including that stamp mark in the guest list footer."

Sera's eyes narrowed. "She saw it."

"She recognised it," I corrected. "I saw the mark first."

Sera's gaze sharpened. "And the target."

Penny's words sat in my chest like a weight. I didn't want them to be true, which meant they probably were.

"She believes she was the intended target," I said. "Melissa asked her to move pre-dessert. Vale took the seat."

Sera's jaw tightened. "Melissa."

"Yes," I said. "Penny also warned me to watch breakfast. She thinks there may be an 'apology dessert' attempt."

Sera's eyes hardened. "All right," she said. "That's enough to act on."

I watched her face, trying to read whether she believed it.

She did. Not because she trusted Penny, but because the mechanics fit. The forged instruction sheet wasn't a one-off mistake. It was a template for control.

Sera said, "You did well," and it sounded uncomfortable in her mouth, like praise was a foreign language.

"I wrote it down," I replied. "That's my only skill."

"It's not," Sera said. "But it's the one we need."

She looked down the stairs toward the door Penny had gone through. "We'll pull old records when we can," she said. "Storm makes it harder. Politics makes it worse."

"And breakfast makes it urgent," I said.

Sera nodded once. "Yes."

She gestured toward the stairwell door. "Back to your room," she said. "Or the lobby if you have to be visible. Do not go anywhere alone. If someone offers you food, you don't touch it. If someone offers Penny food, you stop it."

"I'm not her minder," I said.

Sera's gaze stayed flat. "This isn't about being nice. It's about keeping another body off the floor."

That shut me up.

We went back down the stairs together. At the bottom, Sera paused and looked at me.

"Harriet," she said.

"Yes," I replied.

"Write a clean summary for me," she said. "Seal. Fire year. Melissa. Target. Breakfast warning. Keep it tight."

"I can do tight," I said.

Sera's mouth twitched once. Then she pushed the door open and we stepped back into the corridor, where the hotel's public face waited like a mask.

As we walked toward the lobby, I felt the urge to look around, to clock every staff member, every tray, every smile. Penny's warning had sharpened my senses in a way I didn't enjoy.

I found myself thinking of Pip again, of how he froze and stared before he barked. No drama. No theatre. Just a body telling the truth before the mind could argue.

Pip wasn't here. So I would have to be my own alarm system.

Back in my room, I sat at the desk and wrote the summary Sera wanted, word for word, with times. I slipped the page into a labelled envelope, because habits were safety.

Then I opened my Pocket Log again and wrote one more line for myself.

06:58. Penny scared but deliberate. Seal exists. Food can be weapon. Breakfast is next.

I capped my pen and stared at the wall for a moment, listening to the storm.

The hotel would try to turn the morning into a healing narrative. Coffee. Croissants. A gentle announcement about "support." Hugh would smile. Imogen would nod. Someone would carry a plate like it was kindness.

And if Penny was right, that plate would be anything but.

I stood, pulled on my scarf, and went out.

CHAPTER 14

Second attempt, near miss

Morning at the Mariner's Crown did not arrive so much as it was assembled.

The lobby lights brightened a notch, the scent of coffee was pushed into the air like a public service, and someone somewhere made a decision to call today "breakfast" rather than "a roomful of trapped strangers pretending normality". The storm still battered the windows. The sea still raged beyond the glass. None of that mattered to a hotel that ran on rituals.

Rituals were comforting, right up until someone weaponised them.

I stood outside the breakfast room doors with my Pocket Log open, pen poised, and the unpleasant sense that I was about to walk into a staged photograph. The sort where everyone smiled a little too hard to prove they were coping.

The sign beside the entrance read BREAKFAST SERVICE 07:00–10:00 in looping script, because apparently time was less frightening when it looked romantic. The smaller print underneath stated, PLEASE ADVISE STAFF OF ALLERGIES. That line felt less romantic and more like a warning label.

I wrote the time.

07:03. Breakfast room doors. Storm ongoing. Guests present. Then I went in.

Heat hit first, that thick warmth of too many bodies in a contained space. The room smelt of toasted bread, bacon, and wet wool drying on chair backs. Someone had set out a bowl of peeled oranges, which always struck me as optimistic in a hotel. Oranges wanted to be eaten quickly. If they were not, they went sad and shiny and no one admitted it.

The breakfast room itself was a long space with windows looking out on a slate-grey view of rain and sea. Tables were arranged in neat grids, each one dressed with folded napkins, cutlery aligned, and small jars of jam as if the hotel thought it could distract guests with marmalade.

Hugh Mercer stood near the centre, hands clasped, wearing a charcoal suit at seven in the morning, which was the behaviour of a man who slept in spreadsheets. His smile was on. His eyes were busy.

Near him was Imogen Baird, the Trust sponsor representative, dressed in a pale coat that looked expensive and immune to weather. She held a folder, of course she did. Her hair was smooth. Her expression suggested she was at a memorial service for an inconvenience.

I scanned the room like I always did, the way I used to scan wedding receptions for the cousin who drank too much and the mother of the bride who wanted to rearrange the seating chart with her bare hands. Old habits did not leave. They simply found new targets.

Staff were moving in careful patterns. Chloe at the tea station, shoulders tense, smile fixed. Melissa near the buffet, speaking with the kitchen supervisor, Dean Lomas, who looked like he'd rather wrestle the storm itself than deal with guests. Two servers carried plates in and out of a side corridor. One man in a crisp waistcoat stood by the door with a clipboard and a look that said, I have been told to keep things tidy and I am not sure what that means anymore.

The whole room had a sheen of forced calm.

I chose a table with sightlines to the buffet and the staff corridor. It was not the best view of the sea, but I had not come for scenery. I had come for mechanics.

I set my tote under my chair and kept my Pocket Log on the table, in plain sight. People did not love being watched, but they behaved better when they knew they were being recorded. This was not a moral observation. It was a practical one.

A guest at the next table leaned in to his companion and said, too loudly, "It's all so tragic, isn't it," with the same tone he might use to describe a delayed ferry.

His companion responded, "At least the breakfast looks lovely."

I stared at my place setting, then at the jam jar, and decided that if anyone tried to serve me a story with my toast, I would bite.

I ordered tea from Chloe because tea was my anchor, and because a hot cup gave your hands something to do.

Chloe appeared at my table with a pot and two cups, even though I had not asked for two. Her eyes were red-rimmed and she looked as if she'd been crying in the staff loos and then apologised to the mirror for being unprofessional.

"Ms Crowe," she said, voice careful.

"Hattie," I corrected, because if she was going to be frightened, she might as well be frightened of a person and not a title.

Chloe placed the pot down with a clink. Her hands shook slightly. "I'm sorry about everything," she said.

"That's the hotel's line," I said, and kept my tone mild. "Are you sorry because you did something, or sorry because you were ordered to help cover it?"

Her eyes widened. She looked like a rabbit again.

"I didn't," she started.

I held up a hand. "Chloe. Sit down for one moment."

She glanced over her shoulder toward Hugh. Hugh was laughing at something a guest had said, his smile gleaming. He did not look at Chloe. That told me everything.

Chloe did not sit. She hovered.

"All right," I said. "Then answer me this. Are there any 'special items' being served today."

Chloe blinked. "Special items."

"Apology desserts," I said.

Her face went paler. That was the answer, even before she spoke.

"We have a tray," she whispered. "It's just… a gesture."

"A gesture is a hand movement," I said. "A tray is a plan."

Her mouth trembled. "They said it would help," she murmured.

"Who said," I asked.

Chloe's eyes flicked again, helplessly. Hugh. Always Hugh.

I wrote, without looking down.

07:08. Chloe confirms "apology dessert" tray planned. "Gesture." Visibly frightened.

"Chloe," I said quietly, "if you want to be useful, you tell me who the tray is for."

She swallowed hard. "I don't know," she said quickly. "I just pour tea."

I believed that. She was the sort of employee hotels kept on tea because tea did not require discretion. Tea did not require a seat position.

"Then pour me tea," I said, "and keep your eyes open."

She nodded quickly and escaped, relief flooding her posture.

I sipped, letting the warmth steady me, and watched the room.

Penny Harrow entered ten minutes later, hair brushed into

something that suggested she had tried very hard to look normal. She wore a muted coat and held her phone like a shield. Her expression was calm in the way a person tried to be calm when they'd slept two hours and had spent the rest of the night imagining stamps and seals and poison in pudding.

She spotted me. Her eyes flicked. No wave. No greeting. Just the smallest shift of her chin, as if we were strangers who had once shared a lift.

Good. Subtle meant safer.

She moved toward the buffet first, because that was what normal guests did. She took a plate, picked up a croissant, stared at it as if it contained a moral lesson, then chose toast instead.

I watched. Penny was not stupid. Penny had heard herself say, don't let me take it, and she was already acting accordingly.

She carried her plate to a table near the windows. It was a good table for the sea view. It was also a table that made her visible. Penny always liked to be seen. It was part of her job. It was also part of her armour.

I noted where she sat.

Table 6, near window. Seat facing door.

Then I noted something else.

The table number cards.

Small tent cards, printed in black on cream card stock, with looping script and a flourish. They were not my style. They were the hotel's. They looked sweet. They looked harmless.

I studied the lettering anyway, because once your brain had learned to look for small tells, you could not unlearn it.

The table cards were clean. Proper kerning. Proper spacing. This was the hotel's own brand template, not an imitation.

That was useful. It meant that if anything turned up with off spacing, it would stand out.

Hugh moved through the room like a man doing rounds at

a hospital. He smiled at guests, placed a hand on shoulders, murmured sympathetic phrases. Every so often he glanced at the door as if waiting for someone.

Imogen stood near the buffet, speaking with Melissa in a low voice. Melissa nodded too quickly. Dean walked away from them, jaw tight, as if he'd just been told to do something he found offensive.

I watched the staff corridor.

If an apology tray existed, it would come through there.

I opened my Pocket Log again and wrote a line to steady myself.

07:19. Penny seated, visible. Hugh and Imogen circulating. Staff tense. Watch corridor.

I stood, carrying my tea cup as if I was simply going to refresh it, and moved closer to Penny's line of sight. Not too close. Not obvious. Just near enough that if something happened, I could cross the room in three steps rather than ten.

As I passed Penny's table, I paused.

"Toast is the correct choice," I said, voice light.

Penny's eyes flicked up, cautious. "You sound like you're campaigning," she said.

"I'm campaigning against surprises," I replied.

Her mouth tightened, almost a smile. "Same," she said.

A server approached her then, a young man with neat hair and a grin that looked strained. He held a coffee pot.

"Coffee, madam," he said.

"No thank you," Penny replied, polite.

"Tea," he tried.

"I'm fine," Penny said.

He hesitated. His eyes flicked to the side, toward the buffet.

I saw it. That quick glance for confirmation. For instruction. He was not offering tea because he wanted to. He was offering because someone had told him to keep her engaged. Keep her here. Keep her participating.

I stepped away, refilled my tea at the station, and returned to my table. I did not want to hover over Penny like a bodyguard. That would make her look like a target.

Targets needed to look alone.

The apology tray arrived at 07:31.

I saw it before I understood it. A server emerged from the staff corridor carrying a silver tray covered with a linen cloth. The cloth was pristine. Too pristine. It had that faint starch stiffness that meant it had been ironed recently. It looked like a prop.

The server was Chloe, which surprised me. Chloe was tea. Chloe was safe. Someone had put her on tray duty on purpose.

Chloe walked carefully between tables, smiling with that same polite hotel expression she had worn all weekend. The smile did not reach her eyes. Her eyes were fixed on the tray, not the guests.

Hugh moved a fraction closer, as if shepherding her. Imogen's gaze tracked the tray. Melissa stood by the buffet, hands clasped, watching like someone watching a car approach an ice patch.

My stomach tightened.

This was not kindness. Kindness did not require an audience.

Chloe stopped at Table 6.

Penny.

Chloe lifted the linen cloth with one hand and revealed small glass cups, each one filled with a pale cream dessert topped with a single raspberry. Something like panna cotta, or perhaps a posset. Elegant. Simple. The sort of thing you served when you wanted to look gracious.

Beside the glass cups lay a small folded card.

Not the hotel's usual card stock. Not cream with logo. Bright white. Smooth. Cut slightly uneven, as if trimmed quickly. The text was printed in black in a near-match font. At a distance, it looked like the hotel's script. Up close, I could see even from here that the spacing was wrong.

My pulse kicked.

Penny looked at the tray, then at Chloe. Penny's smile was polite, wary. "What's this," she asked.

Chloe's voice carried. "A special apology dessert, madam. With compliments from the hotel."

Penny's eyes narrowed. "Apology for what."

Chloe's smile faltered. "For... the upset," she said.

"The upset," Penny repeated, and her tone was dry enough to crack glass. "That's a tidy word."

Hugh stepped in, smoothly. "Ms Harrow," he said, voice warm, "I wanted to make sure you felt looked after this morning. We're all shaken. We want to do what we can to comfort guests."

Penny turned her head slightly to look at him. "Comfort," she said.

Hugh nodded, controlled. "Yes."

Imogen drifted closer, her smile thin. "We are a community," she said, as if she were reciting something she'd practised in a mirror. "We support each other."

Penny's gaze flicked to the card on the tray. Her hand moved toward it, almost involuntarily.

My body moved before my mind finished deciding.

I was out of my chair and crossing the room in a straight line, my tea forgotten on the table. I did not run. Running turned you into a spectacle. I walked with purpose, as if I were simply coming over to greet someone.

I reached Penny's table just as her fingers brushed the folded card.

"Morning," I said brightly, loud enough for anyone nearby to hear. "I see the hotel's doing theatre again."

Hugh's smile tightened. "Harriet," he said, like my name tasted inconvenient.

"Hugh," I replied, and gave him the same polite tone I used for difficult mothers of the bride. "Apology desserts. How charming."

Penny looked at me, eyes sharp, trying to read what I was doing.

I looked at the card.

Up close, the kerning was undeniably wrong. The text was set in a serif that mimicked elegance. The spacing between letters had that slight oddness, that mechanical rhythm. A near-match. An imitation.

The paper stock was bright. Too bright. The cut was slightly jagged at the bottom edge.

My stomach went cold.

I did not touch the dessert. I did not touch the glass cup. I touched only the edge of the folded card with my fingernails and lifted it slightly to see the inside.

The inside was not a message of sympathy.

It was a directive.

APOLOGY DESSERT: TABLE 6 SEAT 1. DELIVER IMMEDIATELY. DISCRETION REQUESTED.

Seat. Not person. Seat.

My ears rang with the calm fury of recognition.

I looked up at Hugh. "This is a lovely idea," I said, voice smooth. "Who wrote the card?"

Hugh blinked, smile still on. "It's just a gesture," he said. "Harriet, now is not the time."

"For forged stationery," I said. "I agree."

His smile faltered by a hair. Imogen's eyes sharpened.

Penny's face drained of colour.

Chloe stood frozen, tray still balanced, eyes wide. She looked like she might faint. If she did, the desserts would spill. That would be a mess. Mess was easier for them to dismiss than evidence.

I turned slightly toward Chloe. "Chloe," I said gently, "could you tell me where you got this card."

Chloe's throat worked. She glanced at Hugh. Her eyes filled.

Hugh's voice cut in. "Harriet, you're upsetting staff."

"Yes," I said. "I'm upsetting staff because someone is trying to kill a guest with a printed instruction."

The table nearest us went quiet. A few heads turned. Cameras did not come out yet, but I could feel the itch of them.

Hugh's smile tightened into something brittle. "That is an outrageous statement."

"It's a documented pattern," I replied. "And your printer has already told DI Linley the same story."

The name landed like a stone. Hugh's eyes flicked, for the first time, toward the doorway. Toward police presence. Toward consequences.

Imogen stepped forward, voice silky. "Harriet, you are overreacting. This is an apology dessert. A kindness."

"Kindness doesn't come with seat instructions," I said.

Penny's hands had moved off the table. She was sitting very still, the way people sat still when they were trying not to be sick.

I looked at her. "Don't touch it," I said, quietly.

Penny nodded once, barely moving her head.

Chloe's lips trembled. "I was told," she whispered.

"By who," I asked.

Chloe glanced at Hugh again, then at me, then at the floor.

I did not push her further. Not yet. Chloe was not the hand. Chloe was the glove.

I took my phone from my coat pocket and typed one message

without looking away from the tray.

Hattie: Breakfast room. Apology dessert attempt on Penny. Seat-position card. Forged formatting.

Send.

I heard Sera's voice behind me less than ten seconds later. She moved like a storm of her own, contained and efficient.

"Step away from the tray," she said.

Chloe startled and nearly tipped it. Sera's hand came out, steady, not touching the cups, just guiding Chloe's elbows to keep her upright.

"Chloe," Sera said, calm. "Breathe. Do not move. You are not in trouble if you do exactly what I say."

Chloe's eyes filled with tears and she nodded quickly.

Sera turned her gaze to Hugh. "Mr Mercer," she said. "Why is a seat-targeted dessert being delivered to a guest?"

Hugh's smile tried to return. It failed. "It's a gesture," he said. "We're trying to comfort people after a tragic event."

Sera's eyes were hard. "Why seat-targeted."

Hugh's jaw tightened. "It's just internal wording."

Sera held out an evidence bag to the constable who had followed her in. "Bag the card," she said.

I stepped back half a pace so the constable could access it without bumping Penny or Chloe. The constable donned gloves, took the folded card by the edges, and slid it into the bag without unfolding it further.

Sera said, "Bag the desserts."

Hugh's eyes widened. "You can't confiscate breakfast."

Sera did not look at him. "I can confiscate potential evidence in a suspected attempted poisoning," she said. "Watch me."

The constable began carefully lifting each glass cup off the tray and placing it into a larger evidence container, one by one, keeping them upright. The raspberries trembled slightly with each movement.

A guest at the next table gasped. Someone muttered, "What on earth."

Hugh took a step forward. Sera's head snapped up.

"Do not," she said, voice quiet and lethal. "Take another step."

Hugh froze.

Imogen's mouth tightened. "This is going to look terrible," she said, like that was the real crime.

Sera finally looked at her. "Then stop staging things that look terrible," she replied.

That earned a few quiet murmurs from nearby tables. People loved a police officer who spoke like a person rather than a brochure.

Penny sat very still. Her knuckles were white where they gripped the edge of the table. She did not look at the desserts being bagged. She stared at the jam jar as if it was the only safe object in the room.

I leaned toward her slightly. "Are you all right," I asked.

Penny's voice was flat. "No," she said. "But I'm alive."

That line landed hard. I had written it in my log earlier. Hearing it now felt different. It felt like a cost.

I reached into my tote and pulled out a plain envelope, the kind I used for evidence. I slid it toward Penny without drawing attention.

"If you feel sick," I said quietly, "we document. Time. Symptoms. Everything."

Penny's eyes flicked to the envelope. She nodded once, grateful and furious all at once.

Sera turned to Chloe. "Chloe," she said. "Who told you to deliver this tray to Table 6."

Chloe's lips trembled. She glanced at Hugh again.

Sera's voice stayed even. "Do not look at him. Look at me. Who told you."

Chloe swallowed. "Melissa," she whispered.

Melissa, who had been hovering near the buffet, went pale. Her hands flew to her mouth as if she could physically stop the truth from leaving Chloe's lips.

Sera's gaze cut to Melissa. "Melissa Shaw," she said. "Step forward. Now."

Melissa obeyed, moving like a person walking to a tribunal.

"I didn't," Melissa began, voice cracking. "It was meant to be just a kind thing. I didn't know. I swear."

Sera held up the evidence bag containing the card. "Who wrote this."

Melissa's eyes flicked to the bag. Her face went white. "I didn't," she said again.

Sera's voice was quiet. "Who did."

Melissa's gaze flicked, instinctive, toward Imogen.

Imogen's expression did not change, but her eyes sharpened, warning.

Melissa swallowed. "It was in the folder," she whispered. "It was already printed."

Sera's gaze stayed hard. "Printed where."

Melissa's shoulders collapsed. "Front desk," she said. "They said… it was from management."

Sera's eyes flicked to Hugh. Hugh's jaw tightened.

"Management," Sera repeated. "Meaning you."

Hugh's voice was smooth again, but strained. "Detective Inspector, please. Guests are watching."

Sera's gaze held his. "Good," she said. "Let them watch."

She turned back to Melissa. "Who gave you the card."

Melissa's mouth trembled. "Imogen," she whispered.

The room went very quiet. Quiet in a breakfast room was unnatural. Quiet meant people were listening.

Imogen smiled, small and sharp. "That is absurd," she said. "I would never."

Sera did not argue. She did not need to. She simply nodded to the constable.

"Take Ms Shaw to the conference room," Sera said. "Now. Separate her from everyone. I want a full statement."

Melissa nodded, eyes spilling tears, and allowed herself to be guided away.

Chloe stood shaking, tray still in her hands, as if she did not know what to do without instructions.

Sera turned to her. "You did as you were told," she said, calm. "Now you will do as I tell you. You will go sit in the lobby. You will drink water. You will not speak to Hugh Mercer or Imogen Baird. Understood."

Chloe nodded, sobbing silently, and backed away.

Hugh watched her go, expression tightly controlled.

I watched him watch her. It was the look of a man who measured people by usefulness.

Sera turned back to the room and raised her voice just enough to carry.

"Breakfast service continues," she said. "No special desserts are to be served. If anyone offers you anything not on the standard menu, you decline and you inform a constable."

There was a ripple of discomfort, then reluctant compliance. People did not like being told their croissants might be dangerous. It ruined the butter.

Imogen stepped closer to Hugh, her voice low, but I caught enough to know the shape of it.

"This is out of control," she hissed.

Hugh's smile returned, thin. "We will contain it," he murmured.

Contain. Like a spill. Like a narrative leak.

Sera looked at me then. "Harriet," she said.

"Yes," I replied.

"Tell me what you saw," she said. "And I want it clean."

I opened my Pocket Log, pen steady despite the adrenaline in my fingertips.

"07:31," I said. "Chloe brought apology dessert tray to Table 6, Penny Harrow. Card on tray printed on bright white stock, near-match font, kerning off, same as forged vendor instruction sheets. Inside card: 'TABLE 6 SEAT 1. DELIVER IMMEDIATELY. DISCRETION REQUESTED.'"

Sera's eyes narrowed. "Seat one."

"Yes," I said. "Seat-targeted again."

Sera nodded once. "Photographs."

"I have them," I said.

Sera's gaze flicked to Penny. "Penny touched nothing."

"No," I said. "I stopped her before she took the card."

Penny's mouth twisted. "Like a particularly nosy aunt," she said, voice dry.

I looked at her. "You're welcome," I replied.

That earned a brief, grim smile from her.

Sera turned to Hugh. "Mr Mercer," she said. "You will come with me. Now."

Hugh's smile tightened. "I have guests," he said.

Sera's voice was calm. "You have a problem," she replied. "And it is no longer yours to manage."

Hugh's eyes flicked around the room, calculating. He could not refuse without looking guilty. He could not comply without losing control. He chose compliance, because Hugh always chose optics.

"As you wish," he said, and his tone suggested it was a favour.

Sera did not respond. She simply gestured toward the door.

Imogen moved to follow.

Sera's gaze cut. "Not you," she said. "You stay."

Imogen's smile tightened. "I beg your pardon."

Sera's voice stayed even. "You are not invited to a police interview. You can speak to me later with a solicitor if you like."

Imogen's eyes flashed. Then she smoothed her expression. "Of course," she said. "We will do everything properly."

Properly. The word made me want to bite something.

Sera walked Hugh out of the breakfast room.

The room resumed its murmur, but it was different now. A murmur of fear rather than gossip. People ate more slowly. People watched staff hands more closely. People began to realise that procedure could be a weapon, and they hated that realisation because it made them feel stupid.

Penny finally lifted her tea cup, hands steadier now that the immediate threat had passed. She took a careful sip.

"That was not subtle," she said, voice low.

"No," I agreed. "It was confident."

Penny's eyes narrowed. "They tried again. In public."

"Because the public part is the point," I said. "An apology dessert photographs well. So does an ambulance."

Penny's mouth tightened. "So Vale," she murmured.

My stomach turned. "Vale was collateral," I said.

Penny's gaze flicked to mine, sharp and sad. "He was a person," she corrected, and her voice had a bite of guilt in it. "Obnoxious, yes. Still a person."

I nodded once. "Yes," I said. "And someone thought a 'health incident' was a neat way to scare you. Last night it landed on him."

Penny's fingers tightened around her cup. "So I was meant to be the story," she said.

"Yes," I replied.

She stared out at the rain-lashed windows. "They want me to look reckless," she said. "They want to say I came chasing fire year ghosts and ended up eating something I shouldn't."

"Exactly," I said. "Because if you look careless, no one believes your paperwork."

Penny's jaw worked. "And if I die," she said, voice flat, "they call it tragic."

"They call it tragic and move on," I said. "With a sponsored statement."

Penny's eyes flicked back to me. "You were right," she said quietly.

"About what," I asked.

She gestured slightly with her cup. "About romance branding," she said. "It makes everything look sweeter than it is. Even threats."

I looked down at my Pocket Log. The ink was dark and steady. The page felt solid. It was the only thing in that hotel that felt solid.

"I hate being right," I said.

Penny's mouth twitched. "Same," she replied.

A server approached then, carrying a plate of plain toast. She set it on Penny's table without a word, as if someone had told her, keep it simple, keep it safe, keep it quiet.

Penny stared at it for a second, then let out a breath.

"This is the only toast I've ever been grateful for," she said.

"Don't get sentimental," I replied. "You'll scare it off."

That earned her a small, real smile. The kind that lasted half a second, then disappeared.

I took my phone out and checked messages.

One from Cal.

Cal: Roads still shut. Pip's offended you've abandoned him

for hotel drama. He says your replacement alarm system is terrible.

I stared at the message and felt my throat tighten, not with grief, but with that odd ache of missing something simple. Pip's single bark. Cal's steady presence. The ordinary world.

I typed back.

Hattie: Tell Pip he's correct. Also tell him he's on toast duty when I get home.

Cal: He accepts these terms.

I tucked my phone away.

Penny watched me. "Cal," she said.

"Yes," I replied.

She nodded, eyes thoughtful. "He'll hate this," she said.

"He'll hate the way they're playing it," I corrected.

Penny's mouth tightened. "They play everything," she said.

"Yes," I agreed. "Which is why we stop letting them."

Penny's gaze sharpened. "We," she repeated.

I did not flinch. "You and I," I said. "Because Pip isn't here and Cal can't get through the roads and the police are outnumbered by people with folders."

Penny's eyes held mine. Then she nodded once, slow. "All right," she said. "So what now."

I looked around the breakfast room again, clocking the way Imogen had resumed her position near the buffet, face smooth, eyes cold. Clocking the way staff avoided looking at Penny's table now. Clocking the way guests leaned in to whisper, their phones held low, their thumbs itching.

"We document," I said. "We stay visible. We don't eat anything we didn't watch being made."

Penny snorted. "I'll stick to toast forever," she said.

"It's safer than kindness," I replied.

She laughed once, then stopped, as if laughter itself might be dangerous.

I wrote one more line in my Pocket Log, because it mattered.

07:46. Second attempt prevented. Apology dessert seat-targeted. Confirms intended target likely Penny, not Vale. Pattern repeats. Food used as narrative.

The words sat on the page like a verdict.

Across the room, Imogen's eyes met mine for a brief moment. Her gaze was steady, assessing. It was not panic. It was annoyance. As if I'd spilled tea on her agenda.

I held her gaze, then looked away first, because I had no interest in a staring contest with a woman who treated paper like a weapon. I already knew she was dangerous. I didn't need to prove it with eye contact.

A moment later, Sera re-entered the breakfast room. Hugh was not with her. That was telling.

Sera moved straight to my table. Her expression was controlled, but her eyes had that sharper edge they got when she'd stepped over a line and decided she didn't care who complained.

"Harriet," she said.

"Yes," I replied.

"I'm pulling the portal logs," she said. "Now. Hugh's 'generic admin' account is about to become a very specific problem for someone."

My skin warmed with grim satisfaction. "Good," I said.

Sera's gaze flicked to Penny. "You," she said to Penny, "stay where people can see you. Do not eat anything you didn't choose yourself. If anyone approaches you with a 'gesture', you call out loud enough for half the room to hear."

Penny lifted her tea cup. "Understood," she said, voice dry. "No more desserts with secrets."

Sera's mouth twitched. "Exactly."

Then Sera looked back at me. "And Harriet," she said.

"Yes," I replied.

Her gaze held mine. "You were right," she said. "Seat-targeted. Not person-targeted. Which means last night was an accident of positioning."

The words landed in my chest, heavy and cold. Vale's collapse, the corridor, the rushed privacy, the narrative management. The tragedy of a man who annoyed everyone and still did not deserve what happened to him.

"It means," I said slowly, "that the wrong person died."

Sera nodded once. "Yes," she said. "And it means the person who planned it is still willing to try again."

The breakfast room hummed around us, pretending it was normal. Toast. Tea. Jam jars. Rain against glass. A hotel trying to keep its smile on.

I watched Penny chew a piece of toast like it was an act of defiance.

I watched Imogen stand by the buffet, calm as a knife.

And I realised something else, sharp and unpleasant.

Pip's bark might have saved Penny if he'd been here. But he wasn't. So it was on me.

I was not here to plan romance weekends anymore. I was here to catch the people who used romance weekends as cover.

Sera turned to go, already moving toward the staff corridor and the office beyond, where the portal logs waited like a confession in numbers.

I lifted my pen, wrote the time, and underlined it once.

08:02. DI Linley pulling portal logs. Next move.

Then I looked up at the room again and kept my eyes open, because breakfast was not over and neither was the story they were trying to write with someone else's life.

CHAPTER 15

The portal logs

Sera found me exactly where I knew she would, because she moved through a building like a person who refused to be surprised by it.

I was in the breakfast room doorway, half in, half out, pretending I was deciding whether I wanted another pot of tea, when in fact I was deciding whether to trust any object smaller than my fist. Penny sat by the window with toast and an expression that said she'd never look at a raspberry the same way again. Imogen Baird hovered near the buffet like a decorative menace. Hugh Mercer had vanished from view, which meant he'd gone somewhere private to plan his next public face.

Sera appeared at my shoulder. No announcement. No "excuse me". Just presence.

"Harriet," she said, brisk.

"Yes," I replied, because I'd learned that when Sera used my name, it meant we were done with niceties and moving to evidence.

"Hugh's office," she said. "Now."

I glanced towards Penny. Penny didn't look up, but her shoulders tightened, as if she could feel the room shifting around her. I hated that for her. I also hated that she was right to hate it.

"I'm not leaving her," I said.

Sera's gaze flicked to Penny, then to the uniformed constable standing near the far wall, pretending to read a laminated breakfast menu.

"She's not alone," Sera said. "And you're not her bodyguard. You're my witness."

That last word did it. Witness was something I understood. Witness meant procedure. Procedure meant control, or at least the illusion of it, which was better than chaos.

"All right," I said. "I'm coming."

I walked to Penny's table, keeping my pace ordinary. The quickest way to turn someone into a target was to behave as if they were a target.

Penny looked up at me. Her eyes were bright and tired, the way eyes looked after fear had spent the night rearranging your insides.

"I'm not going anywhere interesting," I said, keeping my voice light. "If anyone offers you anything with the word 'special' in it, you raise your voice and become unbearable."

Penny's mouth twitched. "So I stay myself," she said.

"Exactly," I replied.

Her fingers tightened on her tea cup. "Do what you need to do," she said, and the words sounded like permission she didn't want to grant because she'd rather be safe than brave, but she granted it anyway.

I nodded once and stepped away.

Sera led me out of the breakfast room and into the corridor. The hotel's air changed immediately. Public spaces were warmed and scented and designed to make you forget you were paying too much. Staff corridors were narrow and smelled of detergent, damp wool, and the anxious sweat of people who didn't get to pretend.

We passed a service trolley loaded with stacks of plates. Someone had draped a tea towel over the top like it was a modesty panel. That felt apt.

A staff member I didn't recognise flattened herself against the wall as we went by, eyes down. She had that look of someone trying not to be noticed by authority, which meant she'd been noticed before.

Sera didn't break stride.

"Hugh's been calling people," she said, low.

"Of course he has," I replied. "If his phone stopped working, he'd stop breathing."

Sera gave me a brief sideways look, almost amused, then she turned her attention forward again. "He's also been insisting we can't access the portal because of 'data protection'," she said.

I snorted. "He's very concerned about privacy," I said. "As long as it protects him."

"Exactly," Sera replied.

We reached a door with a brass plaque that read GENERAL MANAGER. The lettering was in that confident font hotels used when they wanted you to believe their decisions were inevitable.

Sera knocked once and opened it without waiting.

Hugh's office smelled of expensive coffee and a particular kind of aftershave that insisted it had never met sweat. It was a neat room, nothing personal, designed to look like efficiency lived here. There were framed photographs of the Mariner's Crown in better weather, a shallow bowl of polished stones on a side table, and a model sailboat that looked like it had never been touched by an actual child.

Hugh stood behind his desk, jacket on, tie perfect, face set in calm concern, as if he'd been waiting to offer condolences to someone who'd dropped a spoon.

"Detective Inspector," he said. "Harriet."

The way he said my name suggested I'd become a problem he hadn't budgeted for.

"Sera," she corrected, because she did not accept titles as armour.

She stepped fully inside. I followed, closing the door behind me. The click sounded too loud.

A laptop sat open on Hugh's desk, screen angled away. Two phones lay to one side, one of them face down. A printer sat in the corner on a small table, the sort of printer that could be blamed for many sins because it was always conveniently "shared".

Hugh's eyes flicked to my Pocket Log, which was out and open already, pen uncapped. He had the sense to look faintly irritated rather than openly threatened. Men like Hugh didn't panic. They controlled.

Sera took a chair without invitation. I took the one beside her, because if Hugh tried to do theatre, I wanted a front row seat.

"Portal access," Sera said.

Hugh's smile returned. Thin. "Detective Inspector, I've told you," he began. "The vendor portal contains sensitive guest data. Names, dietary information, addresses in some cases. We have legal obligations."

Sera's gaze stayed flat. "And I have a death, an attempted poisoning, and forged documents in your building," she said. "Your obligations are not more important than mine."

Hugh spread his hands slightly. "I'm not obstructing you," he said. "I'm trying to protect our guests."

"Protect them from what," I asked, before I could stop myself, "the truth on a spreadsheet."

Hugh's eyes narrowed a fraction. "Harriet," he said, as if I'd spoken out of turn at a wedding rehearsal.

Sera didn't even look at me. She simply said, "Access the portal."

Hugh's jaw tightened. "Our IT provider is not available due to the storm," he said. "The system requires—"

"It requires a password and someone willing to type it," Sera cut in. "Don't mistake my patience for permission."

Hugh's nostrils flared slightly. It was the closest he came to showing anger.

He reached for the laptop and rotated it towards us with a controlled movement, as if he were doing us a favour.

"Fine," he said. "But I want it on record that I object to guest data being handled without proper—"

Sera lifted a hand. "I am recording it," she said. "You object. Noted. Now log in."

Hugh's fingers moved over the keyboard. He typed quickly, practised. The portal's login page was slick and branded with a heart motif that made my skin crawl. A little lock icon sat in the corner, as if that meant anything when the people using it couldn't be trusted.

A dashboard loaded with a list of events, vendors, and files. In the corner of the screen was the account name: VendorAdmin.

Not Hugh Mercer. Not H. Mercer. Not even MarinerCrownGM.

VendorAdmin.

I felt something cold settle in my stomach.

Sera saw it too. Her eyes flicked to Hugh.

"VendorAdmin," she said.

Hugh's smile remained. "It's a shared administrative account," he said smoothly. "Standard practice. It allows our team to manage uploads and correct errors quickly. It's efficient."

"Efficient," I repeated. "Like poisoning."

Hugh's smile faltered. "That's a vile comparison."

"It's accurate," I said.

Sera leaned forward. "Show me the guest list file," she said. "The original upload and every edit."

Hugh clicked through folders, his movements careful. I watched his hands more than the screen. Hands told the truth before faces did. Hugh's hands were steady, but they were slightly too controlled, like a man performing calm.

He opened a file list labelled Second-Chance Romance Weekend. Under that, a subfolder: Guest List and Dietary Notes.

There were multiple files.

Not one final, approved document. Not one version.

Multiple.

I felt my jaw tighten.

Sera pointed. "Which is the one Harriet approved."

Hugh glanced at me as if he expected me to lie for him. It was almost insulting.

"I approved a PDF sent via the portal at 18:42 yesterday," I said, because I had the time. I always had the time. "I saved it, printed it, and recorded the file name. It was labelled GuestList_Final_Approved_HC.pdf."

Hugh clicked.

There it was, in the list. Uploaded at 18:39. Owner: Harriet Crowe.

Sera's eyes flicked to me. "That's your upload."

"Yes," I said. "And my approval sits on my end in ink, not in your portal's feelings."

Sera clicked the file's audit trail. The portal opened a side panel with metadata. Rows of text appeared: upload time, last modified, modified by.

Modified by: VendorAdmin.

Time: 22:57.

Modified by: VendorAdmin.

Time: 23:14.

Modified by: VendorAdmin.

Time: 00:06.

Modified by: VendorAdmin.

Time: 05:21.

My stomach clenched.

I wrote without looking down.

07:?? No, correct yourself. Keep clean. Read.

I leaned closer, squinting at the screen.

The times were precise. The system showed seconds.

22:57:18. 23:14:03. 00:06:51. 05:21:09.

Sera's voice was quiet. "Four modifications," she said. "After Harriet's approval. Overnight."

Hugh's smile tightened again. "Minor corrections," he said. "People change dietary preferences, partners split up, names are misspelled. It happens."

Sera looked at him. "A man died," she said. "And now someone has attempted to poison a guest at breakfast. Stop selling me 'minor corrections'."

Hugh's jaw flexed. "Detective Inspector," he said, "we host hundreds of events. The portal exists because vendors email files in messy formats. We need a central system. A shared admin account is normal."

I felt my pen pause. I looked at him.

"Normal," I said. "Then name the humans who use it."

Hugh spread his hands, wounded. "It's staff," he said. "Events. Front desk. The operations team."

"Names," Sera said.

Hugh's eyes flicked away. "Melissa Shaw has access," he said, reluctantly. "And Martin Goss, our sponsor liaison. Possibly the night manager. It depends."

"Depends on what," I asked. "Who is awake and willing to commit fraud."

Hugh's gaze snapped to me, sharp now. "Harriet, I will not be spoken to like that in my office."

I smiled at him. It was not kind. "Then stop giving me reasons," I said.

Sera cut in. "Export the audit log," she said. "Now."

Hugh blinked. "Export."

"Yes," Sera said. "I want a full export. Not a screen view. An actual file. And I want the portal's access log for the VendorAdmin account. IP addresses. Device identifiers. Anything it stores."

Hugh's expression shifted. "That's not—"

Sera leaned back in her chair, eyes steady. "Try me," she said.

Hugh hesitated, then clicked. A menu opened with options. He selected Export Audit. A download icon appeared, then a prompt.

The export generated as a CSV file.

I could have laughed. A death and an attempted poisoning and the truth reduced to commas.

Sera clicked it open.

Rows of data filled the screen. Each entry showed action type, file name, timestamp, user.

Action: Edit. User: VendorAdmin.

Action: Upload new version. User: VendorAdmin.

Action: Replace file. User: VendorAdmin.

Hugh cleared his throat. "You can see it's just system handling," he said, trying again. "The portal tracks everything. It's transparent."

"It's transparent about the fact someone edited the guest list after I signed off," I said. "That's not the defence you think it is."

Sera scrolled. "Show me the changed versions," she said.

Hugh clicked into version history. Several versions appeared, labelled by the portal with incremental numbers.

Version 1: Harriet upload.

Version 2: VendorAdmin.

Version 3: VendorAdmin.

Version 4: VendorAdmin.

Version 5: VendorAdmin.

Sera selected Version 1 and opened it. A PDF appeared with the guest list, dietary notes, seating tags, and the same faint footer mark that had been bothering me since the file first landed in my inbox.

Even on screen, I could see it. A ghost of a stamp impression in the footer area, like someone had tried to hide a signature by making it almost invisible.

I felt my skin prickle.

Sera looked at me. "That's the mark you mentioned."

"Yes," I said. "It shouldn't exist."

Hugh sighed, as if we were discussing a stain on a tablecloth. "It could be a template artefact," he said. "Some old file reused. These things happen."

"Not in a hotel that sells itself on perfection," I replied. "You don't reuse old templates by accident. You reuse them because it's convenient, or because it gives you something you want."

Hugh's eyes narrowed. "And what would we want."

"A seal," I said, and watched his face.

His control held. Too well. "A seal," he repeated, bland.

Sera's gaze sharpened at the exchange. She didn't ask me to elaborate yet. She kept on task, because that was her strength. She did not chase every thread at once. She chose the one that tightened the net.

She opened Version 2.

The mark in the footer was gone.

Not faded. Not masked.

Gone, as if someone had deliberately removed it.

My throat tightened.

Sera scrolled. "Changes," she said.

The guest list looked similar at a glance. That was the trick. Keep it close enough that no one noticed. Make the real changes small, buried in details people assumed were boring.

Sera zoomed in on the dietary notes.

I leaned in. "That line wasn't there," I said, pointing at an entry beside Penny's name.

"Seat preference: Table 6, Seat 1, Window."

My blood went cold.

"That wasn't on my version," I said, and wrote immediately.

08:19. Version 2 adds "Seat preference: Table 6 Seat 1 Window" on Penny Harrow entry.

Sera's face didn't change much, but her eyes narrowed. "Seat preference," she said. "That's interesting."

"It's convenient," I said. "It's a way to steer service by seat rather than person."

Hugh's voice came in, smooth. "Guests request certain tables," he said. "It's hospitality."

"It's targeting," Sera said.

Hugh's jaw tightened. "Detective Inspector, you are interpreting harmless notes as malicious intent."

Sera clicked to Version 3.

More edits.

A guest with a similar name had been swapped. Two entries were now identical in formatting, down to the same punctuation.

"Copied and pasted," I murmured. "Again."

Sera's gaze flicked to me. "You noticed that in Chapter Three," she said, and I noticed she remembered details. It mattered. It meant she was actually listening, not just collecting.

"Yes," I said. "Some entries look like they were lifted from a different template."

Hugh's fingers tapped the desk once. The sound was small, but it was the first uncontrolled gesture he'd made. Irritation. Not fear.

Sera opened Version 4.

Another seat note appeared, this time under a different name, one of the influencer couple.

"Table 6, Seat 2," Sera read aloud.

My pen scratched.

08:22. Version 4 adds seat mapping notes for influencer couple. Table 6 Seat 2.

Sera's eyes lifted to Hugh. "Why are you adding seat assignments to a guest list?"

Hugh's tone was tight. "It helps staff serve efficiently," he said. "We had... confusion during set-up yesterday. People move seats. It's easier if we track their preferences."

My mouth went dry.

"It's easier," I repeated. "So you can serve a dessert by seat."

Hugh's eyes flicked. "Harriet, you're making accusations."

"Yes," I said. "Because the evidence is sitting on your screen."

Sera scrolled further down the audit log. "Who accessed VendorAdmin overnight," she said, and tapped a link labelled Access Log.

A new panel opened. More rows. This time: login time, user, IP address, device.

VendorAdmin login at 22:53:11.

VendorAdmin login at 23:11:02.

VendorAdmin login at 00:04:20.

VendorAdmin login at 05:19:58.

Each one showed the same internal IP range.

"Hugh," Sera said, voice very calm, "these logins came from inside your network."

Hugh's smile returned, strained. "Of course they did," he said. "Our staff use the portal from the hotel."

"And not from their homes," Sera said. "Not from the Trust's office. Not from a mobile network. From here."

Hugh's jaw flexed. "We have staff on-site," he said. "That's normal."

I leaned back slightly in my chair, pen still poised. I watched him.

Normal was his favourite word. Normal was a rug he tried to pull over everything messy.

Sera clicked one of the access entries. It expanded.

Device: FrontDesk-PC03.

My eyes narrowed.

"Front desk," I said.

Hugh's face stayed composed. "Our front desk team manages guest changes," he said. "If someone's name is misspelled or a dietary note is missing, they correct it. The system is designed for—"

Sera cut him off. "FrontDesk-PC03 was used at 05:19," she said. "Who was on the front desk at 05:19."

Hugh hesitated, then said, "Night shift. It could have been—"

"It could have been Melissa," I said, because that was what he didn't want to say.

Hugh's gaze snapped to me. "You do not know our rota."

"No," I said. "But I know who you put in the line of fire this morning."

Sera's tone was sharper now. "Hugh," she said, "I want the staff rota for last night and this morning. Names. Times. Positions.

And I want it printed."

Hugh opened his mouth. Closed it. Opened it again. "We have privacy policies."

Sera's eyes held his. "I have an investigation. Print it."

Hugh's hand went to the printer, then stopped. He looked at the device as if it might betray him. Then he clicked on his computer and a rota document appeared.

I watched the screen as he scrolled.

Night shift: Melissa Shaw on events. Front desk staffed by Kieran Holt until 06:00. A relief staff member listed as "Temp".

Temp.

No surname.

No agency.

Just Temp.

My pen hovered. That made my skin crawl.

Sera pointed. "Who is Temp."

Hugh's face tightened. "We brought in temporary help because of the weekend," he said. "It's normal."

There it was again.

Normal.

Sera's gaze was cold. "Name," she said.

Hugh's jaw clenched. "I don't have it to hand," he said.

I let out a small laugh. It came out sharper than I intended. "You don't have the name of someone you put on the front desk," I said. "In a storm. During a death. That's either a lie or negligence."

Hugh's eyes flashed. "Harriet, watch yourself."

"No," I said. "You watch your system."

Sera leaned forward. "Print the rota," she said. "Now."

Hugh clicked Print. The printer whirred. Paper slid out, warm and smelling faintly of toner. I watched the sheet emerge as if it were a living thing.

Sera didn't touch it with bare hands. The constable who'd been standing quietly by the door stepped forward, gloved, and lifted it into an evidence bag.

Hugh's gaze lingered on the bag. Something like offence crossed his face. Not fear. Offence that his office had been turned into a scene.

Sera turned back to the laptop. "Version 5," she said.

Hugh clicked, reluctant.

Version 5 was timestamped 05:21.

Five twenty-one.

Two minutes after the VendorAdmin login from FrontDesk-PC03.

I felt my stomach tighten.

Sera opened it and scanned down to Penny's entry again.

A new line had been added.

"Special handling: apology service requested."

My hand tightened around my pen.

"That's breakfast," I said.

Sera's eyes stayed on the screen. "Yes," she said.

Hugh's voice cut in. "That could be a staff note," he said, too quickly. "Someone wanted to make sure a guest felt cared for after last night. This is exactly what I mean. You're taking hospitality notes and—"

Sera lifted her gaze to him. "This isn't hospitality," she said. "This is coordination."

Hugh's smile cracked for a second. "You're determined to see malice," he said. "You've had a long night. Everyone's on edge. It was a tragedy. There's no need to turn the hotel into—"

"A crime scene," I finished for him. "It's a bit late."

Hugh's eyes narrowed. "Harriet," he said, voice low, "you're not police."

"No," I said. "I'm worse. I'm organised."

Sera's mouth twitched, then she smoothed it away. "Harriet," she said, "read me the times."

I looked at the audit log again and spoke clearly.

"Initial upload by me at 18:39," I said. "Approved by me at 18:42. First VendorAdmin modification at 22:57. Second at 23:14. Third at 00:06. Fourth at 05:21. VendorAdmin logins from FrontDesk-PC03 at 05:19. Two minutes before the final edit."

I wrote the same into my Pocket Log as I spoke, because speaking was not enough.

08:33. Portal audit shows post-approval edits at 22:57, 23:14, 00:06, 05:21. VendorAdmin login 05:19 via FrontDesk-PC03. Version 5 adds "special handling: apology service requested" under Penny Harrow.

Sera nodded once. "Good," she said. She clicked another tab labelled Download History.

There was a list of who had downloaded the guest list file and when.

VendorAdmin downloaded Version 1 at 22:55.

VendorAdmin downloaded Version 2 at 23:12.

VendorAdmin downloaded Version 5 at 05:22.

"Printed," I murmured.

Hugh's eyes flicked. "Downloaded doesn't mean printed," he said quickly.

Sera's voice stayed even. "Then show me the print queue," she said.

Hugh stiffened. "The print queue is—"

"In your office," Sera said, glancing to the printer. "And it's going to be very interesting."

Hugh's expression shifted into a forced patience that looked like strain. "Detective Inspector," he said, "with respect, you cannot treat every administrative system as suspect. It's a hotel. We run on procedures."

"And procedures are exactly what someone used," Sera replied.

She stood and walked to the printer. The constable followed. Hugh half rose as if to block them, then thought better of it. Blocking police looked bad. Hugh Mercer did not do things that looked bad.

Sera checked the printer's screen. A job history menu. She navigated with quick, practised taps.

"Recent jobs," she said.

The printer listed file names and times. Not everything, but enough.

GuestList_Final_Approved_HC.pdf printed at 22:56.

GuestList_Final_Approved_HC.pdf printed at 23:13.

GuestList_Final_Approved_HC.pdf printed at 05:23.

The printer didn't show which version had been printed, only the name. The portal, however, did.

Someone had been printing the guest list repeatedly overnight.

I felt cold.

"Hugh," Sera said, eyes on the screen, "who printed the guest list at 05:23."

Hugh's voice went tight. "It could be—"

"The front desk," I said. "Or anyone with that admin account. That's the point."

Sera looked back at him. "Your 'normal' workflow," she said, "created a perfect cover."

Hugh's jaw clenched. "We cannot function with individual logins for every small edit," he said. "It slows everything down. It's not practical."

"It's also how you avoid accountability," I said.

Hugh's eyes flashed. "You're enjoying this," he snapped, and the control slipped just enough to show the man underneath.

"You're enjoying being at the centre of it. You and your little notebook."

There it was. The attack. Not on evidence, but on character.

My hands went still. My voice stayed calm.

"I'm enjoying staying alive," I said. "And keeping other people alive. That's all."

Sera's gaze sharpened. "Careful," she warned Hugh, and the word landed like a blade wrapped in paper. "Harriet is here because your portal put her work into this mess."

Hugh's face smoothed again. He straightened his tie as if that fixed anything.

"I apologise," he said, tone polished. "Stress makes us all speak badly."

I stared at him. "Stress shows what you practise," I said.

Sera returned to the desk and sat again. "Now," she said, "we're going to identify who used VendorAdmin."

Hugh exhaled. "You can't," he said. "That's the whole point. It's shared."

Sera clicked into a deeper log view. "Shared account doesn't mean invisible," she said. "Not if your system records device, location, and session tokens. Which it does."

She scrolled.

Each VendorAdmin session listed a device. The evening edits were from EventsOffice-PC01.

The midnight edit was from EventsOffice-PC01 again.

The dawn edit, the one that added apology service, was from FrontDesk-PC03.

Sera pointed at the screen. "Events office," she said. "Who was in the events office at 22:57."

Hugh hesitated, then said, "Melissa. Martin. Possibly Lorna Beckett, the event coordinator. Imogen could have been in meetings earlier. The Trust—"

"The Trust had no reason to be in your events office late at night," Sera said.

Hugh's eyes tightened. "The Trust is our sponsor," he said. "They have access."

"Exactly," I said.

Sera's gaze flicked to me, then back to Hugh. "Who else has keys to the events office," she asked.

Hugh's smile returned, strained. "It's not locked during event weekends," he said.

My pen scratched again.

08:48. Hugh claims events office not locked during event weekends. Sponsor access possible.

Sera leaned forward. "So anyone could walk in," she said. "Use the shared admin account. Edit a file. Print it. And walk out."

Hugh's voice went defensive. "We are not a fortress," he said. "We are a hotel."

"You're a controlled environment with cameras, staff rosters, and a system designed to make responsibility slippery," I said. "That's better than a fortress if your goal is to hide in plain sight."

Hugh's eyes narrowed. "You speak as if you know our operations."

"I used to coordinate weddings for a living," I replied. "I know exactly how you operate. Everyone smiles and nothing is accidental unless it benefits someone."

Sera clicked on a session entry. Another detail expanded.

Session duration: 12 minutes.

Edits made: 6.

Fields changed: seat preference tags, dietary notes, special handling.

This wasn't a quick typo correction. This was deliberate.

Sera's voice was quiet. "These are targeted edits," she said. "Not generic corrections."

Hugh swallowed. I saw his throat move. It was the first sign of real discomfort.

He tried again. "You're assuming intent," he said. "Someone could have been trying to help staff during a chaotic—"

"No," I cut in. "Chaos looks messy. This is tidy. This is someone who knows how to make a file look normal while changing its function."

Sera nodded once. "Exactly."

She looked at Hugh. "Your portal was used to convert a guest list into a targeting tool," she said. "And the edits were attributed to a generic account. Which means you either permitted a system designed to hide hands, or you benefited from it."

Hugh's eyes went hard. "That's an outrageous allegation," he said, voice clipped.

Sera didn't blink. "Then prove me wrong," she said. "Give me the list of everyone with VendorAdmin credentials. Password change history. MFA settings. Anything."

Hugh's fingers flexed on the edge of the desk. "I don't have that," he said. "It's managed by our provider."

"And yet you logged in without calling them," Sera said. "Which means you have control."

Hugh's smile twitched. "I have access," he corrected.

"You have control," Sera repeated, and the word had weight.

Hugh's phone buzzed on the desk. He glanced down, reflexive.

Sera's gaze snapped. "Don't," she said.

Hugh's hand hovered, then pulled back slowly. He held his palms out, as if surrendering. He did it theatrically, too. A man used to being watched.

I wrote.

08:57. Hugh phone buzz. Sera warns him not to answer. He

complies, performs innocence.

Sera's eyes returned to the screen. She clicked to another area.

File permissions.

The guest list folder had permissions set so VendorAdmin could edit and replace files. Individual vendors, like me, could upload but could not see other vendors' files. The hotel admin could see everything.

Convenient. Central. Powerful.

Sera pointed. "Harriet," she said, "could you have made these edits after your approval."

"No," I said. "I don't have that permission. I can upload. I cannot replace or edit once it's locked."

Hugh's voice was smooth again. "It's for quality control."

"It's for control," I corrected.

Sera clicked to view activity on the vendor instruction sheet folder as well, the one she'd already seized evidence from in Chapter Twelve. The portal showed a file labelled VendorInstructions_ServiceFlow.pdf.

Modified by VendorAdmin at 00:09.

Downloaded by VendorAdmin at 00:10.

I felt the cold settle deeper.

"Midnight," I said.

Hugh's jaw clenched. "We print instructions," he said. "Staff need them. It's normal."

Sera's eyes lifted. "Stop saying normal," she said. "Normal doesn't kill people."

Silence spread across the office. Even the printer seemed to hum less, as if it didn't want to be involved.

I stared at the model sailboat on the shelf. It looked like something from a showroom, not a thing that had ever weathered a storm. Hugh Mercer in miniature.

Sera closed the laptop slightly, not shutting it, just enough to signal a shift.

"We have enough," she said.

Hugh's eyes narrowed. "Enough for what."

"Enough to show that your system was used after Harriet's approval to alter the guest list, and that the edits were performed under a generic admin account from specific hotel devices," Sera said. "Enough to show that someone used those edits to coordinate seat-based service. Enough to show the pattern repeats."

Hugh's smile returned, tight. "Patterns can be coincidences," he said.

I looked at him. "Coincidences don't log in at five in the morning," I said.

Sera stood. The constable mirrored her movement, ready.

"Hugh Mercer," Sera said, "you are not to touch that portal again. You are not to instruct staff to delete anything. You are not to contact your sponsor representative about what we've found. If you do, I will treat it as interference."

Hugh's eyes flicked to the door, to the hall beyond, to the storm pressing against the world outside. For the first time, he looked less like a man managing optics and more like a man realising the optics might not save him.

"I have to run a hotel," he said, voice clipped.

"And I have to stop someone from using your hotel like a weapon," Sera replied.

She nodded at me. "Harriet," she said.

I stood, Pocket Log in hand.

"Keep your notes," she added. "And if anyone asks what we found, your only answer is: speak to DI Linley."

Hugh's eyes cut to me. "You're going to tell the whole breakfast room," he said, sharp.

"No," I said. "I'm going to tell the truth to the right people at the right time. You wouldn't understand the difference."

Sera opened the office door. The corridor air felt damp and cooler, like the building's insides had breathed out.

As we stepped out, I caught sight of Imogen Baird at the far end of the corridor, walking with purpose in our direction. She slowed when she saw us, smile ready.

Sera's gaze fixed on her. "Not now," Sera said, loud enough that the corridor heard it.

Imogen's smile held. "Detective Inspector," she said, smooth. "I simply want to ensure the Trust can assist in any way."

Sera's voice stayed flat. "You can assist by staying away from my witnesses."

Imogen's eyes flicked to me, then away again. "Of course," she said, and it sounded like a promise rather than agreement.

I felt my skin prickle. I didn't like being looked at like an object someone had plans for.

Sera guided me back towards the breakfast room corridor, not rushing, but purposeful.

"You saw his face," I said quietly.

"Yes," Sera replied.

"He wasn't shocked," I said.

"No," Sera said. "He was offended."

"That's worse," I said.

Sera's mouth tightened. "It's useful," she replied. "Offended people make mistakes."

We reached the breakfast room doors again. The murmur inside had risen. News always travelled faster than weather.

Before I stepped back into that room full of knives disguised as jam jars, I looked down at my Pocket Log and wrote one more line, because it mattered.

09:11. Portal proves post-approval edits by VendorAdmin from hotel devices. Seat mapping notes added. Apology handling added. Hugh calls it normal. I do not believe him.

I capped my pen, slipped the notebook back into my coat pocket, and walked into breakfast with my head up, because if someone wanted to write a story over my life, they were going to have to fight me for the ending.

CHAPTER 16

Reveal mechanics

T he ballroom looked as if it had tried to forget what happened in it.

That was the trouble with hotels. They cleaned pain the same way they cleaned spills. Quietly, efficiently, with the sort of practised briskness that suggested they had done it before. The chairs were already being stacked in neat towers, linen tugged straight, cutlery collected into trays. A faint smell of coffee lingered under the polish and detergent, as if the building had decided breakfast should be the dominant mood, no matter what.

Outside the tall windows the storm kept on, rain sliding in relentless sheets across the glass. The view of the sea was reduced to grey movement and occasional white foam. You couldn't tell where sky ended and water began. It was the sort of weather that made a person feel small, which was probably why so many of the guests kept talking loudly. People hated feeling small.

Sera led the way across the empty floor, her shoes quiet on the wood. She moved like she belonged in any room she entered, which was the opposite of how I felt in most rooms lately.

"Ballroom reset area," she said, as if she were reading out a location for a report.

"It's not exactly glamorous," I replied, because the room now looked like the aftermath of a charity raffle rather than a romance weekend.

"It's private," she said. "And it has space. We need space."

"We," I repeated, adjusting my glasses on their chain.

Sera didn't respond. She didn't have to. She simply turned towards the side section near the stage where two trestle tables had been pushed together. A stack of folded chair covers sat nearby, and someone had lined up votive candle holders as if they were embarrassed by their own mess.

A young staff member in a black waistcoat paused mid-fold at the sight of us and looked like she'd like to be anywhere else, including in the sea.

Sera showed her badge without softening her expression.

"We need this area," Sera said. "Now. You can continue on the other side."

The staff member nodded quickly, grateful for clear instructions, and scuttled away with a bundle of linen clutched to her chest like armour.

Sera pointed at the tables. "Set up," she said to me.

I raised an eyebrow. "I'm not your assistant."

"No," she agreed. "You're the person with the evidence and the brain. Use them."

That was Sera. No flattery, no cuddling. Just a blunt instruction. Oddly comforting.

I placed my tote on the table and opened it carefully, as if I were unpacking something delicate. In a way, I was. Paper was always delicate. Not because it tore easily, but because it carried consequences.

I laid my labelled envelopes out in a neat line, each one marked in my handwriting. Place Cards, Seating Plan Drafts, Vendor Instructions, Pocket Log Photographs, Portal Notes. I added the evidence envelope I'd given Penny, unused, and felt a small surge of gratitude that it remained unused.

Sera watched with that stillness she had when she was letting someone else do what they did best.

"You've done this before," she said.

"Not murder," I replied.

"You've done the reconstruction," she clarified.

I looked at the ballroom floor, the stage, the spot near the staff corridor where people moved in and out. "Weddings," I said. "Same ingredients. Different ending."

Sera's mouth twitched. "All right," she said. "Walk me through it. Cleanly."

I uncapped my fountain pen, checked the nib, and felt my shoulders settle. When my hands had something to do, my mind behaved better.

"First," I said, tapping the envelope marked Vendor Instructions, "we have the instruction sheet."

Sera nodded once. "The forged one."

"The forged one," I agreed. "Not mine. Not the hotel's official template. Something made to look like both."

I slid the envelope open and drew out a copy I'd printed from my phone photograph, then another, the seized sheet Sera had bagged and photographed last night. We weren't handling the original without gloves, and I wasn't about to let Hugh Mercer later claim I'd smeared jam on his precious evidence.

Sera passed me a pair of gloves. I pulled them on.

I held both sheets side by side.

"On first glance," I said, "they look the same. That's the point. It's meant to pass at a distance, when staff are moving too quickly to question it."

Sera leaned in. Her bun was severe. Her eyes were tired. Her focus was sharp.

I pointed at the top line. "Look at the font," I said. "Near-match.

It mimics the hotel's script. But the letter spacing is off. The kerning."

Sera's gaze narrowed. "The gaps."

"Yes," I said. "The 'S' in Service sits too far from the next letter. The 'o' in 'position' is tighter. These are small tells, but they matter. They matter because whoever made this didn't have the original file. They were copying."

Sera looked up. "And the paper."

I lifted the forged sheet slightly and let the light catch it. "Brighter," I said. "Smoother. Different stock. The hotel's standard office paper is slightly warmer, not this sharp white. And the cut edge here," I ran a gloved finger along it, "is slightly uneven. Not guillotine clean. Trimmed in a hurry, or on a different machine."

Sera nodded. "This was produced outside the normal print run."

"Exactly," I said. "Which means someone had reason to produce instructions the hotel staff would follow, without asking questions."

Sera's gaze sharpened. "And the instructions were seat-based."

I flipped the sheet over and tapped the middle section. "Here," I said. "Service by seat position, not by name. 'Table six, seat one.' 'Table three, seat four.' That language. It's not normal hospitality. It's workflow. It turns staff into delivery mechanisms."

Sera's eyes stayed on the paper. "And someone then made sure the targeted person was in that seat."

I exhaled. "Or, rather, they made sure the targeted seat was occupied by the person they wanted."

Sera looked at me. "Difference."

"It matters," I said. "Because if you target a person, you need to keep track of them. You need to follow them, approach them, risk being seen. If you target a seat, you let the room do the work for you. You let the seating plan, the place cards, the staff routines deliver the danger."

Sera's jaw tightened. "And last night the wrong person ended up in the targeted seat."

"Yes," I said, and even now the word sat badly in my mouth. Wrong person. As if any death could be reduced to misaddressed post.

Sera didn't push me to say his name yet. She didn't have to. The room carried it.

I set the instruction sheets down and reached for the next envelope.

"Second," I said, "the place cards."

Sera's gaze flicked to the stack. "Your dot pattern."

"My dot pattern," I confirmed.

I pulled out one of my place cards from my own controlled run. Cream card stock, clean cut, printed in my shop, and near the corner, barely visible unless you knew to look, a tiny printer registration dot pattern. Not a deliberate mark, not a flourish, just the fingerprint of my machine.

I held it out to Sera.

She took it carefully. "Tiny," she said.

"Consistent," I replied. "That's the important part. Every card from my run has it in the same placement. If a card appears without it, it didn't come from my printer."

Sera set my card down and gestured. "The replacement."

I pulled the replacement place card from the envelope, the one I'd found on the table last night that lacked my dot pattern. It looked fine at a glance. Good font. Good ink density. But it was too clean. Too perfect. It didn't have the small tell my machine left behind.

"Here," I said, laying it beside mine.

Sera leaned in and looked closely. "No dot."

"No dot," I said. "Which means it was printed elsewhere. Either a different printer, or a different machine with different registration behaviour."

Sera's eyes sharpened. "In this building."

"Almost certainly," I said. "And whoever printed it wanted it to blend. They chose a similar card stock. Similar font. Not exact. Close enough that people who don't spend their lives staring at paper wouldn't notice."

Sera tapped the replacement card. "And this would be used to steer someone into a specific seat."

"Yes," I said. "If you replace a card, you can shift a person's placement without anyone noticing. You can also create confusion. And confusion is where you hide."

Sera's gaze lifted. "Show me the seating plan."

I opened the envelope marked Seating Plan Drafts and slid out my printed plan, the one I'd made for the banquet. Tables labelled. Seats numbered. Names placed. It was clean, logical, and had the feel of something designed to prevent disasters, which was exactly what it was.

I laid it flat and smoothed it with a gloved hand.

Sera stood, leaning over it, eyes scanning.

"Table six," she said.

"Yes," I replied. "Table six was close enough to the stage for Vale's theatrics and far enough from the kitchen door to look exclusive. Hugh likes a room to be easily filmed but not obviously staged."

Sera's mouth tightened. "He likes control."

"He likes applause," I corrected. "Control is just how he gets it."

Sera pointed. "Penny was assigned where."

"Table six, seat one," I said, and felt a small chill. "That was her listed preference after the portal edits. On my original plan, she was table six, seat three. She moved. The plan moved. That matters."

Sera glanced up. "Portal edits again."

"Yes," I said. "Which brings us to the third piece."

I slid my Pocket Log nearer. I didn't hand it over. I never handed my Pocket Log over. It wasn't a trust issue. It was a survival habit.

"I have the portal log times," I said. "And I have my timeline."

Sera gestured. "Read it."

I flipped to the relevant page, my handwriting tight and neat. Time made a person honest. Ink made them accountable.

"Chapter Six," I said, and then stopped myself because Sera didn't think in chapters, she thought in events. "Welcome mixer," I corrected. "At 18:56, staff member approached me with a request. Three place cards. 'VIP preferences.'"

Sera's eyes flicked. "And you refused."

"I refused until I received written approval from my named contact," I said. "Because if I reprint on demand, I lose chain of handling. And because I am not a vending machine."

Sera nodded. "Who asked."

I flipped to the note. "A staff member in a waistcoat. Name tag said 'Ryan'."

Sera made a quick note of her own. "And then."

"At 19:12," I continued, "I saw two handwritten initials added to the seating chart on the staff wall. Different pen. Not the hotel's usual marker. It looked like someone was trying to make changes appear casual. I wrote it down. I also wrote down the exact phrase Ryan used when he asked me to reprint."

Sera looked up sharply. "The phrase matters."

"It always does," I said. "He said, 'It's just easier if we do it by seat, love.'"

Sera held my gaze. "By seat."

"Yes," I said. "Not by name. By seat. That language shows up again and again. It's the thread."

Sera's expression didn't change much, but I could see the anger behind it. Anger at someone using routine to harm.

"So," she said, "the window opens there. You refuse to reprint. Someone else prints replacements."

"Yes," I said. "And because it's a hotel and not a courtroom, people assume the person holding paper is authorised."

Sera's gaze dropped back to the seating plan. "Now explain the swap."

I exhaled slowly. The swap was the part that still sat oddly in my stomach, because it was so simple. Simple was what made it frightening. A small choice in a room full of people, and suddenly someone else was in the wrong place at the wrong minute.

"During the banquet," I said, "Penny Harrow swapped seats with another guest. It was quiet. Fast. She did it after a tense exchange. No raised voices. No obvious drama. But it moved her away from her assigned position."

Sera nodded. "And the staff served dessert according to seat position."

"Yes," I said. "Because the forged instruction sheet told them to."

Sera's gaze sharpened. "So if Penny moved, the dessert still went to the seat, not to Penny."

"Exactly," I said. "The mechanism didn't care who sat there. It cared only that someone sat there."

Sera leaned in, tapping the plan. "Which seat was targeted."

I looked down, then pointed. "Table six, seat one. The seat that the forged instructions flagged. The seat that later had the apology dessert attempt at breakfast."

Sera's jaw tightened. "So Table six, seat one is the kill seat."

I didn't like the phrase, but I didn't correct her. "Yes," I said. "And at the banquet, because of the swap, Vale ended up in that seat at dessert time."

Sera's eyes narrowed. "Vale moved."

"Yes," I said. "He was not meant to. Not originally. But there was a gap in the plan. A person moved a chair. A card was replaced. A staff member followed the printed workflow rather than their own eyes. And Vale paid for it."

Sera's expression shifted slightly then, something hard and tired. "And the person who planned it," she said, "didn't have to touch him. Didn't have to be seen near him. They only had to make sure the paper told everyone else what to do."

I nodded once. "That's why it's so effective," I said. "And why it's so clean. It looks like a tragedy. A medical incident. A terrible coincidence."

Sera's eyes stayed on me. "You're saying it wasn't."

"No," I replied. "I'm saying it was engineered to look like it was."

Sera leaned back. "All right," she said. "Now we bring them in."

I felt my pulse jump. "Them."

"Yes," Sera said. "The people who keep insisting this is normal. The ones with access. The ones with reasons to keep the Trust happy and the weekend smooth. They are going to listen to you explain this. And then they are going to answer questions."

I looked down at my paper evidence spread out on the table, suddenly aware of how ridiculous it could look to an outsider. A woman with envelopes and printer dots, standing in a ballroom, accusing a hotel of weaponising romance stationery.

Then I remembered the apology dessert card with its neat instruction to deliver danger to a seat.

Ridiculous didn't matter. True did.

Sera stepped to the side door and signalled to the constable outside. Low voices. A brief exchange. Then footsteps in the corridor.

I didn't have long to collect myself, so I did what I always did. I straightened the evidence. I aligned the envelopes. I smoothed the seating plan. I made the table orderly because the world wasn't.

The first to arrive was Dean Lomas, the kitchen supervisor. He looked as if he'd been awake for three days and had argued with everyone in the building. His hands were rough, his shoulders tense. He smelled faintly of coffee and onions, which wasn't his fault. Kitchens never let you leave without taking something with you.

Behind him came Lorna Beckett, the event coordinator. Her hair was immaculate, her eyeliner perfect, even now. It should have annoyed me. It did, a bit. Lorna wore competence like jewellery. She stood too straight. She smiled too quickly.

Then Imogen Baird appeared, coat still perfect, folder under her arm as if she'd brought it from her own office to remind us all that she had one. Her expression said she considered the ballroom beneath her, and she would have hated herself for that pun if she noticed it.

Last came Hugh Mercer, jaw set, smile on standby. He looked as if he'd already rehearsed what he would say to a reporter. That made my skin crawl.

Sera stood at the head of the table. I stood beside the evidence like a museum curator who'd discovered the artefacts were still trying to kill people.

"Thank you for coming," Sera said, voice calm.

Hugh's smile flared. "Detective Inspector," he began. "This is highly irregular. Guests are unsettled. Staff are frightened. We should be focusing on reassurance."

Sera looked at him. "We are focusing on prevention," she said. "Sit down."

Hugh's smile tightened, but he sat.

Imogen sat too, slower, controlled. Lorna perched on the edge of a chair, folder on her lap, ready to take notes, which was either habit or theatre. Dean remained standing until Sera's gaze pinned him.

"Sit," Sera repeated, and Dean dropped into a chair as if it might bite.

Sera looked at me. "Harriet," she said. "Explain the mechanics."

Hugh made a small sound, like he'd been forced to swallow something unpleasant.

I ignored him and began, because if I paused now I'd start thinking about how many people were watching, and then I'd start caring about their opinions, and that was a slippery slope straight into silence.

"The dessert last night," I said, "was served according to seat number, not person."

Lorna blinked. "That's not true," she said automatically. "Service follows the place cards."

"Yes," I agreed. "Which are tied to seats."

Hugh opened his mouth. I lifted my hand slightly.

"No," I said. "Let me finish. Then you can perform."

Hugh's eyes flashed. Sera didn't stop me. That was also telling.

I picked up the forged instruction sheet and held it up. "This," I said, "is a vendor instruction sheet printed overnight."

Dean frowned. "That's not ours."

"No," I said. "It's a forgery."

Imogen's eyes narrowed. "That is an accusation."

"It's also accurate," I replied. "Look at the paper stock. Too bright. Look at the font. Near-match. Wrong kerning. And the instructions themselves."

I placed the sheet on the table and tapped the relevant section. "It instructs staff to deliver specific items by table and seat. Table six, seat one. Table six, seat two. It does not say, 'deliver to Dr Vale.' It does not say, 'deliver to Penny Harrow.' It says seat."

Lorna leaned forward, eyes scanning. Her face was composed, but I noticed a faint tension at her jaw.

Hugh scoffed softly. "This is internal wording," he said. "Harriet is making it sound sinister."

I turned to him. "You've said 'internal' and 'normal' so often you might as well have it embroidered on your cuff," I said. "This is not normal. It's engineered."

Dean stared at the sheet, brow furrowed. "We don't write like that," he said, almost to himself. "Kitchen doesn't."

"No," I said. "Because whoever wrote it wasn't writing for the kitchen. They were writing for the staff who follow paper without questioning it."

Imogen's voice was smooth. "Harriet, you're implying someone intended harm through a dessert," she said. "That is an extraordinary claim."

I looked at her. "You saw the apology tray at breakfast," I said. "You watched a seat-targeted dessert almost reach Penny."

Imogen's smile flickered. "That was a kindness," she said, and her eyes said she was already regretting that line because it sounded foolish even to her.

"It came with a seat directive," I said. "Kindness doesn't need a route map."

Sera cut in, voice calm. "Harriet," she said. "Continue."

I nodded. "Now," I said, "place cards."

I took one of my original place cards and slid it across the table. "This is from my controlled print run," I said. "It has a tiny printer registration dot pattern near the corner. My machine leaves it consistently. It's a fingerprint."

Lorna's eyes flicked. "That could be any dot," she said, too quickly.

"It's not any dot," I replied. "It's consistent across my run. If you want, I can produce twenty more cards with the same mark."

I laid the replacement card beside it. "This," I said, "is a replacement place card found on the table last night. It lacks the dot pattern. That means it was printed elsewhere."

Dean leaned in. "Printed here," he said.

"Almost certainly," I agreed.

Hugh's voice turned sharp. "You're basing everything on a dot."

"No," I said. "I'm basing it on a pattern."

Sera slid the portal audit printout forward, the one bagged from Hugh's office. She kept the original bagged, but the photographed copy was enough for now.

"And the pattern," Sera said, "includes portal edits."

Hugh's jaw clenched.

I spoke again, voice steady. "The guest list file I approved was edited multiple times overnight by a generic VendorAdmin account. Those edits added seat preference notes, including Table six, seat one, and a 'special handling' note that coordinated the apology tray at breakfast."

Lorna's eyes widened slightly. Imogen's expression tightened. Dean looked from me to Sera as if trying to decide whether he was allowed to believe any of this.

Hugh leaned back, face controlled. "VendorAdmin is a shared account," he said. "It's used for efficiency. It doesn't mean wrongdoing."

"No," I said. "It means cover."

Hugh's eyes flashed. "Harriet, you have no right to—"

Sera cut him off. "Hugh," she said. "One more interruption and you will wait outside. You do not get to steer this."

Hugh's mouth snapped shut.

I turned to the seating plan, laying it out so they could see. "This was the plan," I said. "Names, tables, seat numbers. It's designed to keep service smooth."

Lorna nodded, too quickly. "Yes," she said. "That's my job."

"And you asked me to reprint place cards at the welcome

mixer," I said.

Lorna blinked. "I did not."

"Not you personally," I replied. "A staff member, Ryan, told me it was 'easier if we do it by seat'. I refused without written approval. That refusal matters because it created a need."

Dean frowned. "A need for what."

"A need for someone else to print replacements," I said. "If you want cards swapped, and the vendor won't reprint, you print them yourself. Quietly. Overnight. Under a generic account. With a near-match font."

I paused and let that settle.

Then I continued, because the next part was the crux.

"During the banquet," I said, "Penny Harrow swapped seats with another guest."

Imogen's eyes sharpened. "That's gossip," she said.

"It's an observed fact," I replied. "I wrote it down at the time."

I opened my Pocket Log to the relevant page and read out, word for word, because accuracy mattered.

"21:14. Penny Harrow exchanged seats with female guest at Table six. Movement swift. No raised voices. Whispered exchange, then chair shift. New seat mapping: Penny now seat three."

Lorna's eyes flicked to the notebook, and I noticed her fingers tighten around her own folder.

I looked up. "If the dessert was intended for Penny," I said, "and the instructions told staff to serve by seat, then Penny's swap protected her by accident."

Dean's brow furrowed. "So who got it."

My throat tightened. I kept my voice even.

"Dr Lucian Vale," I said. "He ended up in the targeted seat at the wrong minute."

Silence fell over the table. Even Hugh didn't speak, and that alone was unsettling.

Sera spoke instead. "This," she said, tapping the instruction sheet, "is why it was clean. Why it looked like a tragedy. Because no one had to be seen near the victim."

Imogen's voice was quiet now, less polished. "You're saying Vale wasn't meant to die."

I looked at her. "I'm saying the mechanism did not care about him," I said. "It cared about where he sat."

Lorna's mouth opened, closed. "That's insane," she said, but her voice lacked conviction.

"It's efficient," Hugh said, softly, and then seemed to realise what he'd revealed. His eyes hardened. "I mean, it's an efficient way to run service. Not… not harm."

I stared at him. "You think efficiency excuses everything," I said.

Sera's gaze stayed on Hugh. "You heard Harriet," she said. "You heard the evidence. Now you are going to tell me who had access to that portal overnight, who had access to the printers, and who had reason to add seat-targeted service instructions."

Hugh lifted his hands, controlled. "As I said, it's shared," he replied. "Staff use it. Vendors use it. The Trust has access. That's why we have it, to avoid chaos."

Imogen's head snapped slightly. "The Trust does not edit guest lists," she said.

"Your credentials can," Sera replied.

Imogen's expression tightened. "We have standards," she said, and the word sounded like a shield.

Dean's voice came in, rough. "Kitchen doesn't do seat nonsense," he said. "We plate. We send. We don't assign poison by chair."

"No one is accusing the kitchen of writing the seat instructions," Sera said. "Unless you give me reason."

Dean's gaze flicked to the forged sheet again, then to Lorna.

"This looks like events," he muttered.

Lorna's eyes flashed. "No," she said. "Absolutely not. We don't forge documents."

I watched her as she spoke. Her hands were too still. Her smile, when it appeared, was too quick. Her eyes kept flicking to Sera rather than to the evidence. That mattered. People who were honestly confused looked at the evidence. People who were managing looked at authority.

Sera's gaze pinned Lorna. "Lorna Beckett," she said. "You are the event coordinator. You manage the seating plan. You liaise with sponsors. You have access to the vendor portal. You also have motive to keep this weekend smooth."

Lorna swallowed. "Everyone has motive to keep it smooth," she said. "A death is bad for business."

"Yes," I said. "But not everyone turns paper into a weapon."

Imogen's eyes cut to me. "Harriet," she said, voice sharp, "you keep insisting the Trust is involved. On what basis."

I met her gaze. "On the basis that your representative has been hostile since day one," I replied. "On the basis that you use romance branding as leverage. On the basis that an old registry seal mark appears in the original guest list footer, which Penny Harrow says should not exist."

Imogen's smile returned, brittle. "Penny Harrow is a journalist," she said. "Journalists see conspiracies because it sells."

"And solicitors see loopholes because it pays," I replied.

Sera's gaze flicked between us. "Enough," she said, not loud, but final. "This is not a debate club."

I took a breath and grounded myself in the paper. Facts. Dates. Ink.

"Let me put it plainly," I said, looking at all of them. "We have a forged instruction sheet that directs service by seat. We have a replacement place card printed outside my run. We have portal edits that add seat mapping and handling notes after my approval. We have a seat swap that moved Penny away from the targeted seat. We have a death that follows the seat-based mechanism. And we have a second attempt at breakfast using the same seat-based language."

I paused. "That is not coincidence," I said. "That is a system."

The ballroom felt suddenly colder, as if the building itself was listening and didn't like what it heard.

Sera nodded once. "Good," she said. "Now, we test the system."

Hugh's eyes narrowed. "Test it how."

Sera looked at him. "We replicate the chain," she said. "We trace who touched what and when. We pull the print queue logs from the events office and front desk printers. We compare ink, paper stock, and file version access. We check CCTV. We check staff keys. We follow the paper trail."

Hugh's smile tried to return. "Detective Inspector," he began, "CCTV is limited in staff corridors, for privacy."

Sera's gaze sharpened. "Stop using privacy as a screen," she said. "You have a dead man and an attempted poisoning. If you want to protect your guests, you will cooperate."

Hugh's jaw tightened.

Lorna's voice came out small. "This is ruining the weekend," she said, as if she couldn't stop herself.

I looked at her. "A man is dead," I said. "The weekend ruined itself."

Lorna blinked quickly, and for a second I saw fear there, real and raw, before she smoothed it away.

Sera stood. "We're done here," she said. "Hugh, you're coming with me. Dean, you're staying available. Imogen, you will not speak to any staff without my permission. Lorna, you will stay in the hotel and you will not touch any documents."

Lorna's eyes widened. "You can't—"

"I can," Sera replied. "Storm lockdown helps."

Hugh rose slowly. "This is unnecessary," he said, voice controlled.

Sera looked at him. "If it's unnecessary," she said, "then you have nothing to fear."

Hugh's smile tightened again, and I thought, not fear. Exposure.

As they moved to leave, I gathered my evidence back into its envelopes with care. I didn't rush. Rushing made mistakes. Mistakes were gifts to people like Hugh.

Sera paused beside me. "You did well," she said, quietly.

"I did paperwork," I replied.

Sera's mouth twitched. "Paperwork saves lives," she said.

It wasn't a comforting line. It was a grim one. But it was true.

I slid my Pocket Log into my coat pocket and followed them towards the side door. The ballroom behind us was already returning to its reset rhythm. Chairs stacked. Linen folded. The room trying to pretend it was only ever meant for romance.

In the corridor outside, I caught sight of Penny at the far end, escorted by the constable. She looked small in the hotel's grandeur, but her eyes were steady when she saw me. She gave a tiny nod, as if to say, keep going.

I nodded back.

Then I noticed something else.

Lorna Beckett, walking just behind Hugh, reached up briefly to touch the side of her neck, fingers pressing where a necklace might sit, though she wore none. It was a gesture of self-soothing, quick and unconscious.

People did it when they were cornered.

Sera saw it too. Her gaze flicked to Lorna, then to me.

"Service corridor," Sera said, low.

My stomach tightened. "You're going to confront her."

"I'm going to ask questions," Sera corrected. "And watch who breaks."

The corridor ahead felt suddenly narrow, the air thick with detergent and tension. The hotel was quiet in that way buildings became quiet when the story inside them changed.

I tightened my grip on my tote strap and kept my face neutral.

Because the paper had spoken.

Now the person behind it would have to.

CHAPTER 17

Culprit cornered

The service corridor had the sort of lighting that made everyone look guilty.

Fluorescent tubes buzzed overhead, casting a flat, uncompromising glare over beige paint, scuffed skirting boards, and a row of fire doors with signs that might as well have read: THIS WAY TO YOUR REGRETS. The air smelled of detergent, damp wool, and the faint metallic tang of catering trolleys that had been wiped down too often and never truly cleaned. Somewhere nearby a machine hummed, steady and indifferent.

I followed Sera at a pace that matched hers, which was to say quick enough to feel purposeful but not so quick we looked like we were chasing someone. There was a difference between a pursuit and a performance. Sera rarely performed.

Hugh Mercer walked ahead of us, shoulders squared, chin lifted, his body doing its usual trick of pretending he was escorting us rather than being escorted. Lorna Beckett was just behind him, folder tight against her chest, the same neatness in her posture that I'd seen when she tried to insist a forged instruction sheet was "internal wording". She kept her eyes forward as if staring at the corridor hard enough might turn it into a stage and give her her lines.

Dean Lomas trailed on the other side, jaw clenched, face drawn. He looked like a man who wanted to go back to his kitchen where the rules made sense, where things either cooked or they didn't, where you could blame a bad sauce on heat rather than human intent.

A young constable walked a few steps behind me, not looming, just there, steady, a quiet promise that if something went sideways it would be handled with the boring competence I preferred.

Sera slowed near the section of corridor that branched towards the ballroom staff doors. I recognised it at once, because my body remembered what my mind wanted to tidy away. The spot where Dr Lucian Vale had collapsed was still marked by a faint shadow on the floorboards, as if something had been scrubbed too quickly and left a difference only a person who looked for differences would notice.

Sera stopped.

Hugh stopped too, a beat later, as if she'd pulled an invisible cord.

Lorna stopped last. She blinked once, slow, and the folder shifted higher against her body, a shield she'd chosen because it looked professional.

Sera turned. Her eyes moved from Hugh to Lorna with the steady patience of someone who had already decided where the pressure belonged.

"Lorna Beckett," she said. "We're going to talk."

Lorna's smile appeared like a reflex. "Of course," she said, bright. "I'm happy to assist. It's all been terribly upsetting."

I felt my mouth tighten. People always wanted to be "happy to assist" when they thought it would keep them in control.

Sera didn't respond to the tone. She responded to the facts.

"You are the event coordinator," she said.

"Yes," Lorna replied. "For this weekend. On behalf of the

Valentine Heritage Trust and the Mariner's Crown. I've managed dozens of events. I have an excellent track record."

"Your track record isn't the issue," Sera said. "Your access is."

Lorna blinked. "Access."

Sera nodded towards the side door that led into the ballroom reset area. "You had access to the seating plans. The staff folders. The printers. The vendor portal."

Hugh's voice cut in smoothly. "Detective Inspector, Lorna has access because she has responsibilities."

Sera's gaze flicked to Hugh like a blade. "Hugh," she said, calm. "Not now."

Hugh's lips pressed together. He looked offended, but he said nothing. That was his style. He stored offence for later.

Sera's attention returned to Lorna. "We have evidence," she said, "that the guest list and service instructions were altered after vendor sign-off. Those alterations were used to coordinate seat-based service."

Lorna's shoulders lifted slightly, then settled. "This again," she said, gently exasperated, as if we were all being very dramatic about a spreadsheet. "Detective Inspector, people swap seats. Staff improvise. Mistakes happen."

"Mistakes don't log in at five in the morning," I said, and regretted it immediately because it made me sound like I was trying to win rather than help. But the words were out.

Sera didn't scold me. She didn't need to. She simply said, "Harriet is here as a witness. She's also the person who can tell a genuine document from a forgery. That's not a mistake. That's intent."

Lorna's eyes flicked to me then, quick and assessing. Not anger. Calculation. It felt like being measured and found inconvenient.

"I don't know what you think I did," Lorna said, voice still smooth, "but I am not responsible for a man's health."

Sera's gaze didn't shift. "We're not discussing his health," she said. "We're discussing your actions."

Lorna swallowed. She recovered quickly. "My actions were professional," she said. "If anything, I've been trying to keep this weekend from falling apart. The storm, the guests, the... tragedy. I've been working around the clock."

"Working around the clock," Sera repeated. "That fits the portal logs nicely."

Lorna's smile faltered, a fraction. "Portal logs."

Sera lifted her phone and tapped once. "VendorAdmin edits," she said. "Multiple. Overnight. From the events office device and the front desk device. Seat mapping notes added. Handling notes added. Service instructions printed. And forged documents with near-match font and wrong kerning."

Lorna's eyes flicked to Hugh again, and there it was, small and sharp. A look that said: do something.

Hugh did not move. He simply stood there, face composed, hands loosely clasped in front of him like a man attending a charity presentation rather than a police confrontation.

I watched him and felt something cold settle in me. Hugh was too calm for someone who'd just seen the foundations of his hotel's "normal workflow" collapse into evidence.

Sera saw Lorna's glance. She stepped half a pace closer, not invading, just asserting space.

"Lorna," Sera said, "you're going to answer questions. If you don't, you'll answer them at the station."

Lorna let out a controlled breath. "This is unnecessary," she said. "I have guests to manage."

"You have police to answer," Sera replied.

Dean shifted slightly. "Just tell her," he muttered, low, as if he wanted this over. "If you didn't do it, just tell her."

Lorna's eyes flicked to him. "I am telling her," she snapped, and then smoothed it immediately. "I'm sorry. Everyone's stressed."

Sera's expression didn't change. "Start with this," she said. "Who created the forged instruction sheet."

Lorna blinked. "I don't know."

"Wrong," Sera said, without raising her voice. "Try again."

Lorna's jaw tightened. "I don't know," she repeated, but the second time it landed less confidently.

Sera nodded once, as if she'd expected that. "All right," she said. "Who had access to the staff-only folder where the seating plan was pinned."

"Hugh," Lorna said quickly. "Hotel staff. Dean. Anyone in operations."

"And you," Sera said.

"And me," Lorna admitted, a touch stiff. "Because it's my job."

Sera's gaze sharpened. "Who requested Harriet reprint three place cards during the welcome mixer."

Lorna frowned. "I didn't."

Sera didn't move. "Who did."

"I don't know," Lorna said, and for the first time her voice carried a hint of irritation that didn't sound rehearsed.

I felt my pen against the spine of my Pocket Log in my coat pocket. I wanted to write. I always wanted to write. Paper made things real.

Sera waited. Silence pressed in, filling the corridor until even the hum of the lights sounded loud.

Lorna lifted her chin. "This is absurd," she said. "A staff member asking for reprints doesn't make me a murderer."

Sera's eyes held hers. "No," she said. "But it shows someone tried to move responsibility away from you and onto Harriet. Harriet refused. So someone else produced replacements. That someone had to know exactly what Harriet's place cards looked like to mimic them."

Lorna's throat moved as she swallowed.

Sera pressed. "And that someone had to know why it mattered, because a place card is only useful if you're directing a person to a specific seat."

Dean's eyes narrowed. "So that's why the seat nonsense," he said, more to himself than anyone else.

Hugh's voice was smooth. "Detective Inspector, you're building a story," he said. "You're asking us to accept a chain of assumptions."

Sera didn't turn to him. "Hugh," she said, tone flat, "you've had enough chances to stop talking."

Hugh's mouth tightened. He looked offended again, but he said nothing.

I studied him anyway. His outrage was neat. His worry, if it existed, stayed hidden. It was all polish.

Sera turned back to Lorna. "Tell me about your credentials," she said.

Lorna's eyes widened, a fraction too quickly. "My credentials."

"Yes," Sera said. "Your event management credentials. Specifically, your connection to the Trust's events grants."

Lorna's face went very still. It was a subtle shift, but I saw it because I spent my life reading people who wanted to appear calm.

"I don't understand," Lorna said.

Sera's tone stayed even. "Penny Harrow recognised you," she said. "Or rather, she recognised your paperwork. She came here for fire year records tied to property ownership on Valentine Row. She also mentioned an old registry seal being used to legitimise forged documents."

Lorna's eyes flicked down. Her fingers tightened on her folder.

Sera took another half step closer. "Penny told Harriet that an old seal should have been destroyed after the fire," she continued. "We saw a registry-style mark embedded in the footer of the original guest list file. Then it vanished in the later versions."

Lorna's breath caught, small, like a hiccup she tried to swallow.

Sera's gaze pinned her. "That tells me someone knows exactly what that mark means," she said. "And someone wanted it hidden once Harriet noticed."

Lorna's lips parted, then closed.

Hugh's head tilted slightly, still calm. "With respect," he said, and Sera's gaze snapped to him so fast I almost admired it.

"Hugh," Sera said, "I will deal with you when I'm finished here."

Hugh lifted his hands slightly, in a gesture that was meant to look cooperative. "Of course," he said, and he sounded like a man agreeing to let a child finish a tantrum.

My dislike sharpened into something more focused. Hugh treated everything as optics, including police work. That was dangerous.

Sera didn't waste more attention on him. She kept the pressure where it belonged.

"Lorna," she said. "Did Penny confront you."

Lorna swallowed. "No."

Sera's eyes stayed on hers. "Did Penny recognise you."

Lorna's voice tightened. "She's a journalist," she said. "She recognises lots of people."

Sera nodded slowly. "Did Penny recognise your credentials," she asked, "as not being yours."

Lorna's cheeks flushed. It was quick and ugly against her carefully applied foundation.

I felt my stomach tighten. That flush was the first honest thing I'd seen from her.

Sera waited. She didn't pounce. She let the silence do the work.

Lorna's eyes flicked to the side, towards the ballroom door, as if she might run. She didn't. She knew she couldn't. Not with the storm, the locked roads, the police presence. There was nowhere to go that wouldn't look like guilt.

Her shoulders sagged slightly, then she straightened again. "This is harassment," she said, but it came out thin.

"No," Sera replied. "This is an opportunity. Tell the truth and it stays tidy. Lie and it becomes a mess."

Lorna's throat moved again. She clutched her folder tighter, then seemed to realise it made her look defensive. She loosened her grip, then tightened it again. Her hands didn't know what to do.

Dean shifted in his spot. "Just say it," he muttered, impatience and fear tangled together. "I've got staff asking if they're next."

Lorna's head snapped towards him. "Don't be dramatic," she said, sharply.

Dean's face hardened. "A man's dead," he snapped back. "You don't get to call anyone dramatic."

That landed. Lorna flinched, small, involuntary.

Sera watched it happen. Her eyes narrowed slightly, not in satisfaction, in focus. She was reading the same thing I was. Lorna wasn't just scared. She was cornered.

Sera spoke again. "What did Penny say to you," she asked, "when she recognised the paperwork."

Lorna's eyes snapped to Sera. "Nothing," she said, too fast.

Sera's voice didn't change. "Lorna."

Lorna's jaw tightened. "She didn't say anything," she insisted. "She didn't have the chance."

"And yet," I said quietly, unable to stop myself, "she swapped seats during the banquet like someone who wanted to avoid being where she'd been placed."

Lorna's gaze flashed at me, hot. "That means nothing," she hissed.

"It means she was afraid," I replied. "People don't change their behaviour for no reason."

Sera's eyes stayed on Lorna. "Tell me about the Trust's events grants," she said.

Lorna's breath left her in a shaky exhale that sounded unplanned. "They're… competitive," she said.

Sera nodded. "And your role."

Lorna's voice went brittle. "I coordinate," she said. "I manage deliverables. I liaise with vendors. I ensure compliance with branding guidelines."

"That's a lot of words for someone who just wants to keep things smooth," I murmured, and I hated myself for the sharpness but my temper had been scraped raw by forged paper and near-miss desserts.

Sera didn't admonish me. She asked the next question.

"Your credentials," she said. "Where did they come from."

Lorna's eyes flicked to Hugh again.

Hugh looked back at her, face perfectly neutral.

It was not a look that said, help her. It was a look that said, don't involve me.

I watched that exchange and understood something. Hugh wasn't surprised by where this was going. He was managing what would touch him.

Lorna swallowed hard. "I have qualifications," she said, stubborn.

Sera's patience thinned, just a fraction. "Lorna," she said. "We can do this now, or we can do it with a solicitor and a tape recorder."

Imogen's voice slid in smoothly. "Detective Inspector," she said, "if you are accusing a Trust contractor of fraud, the Trust will require representation."

Sera's gaze snapped to Imogen. "Imogen," she said. "You will speak when I ask you."

Imogen's smile held, but it tightened at the corners.

Sera turned back to Lorna. "Where did your credentials come from."

Lorna's eyes glistened for a second, then she blinked hard. "They were... borrowed," she said.

The word hung there like damp laundry.

"Borrowed," Sera repeated.

Lorna's voice was suddenly small. "I didn't think it mattered," she said quickly. "I was doing the work. The Trust needed someone reliable. I've been doing this for years. It's not like I wasn't qualified. It's just... paperwork."

It was almost funny. The idea of "just paperwork" being offered as a defence to a police officer and a former registrar. Almost. If someone hadn't died because of paper.

Sera's eyes stayed steady. "Borrowed from who," she asked.

Lorna swallowed. "From a woman who used to work with the Trust," she said. "She owed me. She wasn't using them anymore. It was harmless."

"Harmless," I repeated, and my voice came out flat. "That word is getting a workout this weekend."

Lorna flinched. "It was just to get the contract," she said, voice rising. "The Trust has requirements. People with certain certifications. Certain boxes ticked. I couldn't afford to lose the work."

Sera nodded once. "So you committed fraud to get the contract," she said.

Lorna's face flushed again. "No," she snapped. "It's not like that. It's bureaucracy. Everyone does it."

Sera's gaze didn't soften. "Not everyone," she said. "And certainly not everyone uses it to intimidate a journalist."

Lorna's breath caught. Her eyes flashed. "I didn't intimidate her," she said, too loudly.

Sera's voice stayed low. "Then why did she recognise you," she asked, "and why was she scared."

Lorna's shoulders rose as if she were bracing for a blow.

"She recognised the certificate number," Lorna said, and the words came out quickly now, tumbling. "The grant paperwork, the old files. She's a journalist, she reads everything. She… she looked at me like she'd seen a ghost. She didn't even have to say it. I knew she knew."

Sera's gaze sharpened. "When," she asked.

Lorna swallowed. "On the planning call," she said. "After. When everyone else left. She stayed on a moment. She asked a question. About the Trust's grants. About my name. She said it in that casual way they do when they're pretending it's nothing."

I felt the hairs rise on my arms. Penny's "casual". The kind that was never casual.

"What did she ask," Sera said.

Lorna's mouth tightened. "She said… she said, 'Have you always been Lorna Beckett, or is that just for the weekend.'"

I wrote it down in my Pocket Log without taking it out. My fingers moved in my coat pocket, muscle memory, as if the pen could etch truth through fabric.

Sera's eyes narrowed. "And you panicked," she said.

Lorna's laugh was sharp, humourless. "Of course I panicked," she said. "If she published that, I'd be finished. The Trust would drop me. No one would hire me. I'd be the fraud. I'd be the story."

Imogen's face tightened, a flicker of recognition there, as if she'd just seen her own reflection in the word story.

Sera's voice stayed even. "So you decided to scare her," she said.

Lorna's eyes snapped up. "No," she said. "I decided to protect myself."

"That's what everyone says," I muttered.

Lorna's gaze flicked to me. "You don't understand," she said, voice sharp. "You own a shop. You can refuse a client. You can say no. I can't. I'm disposable. They smile at you and call you 'talented', then they drop you the second you're inconvenient. The Trust, the hotel, the sponsors. They don't care about me. They care about the weekend."

Hugh's expression didn't change. That, more than anything, made my stomach turn.

Sera didn't let the rant move her. "So you created a 'health incident'," she said.

Lorna's face crumpled, then tightened again. "It was meant to be mild," she said quickly. "It was meant to be a scare. A story. You know how these things work. If Penny got ill at a romance weekend, everyone would blame the stress, the storm, the hotel. She'd look dramatic. Unreliable. She'd hesitate before publishing."

Sera's gaze pinned her. "You wanted to discredit her."

"Yes," Lorna whispered, and then she flinched as if she hadn't meant to say it so plainly.

Dean stared at her. "You did something to the food," he said, voice low and dangerous. "You used my kitchen."

"No," Lorna snapped, too quickly. "Not the kitchen. I didn't touch your kitchen."

Sera's eyes narrowed. "Then how," she asked.

Lorna's hands trembled slightly on her folder. "The tray," she said. "Dessert service. Staff follow instructions. They follow paper. If you tell them seat one gets a certain plate, they do it. They don't ask why. They don't know what's in it. They just deliver."

Sera nodded once, as if confirming what we'd already laid out. "You used the seat system," she said.

Lorna nodded, tears rising now, ugly and unwanted. "Yes," she whispered.

Dean looked sick. "What did you put in it," he asked, voice rough.

Lorna shook her head. "I'm not a killer," she said, and her voice broke on the last word. "It wasn't meant to kill. It was meant to make her unwell. For a bit. Just enough to rattle her."

"And Vale," Sera said, quiet.

Lorna's eyes squeezed shut. She shook her head harder. "He wasn't meant," she said. "He wasn't meant. It was Penny. It was always Penny. And then she moved, and I didn't know she'd moved, and the seat stayed the same, and the tray went to the seat and he... he..."

She couldn't finish the sentence. She didn't need to. The corridor itself carried it.

Hugh cleared his throat softly. "Detective Inspector," he said, calm, "this is all very emotional. Lorna is under great stress. We should perhaps ensure she has support. The hotel can arrange a private room."

Private room. Of course. Hugh wanted to tuck the scandal away like a stained napkin.

Sera's gaze snapped to him. "Hugh," she said, voice like ice, "do not offer me a private room. Offer me cooperation."

Hugh lifted his hands slightly. "Of course," he said, still calm. Too calm.

Sera turned back to Lorna. "Lorna Beckett," she said. "You are under arrest on suspicion of murder."

Lorna's eyes flew open. "No," she gasped. "No, you can't. I didn't mean to. I didn't mean to."

Sera's voice didn't soften, but it didn't harden either. It stayed procedural. That was mercy, in its own way.

"Intention will be considered later," Sera said. "Actions are considered now."

She nodded to the constable. He stepped forward, calm, controlled. No drama. No shoving. Just the quiet competence of someone who'd done this before and knew the worst thing you could do was turn it into theatre.

Lorna's hands rose instinctively, then dropped, as if her body couldn't decide whether to fight or surrender.

"I'll cooperate," she said quickly. "I'll tell you everything. The portal, the printer, the files. I'll tell you. I didn't want him to die."

Sera nodded once. "You can tell me," she said. "After caution."

The constable took Lorna's folder from her hands gently and handed it to another officer who'd appeared at the far end of the corridor. Storm lockdown or not, the hotel's staff corridors had become a small ecosystem of authority.

Sera spoke the caution clearly. Lorna nodded, crying now, not the pretty kind, the messy kind that ruined mascara and made a person look human against their will.

I felt a strange tightness in my chest, not sympathy exactly, not absolution, just the ugly reality of someone realising their small act of self-preservation had turned lethal.

Sera held out her hand. "Phone," she said.

Lorna blinked, confused through tears. "My phone."

"Yes," Sera said. "Now."

Lorna fumbled in her pocket and produced it, hand shaking. She passed it to Sera as if handing over her last thread of control.

Sera turned the phone off, bagged it, and handed it to the officer.

"Keys," Sera said.

Lorna's fingers shook again as she produced a keyring. A small fob with the Mariner's Crown logo. Sera looked at it, then at Hugh.

Hugh's expression didn't change. If anything, his smile threatened to return, not in amusement, in relief that the culprit was being packaged neatly.

I watched him and felt my stomach twist.

That reaction was wrong. A normal person, even an irritatingly polished hotel manager, would show something. Shock. Fear. Anger. Disgust. Hugh showed control, and a slight tightening at the corners of his mouth that looked like satisfaction that the mess was being contained.

I noted it in my mind, because my Pocket Log was not just paper. It was also the part of me that refused to forget what mattered.

Lorna made a small sound, half sob, half laugh. "It was meant to be a story," she whispered, and the words sounded like a confession and an accusation in one.

Sera's gaze stayed steady. "Stories have consequences," she said.

Dean sat heavily against the wall, as if his legs had finally given up. "You used my staff," he muttered, voice hollow with anger. "You used my service flow."

Lorna's head lifted sharply. "I didn't use your kitchen," she said, defensive even now. "I used the paperwork. The instructions. The seat numbers. Everyone follows paper. That's what makes it safe."

"That's what makes it dangerous," I said, quietly.

Lorna looked at me then, eyes red, face stripped of polish. "You," she whispered, and there was bitterness there. "You and your little dot patterns. If you hadn't noticed, I would've been fine."

I felt my temper flare. "If you hadn't forged documents and tried to make a person ill to protect your fraud, you would've been fine," I said. "Don't mistake my eyesight for your innocence."

Sera lifted a hand slightly, a silent warning to me. Not to protect Lorna, to keep me from stepping into the mud.

I inhaled slowly and let it go. I could have said more. I chose not to. The best revenge was a clean record.

The constable took Lorna's arm gently. "This way," he said.

Lorna stumbled once, caught herself, and then walked, shoulders shaking. She didn't fight. She didn't scream. She just moved down the corridor, the storm outside still roaring, the hotel inside still trying to pretend it ran on romance rather than control.

As she was led away, Imogen Baird finally spoke, voice tight. "Detective Inspector," she said, "the Trust will need to manage the narrative. Guests must be reassured. This weekend is—"

Sera's gaze cut to her. "This weekend is a crime scene," she said. "If you try to manage anything that touches evidence, I will treat it as interference."

Imogen's smile stiffened. "Of course," she said, and she sounded like she'd file the word interference under inconvenient.

Hugh stepped forward slightly. "Detective Inspector," he said, calm as ever, "I want to express how horrified we are. The Mariner's Crown will cooperate fully. We will issue a statement, we will provide counselling to guests and staff, and we will ensure the Trust understands we acted swiftly."

Acted swiftly. There it was. Hugh trying to write the ending while the ink was still wet.

Sera looked at him. "You didn't act swiftly," she said. "You acted controlled."

Hugh's smile didn't move. "Control is necessary in a crisis," he said.

Sera's eyes were sharp. "Control can be a cover," she replied.

Hugh's jaw tightened, almost imperceptibly. He was annoyed. Not scared. Annoyed.

That was the thing I couldn't shake. He looked like a man who'd lost a staff member, not a man who'd nearly lost his hotel to a scandal that could swallow him.

I watched him with a new, unpleasant clarity. Hugh treated

this as a brand problem, not a moral one. And that meant he would keep treating people as objects in a story as long as the story served him.

Sera turned slightly to me. "Harriet," she said, quieter, "I'm going to need your evidence packaged properly. Your originals, your prints, your notes. You'll do that better than anyone."

"Lucky me," I muttered.

Sera's mouth twitched, almost a smile. "Also," she added, "I want your statement. On record. Seat swap observation, reprint request, dot pattern, forged sheet tells."

I nodded. "I have it," I said. "In ink. With times."

Sera nodded once. "Good."

Dean pushed off the wall slowly, face still drawn. "Detective Inspector," he said, "my staff are going to think they'll be blamed."

Sera's gaze softened a fraction, the rarest thing. "They won't," she said. "They followed instructions. That's what they're trained to do. The person who weaponised it is in custody."

Dean let out a breath that sounded like he'd been holding it since last night. "All right," he said, and it wasn't relief, not quite, but it was a direction his body could follow.

Imogen stood very still, eyes hard. She looked like a person already drafting an email in her head.

Hugh straightened his cuffs, a tiny gesture, neat and pointless, like arranging flowers on a coffin.

Sera's gaze returned to him. "Hugh," she said, "I'll need the vendor portal's full access logs and password change history. Today."

Hugh's smile tightened. "Of course," he said. "We will expedite."

Sera held his gaze. "And Hugh," she added, voice quiet. "If I find a single gap in those logs that looks like someone tried to tidy up after Lorna, I will come back through this building like a storm."

Hugh's smile held. "Detective Inspector," he said, "we have nothing to hide."

I almost laughed. Not because it was funny, because it was so obviously a lie that it became absurd. Hugh always had something to hide. If he didn't, he'd have no reason to exist.

Sera turned away from him. She didn't argue. She didn't need to. Her job wasn't to win a verbal sparring match. It was to build a case.

She looked at me. "You all right," she asked, and it surprised me because it was almost gentle.

I thought of Pip back at home with Cal, probably sulking because no one had brought him a sausage roll. I thought of my shop on Valentine Row, quiet behind its glass, the paper and ink waiting for me like faithful tools. I thought of Penny, still in the hotel somewhere, brave in that exhausted way.

"I'm fine," I said, because fine was what you said when you didn't want to open the cupboard door and see what fell out.

Sera's eyes narrowed slightly. "Fine isn't an answer," she said.

"It's the only one I'm offering," I replied.

She accepted it with a nod, because Sera understood boundaries even when she pushed them.

We walked back towards the ballroom reset area where my envelopes waited. The corridor felt different now. Not safer, not really, but less slippery. The culprit had a name. A motive. A confession. That made the world feel more solid.

But as we passed Hugh, I felt his gaze on me. Not hostile. Not exactly. Assessing, again. As if he were already deciding what role I would play in whatever came next.

I didn't look back.

I didn't give him that satisfaction.

Instead, I slipped my Pocket Log out as we walked and wrote one line, because I trusted ink more than anyone in that building.

09:34. Lorna Beckett arrested. Confessed seat-based 'health incident' plan to discredit Penny due to fake Trust grant credentials. Vale died due to seat swap. Hugh reaction controlled, optics-first. Watch him.

Then I put the notebook away, lifted my chin, and went back to my paper evidence, because if someone wanted to weaponise procedure, I would meet them on their own ground and make it hurt.

CHAPTER 18

Aftermath and hook

The shop smelled the way it always did after a night shut up too long, ink and card stock with a faint trace of damp wool from my coat. Familiar, mildly judgmental, and, if I was honest, a relief.

Valentine Row was still wet enough to shine. The storm had not left politely. It had simply got tired and wandered off, leaving puddles like unanswered questions, wind tugging at bunting that no longer looked festive, and a street full of stranded visitors pretending they were delighted by "a bit of weather" while their shoes filled with seawater.

I unlocked Crowe Cards & Vows with the same care I used for everything that mattered. Key into lock. Turn. Pause. Listen.

Habit from a former life. Habit from a current one too, if we were counting the last twenty four hours.

The bell above the door gave its small, bright chime. I stepped inside and shut the door behind me, then stood with my palm on the wood for a moment, letting the silence settle.

At the hotel there had been noise everywhere. Not just sound, but noise. The sort that clung to you. Laughter that didn't fit, sympathy delivered too loudly, outrage performed because it got attention, and that steady undercurrent of "what does this mean for me" that people tried to pretend was concern for others.

Here, it was only the soft hush of paper. The air felt calmer. The shelves waited. The window display, even slightly crooked from the wind, looked like something designed by a person who believed in second chances.

I did not.

Pip did.

He trotted in behind me, red collar bright against his wiry honey brown coat. He paused just inside the door, body going still, head tilted towards the back office as if checking the place for intruders. Left ear half flopped with its tiny notch at the tip, his little signature detail, as if someone had signed him with a pen. He stared for a long beat, then gave one single bark, satisfied.

"All right," I told him, because it was always easier to speak to a dog than to admit I was glad to be home.

Pip's eyes flicked to the counter.

"You're not getting paid in sausage rolls for barking at stationery," I said.

He stared harder, then moved to the counter anyway, because Pip had never let reality interrupt his negotiations.

I hung my coat on the peg behind the door and rolled my shoulders. My body felt as if it had been clenched since the banquet. I had slept in bits at the hotel, then in corridors, then in rooms that smelled of bleach and panic. The rest I'd had was the sort you got when your brain decided that if you stopped moving you might start feeling.

The shop lights clicked on with a soft hum. Warm yellow spilled across the counter, the display table, the racks of wedding invitations and anniversary cards. All those neat promises in careful typography. All those tidy, romantic scripts that never had to account for the mess of actual people.

I moved behind the counter and opened the drawer where I kept my Pocket Log supplies. Spare ink cartridges. Small envelopes. Labels. A roll of clear tape. The tiny ritual items that made me feel I could keep my life contained on paper.

I placed my tote on the counter and pulled out the envelopes I'd carried back from the hotel, each labelled in my handwriting. Evidence did not belong in a handbag next to a mint and a receipt. Evidence belonged in a system.

I lined the envelopes up, tapped them into a neat edge, and placed them in the metal file tray under the counter, the one I used when clients insisted they wanted "just a quick look" at proofs and then proceeded to reinvent their entire wedding. Different crisis, same method.

Pip watched, then hopped up onto the little mat by my feet and pressed his chest against my boot, climbing onto my foot as if he could pin me to the floor and stop me drifting off into my own head.

There it was. His anchor move.

"Charming," I said, though my voice softened. "You're making me look needy."

He stayed. His whole body leaned into my foot with determined loyalty, as if the storm had taught him that humans were unreliable and boots were not.

I opened my Pocket Log, the actual notebook, not the mental version. My fountain pen felt heavier than usual in my hand, which was ridiculous, because it weighed the same as it always had. What changed was the meaning.

The last page I'd written in the corridor outside the ballroom.

09:34. Lorna Beckett arrested. Confessed seat based 'health incident' plan to discredit Penny due to fake Trust grant credentials. Vale died due to seat swap. Hugh reaction controlled, optics first. Watch him.

I stared at the words and felt that strange sensation again, like my brain was trying to rearrange reality into something I could file. A dead man. A woman in handcuffs. A hotel manager smiling like he could talk his way around anything, including ethics.

My pen hovered.

I added one more line, because it mattered.

10:02. Returned to shop. Pip anchored foot. Started evidence tray. Will not let this become "a medical tragedy" story.

The bell above the door chimed again before I could write more.

My head snapped up. Pip's body went rigid, his stare locking on the entrance, then one single bark.

"Not a burglar," Cal's voice came through the door, calm as the tide. "Just me."

I let out a breath I hadn't realised I was holding. "You could try knocking like a normal person," I called.

"I did," Cal said, opening the door carefully and stepping in with a gust of damp air. "You were busy glowering at paper."

He had a flask in one hand and a paper bag in the other. He wore his usual weathered jacket and that look of a man who had spent decades in wind and salt and never once expected life to be tidy. His presence always made the room feel steadier, which was unfair, because it meant I liked having him around.

Pip's attention shifted instantly from potential threat to potential snack. He stared at the bag with religious devotion.

Cal held it up slightly. "Sausage roll," he said. "Peace offering."

"You're bribing the dog," I said.

"I'm respecting a professional," Cal replied, and Pip gave one more bark as if he agreed.

Cal set the flask on the counter and placed the paper bag beside it. He didn't step closer to me straight away. He never crowded. Cal had a rare talent for being protective without making it about his control.

He looked around the shop, eyes taking in the neatness, the paper racks, the slightly crooked window display.

"You all right," he asked, and his tone was simple, not dramatic.

I could have lied. I did, slightly. "I'm vertical," I said. "That's the main achievement."

Cal's mouth twitched. "Tea," he said, tapping the flask. "Nisha insisted. She said you'd forget to eat and then pretend you didn't."

"Nisha knows me too well," I muttered.

Cal's gaze stayed on my face. He wasn't smiling now. He looked like someone who'd seen too many storms to be fooled by a calm surface.

"You shouldn't have been in the middle of it," he said quietly.

I lifted an eyebrow. "In the middle of what, exactly. The murder. The forgery. The romance branding turned weapon."

Cal exhaled. "All of it," he said. "That hotel is a machine. It chews people up and spits them out with a smile."

"Yes," I said. "And I have spent the last day watching people insist the machine is polite."

Pip pushed harder against my foot, as if reminding me to stay in the room.

Cal noticed. His eyes softened. "He's doing his anchor thing," he said.

"Don't start calling it that," I warned.

Cal's mouth twitched again. "All right," he said. "He's doing his 'you're not allowed to float away' thing."

I didn't answer because it was too accurate.

Cal unscrewed the flask and poured tea into two travel cups he'd brought, practical as always. The scent rose, strong and familiar. Proper tea, not the hotel's lukewarm apologies. I watched the steam and felt my shoulders drop a fraction.

Cal handed me a cup without making a fuss about it.

I took it and drank, and the warmth hit my throat like permission to breathe.

"Better," Cal said, not as a question.

"Don't get excited," I replied. "It's only tea."

Cal leaned his hip against the counter. "Tell me what happened after they took her," he said.

"You mean after Lorna stopped pretending she was 'happy to assist'," I said.

Cal nodded.

I stared down at the tea, watching the surface tremble slightly.

"She confessed," I said, keeping my voice flat. "She admitted the credentials were borrowed. She admitted she wanted to scare Penny, discredit her. She admitted she used seat based service to deliver whatever it was. She kept saying she didn't mean to kill him, as if intention could undo a body."

Cal's jaw tightened. "And Hugh."

I glanced up. "You're asking because you already know the answer," I said.

Cal's gaze stayed steady. "Try me."

"He looked controlled," I said. "Not shocked. Not disgusted. Controlled. Like the whole thing was an inconvenience that needed managing."

Cal's eyes narrowed. "That bothers you."

"It should bother everyone," I said, sharper than I intended. "A man died in his building. A woman tried to poison someone at breakfast. And he's still thinking about statements."

Cal let that sit. He didn't rush to soothe me. He never did, which was why I trusted him more than I trusted most people with my feelings.

"That's his trade," Cal said finally. "Optics. Control. Keeping the machine running."

"Yes," I replied. "And machines don't care who gets crushed."

Pip gave a small huff and shifted his weight, still pressed to my boot, as if he agreed again.

Cal slid the sausage roll out of the bag and held it out to Pip. Pip froze, stared, then took it with delicate precision, as if he were accepting a medal.

"Traitor," I told him.

Pip ignored me completely. Loyalty had limits. Those limits were pastry.

Cal watched him for a moment, then looked back at me. "Sera said she'd keep you posted," he said.

"She did," I replied. "She's the only one in that building who treats facts like facts."

Cal nodded. "She'll do it properly."

I took another sip of tea, then set the cup down. My fingers wanted my pen again. When I didn't know what to do with my mind, I wrote.

Cal noticed my glance towards the Pocket Log. "Go on," he said gently. "Do your thing."

"My thing," I repeated.

"Your paperwork saves lives," Cal said, and he looked faintly amused. "Or at least it stops idiots turning it into nonsense."

I gave him a look. "You've been talking to Sera."

Cal's mouth twitched. "She said it first."

"Of course she did," I muttered, and felt a strange warmth in my chest that was not tea.

I opened the Pocket Log to a new page and started writing, not everything, just the clean timeline. It was the only way I could keep the day from turning into a blur of corridors and faces.

Cal didn't interrupt. He stood with his tea and watched the shop, the windows, the street, as if he were keeping an eye on the world while I put my own back in order.

Outside, Valentine Row was starting to wake up again. A couple in matching waterproof jackets paused to stare at my window display as if love-themed stationery could somehow explain why they were trapped in a coastal town with a dead celebrity in the local hotel. Two teenagers walked past laughing too loudly, phones in hand, trying to get signal. Somewhere down the lane, someone argued about whether the storm made their weekend "more romantic" or "ruined".

It was always about their weekend. Even now.

The bell chimed again.

This time, the sound made my stomach tighten. Pip's head snapped up mid chew. He froze, stared at the door, then gave one bark, sharper.

Cal shifted slightly, not dramatic, just ready.

The door opened.

DI Sera Linley stepped in, rain-damp coat, hair still in its tight bun, eyes tired in that particular way that suggested she'd been dealing with too many people and not enough truth. She paused just long enough to let her gaze move across the shop, the counter, my Pocket Log, Cal's presence, Pip's stubborn boot-anchor position.

Sera's mouth did not smile, but something in her eyes eased a fraction. "Harriet," she said.

"Detective Inspector," I replied. "You're dripping on my floor."

"I'm improving it," she said dryly. "It was too clean."

Cal nodded at her. "Sera."

"Cal," she returned, her tone acknowledging him without inviting conversation. Sera's social skills were efficient, like her policing.

She reached into her coat pocket and pulled out a clear evidence sleeve, the sort that made my spine go straight. Inside was a printed photograph, glossy enough to catch the shop light. Behind it, another smaller sleeve held a torn corner of something, brown paper with a ragged edge.

Sera set the sleeve on the counter and slid it towards me.

"I said I'd bring you something," she said.

My hand hovered above it. "That's either evidence or a threat," I said.

"It's a copy," Sera replied. "A copy you're allowed to have. I'm not handing you originals. Don't make me regret this."

I picked up the sleeve carefully.

The photograph showed a bedside table in what I recognised as a Mariner's Crown hotel room. Expensive lamp, branded notepad, a glass of water untouched. And there, partly cropped in the corner of the frame, was a torn envelope corner, brown and stiff, with a stamp mark pressed into it.

My breath caught, small and sharp.

It was not the modern stamp used for official mail. It was older. A round seal impression with a ring of text. Valentine Row Registry Office, Hartcombe, the letters slightly uneven as if the stamp had aged or been used too many times.

In the centre of the seal, the faint outline of a heart motif, not cute, not modern. A stiff, old-fashioned emblem that looked like it belonged in a filing cabinet, not a romance weekend.

And the date.

My eyes locked on it and my stomach turned.

12 OCT 2007.

The fire year.

My fingers tightened around the sleeve.

Cal's voice softened. "Hattie," he said, not pushing, just noticing.

I swallowed. "That seal," I said, and my voice came out rougher than I intended. "That seal was destroyed."

Sera's gaze stayed on my face. "That's what you said at the hotel," she replied. "Penny said it too."

I forced myself to look up at Sera. "Where did you get this," I asked.

"From Vale's room," Sera said. "Bagged properly. Photographed properly. Logged. I brought you the copy because you're connected to the paper trail and I'd rather you saw it before the rumour mill turns it into something stupid."

"That's thoughtful," I said. "It's also alarming."

Sera nodded once. "Good. Be alarmed."

I looked down at the photo again. The torn edge suggested someone had ripped it off in a hurry, maybe to keep the stamped corner as proof while discarding the rest. The paper looked like an old archive envelope, the kind used for official files, not hotel correspondence.

My mind flicked back, uninvited, to the Registry Office fire. Not the flames themselves, but the aftermath. The smell of wet ash. The warped metal filing cabinets. The people in suits turning up with clipboards and sympathetic faces, asking just enough to look concerned, then manoeuvring to see what could be salvaged, what could be rewritten, what could be quietly bought.

They'd called it a tragedy at the time. They'd said it was a shame. They'd said we'd rebuild.

What they meant was they'd reorganise.

I pressed my thumb against the edge of the sleeve, grounding myself in plastic, because the memory wanted to pull me back.

"That date," I said quietly. "That stamp,"

"It shouldn't exist," Sera finished.

"It shouldn't exist," I agreed.

Cal's voice was careful. "What does it mean," he asked.

I exhaled slowly. "It means," I said, choosing each word like I was placing evidence in an envelope, "someone kept the seal. Or someone recreated it. Either way, it means someone has been stamping documents to make them look official, back to the fire year at least."

Sera's gaze sharpened. "And the Trust."

I didn't answer immediately. It wasn't because I doubted it. It was because saying it out loud made it real.

"The Valentine Heritage Trust has been buying properties on and around Valentine Row for years," I said. "Quietly. Through shell charities, friendly solicitors, opaque 'revitalisation' plans. If you can stamp something with an old registry seal, you can make forged paperwork look legitimate enough to scare people into backing off."

Sera's mouth tightened. "So Vale had this," she said, tapping the photograph sleeve. "Why."

"That's the question," I replied. "Why would a celebrity relationship coach have a registry seal scrap in his hotel room."

Cal frowned. "Blackmail," he said, and it wasn't a question.

Sera's eyes flicked to him. "Likely," she replied.

I stared at the photo again and felt a sick clarity settle. Vale hadn't been here just to play games with couples. He'd been here because something in Hartcombe was valuable, and he'd found a way to make it valuable to him.

"Romance branding," I said, more to myself than them. "A weekend of love stories. A hotel selling a fantasy. A Trust selling 'heritage'. It's the perfect cover. Everyone's distracted by heart-shaped nonsense while the real power moves happen in the paperwork."

Sera's gaze stayed on me. "Harriet," she said. "I'm going to need you to remember everything you know about that fire year. Names. processes. Who had access. Who handled seals."

I let out a short laugh. "You say that like it was a pleasant time."

Sera didn't smile. "I say that like it matters."

It did.

Pip shifted, finished his sausage roll, then climbed harder onto my foot as if he could stop me from being dragged back into

2007 by sheer weight.

Cal reached out and placed his hand near mine on the counter, not touching, just close. A quiet reminder I wasn't alone in the shop, even if I felt like I was.

"What happens now," I asked Sera.

Sera's expression didn't soften. It never really did. But her voice held something that sounded like respect.

"Now," she said, "we process Lorna properly. We verify what she used, how she obtained it, and who helped her. Because I don't believe she acted alone in accessing those systems. Then we follow this." She tapped the photograph sleeve. "This is bigger than a romance weekend gone wrong."

"And bigger than Hugh Mercer's statement," I added.

Sera's mouth twitched. "Yes," she said. "Much bigger."

I looked at her. "Is Penny safe," I asked.

Sera nodded once. "For now," she said. "She's shaken. Angry. Determined. Which is her usual setting, from what I can tell."

"That's Penny," I replied.

Cal's gaze moved to the window. "There'll be talk," he said.

"There's always talk," I said.

As if summoned by the word, a burst of laughter came from outside, followed by the sharp click of a phone camera.

Pip froze. His head snapped towards the window. He stared, body rigid, then gave one single bark, sharper than before.

I turned.

Across the street, near the holiday lets, a woman held her phone up, angling it towards my shop window, the sign, the door. She wasn't taking a casual holiday photo. She was collecting images, deliberate and quick. When Pip barked, she startled, lowered the phone, then raised it again and took another shot, as if defiance mattered more than manners.

Camera flash.

Pip hated camera flashes. I felt it in the way he tensed, his ears pinned, his stare fixed like a nail.

Cal's body shifted, not aggressive, just ready.

Sera followed my gaze and her expression tightened. "That," she said quietly, "is why I brought you the photo. People will spin this. They will pick convenient villains. They will try to make it about you, about your shop, about the 'local vendor' angle."

"Let them try," I said, though my stomach tightened.

The woman outside turned and walked away quickly, phone already in her hand again, thumbs moving.

Gossip as weapon. Optics as oxygen. Hugh's world bleeding into mine.

Sera watched her go, then looked back at me. "Keep your Pocket Log close," she said. "Document anything strange. Anyone taking photos. Any calls. Any messages."

"I always do," I replied.

Sera nodded. "Good. And Harriet," she added, lowering her voice slightly, "do not go looking for this seal alone."

I lifted an eyebrow. "I wouldn't dream of it."

Sera's gaze stayed on mine. "That's a lie," she said.

I didn't deny it. Denial was pointless with Sera. She had the irritating gift of seeing straight through people.

Cal spoke softly. "She won't be alone," he said.

Sera's eyes flicked to him. "I'm holding you to that," she said.

Cal nodded once. "Fair."

Sera slid another small sleeve across the counter, this one containing a printed chain-of-custody note for the copy. She was meticulous. It was one of the things I liked about her. We were both built for systems. The difference was she wore hers like armour. I wore mine like a cardigan.

"Sign," Sera said.

I did. My signature looked too neat for what it meant.

Sera took the note back, tucked it away, then paused, eyes scanning the shop again. She looked tired now, not just in the face, but in the shoulders. It struck me how much she carried, walking into rooms full of people who lied with smiles.

"You did good work," she said, and it sounded almost uncomfortable for her to say.

"I did paperwork," I replied.

"Paperwork caught a killer," Sera said. "And might catch something worse."

She stepped back towards the door, then paused, hand on the handle.

"The fire year date," she said. "If you remember anything specific, anything odd about the seal inventory, anything you didn't like at the time, tell me. I don't care if it feels small."

I swallowed. Memories pressed at the edge of my mind. Not flames. Not drama. Small procedural oddities. A seal log that didn't match. A senior clerk insisting something had been "moved for safekeeping" without signing it out. A solicitor's assistant hovering too close to the salvage boxes.

"Yes," I said quietly. "I remember things."

Sera held my gaze for a beat, then nodded and left, the bell chiming once as the door shut behind her.

The shop felt warmer with her gone, which was odd, because Sera was not what I'd call a cosy presence. But she brought clarity with her, and clarity was a kind of warmth.

Cal remained.

He didn't ask questions right away. He poured more tea and set the cup near my hand.

Pip stayed on my foot, stubborn, like he'd decided this was his job now.

I stared at the photo again, at the stamped seal impression, at the date that dragged me back into a year I'd spent trying to forget.

Hartcombe had always sold stories. Romance weekend was only the loudest version. Underneath the bunting and the script fonts, there were records, lists, and procedures that decided who owned what, who was protected, who was pushed out.

And someone had been forging those procedures for years.

I set the photo down carefully and slid it into my evidence tray.

Cal watched me. "You look like you've just found a crack in the foundation," he said.

"I've found rot," I replied, my voice flat. "The kind that gets painted over and called 'heritage'."

Cal exhaled slowly. "And you're going to dig," he said.

I looked down at Pip, pressed against my boot, and felt that anchor again. I looked at the shelves of paper and ink and the neat rows of cards promising love and second chances.

Then I looked at the evidence tray, at the date, at the seal that should not exist.

"Yes," I said. "I'm going to dig."

Outside, the wind rattled the bunting again, trying to make Valentine Row look cheerful.

Inside, I picked up my fountain pen, opened my Pocket Log, and wrote one more line, because if I didn't record it, someone else would.

12 OCT 2007 seal scrap found in Vale's room. Seal should have been destroyed. Trust and town story sits on forged records. Begin archive thread.

Pip shifted, satisfied, and kept my foot pinned to the floor.

For the first time since the corridor, I felt steady enough to be angry in a useful way.

END OF BOOK 1

AUTHOR

Sherlyn Harlock writes British cozy mysteries with bite: seaside charm without the syrup, romance as a business model, and paperwork as a weapon. In her Valentine Row series, former wedding registrar Harriet "Hattie" Crowe navigates storm-locked hotels, society weddings, and perfectly managed scandals, where forged lists, missing originals, and old seals bend the truth. Harlock leans on dry humour, tight puzzle mechanics, and characters who collect proof instead of gossip. With Hattie's notebook and her scruffy terrier Pip in tow, the stories stay clever, tense, and grounded in one rule: what matters isn't what sounds lovely, but what can be proven.

Printed in Dunstable, United Kingdom